Fame and Infamy

Adventures of an American Maid in Paris

Iva Polansky

Captive
Press
Eden, NC

ISBN: 978-0-9846974-9-6

Library of Congress Control Number: 2012939559

Acknowledgements

Many thanks to the kind curators of the Police Museum of Paris and to the staff of the Bibliothèque Nationale as well as the employees of Gallica.fr, a treasure chest of French books published in the 19th century.
I'm also indebted to my early readers Pat Rowbotham and Penny White for their patience and to my editor V.R. Christensen.

Chapter 1

Montana Territory 1871

Usually, no one paid undue attention to the Chinese laundry, a squat clapboard building with misted windows. This Saturday afternoon however, the laundry's entrance door was being surveyed from the Happy End saloon across the muddy main street. A dozen men in various states of ruggedness lounged about on the covered porch, glasses of beer at reach, puffs of tobacco smoke swirling above their heads.

"Sure Miss McKay's there?"

"Sure, Mitch. Saw her goin' in with a big basket of laundry."

"Sure she likes me?"

"Hey, Pete, you saw the look she gave Mitch last Saturday, didn't you?"

"And a mighty lusty look it was. She turned around to take him from behind the rump too. I'm tellin' you, she's ripe for the pickin'."

"Pete's right, Mitch. This is your opportunity. Why wait another week?"

"O.K. then, I'll try."

"You do that, boy. You do that. Just squeeze her hard and give her a kiss."

Mitch detached himself from the wall, straightened his hat and ambled across the street.

Soft chuckles followed his departure.

The saloon keeper appeared in the door frame. "You're at it again, guys," he said disapprovingly. "That poor ignorant fool."

"Oh, c'mon, it's harmless fun."

"It's harmless as long as she shoots under the feet. One day she might miss and do real damage."

"She's never missed, has she?"

"Can't say she has."

"Never, so far."

"Nah, never . . ."

After a short hesitation, Mitch entered the laundry. The crew in front of the Happy End saloon craned their necks, awaiting the upcoming entertainment. Nothing happened for thirty seconds. Then the door opened and Mitch backed out, hands in the air. He was staring into the shining barrel of a nickel-plated Colt Bisley, first prize in the local sharp-shooting competition. Clutching the revolver was Miss Cornelia McKay, her other hand dragging an empty laundry basket. Passers-by going about their business stopped in their tracks.

Miss McKay aimed at Mitch's feet, ready to pull the trigger, when a premature laugh drew her gaze in the direction of the saloon and the assembly of hoodlums, all of them beaming in anticipation. Mitch profited from the distraction by taking flight along the wooden sidewalk. With the traffic at a standstill, the clatter of his boots was the only noise in the street. Everyone expected well-aimed projectiles to enliven Mitch's escape but it didn't happen. Not this time.

Five rapid-fire bullets shattered beer glasses. The sixth removed a hat from Pete's head and broke the saloon window behind him.

With the chambers empty, Miss McKay lowered the smoking revolver. She surveyed the glass shards scattered in the puddles of beer, the ashen faces, the sweaty brows and shaking hands.

"I hate this town," she said. "I really hate this town."

* * *

Later that afternoon, in the private quarters of the printer's shop farther down the main street, a conference was in progress.

"You must admit, Angus, your niece has become a real problem," said Sheriff Selby. "You know I hate arresting her, but this time I had no choice. Public safety and all."

"It's odd that you should mention public safety, Ned," said Angus McKay. "A young woman should be able to move around freely without being molested."

The sheriff moistened his moustache in a cup of tea served by Angus's wife Teata, who sat with them at the kitchen table with a thumb-sucking toddler in her diminished lap. The latest McKay, thirteenth in succession, was expected to draw first breath in a few weeks time.

"I can't be everywhere," the sheriff complained. "Butte is a gold-mining town crammed with randy bachelors . . . pardon my French, ma'am, but that's a fact. Any single female's fair play. You can't change that. If only Miss Nelly would get married, that would put an end to this."

2

"Married!" Teata exclaimed, her cheeks coloring with anger. "She's just refused Mr. Frobisher's offer. Had she accepted, she could have owned the general store. She could have worn silk to church and our family would have been able to buy fruit again. Today, he got a shipment of prunes and before I got there, they were gone. Since she's humiliated him, he no longer puts anything aside for us. There's nowhere else to shop and God knows what will happen when we get snowed in for months on end. He may even deny us flour for bread."

"That I doubt, Mrs. McKay. Still, your niece seems to have unrealistic expectations. What went wrong this time?"

"According to her, the man has no conversation. He grunts instead of speaking. Now that wouldn't do, would it? Miss must have conversation. That's what they filled her head with in that fancy boarding school back East. French! Piano playing! Money wasted, if you ask me."

"My brother meant well," Angus said. "An only child growing up without a mother and him always on the road, what else could he have done?"

Teata turned to him. "He should've put money aside for her upkeep instead of gambling it away and then getting himself killed. That's what he should've done instead of hanging her around your neck like a dead weight. A pig-headed lass who expects to marry a gentleman! That's not going to happen in Butte."

"You're right, Mrs. McKay," said the sheriff. "I propose the most convenient solution, which is that Miss Nelly should leave Butte for a location where there's a sufficient supply of gentlemen."

"Now look here, Ned Selby!" exclaimed Angus. "If you think I'm going to send my niece away to fend for herself just to save you the effort of keeping order in town, you are very much mistaken. It's my duty to look after my kin."

The sheriff put the tea cup back on its saucer with a clink. "Your kin's only a hair away from supplying bodies for the undertaker. We can't have that."

"I can't keep her inside, Ned. The girl does have a right to fresh air."

"That she does. Only there's an opportunity for her to breathe fresh air away from Butte. A once in a lifetime opportunity."

Angus frowned. "Ned, I told you—"

"Listen to the sheriff, husband," Teata interrupted him. She eyed Ned Selby eagerly. "An opportunity, you said?"

"That's so, ma'am. You heard about the folks who are staying at the hotel?"

"The heiress from the East and her French husband? Everybody talks about them. Only a crazy Frenchman would drag his wife to a place like

3

Butte. Exploring the Wild West, he calls it. With a valet and a maid! And the poor woman so exhausted that she had to take to bed."

"She's mended now but they need a new maid. The one they came with has left them. Up and married. Can't blame the gal. She's nearing forty and by her looks, she's never had such a choice of eager grooms."

"Don't you see, Angus?" Teata said. "There's a hand of destiny in this."

Angus barred her enthusiasm with his ink-stained hand. "Not so fast, wife. We don't know these people. And Nelly must decide for herself."

"That she's already done and she's got the job," said Sheriff Selby. "All that's required of you, Angus, is to write a witnessed permission allowing the Frenchies to travel with an unrelated minor."

"Nelly's set you up, hasn't she, Ned? She's talked you into this."

"Write that permission, husband!"

"Your wife's right. You can do no wrong by signing. It's best for everybody," the sheriff urged.

Months later, when the newspapers from the East reached Butte after the spring thaw, those words came to haunt him. By that time, the *De Chazelle Murder Affair* had made the rounds of the civilized world.

Chapter 2

Paris, three months later

With five billion gold francs of war restitutions owed to Germany after the crushing defeat the year before, all the new French government could afford for an endangered crime witness was a room in a cheap hotel: a room furnished with a sagging bed, the stained coverlet of which had obviously served as a towel, a handkerchief and a shoe-polishing rag to dozens of previous guests. Even that modest arrangement could not last. It was time to move on.

Inspector Savard stroked his walrus mustache as he studied the bundle of sorrow seated across the rickety table. The fate of this Miss Cornelia Jane McKay had been a matter of a prolonged debate between himself and the interrogating magistrate. Was she telling the truth? He was inclined to believe she was. As one of the few in the force fluent in English, he had the opportunity to peruse her diary and found it a blend of self-centered naïveté and ambitious dreams not unusual for a nineteen-year old. Still, it could have been a clever fabrication as the judge pointed out. As a rule, a lady's maid—no matter what nationality—did not pack an expensive revolver in her luggage.

The only reason Miss McKay left the Palais de Justice free of handcuffs was that they had not enough proof against her and His Honor hoped she would make a mistake in the near future. The mighty hand of French justice would remain poised above her head, ready to crush her should she attempt to sell a piece of jewelry or sneak out of the country. However, should she be innocent, Savard was running a considerable risk of finding her murdered. Given the situation, he could be demoted to appease public displeasure with the way the police mishandled the case. So far, there was a French nobleman shot dead, his American wife missing, their valet on the run, and here was this lady's maid with gunpowder sticking to her fingers.

"Better to keep that streaky hair of yours covered," he said. "Is it natural or do you bleach it somehow?"

"It has always been like that. Sun discolors it easily."

"Well, you could pass for a blonde, but only just. Nearly everything else fits that Moncarelli woman's passport. Height five foot five, face oval, eyes blue. It also says blond eyebrows. Yours are brown. Could you bleach them?"

The girl shrugged and leaned her limp body against the back of her chair. She had a tongue on her when he first met her, but two days of loneliness and grief had shrunk it.

Savard folded the identity certificate and handed it across the table. "It was issued by the now defunct Empire. I will get you a new one within a week. The Ministry's office can edit out the discrepancies."

"Amity Moncarelli," she said. "Who is she?"

Savard's eyebrows met in a sorrowful frown. "Was. One of the countless war victims, whose personal papers still pile up at the Ministry of Interior. They are being slowly processed. Her case has just turned up and the American Legation has not been notified yet. A sad story, indeed. A young woman from a good family in Philadelphia eloped with her Italian art teacher. They were married on the ship en route to France, squandered their money, and poverty trapped them in Paris. A letter was found among her personal effects. It seems that she begged her family for help and all she got for an answer was a terse note of refusal. A cold-hearted bunch, her kin. She died of typhoid fever during the Siege of Paris. Her husband was accidentally shot in the popular uprising soon after."

He paused, expecting a reaction, but none was forthcoming. The girl was not coping well. Waxen skin, eyes bloodshot with crying, general apathy.

He sighed and reached for his hat, ready for a few words of advice with which to conclude the visit, when she spoke.

"Thank you for reminding me of the American Legation," she said. "I'll go there and ask for protection. You cannot keep me in France against my will."

Merde. The little bitch still had some fight in her. Savard put his hat back on the table. "Now listen! The Legation has already inquired about you. The judge told them that your passport has been seized because your role in Madame de Chazelle's alleged murder is still under investigation. All the baroness's jewels worth half a million are missing. What about that? Perhaps you shot Baron de Chazelle to increase your share."

She squared her shoulders, her mouth acquiring a harder line. "I thought you were a friend. I was wrong."

"So be it." He rose. "Put on the black dress and gather your things. Agent Levieux is down in the parlor. Don't let him wait too long."

She glanced at the deep mourning attire on the bed and then back at him. "Is that all you have for me? Where's my trunk? And where's my revolver? It's a competition prize and worth a lot of money."

"Confiscated. Have you been planning more shooting sprees?"

She gave him a contemptuous look. "I was thinking of shooting lessons for you and your detectives. You missed Baron de Chazelle by two yards and almost shot me and the cabbie."

Savard swallowed hard. He did not appreciate being reminded of his shortcomings by a gun-packing female from a frontier town in America. A savage land, indeed. Sharp-shooting competitions for women, imagine that!

Granted, leaving the girl in the cab, together with the handcuffed suspect cabbie, was a hasty decision caused by lack of preparation. He couldn't have known that Baron de Chazelle, fleeing from justice, would later leap on the driver's box, unwittingly kidnapping the two people onboard. Try to be accurate exchanging fire while running after a speeding cab!

The newspapers, who liked nothing more than to derogate the police, were still making a feast of it. AMERICAN HEIRESS MISSING! the headlines shouted. MAID SLAYS BARON DE CHAZELLE! CABBIE SPEAKS OF HORROR RIDE! The ink had flown freely with sniggering remarks about the Paris Sûreté being less effective than a lady's maid. Not only did the girl shoot the de Chazelle fellow dead, but she also managed to climb onto the vacant driver's box, calm the bewildered horse, turn the cab around, and collect the handcuffed cabdriver, who had fallen out of the door when the cab hit the sidewalk. The cabbie, proven innocent, was now nursing a broken arm and enjoying reporters' attention. A colossal blunder, all of it.

"I'll have your trunk sent over as soon as possible," Savard said gruffly. "Only remember that you cannot wear color for some time. You're supposed to be a widow."

She did not answer. Savard shifted his weight from one foot to another. "Widowhood is the best disguise," he said. "Always put the veil on when you go out. Don't go out if you don't have to."

Silence and that accusatory stare. Savard sighed again.

"Look, mademoiselle, I know it's hard, but the valet is still on the loose. You are the most important witness we have. He knows that and wants you dead. You want to stay alive, don't you?"

"I want to go back to America."

"And so you shall. When we find Baroness de Chazelle's body. When we catch the baron's accomplice. All we have so far is only your deposition, the

7

physician's report of advanced cyanosis and a hair sample with traces of arsenic."

"It was my mistress's hair in that hairbrush. The doctor told you so."

"A hairbrush is not a reliable proof of murder. We also need a body and you are the only one able to identify it. In the meantime, lie low and don't go anywhere near the American Legation. The valet might have paid someone to look out for you there. And don't socialize with Americans. Not under your real name, nor any other name for that matter."

She lowered her gaze at a cockroach scurrying over the cigarette-burnt carpet, looked at Savard with the same disgust, and turned her head to the wall. Inspector Savard sighed for the third time, gathered his hat, and left.

Chapter 3

Widow Koenig's restaurant *La Tour d'Alsace* spread around the corner of an old five-story building in the rue Saint-André des Arts. The restaurant's newly enlarged windows allowed passersby to feast their eyes on the sight of heavy plates heaped with steaming braised sauerkraut, boiled potatoes, and a variety of meats and sausages. Widow Koenig was a firm believer in the power of glass.

She was a tiny woman with bulging eyes and a monumental voice box. Her staff and customers often wondered how such a large organ could inhabit so small a body. A native Parisian, she had lived in Alsace for twenty-six years, but did not regret her return to Paris. She was French and if Alsace was to be German, she wanted no part of it. She left behind a married daughter as loud-mouthed as her mother; the two did not get along. Her son died at Sedan, his head torn off by a German cannon ball, and the news of his death numbed her better feelings. The only affection her heart still harbored was reserved for her brother Fernand.

Starting anew had been a gamble but it had paid off. Fernand knew the neighborhood like the palm of his hand. A word or two, and he found the ideal location for her restaurant, right in the heart of the Latin Quarter. The Medical School was only a stone's throw away. The Sorbonne, the College of France and many other schools could be reached by a comfortable walk. One only had to cross the Place Saint-Michel and a short bridge to arrive at the Île-de-la-Cité with its Palace of Justice and the police headquarters. Students and ill-paid state functionaries were Widow Koenig's main customers.

Toward nine-thirty that evening the dining room was almost empty, the first wave of patrons gone, the after-theatre crowd not yet there. The tapster and two of the waiters were eating their dinner in the kitchen. The third one, Monsieur Hervé, stood leaning against the bar, alternatively watching both a

9

rowdy party of students and the steps leading to the office upstairs. Roars of laughter filled the room as two youngsters, armed with forks, knocked over a chair during a mock duel over the last piece of bacon remaining on the serving plate. If this went on for much longer, Monsieur Hervé thought, the rascals would get a piece of the old dragon's mind. Would serve them right too.

Widow Koenig took advantage of the mid-evening lull by working on her accounts. Her pen scratched angrily against the paper. If the row downstairs did not stop soon she would have to do something about it. Away from their families, students behaved like wild animals and the waiters would not intervene, fearing for their tips. Her own Gustave, such a well-behaved young man, had been taken away from her, which proved that God ran his business in a capricious way.

She lifted her head when she heard footsteps on the stairs. Soon after, the frosted glass panel of the office door framed the capped silhouette of a policeman.

"Come in, Fernand!" she called.

"I brought her," Fernand said, entering. "She's downstairs."

Widow Koenig rose from her desk. She left the office and leaned against the railing to look down at the dining room. The students carried on with their noisy behavior, pelting each other with bread balls, but their eyes kept straying toward a veiled woman standing by the door, her fingers nervously plucking at the material of her skirt. She was wearing black, a black that commanded no respect with her ankles exposed for everyone to see and her bust straining against a tight bodice. Trouble, thought Widow Koenig, here stands trouble if I ever saw it.

"Stop it at once!" she barked at the students. "This is a restaurant, not a circus. Monsieur Hervé, bring the gentlemen their bill. You," she addressed the woman in black, "sit there!" She pointed at a table far from the young men.

She returned to her office and closed the door.

"This is not going to work," she said.

"But Germaine, you promised."

"She's a hussy."

"A hussy?"

"Haven't you seen the way she's dressed? Advertising her wares like a shameless whore. And silk too! Before the week is over, she'll walk the streets."

"It's not her fault. Inspector Savard bought the dress second hand. She had nothing to do with it."

Widow Koenig sighed. Trust men to choose a female garment! "So I was wrong," she admitted. "All the same, you haven't told me everything. I'm no fool, you know. I read newspapers and I'm capable of putting two and two together."

"Shh . . . quiet . . ." The policeman flapped both hands, looking over his shoulder.

"A foreign widow in distress, my foot!" hissed his sister. "She's the American maid who shot Baron de Chazelle. You have brought a murderess under my roof, Fernand. Shame on you!"

Fernand removed his kepi and patted his balding forehead with a handkerchief. "I'm under a strict order of silence," he said.

"And I'm your sister."

"Orders, Germaine, orders! Anyway, she is no murderess. She shot the man in self-defense. You would have done the same."

"Would I? I would never put myself into such a situation and that's a fact."

"Germaine, your voice! You keep forgetting about your voice. Listen, she's a brave girl. She's shown great courage. Besides, she was the one who brought the doctor to her mistress. Without her, who would have known that there was a crime in the offing?"

"You should have told me all the same."

Fernand's feet shifted uneasily. "Listen, dear, now that Brigadier Lapique is about to retire, I've a shot at promotion. I offered to find work and shelter for the girl. How would I look if you refused? You need kitchen help. Do this for me and everybody will be happy."

Widow Koenig studied her brother. The man was over forty and still only an agent. *Brigadier* Levieux sounded far better. Life had not been easy for Fernand either. His wife had run away with his best friend. During a coup d'état, twenty years ago, he was shot at and since then his right earlobe was missing, making his head look out of balance.

"I'll give her Zidore's attic," she said. "But you, brother, will have to answer to God if she drops arsenic into my coffee."

The cooking smells in the kitchen partly emanated from particles of pork grease, which adhered to every surface of the room. Spices, boiled and roasted meats, and the pungent goat cheese with which the staff had finished their dinner added further aromatic notes. Above it all, immediately fusing with every molecule of fresh air, floated the acidic aroma of sauerkraut.

In the far corner of the kitchen, Monsieur Philippe, an on-and-off philosophy student, bent his thin back over a washbasin. With his hands up to his elbows in greasy water mixed with soda, he scrubbed at a baking dish.

Zidore, a puny boy in pressing need of a haircut, stood at his side, polishing cutlery. Monsieur Jacques, the cook, Monsieur Ludovic, the tapster, and both waiters were in no hurry. They sipped the remains of red wine, smoked, and flicked ashes on their dinner plates to the concert of the cutlery clatter and the slow hiss of a new batch of sauerkraut on the stove. Into this comfortable atmosphere burst Widow Koenig followed by the woman in black.

"Zidore," she boomed, "go up to your room and pack up your things. From now on, you sleep in the alcove under the cellar steps."

The boy froze, his eyes wide open.

"Zidore? Are you deaf?"

Zidore dropped his towel and shot out the door.

The widow addressed her remaining audience. "Messieurs, this is the new kitchen maid. You'll have to be patient with her because she speaks little French," she announced. "You can remove your veil now," she addressed the woman, pulling at the black gauze to make herself understood.

The woman obediently removed her hat.

The men sprung into action. One offered her a chair; another snatched her carpetbag and placed it by her side.

"Aw, poor thing, so young and already a widow," commiserated the cook. "Look how pale she is! I think she needs a little sustenance. A quarter portion?"

"I suppose so," said Widow Koenig. She watched with alarm as the cook filled a plate with sauerkraut, added two potatoes, and then chose the plumpest bratwurst, the meatiest slab of bacon, and the leanest slice of pork shoulder—much more than a quarter portion called for. Men! They all went to pieces at the sight of a pretty face. Trouble. No matter what Fernand said, there was going to be trouble.

She returned upstairs. In her private quarters behind the office, she rummaged through a cavernous linen closet until she found a pair of patched bed sheets, a blanket, and a towel.

Back in the kitchen, she found the girl hunched over her plate, playing with her food rather than eating it. The men—lecherous monkeys, all of them—lingered about. There could not be a greater insult to Widow Koenig than scorning her food. She dropped the bed linen onto an empty chair and set her fists on her hips.

"Monsieur Philippe," she addressed the idling dishwasher, "do I pay you for washing dishes or for admiring the scenery?"

"*Et vera incessu patuit dea.* And her very walk revealed a goddess," declared the philosopher, unperturbed.

12

The widow had no appreciation for Virgil. "None of your Latin nonsense!" she snapped. "As for the woman, she is obviously not hungry. A waste of food, Monsieur Jacques, a waste of food." She turned to the boy cowering by the door. "Have you brought your things down? Then show her up to your room. Her room. Whatever. She won't stay long."

She dispatched the waiters into the dining room, reminding them that Monsieur Hervé was still waiting for his dinner. Fuming, she retired to her office.

No sooner had she sat down at her desk and dipped her pen in the inkwell than she heard a timid knock at the door.

"What now?" she called.

The door opened cautiously and Zidore crept in.

"Well, Zidore, what's the matter?"

The boy was a thorn in her side - a sneaky little creature with fingernails bitten down to the quick and an unpleasant smell about him. He never looked her in the eye, nor did he speak above a whisper. She could not stand him and that was a fact. However, he worked hard and she had no valid reason to send him back to the orphanage.

"The lady's back in the kitchen," he whispered, his gaze fastened to the floor.

"Is she?"

He nodded. Widow Koenig noticed that the child was shaking like a leaf. What mischief had he been up to?

"Any particular reason why I should I be concerned with her where-abouts?"

"She—"

"For heaven's sake, boy, speak up!"

"She doesn't like the room."

The American waited in the kitchen.

"Now, what do I hear?" inquired Widow Koenig. "You don't like the accommodation? I'm sorry, Duchess, but I don't run a luxury hotel. Do I?" she asked rhetorically, turning to the cook, the dishwasher, and Monsieur Hervé who had just sat down to his dinner. They watched attentively, dinner and work forgotten.

The woman stood her ground. "The room is not clean."

"And am I supposed to clean it for you?"

"You must come, please. You must see."

13

"Must I? Who are you to give me orders? Find a brush and a pail of water and don't bother me again!"

"You must come."

Widow Koenig snorted. She turned and began to retrace her steps when a firm hand gripped her wrist. Mercy, the impudent creature was pulling her in the opposite direction!

"What! What!" she gasped. "You, men, don't just stand there! Help me!"

Nobody moved. Was it a false impression or had she seen a sneer on their faces? She had no time to ponder the question as she was dragged out of the kitchen, across the courtyard, and up four flights of steps. By that time, she was out of breath and limply obeying her abductor.

The door at the far end of a winding narrow passage led to a bare attic containing an iron bed, a wobbly chair, and a washbasin standing on a wooden crate. Widow Koenig entered and immediately buried her nose in her apron. Jesus, Marie, and Joseph. The room stank worse than a public urinal!

The girl held a lamp over a yellow-stained mattress and the widow gasped again. Zidore had been wetting his bed. At the age of twelve!

She turned on her heels and scuttled to the nearest landing where she opened a window overlooking the courtyard and leaned out. Her staff stood massed at the kitchen entrance, awaiting further developments.

"Zidore!" she yelled at the top of her lungs. "Come here this minute! Monsieur Philippe, you bring him up! At once!"

She saw the dishwasher reach into the kitchen and extract Zidore from his hiding place behind the door. When they reached her, she grabbed the frightened boy by an ear and dragged him toward the attic. The corridor resonated with loud knocks. Heavens above, was the American demolishing the room? The widow accelerated without releasing Zidore's ear. She was relieved to see that the girl was merely standing on the chair and using the crate as an improvised hammer. She was loosening the handle of a skylight that had not been opened for ages.

Widow Koenig propelled Zidore into the room. "Now see what you have done, you wicked boy!—Monsieur Philippe, come and have a look at the mattress! It has to be thrown out. What a waste, what a —"

"Shut your bloody trap, you old bat!"

"What?" The widow stepped into the corridor to confront a disheveled man, naked but for a towel loosely wrapped around his hips.

"I said shut your trap or I'll do it for you!" he shouted but his voice was no match for the widow.

"Oh, will you?" she yelled. "You don't even live here, so don't you tell me what to do! How dare you expose yourself in a public place? The landlord will hear of this first thing in the morning!"

The last words were addressed past the man's shoulder at the door behind him. The man was about to take a step forward, when a thin female arm emerged from inside the room and yanked him back.

The skylight gave up and a whiff of fresh air passed through the corridor.

"Zidore," said Widow Koenig, "I don't care if it takes you all night, but I want this room scrubbed down and smelling of bleach by tomorrow morning. Understood? Then we shall think about your punishment. What is it you are doing, Monsieur Philippe?"

"Merely leaving your employ, madam," said the philosopher, dropping his apron on the floor. "*Alea jacta est* and I'm not sorry. I shall find a post where a man can provide for his worldly needs without having his eardrums blasted to shreds. Most important of all, I can no longer bear witness to the slow but relentless destruction of an innocent child."

The widow's jaw dropped. "What on earth are you talking about?"

"Zidore is a sensitive boy," the philosopher said. "There was nothing wrong with him until Fate dumped him into your hands to be reduced to a quivering knot of nerves. I detect an utter confusion in your every feature, madam. Let me translate my thoughts into simple terms in accordance with your intellect. You are a loud, heartless bitch and if the boy wets his bed it is your fault. My respects, madam. I shall drop in tomorrow to collect my meager wages."

With a bow of his head, he left her there, aghast and, for once, short of words.

* * *

The clock of the nearby Saint-Séverin church chimed twice. It was two in the morning and Widow Koenig tossed in her bed. The dishwasher's rhetoric still played in her mind, robbing her of sleep. She had never been insulted in such a complicated manner and her failure to respond in kind, or to respond at all, gnawed at her self-esteem. There she had stood, by Zidore's stinky lair, numbed by shock as her world was slipping out of control. First, the girl kidnapped her—yes that was the word, *kidnapped*!—and none of her staff as much as lifted a finger in her defense. One could think that they actually enjoyed themselves! Then the philosopher ganged up with the boy and said such terrible things about her.

She, responsible for Zidore's disgusting habit? Fiddlesticks! The streets were full of homeless brats, far worse off than Zidore. Was it her fault that the boy could not stand a little shouting? She meant nothing wrong by it. True,

15

when she went to confession, the priest had to remind her not to make her sins public. Perhaps she ought to do something about it. But heartless? She had taken an orphan under her wing and given shelter to that foreign girl. Heartless bitch indeed! The world was full of ungrateful, ill-mannered individuals such as the grubby philosopher. But then, if she were right, as she undoubtedly was, why was it that she could not rid herself of the bitter taste of shame?

A suspicious sound in the office intruded on her thoughts. A thief? Everything was locked up as usual. No, it was the girl crying. Oh well, everyone in this world had their own load of sorrows. The important thing was to hold one's head up and go on with one's life.

In the office, the American was blowing her nose. Widow Koenig wished the girl would stop crying and get some sleep. Monsieur Jacques was right—she looked unhealthy. It wouldn't do to have an invalid on one's hands. She should get some sleep herself. Tomorrow, she would have to go and buy a second-hand mattress. Perhaps even a small table. There was none in the attic. Nothing expensive, mind. And a bedspread. No, she had one in the closet, a red one with large yellow roses and a green fringe. That would cheer up the room. There, how could anyone call her heartless?

She turned on her side, patting the pillow under her head, her thoughts dwelling on the bedspread with yellow roses. It had covered her maiden bed in Paris and she took it with her when she moved to the province of Alsace. How lonely and disoriented she felt those first few months! Strange surroundings, strange people and customs, a foreign language. Fortunately, she had her husband to lean on. The girl had no one.

Something stirred in Widow Koenig's shrunken heart. She slipped out of bed, lit a lamp, and threw a shawl over her shoulders. She found her new kitchen maid curled up on the sofa, her head buried into a tear-sodden pillow. She sat on the edge and patted the girl's shoulder.

"Come on, come on," she said.

The girl caught her hand and placed her wet cheek against it. Widow Koenig stroked the mass of wavy hair cascading over the girl's back. She felt strange - mellow and foolish at the same time. How long since she had been so close to anybody? Tomorrow, she would probably regret it. Also, tomorrow she must finally cut Zidore's hair.

Chapter 4

Now living among strangers, you, my diary, are the only one to whom I can talk to without searching for words. How glad I was to find you once I recovered my trunk! I find bitter comfort in your pages, especially in the words written in my carefree days before Father exited this world in such an irresponsible manner, leaving no provision for my future.

I used to face fate with fortitude, even when summarily cast off from school and sent to Butte. Living in a small house bursting at the seams with my uncle's family, I had not lost hope. For two years, I held out in that ugly gold-mining town where nothing ever happened except for a sharp-shooting contest every July 4th. I was biding my time, knowing that my misfortune would not last and that one day I would find a way back to civilization.

So here I am, with civilization all around me yet deprived of everything, including my own name. I cringe when people call me 'Madame Ahmitee' - a dead woman with a family that never cared for her. I ache for company but my boarding school French is of little use here. Reading is not difficult, but conversations are a matter of guessing what the other party is saying. The only exception is Monsieur Jacques, the cook, who speaks slowly and accompanies his orders with gestures to make my life easier. He says 'couper' and his hands mimic slicing, or 'mélanger' and, with his fists atop each other, he performs circles in front of his belly. He inquired about my family and I told him cautiously Amity Moncarelli's story, repeating several times that I was from Philadelphia. Not that it makes any difference. He is under the impression that we Americans live in tents and wear feather head-dresses.

The cook is from Burgundy and his parents are still alive, but they must be very old as he is no longer young. His sister has many children as he demonstrated to me by folding his thick arms and rocking them as if holding a baby. Then he put his palm three feet above the floor and then higher and higher, indicating the respective height of his numerous nieces and nephews. The sister reminds me of Aunt McKay, who has had a child for every year of her marriage.

Monsieur Jacques has an aunt as well. She is very old—he tied a towel over his head and bent forward imitating a frail old woman walking with a cane—and when she dies—stiff body, eyes closed, and arms folded across the chest—he will inherit her house and turn it into a restaurant. He will serve only Burgundian food. "Choucroute, pah! No good," he said. "Burgundy cuisine - mhm!" and he loudly kissed the tips of his fingers, sending the kiss heavenwards. The French tend to do that when talking of food.

The day after my arrival Madame Koenig took me to a large second-hand dress market, where she exchanged my strangling moiré silk for a sensible black bombazine of recent cut. While I dressed behind the dingy curtain, she haggled with the vendor until they reached a satisfactory bargain. She then marched me to yet another market that sold used household goods and chose a mattress and a small table with peeling paint. The two articles are now in my attic along with a garish bedspread, which, if I understood correctly, is of great sentimental value.

I don't know what to think of my new employer. One day she behaves like an angry sergeant, barking at everyone in sight, the next she is as meek as a lamb and the day after that she is back to shouting. Yet I'm grateful for her kindness to me that first night, when my only thoughts were of throwing myself into the river.

Not that I am any happier now, but at least I no longer want to die. Instead, I find relief in work. The hustle and bustle of the kitchen keeps oppressive thoughts at bay, while solitude gives them a free rein. As soon as I close my eyes, determined to sleep, anguish strangles my chest and I chastise myself by replaying scenes from the past.

In hindsight, I recognize the signs that should have alerted me to the suspicious goings on. The road from Butte to Paris was strewn with unheeded warnings. I shrugged off my uncle's misgivings about joining two complete strangers and their creepy valet. When we reached Kitty de Chazelle's hometown, I was amused by the servants' gossip in the Cooper's house. Miss Kitty, they said, had gone and married the French baron without her older brother's knowledge. Even though Mr. Cooper was given six weeks to get used to the fact, he did not greet the eloped couple with kindness. He raged against the fact that hard-earned American money should support an impoverished French aristocrat just so that Miss Kitty could call herself a baroness. When the legal transfer of Kitty's inheritance was completed, my mistress and Mr. Cooper parted like strangers.

I had no cause for concern at that time. Even though it was clear that the baron had married Kitty Cooper for her money, she was in love with her charming husband and happy enough. I, for my part, was enchanted with her castoffs. For the first time in years, I had fashionable clothes, matching stockings, a horsehair bustle, and two fetching hats. I was on my way to France, hoping to catch a distinguished husband of my own. After all, why not? Was I not prettier and smarter than my mistress? Could I not hold my own in domestic science, French, and piano playing?

Smart, I was not. I listened as eagerly as Kitty did to the baron's tales of the French Riviera. I could already see myself strolling along the shore in Nice and meeting the lofty people who spent the winter season there. According to the baron, crossing the path of a prince would be as ordinary an event as meeting a half-breed in Butte. He spoke English with a delightful accent and we could actually hear the buzz of the cicadas and the enchanting song of the nightingale carrying across the velvety southern nights. So absorbed were we in his nightly tales that sometimes I ceased brushing Kitty's hair and she didn't even notice.

"Tell me more. Tell me about the house," she would say, and he would talk about the small town of Saint-Anselme nestled among olive groves. He described the cypress-lined road leading up the hill to a three-story mansion with a view of the sea, a shimmering azure ribbon on the horizon. The château with yellow-ochre façade and the baronial coat of arms carved in stone above the entrance became so real in my mind that I never doubted its existence.

When should I have realized? The seasickness? It was a calm crossing and no one suffered except for my mistress. Or the pregnancy, as suggested by her husband, once we landed, and the 'seasickness' did no longer fit vomiting and stomach cramps? There were other details I chose to ignore. A strangely unconcerned doctor, a bottle of medicine that failed to bring relief and a feeling of uneasiness that grew in me day by day. When blisters appeared on Kitty's skin and her lips turned blue, I finally acted by fetching another doctor. Yet even then, I did not suspect poisoning. When the doctor left and Kitty's silver hairbrush went missing, I reported it to the baron for fear of being mistaken for a thief. I avoid thinking of what happened afterwards, at least during my waking state.

When I do finally fall asleep, I often dream of a dark river. The black water glistens with reflections of gaslights and I fill with terrible foreboding. One of the reflections drifts toward me and as it grows larger, I see that it is a body and the face is that of my mistress. Her body floats by with eyes open; an accusatory finger points at me. I turn and run into a darkened street, past a faceless woman. "I am Amity Moncarelli and you have stolen my name," she says. She follows me as I flee from her. Our steps resonate on the pavement. I turn my head to check the distance between us. Instead of her, I see the sinister chinless face of the valet with his beak of a nose and his dark eyes that burn holes in me. The street squeezes into a narrowing corridor. I must bend forward as the ceiling is descending lower and lower. Soon, I crawl on all fours, then flat on my stomach. I struggle until my shoulders cannot pass through the ever-narrowing space and I'm trapped. With a cry of anguish, I wake up . . . to face another day of gloom.

Chapter 5

Thump, *thump, thump. Thump.* Most days, a mechanical sound woke Nelly from an uneasy sleep. Sometimes at night, when she climbed upstairs with exhaustion weighing her down, other sounds filtered through the thin wall that separated her from her neighbor: male voices, the bed creaking and an occasional quarrel.

Nelly never acknowledged the thin brunette with deep-set black eyes as they passed each other on the steps. On her working days, she was dressed plainly and carried heavy bundles. On other days, her face was painted and her outfit consisted of a red- and black-striped skirt, a loud magenta bodice showing deep cleavage, and a bright-green velvet hat. Everything about the woman was ill kept. By now, Nelly knew how difficult it was to keep clean in the old tenements of Paris, where the only source of water was a pump in the courtyard, yet she could not find an excuse for dirty ears. Everyone could make that much effort.

In the mornings, as she walked down the dim corridor, turning one corner, then another one, taking one step down here and two steps up there—nothing was straight or level in the old house—she could steal glimpses of her neighbors' lives. Some doors were left open, exposing shabby interiors where people worked, slept and ate their meals. Here, a family of Spanish immigrants glued satin lining into smart jeweler's boxes stamped with gold leaf. Elsewhere, swan's down dyed in a variety of colors was assembled into yards of trimming. Two rooms housed a silk flowers factory populated with giggly teenage girls. The supervisor, a short stubby fellow with sparse hair and blue cheeks, stationed himself in the door as she walked by. "When are you coming to work for me, my beauty?" was his daily greeting.

He was essentially harmless, unlike the two students who inhabited a room by the staircase. They were often drunk and, in the early weeks, they used to knock at her door in the middle of the night. One of them waylaid her as she was unlocking her door. She kicked him in the shin and succeeded in locking herself in before he found his footing. Since then, an uneasy truce existed between them. Should he or his roommate try again, she would have to tell Monsieur Jacques. The cook had already dealt with disrespect on her behalf. Everyone witnessed Monsieur Hervé, one of the waiters, being seized by the lapels and repeatedly banged against the wall for trying to kiss her. The stocky cook had an iron grip and she felt safe in his company.

Nelly descended to the main floor and emerged into the courtyard. It was good to be outside even though she missed the immense Montana skies and the bright sun of the prairies. Winter clad Paris with the drab cloak of chilly dampness in which the wet cobblestones shared the same shade of grey with the slate roofs and the leaden sky.

She went round a delivery wagon of the furniture repair firm that rented the main floor of the rear building, crossed the courtyard and entered the restaurant kitchen. It was still cold, but Zidore had the spirit heater going and the aroma of fresh coffee made the room hospitable. She patted him on the back and the boy's thin face lit with a smile. They developed a tacit complicity on the day she secretly rectified his haircut following Widow Koenig's clumsy handiwork. Sitting down, wordlessly sipping coffee, they both enjoyed the quiet spell before the staff arrived and the restaurant erupted with the chaos of a working day.

Lately, the business was thriving. Guests crowded around the zinc counter, sipping aperitifs while waiting for vacant seats. In addition to kitchen duties, Nelly was drafted to help with clearing the tables. She did not mind the extra work as much as she minded being pawed while her hands were full. She no longer had the proper means to demand respect: her confiscated revolver was probably gone forever. To make matters worse, Widow Koenig was in the habit of sitting in a chair at the top of the stairs, keeping one eye on her knitting and the other one on the goings on in the dining room below. She was quick at spotting improper behavior.

"You there," she would shout, "yes, you! Keep your hands to yourself. The only thing we serve is food."

The dining room would ripple with laughter, including the offender who would shield his head as if expecting a blow. It was all good-natured enough if you weren't on the receiving end. On one such occasion, Nelly's neighbor was there in the company of another tart and two students. She was shaking with malicious mirth, enjoying the kitchen maid's humiliation. The next day, upon meeting Nelly on the stairs, the woman exploded with suppressed anger.

"Here she goes, Miss High and Mighty," she sneered with hands on her hips. "Never a smile or even a nod. You think you are better than me, don't you? Let me show you where you can put your stiff upper lip—" she slapped her own behind. "You're pretty stupid if you ask me. Me, at least, when a fellow grabs my ass, I get paid for it!"

Her loud laughter pursued Nelly all the way upstairs. The worst thing about the dreadful encounter was that the woman had a point.

Nelly and Zidore were finishing their breakfast when Inspector Savard, carrying a flat box under his arm, rapped on the kitchen window.

"I need a quiet word with you," he said to Nelly when she let him in.

"Let's sit in the dining room," she said. "Would you like a cup of coffee?"

"That would be very nice, thank you."

The chilly air in the dining room was stale with the odor of cold tobacco and alcohol spills. Savard stirred sugar into his steaming coffee and knocked the spoon against the cup before returning it to the saucer.

"It's possible that Madame de Chazelle's body has been found at last," he said.

Nelly sunk into her chair. "Not again!"

Several times she had been dragged to the morgue and shown bodies in various states of decay. The prospect of yet another such trip filled her with dread.

Savard clutched the cup to warm his hands. "This time it's different. The clothes correspond to your description. As for the body, it's beyond recognition in its present state. However, the doctor will be able to compare the hair with the sample he found in the hair brush. I think we'll have a match. All I want from you is to identify the contents of this box."

He lifted the lid, revealing what was once a colorful Indian shawl. A stinking breath of decay hit Nelly's nostrils.

"Yes," she said, her eyes filling with tears. She discarded the shawl and shook out a torn, discolored beige dress. The box also contained her mistress' shoes and a nightshirt stained with vomit. "Everything is as I told you. I put the dress over the nightshirt. The laudanum the doctor gave her made her so limp that I could not dress her properly and her husband was urging me to hurry." She folded the garments and returned them into the box. "Where was the body found?"

"In a ravine along the Paris-Marseille railway line," Savard said. "But there's more."

He reached into his breast pocket and removed two folded sheets of paper. "I have a game for you," he said, flattening the sheets against the table.

"A game? Now?"

"Let's call it a game. What you see here are two copies from the passport register in Nice. One belongs to Baron de Chazelle and the other to the valet Pierre Blanchard. I will hide their names with my hands. Now, study both passports and tell me which one belongs to the baron and which to the valet."

Nelly went through the documents, item by item. "This is incredible," she said. "The two men were like day and night, one handsome, the other ugly, yet the descriptions are the same. They both were of the same height. They both had brown hair and brown eyes. What does *fuyant* mean?"

"Receding."

"A receding chin. Then this must be the valet's, Pierre Blanchard's, passport."

"Wrong," Savard said and lifted his hands.

Nelly took in a sharp intake of air and clasped her hand over her mouth.

"Two men," the inspector said, "one charming, one repulsive, yet the description is almost identical. This will not happen in the future, I hope. In the future, passports will carry a photographic likeness."

He took a sip of coffee and, arms folded, leaned against the back of his chair. "We received a report from Nice where Pierre Blanchard was known to the police. He was, shall we say, a professional companion. The Riviera is a fertile hunting ground for rich foreign widows in search of diversion. Had it not been for his trips to the nearby Monte Carlo casino, Blanchard could have led a comfortable life. Unfortunately, he tried to patch up his gambling debts by committing fraud and Nice became too hot under his feet. As for Baron de Chazelle, he was another regular at the gambling tables. With his estate laden with debt and likely to go under the hammer, the only thing that could save him was an advantageous marriage. Except, ugly as he was, no rich woman would have him. Somehow, the two clicked together. They decided to exploit the growing trend that brings together Old World titles and new American money."

"So they were plotting Kitty's murder from the beginning," Nelly said. "And I was next."

Savard shook his head. "Only because you caused trouble. Had everything gone according to plan, they would have sent you back to America with a woeful tale of illness and death. There would have been a legitimate grave in Paris and de Chazelle would have returned to his estate a grieving widower, his finances restored."

Nelly sighed. "If only I knew that the doctor had pocketed the silver brush because he suspected arsenic, I'd have kept my mouth shut."

"I truly wish you had," Savard agreed. "The birds would not have panicked and fled. We'd have had them both caged the very same day. Still, you were very fortunate that we arrived in time to follow your cab, Miss McKay." He pocketed the passports and produced another document. "I need your signature. It says here that you have recognized the items presented to you as belonging to Baroness de Chazelle née Cooper."

Nelly went to the counter to pick up a pen and an inkstand. Back at the table, she wrote her name where Savard indicated on the document.

She watched the inspector blowing on the wet signature and broke into tears. "What wrong had she done to suffer so much? What purpose did it serve to drag a dying woman across the country? Tell me, what purpose?"

Savard shrugged. "Obviously, although the odds were against it, the real Baron de Chazelle attempted to take your mistress home and have her buried in the family grave. Very likely, the local doctor would have issued a death certificate attesting to a heart attack. Not all physicians are as perspicacious as Doctor Stein who is an experienced toxicologist. It was a sheer matter of luck that you brought him into the case. As for the rest, one can conclude that once installed in the train compartment, de Chazelle had time to examine the hastily hatched plan and found fault with it. Perhaps the baroness died sooner than he expected and rigor mortis was setting in. He would have had a hard time explaining why he carried his wife off when she was already dead or about to expire. Furthermore, he was unsure how things were developing here. Would his accomplice succeed in getting rid of you before the doctor alerted the police? In the end, de Chazelle decided to call it quits and go into hiding."

Savard returned the document to his pocket and patted it protectively. "In any case, you are definitely cleared, Miss McKay. You will be able to return home as soon as we straighten up the paperwork. Oh, by the way, the Pinkerton Agency is on the case. They have requested your address. Have you been contacted by them?"

"That was last Thursday," Nelly said. "A certain Mr. Dale. He said he was acting on Mr. Cooper's behalf. He wanted to know whether I had seen any financial documents and if so, what they were. Mr. Cooper is mainly interested in recovering his sister's money and jewels."

"Well, let's hope they catch de Chazelle in the process. If he has crossed to Spain or to Italy, our hands are tied. The Pinkerton men are not fenced in by borders nor hampered by lack of funds."

"And what about me?" Nelly said. "How will I return to America? I asked Mr. Dale the intentions Mr. Cooper had regarding me and he said he had no instructions. How am I supposed to make my way back home?"

"Your family cannot help?"

"I don't see how. Once the snow falls, Butte is cut off from the world until mid-April."

Savard thought for a while. "I'll write to Mr. Cooper and mention your plight. Were you owed your last wage?"

She smiled bitterly. "Four dollars. Enough for a railway ticket to Le Havre. And then?"

"Leave it to me," Savard said, rising. "Thank you for the coffee."

Chapter 6

Octave Gaillard whistled cheerfully as he crossed the Saint-Michel bridge. It was a typically grey winter day but Octave's mood was sunny. Thanks to a well-connected friend, he had the privilege of counting the new Prefect of the Seine among his sitters. The fact that the virtual master of Paris and its suburbs commissioned his official portrait from him would open the door to a new kind of customer, those close to the new power. He ought to look for a second studio, this time on the Right Bank. The boulevard des Italiens? No, too many photographers there. The Place de l'Opéra? Very chic but pricy. The Champs Elysées? Now there's an idea! All the *beau monde* passing by on their way to the Bois de Boulogne, and the presidential palace standing conveniently close by. The government could not stay in Versailles forever. Eventually, it was bound to move back to Paris.

In the meantime, he could turn to equestrian photography. Before the war, his arch-rival Disdéri had made a small fortune shooting pictures of thoroughbreds and their proud owners. The work was done outside and required no complicated lighting. He would put one of his assistants in charge of the second studio and pocket the profit. The country might be broke but the private money was still there for a smart entrepreneur. Yes, a studio on the Champs Elysées was a very good idea. He would keep his eyes open for a piece of real estate. Naturally, such premises would not be cheap and, at the moment, he was rather stretched. Not that the business was bad; it picked up quite nicely after the war, but the war itself and the period of unrest which followed had made a serious dent in his finances. The decoration of the rue des Médicis apartment would have to wait. A good excuse to delay the wedding. Amélie would make a perfect life companion but, at thirty-three, he was not entirely ready for family life. He intended to be a faithful husband but another year or two of complete freedom would not come amiss. He enjoyed his women lusty and without restraint and one could not ask the same from a wife. A wife was to be respected.

Yes, Amélie was perfect. What a couple they would make! She beautiful, flawless in appearance and manners; he respected and famous and, even should he say so himself, not bad looking at all. They would produce perfect sons who, through the best education and good connections, would attain success of their own. One day, he would stand in front of his father, a plain country doctor, and say: "Now, tell me again that I'm a failure!"

Besides, Father was beginning to realize, grudgingly at best, that his son's betrayal was not the ultimate crime. A young physician had married one of Octave's sisters and was about to take over the practice. The man was heartily welcome to both. He, himself, was simply not made to be a doctor. The whole business of human misery that was medicine depressed and sickened him. In his heart and soul, he was an artist celebrating nature's beauty in its full bloom. Medicine dealt with decay.

Octave sighed and shuddered at the thought. Then he realized that he had taken a detour by the rue Saint-André des Arts. Funny, how his reflections unconsciously brought him to the old haunts of his student days. Nostalgia seized him just as the church towers across the city chimed noon, reminding him that it was time for a meal.

There used to be a restaurant run by an old Auvergnat couple, an unpretentious place with simple good food. To his disappointment, the Auvergnats were gone, doubtless retired to their province. Instead, the corner was occupied by a brand new business. Gone were the worm-eaten sign and the decrepit façade. The first floor of the building was now an uninterrupted row of windows behind which fluttered the snow-white aprons of waiters.

Octave stared at the sign. *La Tour d'Alsace, Propriétaire Widow Koenig*. Like everyone, he heard about the numerous Alsatian refugees. The countries of Alsace and Lorraine were gone, severed from the body of France. Damn the Prussians. Damn Bismarck. Damn the whole business of politics. However, the pretty country maids painted on the entrance panels smiled invitingly and he had never tasted Alsatian food. A culinary adventure? Why not!

Inside, one of the waiters quickly assessed the cut and quality of Octave's clothes and calculated the size of his tip. With much bowing and scraping, he removed his greatcoat, pulled out one of the small square tables, and paused until Octave took his seat on a padded bench by the wall. He imprisoned the prosperous guest by returning the table to its place, whisked away an ordinary linen napkin, replaced it by starched damask, and awaited orders.

Octave learned that a plate of choucroute could feed two to four people and settled on a half-portion. He ordered a *demi* of Moselle wine and contentedly leaned back against the maroon padding of the bench.

He approved of the change. The mirrors on the walls greatly enlarged the room and magnified the light. The bar counter used to be a sorry sight. Now it was gleaming with new brass fixtures worthy of Tortoni's or the Café Anglais on the Right Bank boulevards. Progress was fighting its way into the heart of the Latin Quarter and Octave was glad. He was a thoroughly modern man.

The place buzzed with lively conversations interspersed with bursts of laughter. It was the vibrant atmosphere of vigor and unbridled life expectations that he remembered from his student days.

To his right, several medics, sporting their first manly beards and mustaches, discussed the merits and dangers of ether. Ten years ago, he was one of them.

To his left, two fine-art students disagreed on differing techniques of *chiaro-oscuro*. Ten years ago, he envied them.

Ten years ago, he was the unhappiest human being alive. He had gone through the motions of learning the craft of medicine because it was expected of him. During the long boring lectures, his restless hands sketched professors and fellow students. The sketches were skillful and sarcastically funny. Still, he was not good enough to consider painting seriously. Worse than anything, he was color-blind. Out of desperation, he turned a hand at sculpture, which proved to be a mistake as the three-dimensional space confused him to no end. What looked perfect from one angle was hideous from another. Defeated, he returned to his medical books, resigning himself to the lackluster fate of a small-town physician.

The waiter brought the first course, a pâté, and a carafe of wine. To Octave's right, the conversation took an unexpected turn as the medics were now discussing the anatomy of a well-known actress. To his left, the dispute was still going on, opposing Rembrandt to Latour.

Chiaro-oscuro, the conflict of light and shadow. He could tell the two greenhorns far more than they knew. But would they listen? Hardly. He was much too familiar with the condescending attitude, the snobbery, and even downright hostility, to which artists subjected photography. Few of them had any insight into its possibilities. Jealousy, nothing but jealousy. Now that everyone could afford an instant portrait, business was down for painters. As for himself, the first time he looked at the world through the eye of a camera, he was forever seduced. This was what he wanted to do. Nothing else mattered.

The choucroute the waiter brought looked like a barbaric offering to the gods.

"Mhm, wouldn't I rather dine on that," said one of the painters.

Surprised by the remark, Octave looked at him. The fellow's gaze was directed toward the kitchen door, through which a girl had entered. Far from shuffling with her head down as was the habit of servants, she was gliding across the room, deftly clearing abandoned tables. Octave's fork, with a piece of sausage skewered on its prongs, remained suspended in mid-air. The girl carried herself with a regal dignity and one had the impression that she was there by mistake; that the humble task she performed was a rehearsal for a play in which a casting error had been made. Octave remembered his manners and completed the fork's trajectory, while his gaze remained on her. Chewing dutifully, he reflected upon the effects of *chiaro-oscuro* on the girl's face. If he mirrored the light from a sharp angle, he could enhance the melancholy of her eyes and, at the same time, outline the perfect oval of the face. A softer light source, a mere reflection, directed at the mouth would bring into focus those eminently kissable lips. Dear God, he had never seen such lips. They asked — no, they begged! — to be devoured with passion. If only the girl would stand still for a moment . . . Now, here was the profile . . . Where had he seen such a profile? It had a touch of familiarity . . . Don't leave yet, he begged silently, but she was gone.

Returned to reality, he decided that he did not care much for Alsatian food. Coming here was a mistake. He declined the dessert and left.

A few days later, he realized that he had developed an inexplicable urge for yet another plate of choucroute. He returned to the restaurant but the girl did not show up.

*   *   *

It was a bad fall and the worst of it was that it happened in front of that awful woman. One moment Nelly was descending the stairs, and the next she knew, she was sprawled at her neighbor's feet. When she tried to get up, a sharp pain in her ankle made her gasp.

The brunette was relishing the situation. "Hey, how do you like it down there?" she asked. "If you want help, you'll have to say 'please'."

"Please," Nelly said.

She staggered into her room, leaning heavily on her helper, who led her to bed and removed her shoe and stocking.

"Seems that you have earned yourself a week on your back," the brunette said, examining the swollen ankle.

She poured water into the basin, submerged a towel, and wrung it out. "I can't promise you a quiet rest," she went on while wrapping the cold compress around the injured ankle. "I have paying guests, while they paw you for nothing downstairs, and I don't mean to stop while you are here. So you'd better stuff cotton into your saintly ears."

Nelly sighed.

"My name is Marie," the brunette said. "And yours?"

* * *

"Monsieur Jacques sends you *un petit quelque chose*," was Zidore's daily greeting. "He says not to worry, everything is just fine down in the kitchen."

Monsieur Jacques's 'little somethings', prepared especially for the invalid, came outside the regular meal times - a caramel cream, an omelet with shrimp stuffing, a sweet pudding, a fruit tart. Not in the mood for food, what Nelly could not finish, which was most of it, she would leave to Zidore.

Widow Koenig visited once, bringing a change of bed linen and a clean towel. She inspected Nelly's ankle, tut-tutted at the size of the swelling, and sighed at the waste of time.

"Try to mend quickly," she said. "They miss you down in the kitchen. Also, I hope that you understand that I have to take this out of your salary."

"What salary?" asked Nelly. "I have yet to be paid."

"I'm paying you one franc a day. Your lodging, food, and laundry amount to ninety centimes. As soon as you reimburse me for your dress, you'll touch your ten centimes a day."

"And when will that be?"

The widow made a swift mental calculation. "Not until mid-April," she said.

It was no use haggling over money when the only option was the street. The widow's visit added a new depth to Nelly's state of melancholy. Alone in her attic that even the garish bedspread could not cheer up, she had time to ponder her present and her future, none of which looked promising. Although nine weeks had passed since Inspector Savard's last visit, she had no news. Had Mr. Cooper answered Savard's letter? How long was she to remain buried alive in a dusty attic with a cheap whore for company?

As if on cue, the door opened and Marie sailed in.

"What's up, Anglaise? Been crying again?"

Nelly quickly wiped her eyes. "Why do you keep calling me Anglaise? I'm not English, I'm American."

"So you know how to speak American?"

"Americans speak English."

"Then you are an Englishwoman," concluded Marie, using her own logic.

She slammed down a bucket she had emptied into the latrine. By now, she was quite at home in Nelly's room. Despite the initial disgust the woman had inspired in her, Nelly had been slowly drawn into her life. Marie came from Ménilmontant, a blue-collar neighborhood outside the city walls. At fifteen, she had 'shacked up' with a shoemaker who used to drink and beat her to a pulp. She left him for Léon, a metalworker who spent most of his time talking politics in cafés. After the Commune uprising, Léon, considered a dangerous agitator, was deported to the colonies and Marie had to fend for herself.

"I make a franc and fifteen centimes for a twelve-hour day stamping eyelets on corsets," she once explained. "Besides, there's not enough work anyway. Sometimes, I deliver a batch only to find that there is no work to take home."

"And how much do you earn on the street?"

"That depends. If it's a gentleman, I ask three francs for a pass and usually get two. With students, I'm lucky if I get one franc. Still, it beats the eyelets, eh?"

Nelly shrugged. "All I know is that I couldn't do it."

"Oh, you couldn't, could you?" Marie bristled. "Try not eating for three days and I guarantee you that at the end of it, you'd spread your legs as well."

Nelly shivered at the idea.

"With Léon, I've got a political education," Marie went on. "I'm a socialist and I don't care who knows it. Léon believes in equality for women. Has it ever occurred to you that women are exploited and grossly underpaid? We earn just about enough to keep body and soul together, never enough to put something aside. When there's no work, we starve. Is that justice or what?"

"No, it isn't," Nelly admitted. "Still, a woman is not meant to be single. She must marry and take care of her family."

"Marry!" Marie snorted. "You still believe in that crap? Marriage is just another form of exploitation. You work like a slave from sunrise to sundown and all you ever get for your pains is the occasional black eye. Bah, being bound to a man for the rest of your life with no more rights than a child! Besides, where I come from, people are too poor to marry anyway. It costs fifty francs just for putting the documents together. Nobody has that kind of money."

"You mean that couples live together without being wed?"

Marie shrugged. "So? It ain't nobody's fault but the government's. They are the ones that make the laws."

Now, with her foot, Marie pushed the bucket into a corner. "Got a pair of scissors?" she asked. "Seems that I've mislaid mine."

And no wonder in that messy room of yours, Nelly thought. "In my trunk there's a sewing basket," she said. "Except that I have only one pair of scissors and I don't want to lose them."

"Eh, don't worry," Marie waved off Nelly's misgivings and opened the trunk. "Oh, my!" she exclaimed, rummaging inside. "Is all this yours?"

"The dresses? Yes. Don't touch them. Just get the basket."

Marie ignored her. "Oh!" she breathed and yanked out a peacock-blue velvet that Kitty de Chazelle had decided was too strong for her coloring. She held the skirt at her waist and admired the abundance of trimmings. "Oh!" she repeated, balancing the bodice against her chest. "This is like a dream. It's so beautiful! Is it really yours? You have fallen on hard times, haven't you?"

Nelly nodded, inwardly suffering at the sight of Marie's grimy hands pawing the rich material. "Put it back, please," she said.

"If I had a dress like this, I could make twenty-franc passes at the Café Anglais," Marie said.

"Well, you don't, and don't even think of borrowing it."

"I'll buy it from you."

"I don't want your sinful money."

"You are a selfish bitch."

"Put it back, will you?"

Marie paused, thinking hard. "Listen," she said with a shrewd smile, "if you give me the dress, I'll tell you a secret."

"I don't want to hear your secrets. What good would they be to me?"

"You don't want to know how to avoid having babies?"

"What?"

"If you give me the dress, I'll tell you how to lie with men without getting yourself into trouble. Isn't it fair enough?"

Nelly propped herself up in the bed. The dreadful business of breeding that made Aunt seem older than her years had somewhat tainted the state of matrimony in her eyes. One or two babies would be lovely, but thirteen?

"Even with one's husband?" she asked.

"Sure. What difference does it make? A man's a man."

This was tempting. Still, Nelly had her doubts. "How do I know it will work? You can tell me a lie."

Clutching the dress, Marie sat on the bed next to her. "I bought the secret from a brothel madam. Before that, I was always pregnant. As you know, I go with men often enough. Do I look pregnant to you?"

"You had been pregnant? Then where are your children?"

"That's none of your business."

"I think it is. Either you tell me or I'll think that you are lying. Then it's no deal."

Marie shrugged. "The eldest is with his father, the shoemaker. The other two were miscarriages. Then I took up with Léon and he had no time for babies. We had a daughter who cried too much and Léon forced me to give her up. After that, he asked me not to get with child again. Going for advice to the brothel madam was actually his idea. So, do we have a deal?"

Nelly nodded.

"After I tell you, the dress is mine. Agreed?"

"Agreed."

And so Marie told her. Nelly could not believe that it was so wonderfully simple. Could a small sponge soaked in vinegar really make all the difference?

"Sure it can," Marie said. "You can also use lemon juice, it works just the same. The acidity kills the seed. After, you just pull on the string, wash the sponge, and let it dry. I'll tell you what. If you let me borrow that pretty little hat of yours, I'll give you two new sponges."

"All right," said Nelly. "But first you'll have to wash your hair."

"Wash my hair? Whatever for?"

"Because it's greasy. And if you want my honest opinion, you should scrub all over. A twenty-franc whore should have clean ears."

"I suppose you are right. I could go to the public bath. I've heard about it but never tried it for myself."

"You do that. And leave the dress behind. It needs to be shortened."

"You'd do that for me? Thanks, you're a real pal!"

I don't believe I'm doing this, thought Nelly as she stitched up the hem. She was making friends with a tart and trying to turn her into a lady. Good thing Aunt was not here to see it. On the other hand, the challenge steered her away from depressing thoughts.

When Marie came back from the public bath, fresh and smelling of soap, Nelly heartened to the task and brought out of hiding beauty aids she had not used since Kitty de Chazelle's illness. She plucked Marie's eyebrows into shape, filed and buffed her nails, patted her face with powder, massaged a drop of castor oil into the lashes and spread glistening pomade on her lips. She lit a spirit heater under a curling iron, and crimped and pinned Marie's hair into cascading curls as the fashion dictated.

"Oh, God, oh!" Marie exclaimed when she saw her face in the mirror. "Oh! I can't believe it. This is fabulous! Don't I look like a picture? Thanks ever so much!" She grabbed Nelly and kissed her on both cheeks. "My name is not Marie if I don't bring at least fifty francs. No, wait! Marie is too ordinary. From now on, I'll be known as Manon. Sounds posh, eh? Anyway, wish me good luck!"

Marie was gone, leaving Nelly with a feeling of emptiness. Again, she was alone with her thoughts and they were of the bitterest variety. She should be the one wearing that beautiful dress. What purpose did good morals serve when life was so obviously unjust?

Chapter 7

On the last day of her confinement, Nelly felt like a caged animal. Outside, the weather had changed. A bright sun warmed up the roof; bird songs and the distant hum of the metropolis streamed in through the open skylight, yet all she could see was the slanting ceiling of her attic and a small square of blue sky.

She longed for a bath, a long luxurious bath, but all she got was the bucket of hot water Zidore brought up along with a message from Monsieur Jacques. Would Madame Amity be agreeable to seeing him at three in the afternoon?

Her visitor came precisely at three, dressed in a new suit and sporting a fresh haircut stiffened with gelatin. He looked strangely nervous, not at all like the friendly cook she knew. In one gloved hand, he held a walking stick and a top hat, the other he kept hidden behind his back.

"Do come in, please," she said as he stood at the threshold, taking in the bareness of her dwelling.

He cleared his throat. "I'm very grateful you have agreed to see me and I apologize for coming up to your room," he said solemnly. "And . . . uh . . ." he lifted his eyes to the ceiling to collect his thoughts, ". . . I'm aware that it could give rise to gossip but I need to talk to you in private and this is the only opportunity before you return to your duties. There is never enough privacy in the kitchen."

"You are welcome, Monsieur Jacques." Nelly offered him her only chair and sat on the bed, hands in her lap.

Still holding a hand behind his back he was about to sit when he remembered something. "For you," he said, handing her a posy of primroses.

"Why, Monsieur Jacques, they are beautiful," she commented weakly, because by then she realized what was coming.

The cook smiled briefly and resumed his solemn expression. "It's like this," he began. "Last week I received a letter from home. My aunt—I had mentioned her, do you remember?—my aunt has taken to her bed. According to my parents, she will not last much longer. She owns a house in a small town not far from Dijon. When she dies, I stand to inherit it. The house sits on the main square. It's a good location and I have already obtained a restaurant license. In a couple of weeks, perhaps even sooner, I'll be leaving here. I've been working in Paris for the past eighteen years and I have quite a bit put by - enough to furnish a restaurant and weather out the first year. And so . . ." he paused and took a deep breath, "And so . . ." he paused again and got on one knee in front of her, "I came here to ask you to do me the great honor of becoming my wife."

She hid her face in the posy, not knowing whether to laugh or cry. The Devil in her kept telling her how ridiculous her swain looked with his sweaty brow, thinning hair, thick legs and prominent belly. *Stupid, stupid,* nagged her reasonable self, *here is a good, hard-working man offering to marry a penniless stranger like you!* To counteract Reason, the Devil conjured a vision of Monsieur Jacques covering her with his body and grunting with passion. The Devil won.

"Madame Amity?" The cook seized her hand and held it in his. He wanted an answer.

"Monsieur Jacques", she said gravely, "I thank you for your offer. Believe me, I'm very flattered . . . very . . . touched by it. But . . ." she hesitated, searching for kind words of refusal.

"But?" He squeezed her fingers with such strength that she gasped with pain. Quickly, he relaxed his grip. "I'm sorry! I didn't intend to—I'm truly sorry. I love you. The last thing I want is to harm you in any way."

She grew uneasy under his intense gaze. To put some distance between them, she motioned to the chair. "Please do sit down and let us discuss the matter calmly."

"Yes, you are right," he said after a brief hesitation. He rose, brushed off his knee, and resumed his seat.

"This is all so sudden," she said. "I must admit that I've never thought of you in this way. You are a friend to me, but no more than that."

"And so I shall remain. A husband and a friend. I hoped to prepare you for what I had in mind, take you for an outing or something of the sort, but the letter came. That puts a new light on the situation. I can wait no longer. And I've missed you, dear heart. You weren't gone for a day and I already felt sad. Don't say no to me! You are alone in the world and I'll take good care of you."

He was right. She was alone in the world. Forsaken by Inspector Savard. Forsaken by Mr. Cooper. As for her family, she could not expect help from them. What else was there for her? Seated again, the cook no longer looked ridiculous, but he remained unattractive. She sighed with relief as an obstacle surged in her mind.

"I cannot marry you. I'm not who you think I am. I live under a false name."

"I know."

"You know who I am?"

"I do. You are the American maid who shot dead that fellow," he said flatly, merely stating a fact.

"You know this and you still want to marry me?"

"I do."

"But I've killed a man!"

"He was a criminal. I'm willing to overlook the whole matter."

Suddenly, she felt nauseated. She got up. "Who else knows?"

"Nobody, nobody," he said quickly, rising as well.

"Then how do you know?"

"Agent Levieux. He told me over a bottle of wine. Drink loosens his tongue." He caught her in his arms. "Don't worry, I'll never hold this against you. I'll always be there for you. I'll protect you against the world. Just say yes."

She wanted very urgently to say 'no' but she was in no position to do it. There was a strange glint in the cook's eyes, he breathed hard, and his arms felt like a prison.

"Why, Monsieur Jacques, you are crushing the primroses," she said and giggled as prettily as she could. The remark put an end to the tension.

"Oh. I'm sorry." His embrace relaxed and she was able to wiggle out of it.

"I cannot give you an answer today," she said, stepping out of his reach. "As I've said, this is too sudden. But," she added quickly as he took a step forward, "I'll give it serious thought, I promise."

"When?" he asked, taking another step toward her. "When can I expect a definite answer?"

"A week," she said, stepping to the side because by then she was nearly wedged into a corner. "Give me a week."

"You need a whole week?"

"Monsieur Jacques, marriage is a serious life decision. Surely, we agree on this point?"

"Yes, indeed," he conceded. "Still, a whole week . . ."

"Tomorrow then," she said, tired of the strange dance and eager to end it. "Tomorrow, agreed?"

He caught her hand and kissed it. "We're not yet married and already you make me suffer," he complained.

He left smiling as if he had won a victory. That only added to her uneasiness, which had been building up during the encounter. The man did not expect a negative answer. 'We are not yet married,' he said, implying that, eventually, they would be. In his mind, she was in no position to refuse.

* * *

At his third visit to the restaurant, Octave was thoroughly sick of the choucroute. He ate a potato, played with the blood sausage, picked at the pork shoulder and ignored the cabbage. As far as he was concerned, the Germans were welcome to Alsace and its food. However, all that was forgotten when the girl finally came in.

She had lost some weight, he noticed, and the melancholy that previously dwelt solely in her eyes was now enveloping her like an invisible blanket. Something was distressing the girl, of that he was sure. Perhaps it was Widow Koenig's doing. He had already experienced the loud-mouthed shrew's act when, on his last visit, she threw out a pair of drunken guests.

His gaze went to the counter, where the diminutive battle-ax had been managing the receipts a short while ago. She was still there, but she was watching the girl with a frown on her clownish face. The next moment, Octave witnessed a strange pantomime. When the girl looked at her employer, the widow shook her head in disapproval. Then she put a finger in each corner of her mouth and pushed her lips upward. The girl understood and composed a smile on her face. Widow Koenig nodded, satisfied, and went on with her paperwork. The girl continued collecting dirty dishes on her tray, now turning her back to Octave.

He saw the hand clearly as it shot out from a nearby table and pinched the girl's behind. The culprit laughed but his laugh suddenly changed into a shriek of pain.

"What's that?" inquired Widow Koenig.

"The waitress stomped on my foot. She crushed my toes." complained the youth.

"Stop damaging the guests, girl," shouted the widow. "It's not what I pay you for!"

The room roared with laughter, which died out when Octave grabbed the youngster by the lapels and dragged him up.

"Apologize for what you've done, you blackguard!"

Shorter than his captor and of a slighter build, the youth squirmed, but Octave held him tight.

"I'm waiting," he said.

39

"Fuck you!" blurted out the student, fighting humiliation.

"Now listen, you!" boomed the widow. "I want no brawls in my restaurant, is that clear?"

"Absolutely, madam," said Octave and pressed the youth's face into a plate of choucroute, holding him down by the hair. "A simple apology will do."

"What apology? She is the one that caused the trouble," the widow countered.

"I did not," protested the girl. "And I never asked for this job!"

She dropped her tray and, as the china broke with a deafening crash followed by Widow Koenig's earsplitting wails, she ran toward the door and out into the street. Octave released his prisoner's hair, grabbed his hat and followed in her wake.

He saw the girl running in the direction of the Saint-Michel Square and sobbing into her apron. Octave trailed her at a distance. At the corner of the square, he encountered a flower vendor selling her last three bunches of white daffodils. He emptied her basket, threw a few coins into it and, armed with the bouquet, pursued his prey.

He did not have far to go. The girl sat on the surround of the Saint-Michel fountain, dwarfed by the monumental archangel statue behind her. She rested her elbows on her knees, supporting her head in her hands.

"Mademoiselle—"

"Leave me alone," she snapped without looking at him.

He brought the flowers forward. "For you."

She looked up, recognized her gallant defender, and smiled through her tears. "For me? Why?"

"Because you have such a sad smile."

She accepted the offering. Burying her head into the flowers, she shook with a new bout of weeping.

"There, there," said Octave. "I'm sorry. This was meant to cheer you up."

"Amity!" someone shouted.

"Oh, no!" the girl exclaimed, clasping a hand around her mouth.

A short stout man in a cook's apron ran toward them, followed by one of the restaurant waiters.

"That's Monsieur Jacques! I don't want to see him."

The two men were quickly crossing the few yards that separated them from the fountain.

"Come!" said Octave.

Hand in hand, the two ran along the sidewalk until they reached a cab station. The pursuers were gaining on them while he helped the girl into a waiting cab.

"Drive fast!" he shouted at the cabbie.

"Where to?"

"Never mind, just drive!"

The man shrugged and cracked his whip. The cab lurched forward and merged into the southbound traffic.

"Wait! Amity! Wait!"

Monsieur Jacques managed to reach the cab window. He was nearing exhaustion but struggling valiantly.

"Where are you going?" he shouted.

"Away," said the girl.

"Where?"

"I don't know."

"When will you be back?"

"Never!"

The cook fell behind as the cab gained speed and drove away, nobody knew where.

Chapter 8

Nelly lifted her leg and wiggled her toes. She ran a palm along her shin and around the knee. It was the leg of a woman. No longer a girl, a maid, a virgin. A woman! The pink toes had been kissed one by one. She had been caressed and gently nibbled on, tasted, savored, relished, softened, crushed and ravished until exhaustion. Her beauty was so great, Octave declared, that it had to be honored at least a half a dozen times. He fell into a heavy slumber after the fourth round and was still asleep although the large hand of the ormolu clock standing on the mantelshelf was approaching the cipher twelve while the small one was already firmly set on nine.

She turned on her side and gently ran her finger along Octave's eyebrows that swept in two thick graceful arches above the long-lashed lids. The nose was a little too long, a little too aquiline, reminding her of a Roman bust she had seen in a picture book. Some emperor or other. His brown hair, tousled by sleep, fell over his forehead. She combed it back with her fingers. Octave reacted by tightening his arm around her waist. His eyelids fluttered briefly and then his muscles relaxed. He was back in the realm of dreams.

He was tired and no wonder. What a hard worker he was! All she knew of lovemaking was completely shattered by last night's experience. But, of course, her only point of reference had been Marie's pathetic business. No more than a brief creaking of the bed, accompanied with Marie's contrived moans and encouragements, often followed by a sordid squabble about money.

A knight in shining armor, elegant and handsome, that's how Octave appeared to her at the Saint-Michel fountain. When he gripped her hand, she followed him without hesitation. At last, she was being rescued from a life of drudgery. No more Widow Koenig, no more Monsieur Jacques expecting an answer. She was free!

Octave brought her here, into his apartment on the boulevard Saint-Germain, furnished with discreet luxury and the latest modern comfort. The bathroom was her undoing. The zinc tub encased in mahogany, the ceramic sink sitting on an ornate pedestal, the snow-white towels with fringes and monograms, all of that contributed to her surrender. She had soaked in rose-scented water, soaped the kitchen smell out of her hair and brushed grease stains from under her nails. How could she go back to her miserly attic after such bliss?

The situation was redeemable, she hoped. She must make Octave marry her. She knew she wanted none other. Already, when he laughed as the cab sped away from the crest-fallen Monsieur Jacques and the seething Monsieur Hervé, the sight of his strong white teeth sent a shiver of delight down to the tips of her toes.

"Tonerre!" he exclaimed. "They were running after me. I forgot to pay."

"Damn!" he said now, awakened by the chiming clock. "I've important sitters at half past nine." He planted a careless kiss on her brow. "You are quite a kitten," he said and jumped out of bed.

A kitten? Was that all he had to say after what they had been through? Only last night, she had been his idol, his queen, his goddess, fairer than Helen of Troy, sweeter than Titania, and more graceful than Artemis, the godly huntress. Her head had spun with the sound of all those majestic names. Now he demoted her to a mere kitten.

She heard the swishing sound as he pulled at the chain in the water closet, then the faucet being turned on in the bathroom, the water splashing loudly into the sink. Something metallic clattered on the hard floor and Octave swore with impatience.

The enormity of what she had done suddenly sank in. She was no better than Marie!

Quickly, she picked up her chemise and petticoat. Her clothes hung over a padded chair by the window, embarrassingly shabby against the opulent brocade of the curtains. Her apron was gone. "You don't need that anymore," Octave said and tossed it out of the cab window. "From now on, I'll take care of you."

Dizzy with freedom, she believed him. But what did she know about this man other than that he was gallant and handsome? What was in her blood, what seed of moral abandon that made her take reckless decisions and follow them without thinking? Tears invaded her eyes. With trembling fingers, she hooked up her bodice. She never felt more ashamed, more abandoned, or more lonely.

"What is it, kitten?" Octave was back in the bedroom, struggling into his clothes.

"I'm ruined," she said.

"Now, now," he took her hand, turned it, and kissed the palm, "I said I'd take care of you and Octave Gaillard has never gone back on his word. Now let me finish what I'm doing. Jesus, it's quarter past nine!"

He opened a drawer in search of a fresh collar. "Mother Laforge, the concierge, comes at ten to do the cleaning," he said, buttoning the collar to his shirt. "Tell her to bring you a breakfast. There's some money in the malachite box in the sitting room."

He reached into another drawer and handed her a handkerchief. "Here, blow your nose, you little goose."

She was sliding further down the scale, from kitten to goose.

"My cufflinks! Pass me the cufflinks. There! Under the lamp."

He took the gold cufflinks from her and inserted them into his cuffs. "No more tears, understood? What's done is done. And was it not well done? Dear God, what a night!"

The knot of his cravat finished, he grabbed her to him and kissed the base of her neck. "Oh, you delectable dish," he said, pressing his loins against her, "look what you are doing to me!" Even through her skirt, she could feel the swelling. "Maybe those chaps could wait ten more minutes."

"No," she said and pushed him away.

"No. You are right. The Engineering School Board. Those people have Swiss clocks for brains." He released her, buttoned up his vest and reached for his jacket. "Have you seen my watch?"

"No, I haven't. Listen, you promised me a job."

"Now, kitten, that can wait. First, I must find you a room.— Where's that watch?— You cannot stay here. My mother and sisters descend on me now and then. It would be extremely awkward if they found you here. Then there's Cousin Émile, he is at the Polytechnic School, wants to be a civil engineer. I don't trust his big mouth.— There it is!"

The watch in his vest pocket, the gold chain secured through a button hole, Octave threw on his overcoat and grabbed a pair of gloves, his walking stick, and his hat.

"Now, be a good girl and wait for me. Don't expect me for a while, I've a full day. And don't worry at all. We'll work something out."

The main door slammed behind him as the clock struck half past nine.

His last words killed the romance dead. Nelly sat down and buried her head in her hands. The room was quiet—too quiet now—filled only with the indifferent ticking of the mantel clock. On one point, her lover was right. What was done was done. If only the shame of it could go away. A fallen woman. She was that and no mistake! Until yesterday, she knew nothing of the dangerous currents in her body that responded hungrily to a man's touch, overrode scruples and did away with reason.

Unable to sit still, she began to pace the room, half-aware that despite her self-castigating mood, her bare feet unabashedly enjoyed the thick pile of the carpet. She threw open the window and the dynamic noise of a busy boulevard invaded the room. Leaning against the cast-iron railing, she looked across the wide avenue where she could read the golden letters on two black panels fixed high above the line of trees. Over five feet in height, the panels filled the entire width of a corner building, both on the boulevard façade and that of the adjoining street.

OCTAVE GAILLARD / ARTIST - PHOTOGRAPHER
Individual and group portraits - Miniatures - Fine Art Models

She, too, could be a fine art model, Octave said, but when she asked what the job involved, he glossed over the subject and replenished her wine glass. Four glasses were enough to muddle her brain. Life was to be lived, not endured, Octave said. He said many other things while his fingers were busy unhooking her bodice. It felt so good, yesterday, to let go of the struggle that had been her life and to surrender to what she thought was a safe harbor of this smooth-talking man's arms. Today, she was an embarrassing object to be hidden away in some obscure room.

A movement to her right caught her eye. An elderly woman, leaning from a window of the neighboring house, was watching her with keen interest. Suddenly conscious of her stained work dress and her loose tousled hair, Nelly quickly stepped back into the room. The woman knew! She clearly saw the disapproving look. In the future, she would have to face more of the same. She had landed on the other side of the moral barrier, together with Marie and other women without a wedding ring on their finger. Would she ever get used to it? No, such a thought was much too painful. Octave must marry her. She must make sure that he would.

* * *

Octave's mind kept wandering back to his rooms across the boulevard and played over the previous night performance. Jesus, that girl had an inspiring body! He felt tired but it was a good, liberating fatigue. However, his good mood did not last long. The old farts from the School Board irritated him no end. First, they could not agree on the backdrop. Should it be a library, a

45

Gothic window, or a plain curtain? Then there was the shuffle for positions. Who would be seated and who would remain standing? They bowed to each other—*After you, monsieur! No, no, after you!*—but the tension between them, the jealousy, and the covert fight for prestige were almost palpable. With a diplomatic skill one had to learn fast in a profession that catered to human vanity, he herded them into a well-balanced pose. Just as he exposed the plate, one of the sitters sneezed and the plate was ruined. During the time it took for the apprentice to slide in the replacement, the sitters moved and all the hard work was lost. Again, he went around, adjusting a hand here, lifting a head there. Above the glass ceiling of the studio the clouds were gathering. That meant longer exposures and more frustrations ahead.

The venerable school board gone, he left his assistant in charge and repaired to La Tour d'Alsace to pick up the girl's trunk. What followed was one of the worst hours of his life. Widow Koenig threatened to call the police on him. Abduction of a minor, with two reliable witnesses to corroborate the fact, she said. In the end, all she wanted was money. He paid her, but his thrifty provincial blood boiled at such extortion. Then he ran into the cook. The chap had murderous designs on him. According to the cook, the girl was his fiancée and he, the abductor, the defiler, was about to be cut to pieces. The kick-boxing lessons at the gym served him well in the circumstance for he was able to kick the knife out of the man's hand. The waiters and some of the bystanders held the enraged cook until a policeman arrived. He happened to be none other than a brother of the harpy whose enormous voice alerted the whole neighborhood.

"Haven't I told you that there would be trouble? Haven't I?" she shouted at the policeman. "That girl's nothing but trouble," she confided to Octave in a travesty of whisper. "You'll be surprised when you find who she really is. But that's your problem now," she ran her palms against each other in a slicing gesture of good riddance. By then, he was inclined to believe her.

The affair was concluded then and there, with Octave declining to lay charges against the cook. While the latter was plied with cognac at the bar counter, the trunk was brought down and loaded on a handcart. The concierge, a sly character, was charged with conveying it to Octave's address and tipped handsomely for keeping his mouth shut. It would not do to find the cook, knife in hand, at one's doorstep. In any case, Octave was certain that whatever was in that trunk was not half worth the trouble. He was glad to put the restaurant behind him and hoped never to hear of it again.

"Monsieur! Please, monsieur!"

Octave turned. A skinny boy was running behind him.

"Monsieur, are you Madame Amity's friend?"

"Who is Madame Amity?" inquired Octave.

"Why, she is the one that has broken Monsieur Jacques' heart, although I'm sure she did not mean to. Are you her friend?"

The boy was obviously referring to the same woman who had claimed that her name was Nelly.

"I have the doubtful distinction of knowing her," Octave said at last.

"Tell her not to worry. Tell her Monsieur Jacques is leaving tomorrow. He's not bad, you know. Only unhappy."

"Hm. And who are you?"

"Zidore. I work in the kitchen. Please, tell Madame Amity that I wish her well."

"I'll do that, Zidore. I take it you like her?"

The boy blushed and found a sudden interest in his disintegrating shoes. "She's very nice."

"How old are you, Zidore?"

"Twelve and three quarters."

"Do you like to work for Widow Koenig?"

"She shouts all the time."

"Don't I know it," Octave agreed wholeheartedly. "Listen," he added, feeling exceptionally sorry for the boy, "when you are fourteen, come and find me. Octave Gaillard, photographer, boulevard Saint-Germain. Remember that, but keep your mouth shut!"

"I will monsieur. I will!" said the boy eagerly and smiled from ear to ear.

Back in the studio, Octave sent the apprentice for lunch and ate it in his office while listening to the musical photo-albums salesman, who had been waiting for him since eleven o'clock. The albums proved to be an amusing novelty and Octave ordered four dozen for the shop.

The afternoon opened with a nude group study for a mural. Octave had chalked off two hours for the session but the painter who ordered it happened to be twenty minutes late and the waiting models, men, women and children, all of them Italian immigrants, got themselves into a vociferous dispute. After they left, a strong odor of unwashed underwear infested the studio for hours.

The last sitter was an Oriental potentate with a suite of servants, some of them armed to the teeth. Octave decided that he had seen his fill of knives for one day. He was about to pour himself a drink when a rotund man in his fifties, clutching a blue umbrella, walked into his office.

"Octave, my boy!"

"Uncle Maurice?"

"Surprised, eh?"

Surprised? Flabbergasted was the word. Was there no end to his annoyances for one day?

"What are you doing in Paris?" he asked after they exchanged kisses: left cheek, right cheek, and left again.

"A little spying, as usual. The Magazines du Louvre has gotten a new line of goods, I've been told. I thought I would check to see how it sells before ordering any of it."

Uncle Maurice owned a haberdashery in Yvetot, Octave's hometown. Once or twice a year, he made a foraging visit to Paris and Octave knew what was coming.

"I thought you could put me up for a couple of nights. I left my bag and a basket of preserves at the concierge's. The daft woman wouldn't let me in."

God bless her, thought Octave. "You should've let me know, Uncle. A telegram—"

"Bah, a waste of money, my boy. Am I putting you out of joint?"

Not at all, only completely screwing up my plans, Octave thought. "No. You are welcome, naturally. A glass of armagnac?"

"That I don't mind," said his uncle, installing himself in an armchair. "Good stuff," he said after tasting the amber liquid. "Nothing but the best for our Octave, eh? So, now, how about you telling that Cerberus of yours to let me in to wash off the dust of the journey, so to speak?"

Octave reached for a box. "Have a cigar."

"A Corona de Luxe? You don't deny yourself a thing."

The cigars were there for important clients. He never smoked them. "Are you hungry?" he asked.

"Ravenous."

"Oh, good. How about an early dinner then? At the Chaillot's?"

"What's that?"

"A good place." *At least a couple of hours gained. That would give him time to dispose of the girl.* "You would not believe their salmon mousse. A poem! An excellent cave as well."

"Hm, isn't it one of those luxury restaurants with a waiter behind every chair?"

"God, no. Besides, I'm inviting you."

"Well then, what are we waiting for?"

"I've some business to take care of. I'll be back before you finish your cigar. Have another glass."

Octave descended the two flights of steps that separated the courtyard studio from the shop. Mother Laforge, a mustachioed matron with cunning eyes, was already waiting in the storage room. The woman was worth her weight in gold.

"I have a house-guest," he said.

Mother Laforge smiled appreciatively. "I've seen her."

"What was she doing?

"Crying. Later on, taking a bath and curling her hair."

"Hm. Have you brought her breakfast?"

"I have. And her lunch too."

"Very good. Has her trunk been brought up?"

"It has. The man wanted a tip but I gave him nothing."

"Well done. He's been paid."

"I figured as much."

"You are as smart as you are reliable," said Octave warmly and pressed a coin into her palm. "Now tell me, to your knowledge, is there a place nearby the young lady could be transferred to? Preferably with close access to water."

"There's the two-room suite in the rue Danton, but it's not furnished. It wouldn't do."

"No, it would not."

"Why not the Quay de la Tournelle? It sits empty at the moment."

"Quay de la Tournelle! Of course!" He reached into his pocket and removed two coins. "For the cab. The driver will help with the trunk."

The concierge was already half way across the boulevard when Octave remembered something. "Mother Laforge!"

"Be so good and stop at the Beaussire's," he said when she came back. "Have them deliver a dozen long-stemmed roses to the Quay and put them on my account. And tell her that I'm sorry but I won't be able to see her tonight. And that I shall definitely make up for it tomorrow."

"Monsieur Gaillard, it's not my place to voice an opinion, but . . ."

"On the contrary. I'm listening."

"She can't eat roses."

"Mother Laforge, you are infinitely practical. You think of everything," said Octave and, once again, he reached into his pocket.

* * *

Uncle Maurice raked the serving dish with a spoon and deposited the gleanings on his plate.

"This *nègre en chemise* is not unlike your aunt's," he commented, "except for the grated lemon zest in the whipped cream. A nice touch. I must tell her about it."

Octave glanced at the plate with unseeing eyes. The puréed chestnuts held no interest for him, nor did the health problems of the mayor of Yvetot's wife and other local gossip. He uttered a non-committal sound and sipped his cognac.

"Oh, but I haven't told you who I saw the other day," Uncle Maurice went on. "Your future mother-in-law! She bought fifteen yards of Valenciennes lace. At twenty-eight francs a yard, that's a lot of money. If I were you, I'd watch out. The woman's a spender and daughters often turn out like their mothers."

"Amélie is perfect," said Octave firmly.

"All the same, she doesn't bring you a sufficient dowry. You could have done better for yourself. Well, after all that courting, it's too late anyway."

"Amélie is perfect," repeated Octave with a frown.

Uncle Maurice sighed. "*Très bien, très bien*. Don't get yourself worked up for so little." He lifted a glass of brandy and poured it into his coffee. "Not a bad meal altogether, although I'm not sure about the escargots. I feel them sitting down there like pebbles," he patted his stomach.

It was a good time to ask for the bill and Octave nodded to the waiter. Uncle Maurice returned to the previous topic.

"Your mother says you spoil her too much."

"I spoil Mother too much?"

"Hah. Wouldn't that be something! No, I mean Amélie. All that waiting until the girl is good and ready makes no sense to me."

Octave suppressed a smile. So Mother was covering his tracks. It would not do for her to admit that her son was the one dragging his feet.

"Amélie is too young," he said.

"She's nineteen, for God's sake! Your mother was having her second child at the same age."

"She wants to be married on her twentieth birthday. I'm not going to force her hand. I can wait."

"What a bloodless generation you are," commented Uncle Maurice, shaking his head. "When I was your age, a couple of oxen could not keep me away from my bride. And here you are, seeing your sweetheart once a month and content to hold her hand. I'm sure what the newspapers say is true. They say—"

The waiter brought the bill and Octave was grateful for the interruption. He knew what the newspapers were saying—what everyone was saying—and hoped not to hear it again.

"—they say that the French nation is degenerating," resumed his uncle as soon as the waiter was gone. "Low birth-rate, low morality, sin and corruption. How else could we have lost the war? Ah, the Empire has led us into perdition, no doubt about it."

"The Empire also gave us eighteen years of prosperity. Shall we go?" Octave asked, already putting on his gloves.

"Sin and corruption," Uncle Maurice repeated doggedly. "Don't try to dodge the issue, my boy! When a man's not married by the age of thirty, one has to wonder what he does with himself in his free time."

"There's nothing to worry about."

"Loose women. Brothels. Shameful diseases."

"There's no need for specifications," Octave said gruffly. "I studied medicine, remember? If you want the truth, I never go to such places. I'm not stupid."

"I'm afraid those escargots have not agreed with me at all," said his uncle with an anxious frown. "It would not do to suffer a liver crisis on my first day in Paris." He probed his stomach with inquisitive fingers. "I think I shall make an early night of it."

"Let's take a cab then," proposed Octave, suddenly reviving. Perhaps the evening was not altogether lost.

It was only eight o'clock when he emerged from his quarters, refreshed by a quick shave and wearing a clean shirt. The night was descending on a boulevard alive with traffic and relaxed pedestrians. Rain had washed the city and the streetlights reflected in the dark mirror of wet asphalt. Octave inhaled the moist spring air with delight. Whistling, and playfully whirling his walking stick, he turned to his right in the direction of the Quay de la Tournelle.

At the same moment, as she was crossing the street, a brunette with a classic profile paused. She was about to call his name and then changed her mind. She began to follow him at a distance.

51

Chapter 9

A nice place, Mother Laforge had said. Nelly found it more than nice. Lovely, was the word. She had been taken to a third-floor apartment with the most breath-taking view of the river and the Saint-Louis Island opposite. To the left, the cathedral of Notre Dame had its back to her, displaying a wealth of buttresses, finials, and arched windows. At her feet stretched the busy Quay de la Tournelle and the river Seine spanned by numerous bridges: a highway for boats of all shapes making their way upstream and down.

"This place used to be a gold mine under the Empire," said Madame Perrichon, the concierge, as she opened windows to freshen the stale air. "The city was always packed with tourists and those who stayed longer than a fortnight preferred to rent furnished apartments like this one. Nowadays, they come for short visits to stare at the ruins and then it's off and away to Switzerland or Italy."

She was in her forties, a gaunt woman with a perpetually runny nose and deep lines of worry etched across her forehead. "Nothing is like it used to be," she added mournfully.

The bedroom communicated with the sitting room, both facing the river. The striped wallpaper of coral pink showed a couple of lighter rectangles where some personal pictures had once hung. The window hangings and those of the bed were of light green chintz with floral motifs. There was a fireplace with a mantel of polished gray granite, a couple of velvet chairs, a dresser with a marble top, a floor-length mirror and an oak wardrobe with three doors.

The concierge turned down the folded mattress. "I hope the bed linen hasn't caught mildew with the damp winter and no heating." She opened a hidden closet, removed a stack of sheets, and sniffed at them. "No," she said, "they're all right. A nice lavender scent. There," she sighed contentedly when the bed was done. "You'll be nice and cozy. It's good to have someone in here. How long do you think you'll be staying?"

"I don't know," Nelly said.

"Well, in any case, a lady like you should have a maid. There's an alcove with a cot in the kitchen so you don't have to pay extra for an attic room."

"I don't think I shall take a maid right now," Nelly said, glad that a pair of gloves hid her chapped hands. A pretty hat perching on a fashionable hairdo and one of Kitty's discarded dresses had worked wonders for her self-esteem, but this was too much too soon.

"Let me know if you do. I've just the right girl for you."

"Certainly."

"The furniture needs a bit of polish. I can pass the rag around for you."

"That will not be necessary."

"As you wish," said the concierge, showing no signs of leaving. "You said that your name was Woodridge? Is that English?"

"No, I'm an American." Woodridge was her mother's maiden name. She'd had enough of Amity Moncarelli and her dark world, but was reluctant to use her own name soiled by the murder affair.

"An American! Well, I'm glad. The English are not much liked here. A penny-pinching, fault-finding bunch they are. We used to have mainly Americans because of the bathroom. Americans are very keen on bathing. You won't find bathrooms elsewhere in town. The last family spent eight months here and they knew how to reward good service. Pity that with the Prussians closing in on Paris they had to evacuate so quickly that they had to leave behind the piano and the pair of Sèvres vases on the mantelpiece. Anyway, the English are not good tippers. Very tight with their money they are. On the other hand, Americans are very nice, easy-going and generous folk . . ."

Nelly finally grasped the purpose of the concierge's speech and gave the woman a coin from the money Mother Laforge had provided her.

When the door closed behind the woman, Nelly pressed her hands to her cheeks and let out a squeal of joy. Although she had been shown around, now she could explore everything at her leisure. In the sitting room, the warm golden-yellow brocade on the walls compensated for northern exposure and the cut-velvet draperies of the two windows framed the magnificent view of the river. She opened the lid of the upright piano and tried a few chords. She had not played since leaving the boarding school. Would she remember how? Unfortunately, the piano needed tuning.

Across from the hall was the dining room where the windows revealed the budding crown of a chestnut tree. The rear façade of another building framed the courtyard. On the third floor, by a window, a blonde woman of Nelly's age was repotting a sickly-looking aspidistra. Their eyes met and the young woman smiled. Nelly returned the smile and lifted a hand in greeting. One of her new neighbors.

The oval dining room table was ready to seat six and there were two more padded chairs by the sideboard containing cutlery, china, and serving plates. A door led to a corridor accessing more bedrooms, one of which was converted into a modern bathroom with black and white floor tiles. The etched-glass of the window let in daylight while providing privacy. A hopelessly dead palm tree spread its brown branches over the bathtub.

In the kitchen she found dusty pots and pans and, in the broom closet, some cleaning tools and a jar of dried-out furniture polish. She took a dust-cloth to the sitting room and was about to go and change into her working clothes when the doorbell rang. Out on the landing stood a delivery boy in a smart uniform, holding a basket of roses. Dear, dear Octave! How badly she had misjudged him. He was in love with her after all!

She had barely set the basket on the sitting room table when the bell rang again. This time she opened the door to a frowning bull of a man.

"What do you think you are doing?" he said.

"Inspector Savard?"

"Don't just stand there, mademoiselle. Kindly let me in!"

She ushered him into the sitting room. He chose to sit in an armchair, while Nelly remained standing as if ready for flight. "How did you find me?" she asked.

"Agent Levieux. The rest was police routine. Do you think you can hide from us?"

"I'm not hiding."

"You are acting like a fool and adding to my already busy schedule. I've no time for your amorous adventures, Miss McKay." He took in the comfortably furnished room and the bouquet. "Of course, I'm too late."

Nelly felt herself blush.

"Well, that's neither here nor there," he said gruffly. "You are going home, young woman, and from what I see, the sooner the better."

"Going home?"

"Yes. Last week, I received an answer from Mr. Cooper. He's sending you a letter of credit. Sixty dollars for a second-class cabin ticket, plus forty more for expenses. Mr. Cooper is willing to employ you as a maid, although I'm not sure he would be as willing if he knew how you've turned out."

"Say that again?"

"I think we understand each other."

"No, not that. The part about last week.

"Last week?"

"You said that Mr. Cooper's answer came last week?"

"That's so. What—"

"You have known this for a whole week and you did not tell me?"

"What do you take me for, Miss McKay? I'm a busy man, not a carrier pigeon. Besides, what difference does it make?"

"What difference?" Nelly threw up her hands in anger. "What difference does a week make? One more week of loneliness and misery for me, that's all. One week of slaving without ever seeing a franc, of living next door to a prostitute and having to hear everything that went on in her room. One more week of living with nightmares, alone, always alone." She pointed a finger at him. "You used me. Yes, you did! You blackened my name at the American Legation yet you knew that I was blameless. But you don't care at all. One week could have made a difference between what I used to be and what I've become. What I'm now is the result of your schemes. You've driven me to it!"

In the silence that followed Savard ran his knuckles across both sides of his graying mustache and brushed his lapel. He cleared his throat, reached into his breast pocket, and removed several documents.

"You have a peculiar way of thanking me for arranging your affairs, Miss McKay. Your passport . . . your birth certificate . . . the letter of credit . . . a letter of release for the fourteen trunks held in storage. You have to sign this one in duplicate."

"Trunks? Storage?"

"Mr. Cooper does not care for female frippery. His own words. You are to keep the baroness's personal effects or dispose of them as you please. I suggested that sending them over would probably cost more than they are worth. Mr. Cooper made a sensible decision, don't you think?— Do I see a smile? It suits you better than an angry frown."

"Why," said Nelly, finally sitting down. "This is indeed good news. Thank you, Inspector."

"My pleasure."

"The fact is that I have nothing to sign with," she said, looking around. "You see, I've just moved in—"

"Under a false name."

"At least it's my mother's maiden name, not one stolen from a stranger."

He shrugged and produced an ink pencil. "As long as you don't use it on official documents."

Nelly moistened the pencil tip with her tongue and signed as Cornelia J. McKay. The document made her the owner of fourteen trunks packed with riches. Female frippery indeed! There were furs, lace, exotic bird feathers and fine embroidery, not to speak of expensive hats, gloves, shoes and stockings, reticules, muffs, shawls, and elaborate lingerie. Mr. Cooper had never had a wife with fashionable seamstress's bills to be taken care of; otherwise he would not have been so generous.

"I shall write to Mr. Cooper and thank him," she said.

"You can do it personally, since you are going home."

"I'm not going home."

"Is that so?" Savard asked. "And what do you intend to do instead?"

"My intention is to marry Monsieur Octave Gaillard."

"The man who—"

"Yes," she said quickly.

"Did he ask you?"

"Not yet."

"Has it occurred to you that he may have other plans?"

"If he does, he will have to change them."

Savard sighed and passed his palm over his tired face. "Miss McKay," he said, "you will save yourself a lot of misery by going home. As a rule, men do not marry their mistresses."

"Are you saying that it has never happened?"

"Strange things do happen. Calves born with two heads. Dead people resurrecting. A man marrying his mistress belongs to that category. There's a lot you don't know about France, my dear."

"There's a lot you don't know about Americans," Nelly fired back.

Savard raised his hands in a gesture of surrender. "I bow to your superior knowledge, Miss McKay . . . uh, Woodridge. However, let me point out that according to French law you are a minor until you reach the age of twenty-five. In the absence of your family, the judge has the authority to pack you home to Butte, wherever that is."

She opened her mouth to protest but he shook his finger at her. "However, since you are inclined to believe the worst of me, I've decided to look the other way." He picked up his hat and rose. "I will not stand between you and your aspirations. Ah, I almost forgot," he removed a bunch of keys out of his side pocket. "For your trunks."

* * *

It was past seven when Nelly reached the storage facility. To her relief, she found the business still open, but she had to grease the owner's palm before he agreed to organize the delivery that same night. She parted with the money because she could not wait to have the trunks in her possession, as if another night in storage would make them disappear, never to be seen again.

On her way home, she stopped at the grocery. She bought oat flakes, butter, sugar and coffee, salt, eggs, candles and a box of matches, soda powder, a bar of coarse soap, furniture polish, bleach, a bottle of kerosene, and other paraphernalia of good housekeeping. She had begun her married life prematurely, but this unsatisfactory situation would be rectified as soon as possible, if only to prove Inspector Savard wrong.

"And could you please recommend a piano tuner?" she asked the grocer.

As she approached home, her attention held by the fact that her sitting room windows were alight, she did not notice a brunette in a plum silk dress strolling along the quay. Upstairs, she found Octave sprawled on the sofa, a glass in hand. On the table, next to the roses, a bottle of champagne protruded from an ice bucket.

"I came here with the expectation of your warm embrace and all I have found was a chilly absence," he complained. "Here I am, perched in a panther-like readiness, waiting to pounce and devour, and growing impatient. Come," he patted the cushion at his side, "and let's have a glass of champagne. Where have you been?"

"Grocery shopping."

"I see. Settling in. How do you like your new home?"

"Very well, thank you. I hope the rent is not too high. I don't want to abuse your generosity."

"It's not really a rental since I'm the landlord. You may stay here for the time being. You do agree, I hope, that I'm taking good care of you?"

She nodded.

"Then why do you stand there with that severe expression on your face? Doesn't your Octave deserve a hug and a cuddle?"

"We must talk," she said.

"I agree absolutely." He discarded his glass on the side table. "We shall talk all you want but, first, let's do some pouncing—" he shot up with lightning speed, caught her hand, and pulled her with him onto the sofa, "—and devouring!" His lips landed on hers and it was a while before she could recover her breath. When Octave's hands reached for the hooks of her bodice, she caught his wrists.

"What is it, kitten?"

"We really have to talk."

"Not now," he pleaded, grabbing the hem of her skirt. "Talking means thinking and I'm not in a thinking mood. I'm the slave of your beauty, a mindless love apparatus. Let me pursue my mission." His hand was sliding along her calf and circling the knee. It crept up her thigh when the doorbell rang. "Damn!" he said. "Who is it? Are you expecting anyone?"

"Probably the grocer's boy."

"Oh, very well then," he said, annoyed, and released her.

"Mamz'elle Woodridge?" inquired a burly man in a worker's cap and blouse, with a frayed blue kerchief around his neck. He was leaning against a trunk, catching his breath and exuding a cloud of garlic and wine vapors. Clad with similar casualness, a companion with purplish nose stood by his side.

"My trunks!" Nelly exclaimed, elated.

Somewhere below, another of her precious trunks was being dragged unceremoniously over the steps. She cringed as if her own ribs were suffering the same fate.

"What on earth . . . ?" Octave appeared in the sitting room door.

"Evening, m'sieu," Blue Kerchief touched his cap to him and then addressed Nelly. "Where do you want this mamz'elle . . . er, ma'am?"

"I'll show you the way." Nelly stepped back to allow the deliverymen in. Two more, huffing and puffing, reached the door with a second trunk.

"How many of these monsters do you own?" Octave asked when she came back.

"Fourteen."

"Fourteen?" He steered her into the sitting room. "Where does it all come from? God, I know nothing about you. We really do have to talk."

"No, *we* have to talk."

Both Nelly and Octave turned as a brunette in a plum silk dress came to plant herself in front of them.

"Loulou," said Octave in a small voice.

"You rotten double-dealing bastard!" the woman yelled. "I'll cut your balls off, I swear I will."

"Loulou . . ."

"A bitch with an accent, no less!" She hit him in the chest with both palms. "What, tired of French meat? Want some spice? I'll give you spice." She sprang for the mantelpiece.

"No! Loulou! Louise! Put that down, do you hear me? It's a Sèvres!"

"Good!" said Loulou and threw the vase at him.

Nelly, who followed the exchange with a detachment caused by shock, saw the heavy object describe a circle in the air. She saw Octave leaping forward in a desperate attempt at saving the precious porcelain. The two met halfway, the vase shattering against his skull. Octave's knees folded under him and he landed on the floor with a heavy thud.

"Ouch," said one of the deliverymen. Their heads, all four of them, were unabashedly stuck in the door opening.

"My God," breathed Nelly. "He's dead."

Purple Nose detached himself from the group and knelt by Octave's body. "Nah," he said, "he's breathing. He's gonna have a bad headache, thass all."

As if willing to reassure his audience, Octave moaned.

"There, you see," said Purple Nose. "Pity for the vase though. A nice piece, eh, Gugus?"

"Must have cost a fortune," agreed Blue Kerchief.

"You," said Nelly to Loulou, "get out!"

The brunette tossed her head and shrugged. "I was going anyway. You can keep this heap of rot. When he wakes up, tell him I've been cheating on him with an art critic."

"What?" said Octave and briskly sat up.

"That's right. With Alfred Toussaint from *Le Gaulois*. Choke on it!"

She backed toward the fireplace and, malevolently looking Nelly in the eye, slowly, deliberately, she pushed the second Sèvres vase from the mantelpiece. Then she swept toward the door, where the men gave her a wide berth.

"Women!" wailed Octave, holding his bruised head.

"Tell me about them," nodded Blue Kerchief, accompanied by a chorus of sympathetic noises from the rest of the males.

Somewhere in the midst of the chaos, the groceries were delivered. Nelly made a cup of coffee and took it to the bedroom where Octave, propped against the headrest, nursed his bruise with an ice pack.

"Alfred Toussaint," he grumbled. "I cannot believe it. She cheated on me with that venom-spewing bastard. It hurts me to the core."

"You are disgusting," she said and slammed the cup on the night table. "Here's your coffee. Drink it and go home."

He caught her hand and pulled her on the bed next to him. "You didn't find me disgusting last night."

She tugged at his grip. "Last night, I knew nothing about you."

"And now you think you've got my measure?"

"Exactly. And to think that I wanted to marry you!"

"Marry me? Why, that's absurd."

She bristled. "Absurd? What's absurd about it, I ask you? You seduced me. You've taken my virginity. If we were in America and I had my family around me, you'd be forced to marry me. With a shotgun between your shoulder blades, if need be."

"That's positively barbaric."

"It makes men think twice before playing games with honest girls."

"How can a poor chap think when dealing with an honest girl like you? You did not exactly fight me off. If my memory serves me well, you actually enjoyed yourself. Come on, admit it! All I had to do was to undo a few hooks like this—"

She slapped his hand off. "Stop it! Can't you be serious for a minute?"

"Very well, let's be serious. Just don't sit too close, you are distracting me.—Well now, where were we? To begin with, we've both labored under a false impression. I have taken under my protection a poor servant girl only to find out that she comes with a load of mysterious possessions, a knife-wielding fiancé, and a long string of names. The concierge told me that you've moved in under the name of Miss Woodridge. I took care not to contradict her. However, Widow Koenig speaks of you as 'that Moncarelli creature' and your little friend Zidore refers to you as 'Madame Amity'. As for me, I'm supposed to call you Nelly. Personally, I like the name Nelly. It rolls over the tongue like a caramel, but I demand an explanation."

"My true name is Cornelia McKay. Nelly for short."

"Go on."

"The cook is not my fiancé. It's his invention."

"Like your tale of being stranded in Paris when your mistress died? A maid with fourteen trunks?"

"They are my inheritance. Have you ever heard of the de Chazelle murder?"

"Have I ever! The first interesting criminal case after the war. We all needed a decent distraction. I beg your pardon. That was rather tactless of me. I suppose you were somewhat involved. Wait a minute!" The ice pack slipped as he sat up. "McKay? *The* Nelly McKay? Was that you?—I'll be damned."

"Does it bother you?" she asked defiantly.

"No. Quite the contrary. I find it intriguing. Where's that fellow, de Chazelle? Still on the run?"

"It seems so. I've been hiding from him."

"You are in danger? Now I understand your need for secrecy. You can count on my help."

"Why, Monsieur Gaillard," she said, replacing the ice pack a little too harshly, "I do believe you are capable of noble sentiment after all."

"Ouch! Kindly throw this thing away, will you? It's dripping."

She emptied the ice back into the champagne bucket.

"Come," Octave said with a conciliatory smile, "let's each have a glass. It would be a pity to waste good champagne. You are judging me altogether too harshly, dear kitten. I was acting in good faith. I've not promised you marriage and it had not occurred to me that you would entertain such an idea. Any Parisian girl in your position would understand that without saying. Had I known your real circumstances—"

"Rest assured that I don't entertain the idea anymore, Monsieur Gaillard," she interrupted him bitterly. "I've grown a little wiser about your French ways. Not that I find them to my taste."

He crossed his arms and shrugged. "Just what is it you disapprove of? My ex-mistress? Surely, you do not expect a man of my age to live like a monk? On the other hand, neither she nor I will lose any sleep over the breakup."

"Is this supposed to be a civilized way of life?"

"Is this a serious question or a nasty remark?"

She shrugged. "What do you think?"

"I choose to answer it seriously," he said. "Tell me, is divorce allowed in your land of shotgun weddings?"

She nodded.

"Not here," he said. "In France, marriage is an institution from which there is no escape. Therefore, a Frenchman pays close attention to the choice of his spouse. She has to satisfy all his criteria for a good wife. In the meantime, a man enjoys a series of fleeting affections provided by women of a certain class. It is a system in which everyone knows his place. As for you, dear kitten, except for a marriage, I'm willing to go along with your wishes. Just tell me what they are."

She thought for a moment and shrugged again. "At this point, I have no wishes left. I'll listen to the voice of reason and take myself back to America. A post has been offered to me, but first I must sell most of my possessions. I cannot afford to carry them with me. This reminds me that I should go and check on the deliverymen. They ought to be done soon."

"Let me deal with it." He got up and smoothed his hair in front of the mirror. "What kind of post is that?"

"A maid to Baroness de Chazelle's brother."

"A maid? Come on, you cannot be serious. Is that what you want?"

A maid in Mr. Cooper's household? She remembered the kitchen in the gloomy brick mansion, where she briefly had taken her meals with the servants. She used to be a lady's maid with a bright future. Now she would have to wield a duster. What happened to her ambitions?

"What should I do then?" she asked.

He squeezed her shoulders. "Stay in France for a while. Be a student of life. Enjoy yourself, perfect your French, polish your style. Return to America as a respectable French teacher. No one will know of your little slip up."

"Respectable?" She pushed him away. "It doesn't work that way. Respectability dwells within the soul. I've already stepped over the line."

"Then what else do you have to lose? From now on, you can only gain. Come with me!"

He led her to the window. "Look at that," he said, pointing at the scintillating lights. "This is Paris with its theaters, museums, restaurants, cafés, and boulevards. There is a pulse in this city you'll find nowhere else. It's all yours for the taking."

"You are a smooth talker, Monsieur Gaillard," she said and pried his hand off. "The trouble is that you come with the package."

"Is that a problem? I'm a reasonably good-looking fellow and I'm quite taken with you. In fact, I'm very much taken with you."

"Taken with me? What does that mean in plain speech? And how long do you think you will be *taken* with me? How long before you decide that my French studies have come to an end?"

"I see," he said. "Let's speak in numbers. Would you consider one year of my protection as a fair amount of time?"

A rough knocking interrupted them. "Beg yer pardon," said Blue Kerchief, sticking his head into the door, "we're done."

"I'll settle with you presently," Octave said. He squeezed her arm. "Think of my offer, sweet kitten!"

When he returned, she was waiting for him in the sitting room, holding his jacket.

"Are you sending me away?" he asked.

"Until tomorrow," she said. "You've asked me to think about your offer. I cannot do it with you around. I want to ponder the matter quietly on my own."

"Kitten . . ."

"Please, go."

Silently, he put on his jacket and made for the door. As he was reaching for the door handle he reeled and had to steady himself against the wall.

"Surely, you cannot be heartless to the point of sending me away in my weakened state?" he pleaded.

"It's an awkward ploy."

"No, I assure you. Suddenly, my head is spinning."

She grew alarmed. "Is it?"

"Yes, I need to lie down. Come and help me!"

She supported him by the elbow and led him to the sofa.

"No, not there," he said. "To the bedroom. I need something soft under my head." He leaned on her, almost crushing her by his weight. "Hurry up! I feel faint."

She deposited him on the bed and removed his shoes. "Should I send for a doctor?" she asked.

"Why, no!" He smiled weakly. "All I need is a good sleep, I'm sure. I shall be perfectly all right in the morning."

She eyed him with suspicion as he unbuttoned his collar. "There are three more beds in this place. All doors have locks in them. I will not disturb you and I hope you will not disturb me."

She felt a malicious satisfaction when the corners of his mouth turned down.

"I've had a very rotten day," he complained. "Most of it thanks to you. Why don't you appreciate me at my true value?"

"Good night," she said.

In the kitchen, Nelly sat down to a late dinner of biscuits and coffee. To-morrow morning, she promised herself, she would go to a market and shop for meat and vegetables. What would be the first honest American dish she would cook in her own kitchen? Her own kitchen. She liked the sound of it. Her own kitchen, her own sitting room, her own everything! No, wrong. It all belonged to one Octave Gaillard. Only marriage could make it right and that was out of question. Or was it, really?

Her thoughts went to Loulou. She had recognized that wretched woman from the photographs in picture albums she had seen in Octave's rooms. One of them bore the title *The Beauties of France* and contained photographs of scantily dressed pretty women with names like Bon Coeur, Jolie Yvette, Unforgettable Mireille — and Loulou de Montmartre. A name as vulgar as the woman herself. What was Loulou doing at this moment? Crying over Octave or sleeping with her art critic? How lightly the French took such matters! On the other hand, now that Octave was free of that harlot, she had him to herself. He was looking for a perfect wife and she felt qualified for that post. Sooner or later, he would realize it himself. *Calves born with two heads. Dead men resurrecting.* She had one year to accomplish the miracle and trunks full of seductive clothes.

Candle in hand, she turned off the gaslights. In the sitting room, she stopped by the window to close the shutters. She watched the dark waters of the river, speckled by the silvery reflections of the moon. A lone barge labored against the current, a dog running back and forth on board, barking. His owner shouted a reprimand, the voice carrying across the water, unimpeded by the sound barrier of the day's activity. A faint clip clop of horse hooves grew stronger and she saw a carriage crossing the nearest bridge. A church clock somewhere nearby struck midnight, followed by others across the city. Paris! What had she seen of it so far? Why leave, indeed? Did she not deserve a break after a long period of darkness and a pair of strong arms as a barrier against her loneliness? Mentally, she revived the experience of the previous night, sighed with anticipation, and closed the window against the night chill.

In the bedroom, she held the candle above the bed. He slept on his stomach, one arm around a pillow, the other stretched across the bed. Abandoned to sleep, he looked much younger, merely an overgrown boy, and completely harmless.

"Octave Gaillard," she whispered, "say good-bye to your old life!"

He woke up instantly when she extinguished the candle and slipped into the bed at his side. The arm she had wrapped around herself came to life, the hand following the outline of her hips.

"So you've come to a decision?" he asked.

"Yes. I will become a student of life."

He chuckled. "What time is it?"

"About five after midnight."

"A new day. My luck has turned."

Chapter 10

"McKay?" asked the clerk, his eyes narrowing as if he searched for a half-buried memory.

"Why, yes. Here's my passport." Nelly lowered her voice to a whisper, hoping that the man would follow her example.

The offices of Johnson & Morris proved to be a meeting ground for Americans. There were at least two dozen people present, scanning newspapers to catch up with the news from home, exchanging tips about places to go and things to do, picking up personal messages or, like her, cashing letters of credit.

"Miss Cornelia McKay," repeated the man behind the desk, his voice booming. "Jacobs," he addressed a colleague, "see if we have a copy from the bank!"

Was it her impression, or had the room grown quiet? It has been months since the newspapers shouted her name and by now it should be water under the bridge. Yet Octave had known immediately who she was.

"Take a seat, miss. This will take a few minutes."

Gradually, hushed conversations replaced the embarrassing silence. Nelly snatched a copy of *The Washington Post* from a nearby table and hid her face behind it.

REPUBLICANS DISSATISFIED WITH THE GRANT ADMINISTRATION.

She was pretending to read the small print under the headline when, from the corner of her eye, she saw the clerk nodding in her direction and whispering into an eager ear of a man with ginger sideburns, who approached the counter as soon as she had left it.

"Can't be. I thought she was back in the States," said a piercing female voice in the far end of the room.

"Miss McKay!"

Nelly discarded the newspaper, rose, and smoothed her skirts, her movements deliberately slow. Was she looking sufficiently unconcerned? The rustle of stiff silk as she walked toward the desk was the only noise in the room.

"French or American currency?"

"French, please."

The clerk counted the money.

"This time she hasn't got a gun," she heard.

"What do you know? There could be whole artillery hidden in her skirts . . ."

". . . has done well for herself. Look at that dress . . ."

Loud whispers. Sniggers, chuckles. Did they think she was deaf?

"Sign here, please."

She put down the pen, gathered the banknotes and stuffed them into her reticule without recounting them. Avoiding curious eyes, she swept out of the office onto the busy boulevard. An omnibus was coming to a halt a few yards away. She boarded it without inquiring about its destination, purchased her ticket, and sat on the long wooden bench next to a peasant woman who was hugging a basket of eggs. A white-haired gentleman with the red ribbon of the Legion of Honor in his buttonhole joined an officer and two nuns on the opposite bench. At the last moment, the man with ginger sideburns got in. He landed with a flop at Nelly's side as the omnibus jerked forward.

"I beg your pardon," he said. "Ronald J. Briggs, correspondent of The Chicago Tribune. Glad to see that you've come out of your retirement, Miss McKay. Our readers will be interested in your story."

"I don't want to be in the newspapers."

"Would ten dollars change your mind?"

"I have nothing to say to you," she said, siding closer to the peasant woman.

He slid on his backside to fill the gap. "Come, come. Twenty dollars?"

She stood up but he caught her wrist and pulled her back on the bench. "A hundred smackers," he whispered into her ear. "Just think of all the pretty things you can buy for that kind of money."

Nelly's gaze landed on the peasant's basket, assessing the eggs as a weapon, when a walking stick inserted itself between her and Mr. Briggs. "Is that man bothering you, mademoiselle?" the white-haired gentleman asked.

"Yes, he is. I appeal to you, monsieur!"

Mr. Briggs released Nelly's wrist. "Now, now," he said, switching into French, "this is a personal matter, monsieur. Kindly mind your own business!"

"The young lady has clearly made it my business. I must insist that you leave her alone."

Mr. Briggs bared his teeth in a conciliatory smile. "This is a mistake, I assure you. The lady is a friend of mine. We are both Americans. I repeat that ours is a personal business."

"I don't know this man," declared Nelly. "He's been offering me money."

The nuns sucked in their breath.

Mr. Briggs's jaw dropped. "I . . . that is . . ."

"You ought to be whipped!" said the old man.

His walking stick pinned the reporter against the seat. The peasant woman hunched over to protect her eggs. Nelly got up and darted toward the exit. The conductor pulled on the bell rope, the driver shouted at the horses, and the omnibus slowed down. She turned to see what was going on behind her back. Mr. Briggs had slapped the walking stick aside and made a move for the exit when he was stopped by a rasping sound. Nelly glimpsed the glint of steel, some ten inches of it menacingly sliding out of the officer's scabbard. Mr. Briggs reconsidered. He slouched back against his seat and the officer let his sword fall back with a decisive click.

"Thank you," Nelly said to no one in particular and alighted.

She stood on the sidewalk, watching the back of the receding omnibus until she was sure that Mr. Briggs remained aboard and then she looked around. A noisy street with tall houses, shops, people, carriages and horses. She had no idea where she was. It did not matter. She was back in the safe world of the anonymous Miss Woodridge.

* * *

"Tell me, why is that?"

"What?"

"You haven't been listening to me!"

"I find the curve of your calf completely absorbing. Look how gracefully it joins the back of your knee! What was the question again?"

Nelly sighed and pulled the bed sheet over her legs. "What happened this morning. They sneered at me. My own people did that to me while it seems of little matter to the French."

Deprived of her calf, Octave gently nibbled at her shoulder. "Mhm, it doesn't matter to me."

"It did not matter to Monsieur Jacques either."

He lifted his head. "Oh, your 'fiancé' — "

"Stop saying that, please!"

"I suppose it doesn't matter to chaps who have designs on you."

"Why?"

"It's exciting, like bedding a cheetah."

"A cheetah? What's that?"

"A wild cat. Similar to a tiger, only more graceful."

She was perplexed. "I did not do it on purpose. I don't enjoy killing. Not even a fly, let alone a man."

"You did it. Another woman would have swooned. You climbed up on that cab roof and shot the man."

"I did not mean to kill him. It happened too quickly. The detectives were running after him, shooting, when he leaped on the driver's box and whipped the horse. I don't think he realized there was still someone inside the cab. He was surprised when I aimed at him and asked him to give himself up. He reacted by turning his gun at me and I had no other choice than to pull the trigger."

She had his full attention now, his head propped against his palm, his hazel eyes boring into hers.

"Do you regret it?" he asked.

"I used to have nightmares. Always the same dream. He wasn't in it, ever."

Octave ran a finger around her lips. "Had he been caught, he'd be guillotined. You have saved the French justice a great deal of money."

"If that's so, why was I treated like a leper?"

"That's human nature. The very fact of living with criminals has somewhat tainted you in the public eye."

"That's unjust!"

"Who says that life is just?"

"What do you think will happen when they find Baron de Chazelle? Will there be a trial?"

"Of course."

She buried her head in the pillow. "Then I hope they never find him. I cannot stand the idea of having my name in the newspapers. It's an honest name. It used to be," she corrected herself.

"It still is," he said unconvincingly.

"You know that it's not true! But it's in your power to make it honest again."

"Frankly, kitten, this conversation is turning in the wrong direction." He stretched his arm to reach his pocket watch on the night table. "Ten past seven. Time to go."

She understood her mistake. She must not pester him. The idea of marriage should be born in his own head. She watched him dressing, the intricacies of fashionable male wardrobe still a novelty to her.

"Will you come back tonight?"

"No. These gatherings rarely end before midnight."

"What is it again?"

"A preliminary meeting of the Society of Photography. Boring stuff."

"Why go if it's boring?"

"I mean it would be boring for you."

"Maybe it wouldn't. Hardly less boring than sitting at home alone."

"I will take you out, I promise."

"When?"

"The day after tomorrow. An opera and a good restaurant. How is that?"

A low-cut evening dress. An ermine cape. Who is that queenly apparition at Octave Gaillard's elbow, people would ask. He would beg her to marry him.

"Yes, that would be very nice," she said.

* * *

It was not altogether nice. Judging by Octave's frown, as he sat at her side in the cab, the evening had been a fiasco and she suspected she was being held responsible. Yet it had begun so grandly at the Italian Theatre!

From the moment they made their entrance, she was dazzled by the collection of sumptuous dresses, sparkling jewelry and elaborate hairstyles. She had been told that France was a country with an astronomical debt but from what she saw there was still much wealth about. They were seated on the balcony, as no women sat in the orchestra, and she pointed her opera glasses at the audience only to see other glasses directed back at her. It was an amusing game, in which she was by no means a loser as her hair was done in the latest style and her dress with silver embroidery could compete with the best. On her ears dangled two teardrop pearls, a gift from Octave. He had insisted that she should look her best and appeared as proud of her as she was of him in his faultless evening suit. They belonged together, that much was clear.

The lights dimmed off which was a modern procedure, Octave explained to her. In the past they stayed on so that people could go on admiring each other. She did not mind the obscurity, for once the music began she paid attention to nothing else. Her only experience of a full orchestra had been a marching band. This was different. She had not known that music could caress like a lover's hand and, a moment later, attack with full force like the thunder of a wrathful God. When, after the overture, the curtain went up and the singers' voices penetrated deep into her soul, she merged with the story unfolding on the stage. They sang in Italian and yet she understood their passion and despair. How beautiful and cruel was love! Poor, poor Violetta, the noble-hearted courtesan! How she felt for her! So much more so because she, too, was a kind of a courtesan until Octave should see the light. By the time Violetta collapsed dead, Nelly was sobbing aloud.

Octave was embarrassed. He said she was a social liability, but that did not stop her sobs. It was as though all the bad experiences of the past months found a final outlet in the tears shed for the brave woman on the stage. Goodness had a healing effect on her soul, she said, and she felt inspired by Violetta's noble sentiments. To which Octave replied that he had never heard of a courtesan behaving selflessly. The real woman after whom the La Traviata character was fashioned used to live in Paris in the forties. Her name was Marie Duplessis and her love affair with that young fellow was unwittingly financed by a count and a duke. They were the only two for whom he felt truly sorry. And would Nelly—please!—stop making a spectacle of herself, go to the powder room and do something with her face? He had booked a private room at the Maison d'Or, where a sniffling, red-eyed creature would not give him credit. Had she forgotten that he was to meet with influential people?

Nelly swallowed her tears and acknowledged her responsibility. She was supposed to be part of Octave's scheme. He was anxious to be elected to the committee of the International Society of Photography and, as the general meeting approached, he needed to whip up support for his candidature. The two men he had invited to dinner could sway the vote in his favor.

"What do you want me to do?" she asked.

"Smile," he said.

She was determined to be on her best behavior and anxious to please, but the dinner turned out to be an ordeal. She could not help feeling uneasy under Octave's watchful eye, while most of the conversation escaped her. They talked about people she knew nothing about and laughed at jokes she did not understand. She kept smiling, since that was her assignment, but as the dinner progressed, it became harder to keep the smile in place.

The other woman in the room, a willowy brunette with a disdainful expression, glanced at her once from under her lids and then ignored her for the rest of the meal. With her glittering jewels and languid manners, she looked like a goddess who had descended from Mount Olympus to study the mortals. She did not smile once. It occurred to Nelly that it could have been an act, but it seemed to work as she had her man, a manufacturer of photographic equipment, wrapped around her little finger.

"*La femme fatale*. She's ruining him," Octave whispered into her ear. She could tell that he was impressed. And there was she, with her stiff smile, feeling utterly inadequate. But the worst was yet to come. When the coffee and liquor were served and the men lit their cigars, someone proposed that they should listen to music. The Femme Fatale pulled at her Turkish cigarette and blew the smoke through her pursed lips.

"Perhaps we could listen to American music if our little friend can handle the piano."

The way she said it, flatly, but with an amused twitch to the corner of her mouth, set Nelly into motion.

"As a matter of fact I can," she said.

She sat at the piano, played a simple quadrille by Steven Foster and missed twice. It took a supernatural effort to close the lid and return to her seat while they clapped politely and resumed the conversation.

The other man, the treasurer of the society, who had an aristocratic particle appended to his name, kissed her hand.

"Charming," he said in English. "You Americans bring a fresh breeze to the miasma of the Old World. Tell me, are you planning to waste your beauty on that ambitious pup? If so, you underestimate yourself. He cannot afford you. There's room around your graceful neck for a diamond *rivière* and I would feel privileged to clasp it on. What say you?"

She was so flabbergasted that she said nothing.

"You are frowning. Have I shocked you?" he asked. "How refreshing, indeed."

He was the most disagreeable man she ever met. It amused him to tell her that time would come when her lips would wrinkle with age and deep furrows would run from her nose down to the corners of her mouth. It was his friendly advice, he said, that she should keep that in mind while her looks were marketable. After his insulting speech, she lost all desire to smile.

"What was he telling you?" Octave asked when they boarded the cab that was taking them home.

"Nothing," she said. "Small talk."

She expected him to wind his arm around her as he had done when they set off for the evening, but he sat huddled in his corner.

"Is something wrong?" she asked, no longer able to bear his silence.

"You must correct your table manners. They are odd."

"What's odd about them?"

"You cut a piece of food, then put the knife down, turn the fork to the right, seize it with your right hand, carry the morsel to your mouth, then put the fork down, turn it left, pick up the knife and start again. When you do it several times in a row, it looks as if you were knitting. So many useless movements while you could simply use your left hand for the task."

"This is what we were taught at the Misses Weinhardt's Academy. All polite Americans handle the cutlery this way."

"I know. I've seen it before. Believe me, it's distracting. Please, don't do it."

"Very well," she said with a lump in her throat. "Anything else you don't approve of?"

"As a matter of fact, yes. Watch how you handle the fork. The prongs do not have to point down at all times. It's a matter of judgment. Seeing you balancing peas on a fork pointed downwards was an unsettling experience."

It dawned on her that she might not be the perfect wife Octave had been looking for. She cried in public and had contemptible table manners. She searched for a means to lash back at him.

"Do you want to know what that man said to me?" she asked.

"Tell me."

"He propositioned me."

Instead of frowning, as she expected, he looked pleased.

"Does it not bother you?" she asked. "He offered me a diamond necklace."

"Did he, indeed?"

"Is that all you have to say? You should be raging mad!"

He chuckled and drew her to him. "Of course I'm raging mad. But it pleases me nevertheless to have my taste confirmed. You are a diamond in the rough and it will be a pleasure to polish you into high shine."

She relaxed against his arm but her mind kept churning gloomy thoughts. That awful man and the ravages of old age. Surely, it cannot happen to her? Not for a long, long time!

Chapter 11

Mademoiselle de la Pelletière, whose ancestors dated back to the First Crusade, was probably the thinnest human being Nelly had ever encountered.

"Her kind would rather eat dry bread than live in a bed-sitter," Octave had said. "She and her mother were already hard up before the war. I suggested they should move into something more suited to their means, but no! She digs her heels in and waves a thirty-year contract in my face. Nobody paid rent during the siege because food was too expensive. Now the law is out and all the arrears have to be paid. Don't take any nonsense from her. Either she will work her debt off or I'll have the bailiff on her."

Mademoiselle had perfectly dressed dark hair that Nelly suspected to be a wig as the color was far too vigorous for her pale wrinkled face. Her flat chest was encased in a black dress the skirt of which fell down to the floor like an iron plate. With her long arms in tight black sleeves and with the palms of her hands pressed together, she reminded Nelly of a praying mantis.

"Be seated," she said and indicated a chair.

Nelly obeyed. The door discretely clicked behind the aged servant who had introduced her into the salon. It was a cluttered room with dusty draperies framing the same view as her own on the floor above. Chipped gilt accents on the carved wall panels and a full-length coat of armor with a clutch of disintegrating ostrich feathers sprouting from the helmet lent it a feeling of faded grandeur. The room reeked of old age, cat's urine, and mothballs. Through the half-opened door leading to the adjoining room, she had glimpsed a carved bed post and the corner of a mattress with a chamber pot underneath. Someone coughed, probably Mademoiselle's mother. Octave said she was close to ninety and completely deaf. Nelly felt depression settling upon her and wished to be miles away. A Persian cat rubbed his back against her legs, leaving a trail of white hair on her skirt.

"Do not bother our guest, Perseus," said Mademoiselle. She sat down facing Nelly, a polished mahogany table between them. They looked at each other, both disliking what they saw, until Nelly lowered her eyes.

Mademoiselle cleared her throat. "Let's make one thing perfectly clear, Miss Woodridge. Extraordinary circumstances force me to accept you into the privacy of my home. That is where our business starts and ends. Should we meet in public, I shall ignore you and you shall oblige me by doing the same."

Nelly's cheeks flushed. "It seems that we have been forced on each other, mademoiselle. I have no wish to blacken your reputation."

"Very well. We shall not mention this anymore." The woman folded her hands in her lap. "Let it also be known that I have no teaching experience. Monsieur Gaillard was very vague about his requirements. Since I do not know what your failings are, we shall have to find out. Therefore, we shall spend the first hour in conversation. Feel free to ask me a question."

A question? What question? This was awkward. Nelly's gaze roamed about the room, slid down Mademoiselle's long nose and landed on an enameled brooch that adorned her bodice.

"I've seen this brooch before. Does it mean something?"

"Indeed, it does. A white fleur-de-lis on blue background is the symbol of the French royalty and is proudly displayed by all partisans of justice. The print behind you," Nelly turned to the framed likeness of an obese gentleman, "represents the Count of Chambord, a descendant of the Bourbon dynasty, and by the grace of God the rightful king of France."

"But France is a republic."

Mademoiselle consented to smile. "Not for long, Miss Woodridge, not for long! Things shall be restored to the order which God intended."

"But why? Hasn't there been enough bloodshed already?"

* * *

"The old stick may be right," said Octave that same evening. "Nothing is carved in stone. We may have a republic for now, but most of the deputies have royalist sympathies. What's more, it is said that the army still supports the exiled emperor. Only God knows what we are going to end up with after the next elections."

"Don't send me back there! She's awful. She says that I'm insolent, my pronunciation is atrocious, my spelling barbaric, and my grammar non-existent. I was made to repeat the past tenses of irregular verbs while balancing a book on my head to prevent slouching. I don't slouch, do I?"

"There is always room for improvement."

"And because she doesn't want you to feel short-changed, I must do homework. Am I really slouching?"

"Of course not. You just make yourself a little too comfortable when sitting. What kind of homework?"

"We had a little quarrel about democracy and now I have to write an essay on the advantages of republic versus monarchy. I don't even know where to begin. She makes me feel so stupid."

"Does she? We will see to that. Take a pen and a sheet of paper!"

"But—"

"Do as I say!—Now, write! Let's see . . . Ah, let's throw in a short introduction. At the dawn of the ages . . . comma . . . men hunted to satisfy their hunger. Later . . . comma . . . they settled down . . . comma . . . grew wheat and baked bread. Am I too fast for you?"

"I don't know how to spell most of the words."

"Never mind that, just go on! — It was not long before certain individuals realized that taking bread by force was less tiring than toiling on the land. They took the land itself and ruled those who worked it. To justify the robbery . . . comma . . . the ruling class claimed a divine right to their privileges. By distancing themselves from work and the creation of values . . . comma . . . the aristocrats have become a burden on society and the antithesis of the divine. There are no advantages to the monarchic rule other than pomp and display. In sharp contrast . . . comma . . . the republic brings to the top men of talent and industry regardless of their origin. There! That will show her."

* * *

Mademoiselle de la Pelletière read the essay without flinching.

"You do realize, I hope, that your spelling makes the text practically illegible?" she said. "After I have corrected it, you shall rewrite it repeatedly until it is flawless. Then you shall read it aloud and I shall correct your pronunciation until that, too, is flawless. Since Monsieur Gaillard had the goodness to dictate your homework to you, we must not disappoint him. Our next essay will discuss the advantage of good manners over boorishness."

* * *

"The royalist cow! Good manners include paying rent on time. Kitten, sit down and write the following . . ."

In Nelly's humble opinion, neither Octave nor Mademoiselle de la Pelletière displayed good manners, but the ongoing war between them accidentally produced good results.

"I have to give it to the old girl," Octave was to say later. "Her method is unorthodox but your spelling is good and she has refined your accent. What are you doing now?"

"Reciting Racine."

"Very well. Carry on."

* * *

As the weather warmed up, the tall blonde who lived across the courtyard could be often seen at her window with a piece of sewing in her hands or idly leaning out, fiddling with a lock of her hair. She radiated the pent-up energy of a racing horse confined to its stall. Her face with an aquiline nose and almost colorless eyebrows did not match the conventional blueprint of prettiness. For the same reason, it deserved a second look. Whether one found it beautiful or merely interesting depended on individual taste.

Nelly liked her at the first sight. They used to wave to each other across the courtyard before they met at the market. Modestly dressed as she was, in a dove-grey gown with a prim white collar and a moss-green cape, the blonde had a servant with her, a stout girl as dark as her mistress was fair, with a shadow of moustache on her upper lip. Nelly felt vaguely embarrassed for carrying her purchases herself.

"We meet at last," she said boldly. "I've been thinking of visiting you but I was not sure of your welcome."

"And I have been thinking the same!"

They laughed and locked arms like old friends.

"Cécile," the blonde said to the maid, "run along and put the pot on the fire! I hope," she turned to Nelly, "that you shall accept an invitation for a cup of coffee? Or should it be tea since you are English? I think I've detected an accent."

"I'm an American and coffee would do just fine."

"An American!" the blonde exclaimed. "How exciting! Do you know that I've never met an American? But then, I've been in Paris for such a short time that I've not met anyone. My name is Madame Babeau, but you must call me Géraldine since we are of the same age. I'm nineteen. How old are you?"

Géraldine was an unstoppable talker. A newly married provincial, she and her husband had moved into their apartment a week before Nelly moved into hers. She knew no one in Paris, had only her maid for company and felt painfully lonely.

"See, this is my wedding picture," she said when they were seated at the table in her dining room, which doubled as a parlor. Its modest dimensions and cheap furniture spoke of limited means yet everything was spotlessly clean and, except for a few family photographs, there were none of the sentimental mementos and useless knickknacks accumulated by years of married life. In that aspect, her home was equal to Nelly's.

76

"A very nice picture," Nelly said, unable to think of a better compliment. Her new friend's husband was apparently a pudgy, already balding man with a severe black beard. "Your wedding dress is very pretty."

"Isn't it?" Géraldine nodded, pleased. "Mama had it made in Orléans. My father is a public notary in Beaugency, some twenty miles east of Orléans. Ours is a small town. Nothing ever happens there. My sisters envy me for having married a Parisian. Except that nothing ever happens here either. Monsieur Babeau is a clerk at the Ministry of Finance. When he comes home at night, he is too tired to go anywhere. Except on Saturdays when he plays billiards with his friends. That leaves only Sundays for our walks. Last Sunday, we went to the Jardin des Plantes. That's a zoo, and all the animals were slaughtered for food during the Prussian siege. They've replaced some of them but it is far from what it used to be. At least that's what Monsieur Babeau says. Imagine eating an elephant! I wonder how it tastes. Don't you? Do you know that the Parisians ate cats, dogs, and rats? Now, there's something! I would rather die than eat such horrors! Well, I suppose one sees things differently when one is starving. Have you been to the Jardin des Plantes? It's not far from here, just down the Quay de la Tournelle and past the Wine Market. Have you seen the Wine Market? It's huge! There are entire streets and blocks where nothing else is sold but wine and liquor. Well, this is all I've seen of Paris so far. Precious little, isn't it? I have to wait until next Sunday, provided there's no rain. I never thought life in Paris would be like that, so boring, so dreary."

Tears stood in her eyes, but before she could give full way to her misery, Cécile came in with a tray. Géraldine poured coffee into small cups with a forget-me-not pattern and pushed a serving plate toward her guest.

"These are called madeleines. Do you have biscuits in America as well? You must tell me all about America. Oh, this is so exciting!" she clapped her hands like a child.

"Well . . ." Nelly began, munching on a biscuit and trying to think of something American that could be of interest, but before she could go any farther, Géraldine's curiosity was already exhausted.

"Oh, what use is it?" she complained. "I shall never go anywhere. I shall be forever frozen in this dark apartment. At least, at home we had a garden."

"Why don't you go out by yourself? I do it all the time."

"Do you? But that's dangerous! The traffic is horrendous and if you are not careful, you can get yourself run over by horses. Here, a pedestrian counts for nothing! Or you may get robbed or worse. Monsieur Babeau allows me to go to the market and to the Luxembourg Garden, but I have to take Cécile along. We cannot stay long as she has work to do."

"Would you like to go out with me?"

Géraldine caught Nelly's wrist, a smile brightening her face. "Would I? I would love it! When? Tomorrow? . . . Tomorrow afternoon? How wonderful! I can hardly wait!"

Nelly was looking forward to the prospect. Going out alone was not dangerous but a lone woman had to walk at a steady pace, looking straight ahead. Slowing down or exchanging what a man would think an inviting look meant trouble. On her early forays into the town, she used to pause at shop windows to enjoy the displayed goods until she realized that she made herself vulnerable to advances. Once, a man pursued her for three blocks with a sickening insistence until she asked a policeman for help.

"Naturally, you are an American," said the arm of the law after having sent the lecher on his way. "You American women cause problems with your independent ways. Next time, bring a chaperone or stay indoors if you are as respectable as you claim to be. There are loose women about, as well-dressed as you are, and how can a poor fellow tell which is which?"

Mollified by the tears that stood in her eyes—he did not realize they were tears of rage—he took a paternal tone with her. "If you go out, you must leave your finery at home. Dress plainly in dark colors, preferably in black like a widow or a working girl. Don't loiter in front of the shop windows for that's how the disreputable women conduct their business. Understood?"

She nodded.

"Well then," he twirled his moustache, suddenly imbued with Gallic charm. "The fact is that, to a Frenchman, a pretty face and a well-turned out figure are a work of art. Don't take it too seriously, mademoiselle, it's just the way we are. Most of the time, there's no harm in it." He touched his kepi. "Good day to you, and enjoy your stay in Paris."

Once again, Nelly dug out her dreary black dress. The policeman was right. As long as she looked modest and purposeful, she was left alone. Still, what fun was it to own an elegant wardrobe without making use of it?

Despite all, she ravenously enjoyed her freedom. She was, as Octave said, an urban explorer. With a Baedeker guide under her arm, she visited places of interest and whenever she could, she attached herself to a group of tourists and listened to the guide's comments. She already knew her way around the Île de la Cité and the main boulevards. The Baedeker said that there were fifty-seven of them running in all directions, but the most important ones circled the city in two rings, turning into bridges where they crossed the river.

One of the first trips led her past the burnt-out Hôtel de Ville to the soot-blackened wing of the Louvre and the hollow skeleton of the Tuileries Palace, which attracted the first trickle of tourists Paris saw after the war. Clutching guide booklets to the ruins of Paris, they scaled the rubble, shook their heads, and exchanged loud comments.

"I say, Martha," Nelly heard someone say in English as she stared at the impressive carcass of the former imperial palace, "I cannot believe the Frenchmen did this to themselves. What a hysterical nation! Even the Prussians behaved with more decorum when they entered Paris. To have such savagery at the doorstep of England is a most unsettling thought."

The bruised city with its gaping wounds, subjected to the humiliation of thrill-seeking foreign visitors, responded with glances of powerless rage. An elderly couple, the woman in deep mourning, passed Nelly and the group of tourists. As their eyes met, Nelly was transfixed by the couple's obvious distress and realized what such behavior meant to the proud inhabitants of Paris.

Yet the City of Light was already awakening from the cataclysm of war and revolution. The ruins were being cleared out and scaffoldings went up, alive with human ants - bricklaying, repairing, repainting. As the first green leaves appeared on the trees and sun heated the asphalt of the boulevards, the cafés spilled their chairs and tables onto the sidewalks and Paris became a vast, entertaining living room. Nelly was falling in love with it.

Chapter 12

Félicie Perrichon finished sweeping the sidewalk. She had worked slowly while pretending not to pay attention to the spectacle across the street, but now she had no other pretext to linger in front of the building unless she wanted to be caught gaping. Yet she could not help doing just that. There, on the quay, standing by the railing, was the most incredible creature she had ever seen. Bands of gypsies sometimes roamed the streets, seeking strength in numbers, but this one was alone as if even her own folks had rejected her.

Her? There was no telling whether the freak was a man or a woman. Black tangle of long hair escaping from a bright-colored head-scarf, pendulous breasts under the bodice, as well as numerous skirts thickening the gypsy's hips - all this clashed with a full black beard that ate half of the creature's face. A deep gash, probably acquired in a fight, had ruined her nose. She—Félicie had to decide on a gender, however reluctantly—stood by a folding stand hung with small colorful prints that flapped in the lively breeze of the spring afternoon. Devotional pictures, the concierge guessed. She had a number of them lodged between the pages of her missal; they were sources of comfort and beauty. She twiddled the handle of her broom, hesitating. The pictures would give her an opportunity to approach the creature and study her at close range.

A wagon loaded with wine barrels lumbered past her, temporarily obstructing the view. When it passed, a couple of young women were inspecting the stand, touching the prints and giggling nervously, while a group of barefoot *gavroches*—ragged bundles of mischief—gathered around, elbowing each other, smirking, guffawing. The boys were every concierge's nightmare. They peed in house entrances, rang doorbells for fun, and stole everything not nailed down. Now they had driven away the gypsy's clients. They were pulling faces at her, laughing and jumping back and forth, displaying bravado while staying out of reach.

Félicie had already experienced the powerless rage of a victim tormented by boys too swift on their feet. Muttering a curse, she was turning her back on the sorry scene when she heard a piercing shriek. Wincing with pain and holding his thigh, one of the urchins wailed as the gypsy's whip caught him again. The scared boys stampeded across the road toward Félicie. Delighted, the concierge brandished her broom and managed to hit a couple of backs before the herd disappeared behind the next corner.

The gypsy calmly coiled her weapon, stacked it into the stand, and motioned to Félicie to cross the street. The latter obeyed as if drawn by a magnet.

"Choose a picture," the gypsy ordered. The command was softly voiced but it was a command nevertheless.

"How much?" Félicie asked, her gaze meeting a pair of intense dark eyes.

"It's a gift. You helped me to get rid of the pests."

The bright colors of the prints appealed to Félicie. The subjects were familiar to her. Saint-Sebastian attached to a tree trunk, his muscular body pierced with numerous arrows, and Saint-Catherine holding the wheel on which she had been martyred, headed a gallery of ecstatic saints. There was also the Savior exposing his bleeding heart, the Virgin Mary with tearstained cheeks, the Holy Family fleeing to Egypt, and a Nativity scene. She settled on Saint-Geneviève, a heroic nun, clutching a sword in her delicate hand.

"The defender and patron saint of Paris," the gypsy said. "May she protect you in all circumstances."

Félicie nodded and reverently kissed the print. "You read tarot?" she asked, pointing at a sign.

"I give advice using tarot as guidance. I tell people what paths they should take to achieve wealth and happiness. I see opportunities where others don't."

Félicie eyed the heavy necklace of gold coins around the gypsy's neck. Despite her coarse look, the creature exuded prosperity. "There are no opportunities for people like me," she said plaintively.

"That's the wrong way to think. The way of the poor. You allow yourself to be carried by the current of misery, ignoring branches that could help you to hoist yourself onto dry land."

The flowery speech confused Félicie. "What branches?" she asked.

"The branches of opportunity."

"Huh?"

"Every day brings us an opportunity to better ourselves," the gypsy explained patiently. "Except that most people don't recognize it. That's why they are poor."

"And you tell them what to do?"

"Exactly."

Félicie scratched her forehead, helping the information sink into the folds of her brain.

Seeing her hesitate, the gypsy leaned closer. "I'll do a reading for free just to show you how it works. Do you know why?"

Félicie shook her head.

"Because my advice always works. Next time I see you, you will ask for more and gladly pay for it."

There was no reason for resisting such an offer. Minutes later, they were both seated at a table in Félicie's cramped loge under the stairs. She eagerly removed a chipped coffee cup and a sewing basket to make room for the gypsy's tarot. The latter fastidiously scratched candle drippings off the wooden surface with her nail and swept them on the floor before reaching into the tangle of her skirts and bringing forth a small package wrapped in a square of royal-blue silk. She smoothed the fabric on the table and placed a deck of cards in the middle. With the palms of her hands, she stirred the cards. Félicie noticed that the gypsy had a peculiar odor about her; she smelled of something medicinal. A camphor ointment, perhaps.

The gypsy swept the cards together, shuffled them, and pushed the deck across the table. "Cut the deck into three piles with your left hand, the one of the heart. Now put the bottom pile on top of the middle one and the two together on top of the first."

When Félicie executed the orders, the gypsy dealt out nine cards in three rows. "Past . . . present . . . future," she explained and turned the top row face up. "A reversed Hanging Man, the Page of Cups and the Final Judgment," she said. "This means you have missed a good opportunity. Some change occurred in your life and you did not take advantage of it. Had you acted wisely, a young person," her finger tapped the Page of Cups, "would have brought you financial comfort in your old age."

Félicie studied the Page of Cups with a doubtful frown. "I don't know anyone of that sort. Young fellows bring nothing but trouble. They get drunk and leave vomit on the stairs."

"I said a young *person*. It may be a woman. That person is close to you, perhaps living in this house. Think of something that happened in the recent past."

Félicie thought hard, her face screwed up with the effort, and shook her head.

The gypsy shrugged. "Never mind, it's in the past. We'll look at your present." She turned over the cards in the middle row, exposing a Five of Wands, a reversed King of Pentacles, and a Ten of Pentacles. "Your present says that you are meeting with opposition from this King of Pentacles. It seems that this situation has been going on for some time and I feel that it's somehow connected to the Page of Cups."

Félicie opened her mouth to protest—no king would carry on a personal dispute with her and all this was just a lot of nonsense—but the gypsy shushed her sharply.

"The King of Pentacles represents a young, blue-eyed person with fair complexion. Since the card is reversed, that person is lacking foresight." The gypsy brought the card to her forehead and closed her eyes. "It's definitely a woman. A young, attractive woman. She is coming from a great distance. She may be a foreigner but she is close, very close. She's living in this house."

Félicie's jaw dropped. "God Almighty, that's the American from third floor. That's her, dead on! What did you say she was? Lacking foresight? Does it mean she's plain silly? Because she's that and no mistake."

Now that Félicie had thrown open the gate of her opinion, resentment gushed out in a precipitous stream of words. "Whatever money she has, she sits on it tight," she complained. "Nothing to gain there. Just this morning, I met her on the stairs hauling a basket of potatoes. Thirty francs a month, I said, thirty francs is all you need to pay for a maid and our Julie's just right for you. No, she says, she can't afford it. 'Look, Miss Woodridge,' I said to her, 'a woman in your position should have a maid, a cook, and even a carriage with a pair. That's how things are done in France.' And she says, 'You know what my position is and I will not make it any worse by taking his money.' Well," Félicie leaned over the table and lowered her voice, "that man of hers owns this house and one more beside it. He's got a successful business and I heard that he had luck at the bourse during the Empire. What's thirty francs to him? You know what I think? I think she hopes he'd marry her."

She chuckled contemptuously. "In the meantime," she went on, the wrinkles on her forehead deepening, "poor Julie is working for a widower with two grown up boys. Her mistress died a couple of months ago and since then I don't sleep with worry. The way things are now it's only a matter of time before the girl shows up at my door with a swollen belly."

The gypsy waved her hand dismissively. "Well, if that's the problem, there's a way around it. If you follow my advice, we'll have that Julie of yours settled upstairs by tomorrow. It's well worth the effort. See this?" she pointed at the Ten of Pentacles. "There's a fortune attached to that American woman. Let's see where it comes from and what's in it for you."

She pressed the card against her forehead and lapsed into silence. Félicie sat with her fingers entwined, her cheeks flushed with excitement. This was real. The gypsy had a gift of clairvoyance.

A nerve-wracking minute later, the gypsy spoke, her voice hoarse with awe. "This matter is far more important than I expected. We are speaking of a *great* fortune. It will come by tortuous ways but if you become connected with that woman through your daughter—"

"Niece. Julie's my niece."

"Niece, then. In any case, she's the Page of Cups through whom you'll enjoy a comfortable old age. You have a second chance to grab at the opportunity and this time you must do it right."

"But how?" Félicie asked anxiously.

"Let me tell you something about men . . ."

* * *

Blissfully unaware of the conspiracy downstairs, Nelly opened the oven and inspected the roast, while the cover clattered on a pot of boiling potatoes on the kitchen stove and an apple pie cooled on the windowsill. She was working hard at conquering Octave's reluctance to eat at home. Restaurants were entertaining to a point, but he must see her as a good housewife, anxious to save his money. Besides, at Widow Koenig's she had seen food accidentally dropped on the kitchen floor and replaced on the serving plate. Who knew what was going on elsewhere?

She had splurged on a bouquet of red tulips, which she now carried to the dining room. Fresh flowers made the table more inviting. However, with such expenses, Mr. Cooper's money would not last forever and she had begun to think about selling a part of her wardrobe while it was still fashionable. She had seen Octave's portraits of actresses parading their finery, and she questioned him carefully, gathering a few leads. Poorly paid yet pressed to look their best, the women would not resist a good bargain. She still had to figure out how to approach them.

A key rattled in the lock of the main door. She smoothed her apron, patted her hair, and eagerly stepped into the hall. The smile died on her face when Octave ignored her greeting and, scowling, resolutely went into the sitting room. She followed him and paused on the threshold while he approached the piano, seized a small box standing on top of it, and inspected its contents.

"Come here," he ordered.

Was this the man that was supposed to kiss her and call her his sweet kitten? She took a tentative step forward.

"What's this?" he barked and threw the contents out. Gold and silver coins landed on the carpet, others rolled under furniture.

"Money," she piped, intimidated by his inexplicable anger.

"Never," he said icily, "never—do you hear me—never say that you can't afford a maid."

"This is not my money."

"Like hell it is not! I've been playing your silly little games long enough, Miss Respectable! However, I'm drawing a line at this one. I will not have you spreading the tale that I don't give you enough money."

"I said nothing of the sort."

"The way you put it, it sounds the same. You are shedding bad light on me. It is known that Octave Gaillard always pays his dues and I will not have my reputation tarnished. The money is yours and you will use it to run this household properly. I never again want to hear from the concierge that you take carpets down to the courtyard and beat the dust out of them in front of everyone. Understood?"

She choked with indignation. "I don't want to live on your money. It's not proper. It would make me a kept woman."

"Too late, you already are. Unless, of course, you start paying rent for this apartment."

She had nothing to say in response to that. The rent was beyond her means. Moving into some smelly, bug-infested attic . . . No, she was not ready for the sacrifice.

"I told the concierge to bring the girl tomorrow. You will pay her thirty francs a month. Next time, I want to see this box empty."

He adjusted his hat and headed for the door.

"Where are you going?" she asked, fighting tears.

"I need fresh air to calm down."

"But the dinner is almost ready."

"That's another thing," he said. "I will no longer suffer your deplorable cooking. From now on, stay away from the kitchen. Had I wanted a cook, I would have hired one."

Chapter 13

Although her aunt said that she was nearly seventeen, the scrawny Julie looked closer to fifteen. She had lackluster brown hair, dull brown eyes sunk deep into the eye-sockets, and the vitality of a turtle. To make matters worse, she was a liar.

Early in the morning after Julie's first night in her new home, Nelly found the kitchen floor scrubbed raw and stinking of bleach, a bucket upturned in the sink, and the girl claiming that she did not do it. The same thing happened the next day. Why did she need to lie? What was her game? Disturbed, Nelly went to question the concierge.

"Scrubbing the kitchen floor during the night?" the latter asked. "I swear I had no idea! No wonder she looks so tired. I thought it was overwork. Poor Julie," she added, her face contorting as tears appeared in her eyes. "She had a bad experience during the Bloody Week last May. Caught in the shooting she was, and has never been the same. They found her wandering the streets covered in blood. Fortunately, it was not her own. Someone recognized her and brought her back to her employers. She doesn't remember what happened. Maybe she just got confused after her mistress died and there was no one to give her guidance. As long as there's food on the table and their shoes are clean, men don't care. I'm sure this will stop as soon as she settles down and gets used to your ways."

"I finally caught her at it last night," Nelly said to Octave the next day. "At first, I thought she was lying, but now I think that she does not remember what she has done. 'Why are you doing this', I asked. 'It has to be done,' she said. I ordered her to stop, but she went on with the scrubbing. It was only when I shook her by the arm, and called her name that she became confused.

All of a sudden, she seemed surprised to be in the kitchen in the middle of the night. I saw her to bed and she fell asleep soon after."

"An interesting case of somnambulism," Octave said.

"Somnambulism?"

"The girl is a sleepwalker."

"Sleepwalkers stroll on the roof with outstretched arms and there has to be a full moon."

"That's a popular myth. Sleepwalkers can do anything. This one has chosen to scrub the kitchen."

"But why?"

He shrugged. "I don't know. It could be some kind of purification ritual."

"With all that, she seems to be sleepwalking during the day. What am I to do?"

"Get rid of her. Maids are thirteen to a dozen. I'll find you someone suitable."

"No," Nelly said. "I must find a way to stop those night-scrubbing binges. Once she sleeps properly, she will improve."

In the end, she took Julie into her bed and attached their ankles with a rope. Each night, at about two in the morning, a tug on the rope would wake her up. She would pull at the rope, a hard tug or two. "Come back to bed, Julie," she would say.

Each time, the girl obediently stretched herself at Nelly's side and, within five minutes her regular breathing allowed Nelly to resume her own sleep. On Saturday, when Octave stayed overnight, Julie regained her own bed. On Sunday morning, the kitchen stank of bleach again.

* * *

"I wouldn't take Cécile into my bed if my life depended on it," said Géraldine. "It is not proper. How can you expect respect from servants if you treat them as your equals? You foreigners do amaze me."

"She needs help," Nelly said.

"That too would worry me. Who knows what is going on in that sick head of hers? What if she slices your throat open while you are asleep?"

"Julie wouldn't hurt a fly."

Géraldine cut a length of poppy-red yarn and concentrated on threading her tapestry needle. "In my opinion," she said when she was done, "the girl belongs in a lunatic asylum. Her aunt is taking advantage of you."

"You've never been through real hardship, have you?"

"No, I cannot say I have. Have you? Of course, with your father dying and leaving you stranded in a foreign country, it must have been very hard on you. Although I must say that you weathered it well and you seem to enjoy your freedom. In a way, I envy you."

Nelly put her work down. Following Géraldine's example, she was embroidering a pair of slippers in Berlin wool. Her friend's canvas flamed with wild poppies and the slippers were intended for Monsieur Babeau's anniversary in June. Nelly had chosen a pattern of cornflowers on a cream background.

Yes, she had weathered her crisis as well as she could. Now she was sitting with the needlepoint in her lap, surrounded by the fragrant springtime splendor of the Luxembourg Garden. The gravel walks were teaming with hundreds of children, nursemaids, and well-to-do couples enjoying an afternoon constitutional. A tall iron fence protected the vast garden from beggars. Behind the golden clouds of blooming forsythia bushes, she could hear the distant thunder of vehicles going up and down the boulevard Saint-Michel. For a few *sous*, she could rent a lawn chair and play the role of an irreproachable *bourgeoise* like Géraldine. It was a sham, a pitiful sham, yet she needed these respectable afternoons as a soothing balm for the discomfort of her sinful life. She felt sorry for deceiving her new friend, but would she have a friend if Géraldine knew the truth? And to think that Géraldine actually envied her freedom!

"You Americans are so independent," the latter said. "My family would never allow me to live alone. This is unheard of in our circles. But since you have your cousin to look after you, I suppose it's all right. Except that people could interpret it the wrong way. I took the liberty of telling Monsieur Babeau that your father is alive and traveling abroad. I hope you don't mind me telling such a lie because I am afraid my husband would not allow me to speak to you otherwise. Already, the fact that you are a foreigner does not sit well with him. But when he heard that you have Mademoiselle de la Pelletière for company, he was less worried."

Oh good, there goes Mademoiselle's reputation, thought Nelly with a pang of guilt. Should Monsieur Babeau ever learn the truth about *Cousin* Octave . . . And now Géraldine has added her own contribution to an already thick tangle of lies.

The story of her life, as told in the neighborhood with the complicity of the concierge, made her out to be the daughter of an American businessman, struck by a heart-attack in Paris, and of a long-deceased French mother. At her demand, Octave had supplied her with a couple of tastefully framed photographs representing her fictitious parents: a very proper lady bearing a faint resemblance to her and a distinguished pot-bellied gentleman with a beard. The pictures were prominently displayed above the fireplace of her sitting room where the Sèvres vases once stood.

Nelly sighed. Apparently, the story was not good enough for her friend, as she had to resuscitate the late Mr. Woodridge in order to make Nelly more palatable to her husband.

"At least, you should have an older woman living with you," said Géraldine, while busily filling in a poppy leaf with fine tent stitches. "A widowed aunt or an older cousin. In every family, there's an old maid just good enough for the task. I'm surprised that Monsieur Gaillard has not thought of that. He's French and he knows our customs."

Monsieur Gaillard does not care enough, Nelly mused. Monsieur Gaillard changes into an eel every time I mention love. Yet I love him and cannot help it!

The day after the ugly scene, Octave sent a jeweler's box to smooth things over. The opal ring now sparkled on her finger, its rainbow colors intensified by sunshine. The wages of sin.

She watched a starchy nursemaid pushing a baby pram past them, the wheels revolving with a crunching sound on the fine gravel. Everything in this public garden was so proper, so unlike herself. What was she doing here? The sedate activity no longer satisfied her. Suddenly, she ached for a change.

"Must we always come here? There are other places."

Géraldine stabbed her needle into the canvas and lifted her head. "You know that Monsieur Babeau does not want me to go anywhere else. The Luxembourg Garden is a safe place. I told him I first met you here."

"That's the second lie you told him in my behalf."

"Only because I value your friendship. We are friends, aren't we?"

"Of course, we are. But don't you want to see more?"

"You know I do. But Monsieur Babeau—"

"He doesn't have to know, does he?"

"Well, I suppose that close friends like us are entitled to share a few secrets," conceded Géraldine. "If I don't tell him it's not actually a lie, is it?"

"I'm not sure about that. But since you've already started on the path of falsehood, why should that worry you?"

Géraldine thought it over. "I suppose you are right. Yes, let's do it! Let's go somewhere we've never been before!"

Chapter 14

"**A** dessert? I cannot possibly eat another bite," protested Géraldine. "Except perhaps some fruit."

"May I suggest Mandarins Napoleon?" offered the dignified waiter. "They are sections of mandarins dusted with confectionary sugar and soaked with cognac."

Géraldine covered her mouth to hold in a burp and dissolved into uncontrollable giggling.

"Madame is in a joyous mood," commented the waiter, his face strictly expressionless. "Mandarins Napoléon may also be served flambé," he addressed Nelly, "which would considerably reduce the alcohol content."

"Definitely flambé," said the latter, casting an anxious glance at her friend. "And strong coffee, please."

She felt tipsy as well. They had drunk half a bottle of champagne on top of their aperitifs. What fun they'd had dressing for this lunch, deciding on appropriate dresses, building fashionable hairdos, and trying on numerous hats! Spending Octave's money was not hard after all.

"I wish Babeau could see us now," Géraldine mused later, while they were watching the play of bluish flames in the serving plate. "He would turn into a salt statue like Lot's wife!" The idea seemed to please her.

"How did you two meet?" asked Nelly when the waiter was gone and the dessert ready for consumption.

"Through a matrimonial agency."

"You are joking!"

"Why would I? A girl cannot walk around with her dowry written on her forehead, can she? So, how else would she meet suitable marriage prospects? Don't you have matrimonial agencies in America? No, I suppose you would not, being such a savage country. Is it true that American men spit tobacco on the floor? I once read about it in the newspaper. How disgusting!"

"Your coffee is getting cold," said Nelly sharply.

"Oh yes, the coffee," Géraldine took a sip and returned to her topic. "There were not many inquiries in my case. I had only a small dowry because I have four more sisters. Babeau was by far the best prospect except that he turned out to be shorter than myself. Still, being an old maid was a far worse fate. And I was looking forward to living in Paris."

She poked her finger through the handle and proceeded to turn the cup back and forth, producing an irritating sound. "Things did not turn out as I expected," she commented moodily. "He's very careful with his money. Every franc he gives me has to be accounted for. I can never repay an invitation such as this one."

"You don't need to. This lunch has been my pleasure."

"Still, it's not right."

Once they left the restaurant, the fresh air made them both realize how drunk they were.

"My head turns," Géraldine complained.

"So does mine. Let's walk it off. The faster we walk the better." Nelly took her bearings. "Let's see. We can cross the Pont Neuf to the Quay du Louvre, walk as far as the Place de la Concorde, cross the bridge there and return by the Left Bank. That's a good hour of brisk walk. By the time we are done, we should be all right.—Géraldine?"

"Over here!"

Her friend was swaying in front of a confectionery, admiring the window display. "Look," she pointed at the artfully arranged boxes in which miniature marzipan fruits reposed on paper lace. "Isn't it pretty? Look at those little apples, peaches, pears, and oranges! I so wish I could buy a box for Mama. She would love it, I'm sure."

"And does your mother know that you two are out alone?"

This came from an imperious elderly woman, dressed in silk and black lace, who just stepped out of the shop. She looked from one girl to another. "Which one of you is the elder?" she asked.

As they both stood there with their mouths hanging open, she targeted Nelly. "The youth of today!" she said indignantly. "Out for mischief, I shouldn't be surprised. Take your sister home for your mother must be worried sick."

"The crazy old crone," murmured Géraldine as they watched the old woman being helped into a solid barouche with a coat of arms on the door.

"She must have left her glasses at home. Anyhow, she has no business telling us off in public. How embarrassing. And she thought we were sisters! It is actually kind of nice, isn't it? I mean, being like sisters . . ."

Once they reached the Place de la Concorde, they forgot all about their projected itinerary. The whole stretch of the Champs Elysées, from La Concorde up to the Arc de Triomphe, was a vast amusement ground. They watched jugglers and contortionists, dancing dogs, monkeys dressed as humans, and even a tame bear balancing on a wooden ball. They wove their way between rows of fashionable vehicles, sampled fresh cheese and each drank a glass of milk still warm from a goat. Nelly found it nauseating but Géraldine swore that it would definitely clear their heads. They rode a pair of foul-smelling donkeys and shook their skirts in disgust when they dismounted. They watched a Punch and Judy show amidst delighted children and laughed at the silly jokes. Exhausted, they fell on a bench and stretched out their aching feet.

"I'm so happy I could weep!" declared Géraldine. "I've never had so much fun!"

"That won't last another minute."

"What do you mean?"

"Don't look, but there is a fellow who has been following us for the past ten minutes. He's moving in for the kill."

"What—"

"Good afternoon, ladies!" The man about town briefly lifted his hat and stood in front of them, twirling his walking stick. "You seem to be having a nice time," he went on. "Would you include me in the fun? I could make it worth your while."

Géraldine eyed him gravely, and then leaned forward as if inhabited by a serious concern. "And does your mama know that you are out alone?" she asked.

The look of surprise that wiped out his smug smile was priceless. Both girls exploded with laughter.

Angry, the man said something about lack of manners, which sent them into another spasm of mirth. When they wiped their eyes, the pleasure-seeker was gone.

"I didn't know you had such a devil in you," said Nelly, clutching her aching ribs. "This is by far the funniest thing that has ever happened to me! Take care! There goes another one."

They took a slow way back home by the busy street of Saint-Honoré and by the boulevard de Sébastopol. They lingered in front of shop windows, pretending to admire the displays, ready for the next victim. Géraldine refined her act to perfection and each time she had the same success. They laughed as they ran away from the confused men, jostling the crowd and oblivious to critical glances from the passers-by. It was a splendid revenge for Nelly's past humiliations.

They passed the ruin of the Hotel de Ville and emerged on the quay. It was then that they realized that the sun was setting. And there, on the opposite sidewalk, was Monsieur Babeau on his way home.

"Jesus," breathed Géraldine.

They both made a sharp turn and took cover behind a kiosk. Nelly poked her head out.

"He is heading for the Pont d'Arcole," she reported. "We cannot run past him. Let's wait till he's gone and then make for the Louis Philippe bridge."

"We'll never make it on time," Géraldine's voice had a touch of hysteria. "What if we run into him on the opposite side? He'll see me in this dress!"

"Wait here," Nelly ordered. She stepped into the street and hailed passing cab. "To the Quay de la Tournelle, as fast as you can!" she called to the cabbie, herding Géraldine inside.

The cab overtook the short, squat figure of Monsieur Babeau half way across the bridge and hurled at all speed toward Notre Dame with Géraldine hiding in a corner. Ten minutes later, she stood in Nelly's bedroom, struggling into her gray dress, while Nelly was leaning far out of the window.

"I see him," she announced. "He is passing the corner of the rue de la Bièvre."

"Then I've about ten minutes left. He always stops at the tobacconist's. Oh, come and help me, please! I'm so nervous that my fingers refuse to obey me."

Nelly hooked up her friend's bodice while Géraldine tied the ribbon of her bonnet.

"I want you to know, Nelly," she said, "that whatever happens, this has been the most exciting day of my life. Today, I've lived."

They embraced, holding each other for a few precious seconds, then Géraldine grabbed a bag containing her embroidery frame and left.

Later in the evening, Cécile brought a secret note.

Dearest Nelly, Géraldine wrote, *I reached home with time to spare. What a wonderful day! However, I have to warn you: Those confounded donkeys were infested with fleas! I have caught one right now. I have a couple of bites on my leg, which will be hard to explain. Your friend who loves you, G.*

Chapter 15

Sunday, after the excursion to Champs Elysées, Nelly woke to bright sunshine with Octave at her side. She thought of shaking him awake and then changed her mind. Since the poor darling had paid her so many attentions during the night, he should have his restorative sleep.

She fell back into the comfortable cradle of her down pillow and began to plan her day. They would have a lazy breakfast and then drive to the Bois de Boulogne. Arm in arm, they would stroll with other elegant people down the long winding paths of the park, stop for lunch, and then board a rowing boat that would take them to one of the islands where a band would play a selection from fizzy Offenbach's operas. In the evening, they would ride back to the Arc de Triomphe, down the Champs Elysées, and onto the boulevards to dine in one of the better restaurants. Yes, today was going to be a splendid day.

She stretched voluptuously, slipped into her morning wrap and opened the window. A fresh breeze scented with sun and water entered the bedroom. She exposed her face to the gentle wind and allowed it to ruffle her loose hair. It was an exquisite sensation.

"Don't move!"

She turned and saw Octave propped on his elbows. He was observing her with a feverish intensity.

"I said don't move."

"Why?"

"Just do what you have been doing."

Puzzled, she turned back to the window.

"No, no! Tilt your head back and let the wind kiss your face. There. Now, stand still!"

He threw off the sheet and jumped out of the bed. He circled her like a predator, his hands improvising a frame through which he peered at her from different angles.

"This is perfect," he said.

"That's enough," Nelly said. "There's a *bateau-mouche* full of people coming up the stream. They'll see me undressed. Besides, I'm getting cold."

"Then come and I'll warm you up," he offered.

"A cup of coffee will do the job perfectly," she said, closing the window and drawing the drapes. "What was that all about?"

"You, *ma belle*," he said with enthusiasm, "are going to win me a prize at the Salon. If I work fast, I can still replace this year's entry, but only just. The Salon opens in ten days."

"What salon? What are you talking about?"

"The annual Salon of Photography. The first one after the war. There's no better place to forge an international name. And you, kitten, are going to be my calling card. I want to recreate the situation at the window. I'll call it *Morning Breeze*."

"No, dear. I'm not going to be gaped at by a bunch of strangers. Especially not while dressed in flimsy lingerie."

"What's wrong with that?"

"Everything. I'm not going to pose for a filthy photograph."

"A filthy photograph? How dare you call filth what's nothing but art?"

"Please, let's not talk about it anymore. You have already spoiled what looked like a beautiful morning. What do you want for breakfast? Fried eggs or the usual?"

"You know that I don't care for eggs in the morning. Please, kitten, listen to me!"

He threw on his dressing gown and followed her into the kitchen.

"Eggs only for me, Julie," Nelly said to the maid who busied herself with grinding coffee beans.

"Listen to me," Octave repeated. "It's about a young woman and the promise of a beautiful day—"

"What is it going to be for you, dear? Strawberry preserve or plum jam?" she interrupted him.

"I want to capture a moment of pure enchantment with life, do you understand?"

"I understand very well."

"Well then?"

"I said no. You will not turn me into another Loulou de Montmartre. Is that clear?"

* * *

The one-legged Monsieur Goubert came on Mondays. Unlike Mademoiselle de la Pelletière, he was eager to repay his debt to Octave by improving Nelly's piano skills. Her heart bled each time she saw the sweet old man hobbling down the stairs from his fifth-floor apartment. The floor on which one lived, she noticed, was determined by status and wealth. There was a wide social gap between the second and fifth floors, while the garrets under the eaves were reserved for servitude and misery.

"Would you rather that I came up for my lessons?" she asked when she first met him.

Monsieur Goubert shook his white head. "My dear Miss Woodridge, my piano has been sold a long time ago. I'm an ambulant teacher and I don't mind the exercise. It keeps one young."

When she finally summoned up enough courage to ask about his leg, he explained that he had been buried under the rubble of a shelled house during the Bloody Week, but he refused to supply details.

"Such memories are best left alone," he said. "In human history, there have always been brief episodes of madness when even honest brains caught fire. When the blaze is extinguished, people stare in horror at what they have done."

"Very good, Miss Woodridge," he said now. "Except for the last four measures where you have slipped into adagio. You have to maintain the rhythm firmly in allegro. Work on it and when you improve, we shall attack the Moonlight Sonata by Beethoven. There are four sharps that will certainly sharpen your fingers, if you allow me a little levity."

He chuckled, pleased with his modest joke, and contentedly rubbed his hands together. The lesson was over and he knew what was coming. Rare were the households where he was offered a bite to eat.

The door opened and a neat little maid laden with a tray came in. An aroma of cinnamon buns and fresh coffee entered Monsieur Goubert's receptive nostrils. When he took a second look at the girl, his jaw dropped.

"Gracious God," he said, "is that you, Julie?"

Nelly looked at him, surprised. "You know Julie?"

"I do indeed." He hobbled closer to the girl. "Julie, my poor Julie, how are you?"

Clutching her tray, the maid backed away from him.

"Don't you remember me, little Julie?" insisted the old man.

All he got for an answer was a dangerous rattle of china. Quickly, Nelly snatched the tray out of the girl's hands. "Julie has trouble remembering," she said.

"Impossible! The ambulance," he insisted, "the man with the crushed foot, that was I! Stretched on the bed I was and you, Julie, standing with that boy in your arms—"

"No," said Julie in a hoarse voice while backing toward the door. "No!" And she fled the room.

Nelly, Julie's aunt, and Monsieur Goubert gathered around the sitting-room table in an atmosphere of concerned conspiracy.

"She brought that injured boy in. He was about seven years old," the old man said. "All was confusion. The shots in the street were ringing close by, but no one could tell whether they came from the Communards or from the government troops. The ambulance was packed to capacity so the nurses told her to put the child in bed with me. Just then, the door flew open and the soldiers stormed in. They must have had orders, for the shooting started immediately. No one was spared—men, women, children—neither patients nor nurses. 'Death to the Communard vermin,' they were shouting.

"The soldiers shot the boy in Julie's arms and they both fell to the floor. The patient in the bed next to mine was shot through the head as he tried to escape. He fell over Julie and the child. His blood and brains had spattered all over me. I had the presence of mind to play dead.

"The shooting stopped. There was a brief silence, followed by the moaning of the injured. Soon after, the soldiers went around the room, executing everyone who moved. When they left, I heard the girl stirring under the two bodies. I spoke to her in a soft voice, told her not to move, to wait. I asked her name and she told me. She was terrified, but she kept quiet. There was no one left alive in that hospital room except for the two of us, but we could not escape because there were guards posted outside.

"Later, an officer came in with a half-dozen men. He ordered them to remove the bodies and place them onto a wagon in the street. It was then I knew that God had listened to my prayers. I recognized the officer's voice. He was a former pupil of mine, a young lad from a good family. I called him by name. He was surprised to find me in that 'rat's nest' as he put it. I told him I had been carried there after having been trapped under the rubble fallen from the roof of the Ministry of Finance. I told him about Julie, still buried under the corpses. He had her pulled out, untouched but covered in blood. She could barely stand on her two feet.

"'You have nothing to fear, Julie,' I said.

"'That remains to be seen,' the lad replied. 'Do you know her?'

"I said I did not but I told him about Julie's bravery in trying to save the child.

"'Yes, they are brave, those demented Communard hellcats,' he conceded. 'They fight on the barricades along with their men and crawl across Paris with bottles of kerosene, setting buildings on fire. Don't you smell the smoke? The city is burning and it's their work.' He pointed at Julie, held by two of his men. 'I'm sure she's one of them. A *pétroleuse!*'

"'For God's sake, Lieutenant,' I said, 'was the war not enough? Why should we French be killing each other? I'm not a Communard, as you well know, and yet I'm here. How many innocents are among these dead? Don't add to the carnage by shooting another child! Think of your sister Paulette — she must be this girl's age.'

"I think his sister's name did it. He snapped out of his rage and ordered Julie released, but that was not the end of the girl's ordeal. Before she was allowed to go, she had to scrub the blood-soaked floor. By that time, I was drifting in and out of consciousness because my injured foot had turned septic. In one of my clear moments I realized that Julie was gone."

The old man lifted a glass to his lips and took a sip of wine. They sat in silence, Nelly's cheeks wet with tears, Félicie sobbing into her apron.

"When I saw her today," he went on, "I didn't know that she had buried it inside. In a way, I'm not surprised. It's hard to live with such memories. I had nightmares, night after night. In fact, I still do at times."

"You are a good man, Monsieur Goubert, and God bless you," said the concierge as she dried her eyes with her apron. "Poor dear," she said, rising, "I must go and see how she's doing."

Monsieur Goubert shook his head. "It hurt my feelings when Julie ran away from me. I have done her no harm, quite the contrary. Why is she afraid of me?"

This was true. Nelly had found Julie in a dark corner, arms tightly wrapped around her knees. "Please, make him go away," she pleaded.

"Why, Julie? Has he done something wrong to you?"

"I don't know. It's his voice. Please, send him away!"

She was now in bed, sedated by a strong poppy seed infusion.

"I'd better go as well," Monsieur Goubert reached for his crutch. "I'm glad that the girl is alive. It's a sad business all the same."

* * *

"Why? Why do people do such horrible things?" Nelly asked. "Swear to me that you had nothing to do with it!"

"That I can do with clear conscience," Octave said. "I spent the whole uprising in jail, along with other officers of the National Guard. We were not liberated until the Versailles troops had dealt with the Communards. I agree that mistakes were made, but dwelling on them will change nothing."

"Mistakes? You call such horror mistakes?"

"Come," he said. "Let's forget it. Life goes on." He closed his arms around her waist and attempted to kiss her.

"But Julie—"

"She'll be fine. Time heals all wounds."

"I tried to picture what's happening in Julie's head," she said. "And do you know what I saw?"

"No, what?"

"I had a vision of a room. There was a carpet on the floor. It was bulging with life as if an unclean beast had been swept under it. There it was, living, breathing, hidden. All I could make of it was its uncertain shape. Do you know what I mean?"

"Hm, interesting."

"For a moment, I actually lived Julie's terror." Nelly crossed her arms and grabbed her shoulders as if she needed protection from such a thought. "Today, when she met the music teacher, I think that a corner of the carpet was lifted. The beast was there, ready to pounce from its hiding place. That's what scared her."

"You have a wild imagination."

"I may be wrong, but I'm convinced that as long as the thing hides in her head, Julie will suffer. It has to be chased out. Except I don't know how."

"Neither do I and I don't want to think about it anymore. Let sleeping dogs lie. She's not the only one to suffer. Thousands did. Time will take care of everything. Enough said!"

He swept her in his arms and carried her to bed.

"I'll try to talk to her," Nelly went on doggedly while Octave removed her shoes. "Or perhaps Monsieur Goubert should—"

"Kitten, shut up, will you?"

"I need advice."

"All right, all right. I'll talk to someone," he promised while stripping off her stockings. "A friend of mine."

"Who? Is he the man you play chess with every Thursday?"

"Yes, Henri. The chap's a walking encyclopedia. He might come up with something."

"Then ask him what to do."

He ran his hand along her calf. "I will. On Thursday."

"No, today!"

"Today?"

"You said you meet him at a café in the rue Sommerard. That means he lives somewhere nearby."

"He lives close to La Sorbonne, by the Luxembourg Garden."

"Then it's a short walk."

"All right, I'll see him tomorrow." He released her foot and transferred his attention to the hooks on her bodice.

"Please, go now!"

"Now?" He swore and straightened up. "Look here, princess! I worked hard all day long. Then I dropped into the middle of a domestic crisis. And now, when it's over, you treat me like an errand boy." Angrily, he stretched himself at her side, hands under his head. "I'm going nowhere."

"It is not over. Julie—"

"Julie this and Julie that! Julie can wait and so will you. Yesterday, I asked you to do something for me. It was not much and still you refused. Why should I lift a finger for you?"

"I'm not asking you to strip to your underwear in front of a camera. But what do you know about decency? How can you even think of making love at this moment?"

"So now I'm a monster!" Abruptly, he got up. Standing in front of the mirror, he adjusted his cravat.

"Are you going then?"

"What else can I do? I'll have no peace otherwise."

"Thank you."

Sulking, Octave inserted his arms into the jacket she was holding for him. "He may not be at home," he commented.

"You'll find him somehow."

"I'm not so sure."

"You said you wanted my picture taken in the morning wrap."

"That's correct."

"Then I'll do it."

He paused, his fingers resting on his jacket buttons, a pleasant surprise spreading over his face. "You will do it?" he repeated, still incredulous.

"Yes, I promise. I need your help and your heart is not in it. If posing in my negligee will get you going, then so be it. But don't come back without an answer."

"That doesn't explain why you are so keen on purging that girl's head. What is she to you?" His eyes narrowed. "No, don't answer that one! I think I know. It has something to do with the de Chazelle murder. Tell me, is Julie your ticket to redemption?"

"For the shooting? No, that could not be avoided. But for Kitty de Chazelle, yes. Instinct kept telling me that something was wrong, but I shrugged it off. Perhaps I could've saved her life had I not been lying to myself. Now God has sent me Julie. If I fail her in her need, then I'm a worthless human being. Now go and find that man!"

Chapter 16

I hate Octave-the-artist! He is a creature from hell! Nelly wrote in her diary. Things went wrong from the beginning. When she promised to pose for him she thought he would bring his camera to the bedroom. Why not, after all? The previous summer in Butte, an itinerant photographer set his camera where needed and took quite a good picture of her family, except for the twins Billy and Teddy, who were never able to stand still.

Octave would not hear of it. He had a set built in his studio. It consisted of two converging wooden walls, covered with wallpaper and with a genuine full-length window set in. He rented a large fan from the Variétés Theatre, which came with its own operator, an unsavory leering character in a blue workers' blouse. At Octave's order, the man would crank the handle and the fan would produce an artificial breeze. In addition to the man with the air contraption, there were an assistant and a pimply apprentice. This assembly awaited Nelly at eleven sharp, as Octave wanted the advantage of strong mid-day light. She was only ten minutes late because she could not decide between two hats, but even for this small infraction she had to face Octave's wrath. Clouds had appeared on the horizon, jeopardizing the project, he complained, while pushing her unceremoniously into the dressing room. Every couple of minutes, he would knock at the door and ask, "Are you not finished yet?"

When she emerged in her white wrap, he led her across the vast studio, through a maze of photographic equipment, mirrors, props and curtains to a camera of elephantine proportions. The glass ceiling was obscured with movable shades while bright daylight was flooding the studio through the large windows facing the set. Nelly was asked to put her hands on the opened windowpanes, tilt her head back as she had done in her bedroom and hold still.

"The wind!" Octave called.

The man at the wheel in front of her began to turn the handle and a gentle breeze caressed her face.

"Lavisse, adjust the mirror," Octave called to the assistant. "I want more light on the chair. Stop! Who the hell brought the fresh carnation? Bébert," he addressed the apprentice, "come here! Did I say fresh carnation? I did not, did I? I said *wilted*. W-i-l-t-e-d! Now, get your ass out of here and bring me a wilted carnation, understood?"

Nelly had no idea what he was talking about until she noticed a chair by her side and an evening jacket with a fresh carnation stuck in the buttonhole thrown over the seat.

"What is this jacket doing here?" she asked. "I don't think it belongs to the picture."

"Don't tell me what belongs in the picture," Octave barked. "All right everybody, take a rest until the lad gets back from the florist's."

As there was nowhere to sit, she took the jacket and hung it over the back of the chair. Octave pressed his palms against his temples and growled.

"What have I done?" she asked.

"The jacket! Do you have any idea how long it took to arrange the jacket? Get out of my way!"

He spent the next ten minutes throwing the garment on the chair until it fell just right. By that time, the apprentice was back and the carnations switched.

"Everybody to his post!" the despot clapped his hands. "You," he addressed Nelly, "close the window, open it again and freeze at the end of the act. That will do for a more natural pose. The wind!"

The man at the wheel set to work while she opened the window. Again, the gentle movement of air ran over her face.

"Faster!"

The creaking of the wheel quickened and what had been a breeze changed into a wind that lifted her loose hair and plastered the white fabric against her body.

"Good. I want you to look happy. Try to think of something enjoyable and arch your body forward as if seeking a lover's embrace. Forward . . . Forward . . . Stop! Stop the machine! — Are you wearing stays under that wrap?"

"I am," she said in a small voice.

"Go back into the dressing room and remove it. I don't want a stitch of clothing underneath. I need natural curves."

She did not walk to the dressing room. She ran there, driven by anger and shame. Locking herself in, she proceeded to change into her street clothes. Octave knocked at the door several times.

"What's taking you so long?" he kept asking. "Nelly? Kitten?"

She tied the bow of her hat, stuffed the wrap into a bag she had brought for that purpose and unlocked the door.

"What is it?" he inquired as she attempted to push past him. "Where are you going?"

"Get out of my way! It's finished."

"No, it is not!" He caught her arm and dragged her back into the dressing room. "What's got into you?"

She was choking with humiliation. "I have never been so ill-treated in my life. You shout at me, you talk about lover's embrace in front of strange men and, to top it all off, you discuss my underwear in public. That, plus being near naked, is more than I can stand."

"But kitten—"

"You are despicable!"

"You unbearable goose!" he thundered. "I'm in the process of creation and have no time for your silly sensibility. My men have seen it all and more. Stop this capricious behavior and get out of your clothes!"

They stared at each other in a silence charged with electricity before she made another escape attempt. He reached the door ahead of her and barred her way.

She slapped his cheek.

He slapped hers.

Nelly froze, her anger gone, tears on hold, disbelieving.

"I did go and see my friend, did I not?" Octave asked.

She nodded.

"He recommended mesmerism, is that right?"

"It is."

"And have I not arranged for an appointment with the distinguished Professor Charcot?"

"You have."

"Then remember that I can still call it off."

He left the dressing room and softly closed the door behind him.

She did what he wanted. She even managed to look happy for the sake of the art. The picture would not show the block of ice that occupied her ribcage.

* * *

As if to agree with Nelly's dark mood, the clouds that had menaced Octave's enterprise later released a relentless rain. Nelly and Julie, their shoulders rubbing together with the swaying of the cab, the raindrops beating a steady rhythm on the roof, traveled silently along the Left Bank, each occupied with her own thoughts. Julie's state of mind could be easily guessed from the way she kept crumbling her aunt's Sunday handkerchief. The freshly laundered and starched white cloth was already limp with the moisture of her sweaty palms. In spite of her distress, she held her head up and stiffly stared straight in front of her. Nelly was no less nervous. She now castigated herself for having refused Octave's offer.

When they had separated two days earlier, they barely spoke. The next morning, he sent Bébert to the quay. Dripping water on the carpet in the hall, the gangly apprentice handed her a note from his master. Would she want him to attend Julie's appointment with Professor Charcot at La Salpêtrière? She stared at the cold words, reading them repeatedly as if expecting that an apology, written in sympathetic ink, would suddenly materialize on the page.

"How is Monsieur Gaillard?" she asked and instantly regretted her question. It was not up to her to show curiosity. *She* was the injured party.

"Very tired, ma'am," replied Bébert. "He spent the night in the laboratory."

"The laboratory?"

"Developing the photographs and the like. Supervising the mounting. It's a great picture, ma'am. It will make a killing!"

Remembering that this teenager had seen her without stays, defeated and in tears, Nelly blushed with embarrassment. To create a diversion, she rang the bell and ordered a cup of tea for Bébert and a towel for his wet hair. Why, the boy could catch cold, running in the rain without an umbrella! While Bébert gladly followed Julie into the kitchen, she busied herself with a reply. Octave's presence was not necessary, she wrote in the same icy tone. Having come all the way across a vast ocean, she considered the trip to La Salpêtrière a simple matter. She wrote this in spite of the fact that she had no idea where La Salpêtrière was or, indeed, what it was. She would find out somehow.

"La Salpêtrière!" exclaimed Félicie when she heard the news. She crossed herself. "I'll go nowhere near it. The horrible things that went on there! Rape and murder and madwomen chained down in the caves! It's a cursed place, Miss Woodridge."

"Oh, come, come," said Monsieur Goubert, who was passing by the concierge's loge and overheard the conversation. "That happened a hundred years ago, during the first revolution. Nowadays, it is a respectable hospital."

"With all due respect," Félicie replied tartly, "it's still a madhouse. And to think of Julie, our little Julie, in there!"

"Julie will be perfectly safe. The hospital has an excellent reputation for treating illnesses of the mind. Doctors from all over the world study with Professor Charcot. You could not ask for a better man."

"Ah? And how do you know all this?"

"Because, instead of wasting time in idle gossip like women do, I read newspapers. I consider it every man's duty to seek knowledge and self-improvement. Professor Charcot is a highly esteemed scientist, Madame Félicie, and I ask you, for Julie's sake, to take my word for it."

Despite the music teacher's assurances, the concierge's calloused hands nervously wrung her apron.

"It seems to be the only way to help your niece," Nelly said, fighting her own creeping doubts.

"What is this mesmerism anyway? What are they going to do to our Julie?"

"I've been told it's a sleep therapy," Nelly said.

"The correct term is hypnosis," added Monsieur Goubert.

"I don't like it one bit," Félicie sighed. "This is too much for me to decide. My head is splitting."

In the end, she added her clumsy signature to the consent form on the condition that Julie would wear a chemise touched at the Saint-Geneviève's altar in the church of Panthéon.

"And you'd better wear one as well, Miss Woodridge," she added.

Armed only with the saint's protection, Nelly and Julie faced a monumental task. The cab had been fifteen minutes late, the driver complaining about a traffic jam at the intersection of boulevard Saint-Germain caused by a burst water pipe. A bad sign, Nelly mused. She glanced at Julie at her side. At first, the girl was convinced that she was going to the hospital for a surgery.

"They'll bore a hole in my head. What if I die?" she had asked. No matter how Nelly insisted, she could not grasp the idea of hypnotherapy. "How else would they chase the beast out?" she asked.

Nelly tried another approach. "Professor Charcot is a powerful magician," she said. "He will charm the beast out of your head like this—" she clicked her fingers.

This worked better. In any case, the fact that despite her fear Julie was willing to submit herself to the therapy was a small victory.

After reaching the busy Gare d'Austerlitz, the cab turned away from the river and left them in front of a massive complex of stone buildings topped with a majestic dome.

"Come!" Nelly took Julie by the elbow and resolutely stepped forward. Huddling under an umbrella, they passed through the archway and approached the main building through the formal garden of the entrance court. Despite the rain, it was teaming with life, but the silent comings and goings between the crushing weight of stone walls added to Nelly's anxiety. She could easily identify with the fear and despair of the thousands of young women, orphans and criminals, who used to be held in this former gunpowder storehouse as breeding stock for the colonies. The complex now housed six thousand patients. So Monsieur Goubert had said.

They paused in the entrance hall, taking their bearings in the hustle and bustle. Nelly hailed a nurse in a black bonnet, white arm cuffs, and a voluminous starched apron.

"Professor Charcot? You must go to the Neurological Clinic," the woman said.

"You may come with me," offered a brunette, who was passing by, a stack of files under her arm. "It's on my way."

They followed her, Julie clinging to Nelly and dragging her feet, until they reached a corridor with sturdy carved benches, occupied by various examples of human misery. Nelly, too, slowed down as they passed the collection of faces distorted by lasting spasms and bodies animated by violent tics.

Their escort paused to look over her shoulder. "Hurry up!" she said. "The lecture begins soon and you've not been processed yet."

"We are not here for a lecture," Nelly said. "We've come to see Professor Charcot."

"Of course you have. Nevertheless, you must go to the triage room and talk to one of the physicians. Be quick about it! They are wrapping up for this morning. Do you have your consent form ready?"

While Nelly fumbled with the strings of her reticule, the young woman glanced at the clock above the door. "I have to leave you here. I hope you'll not miss the lecture. The professor is very strict with his schedule."

What lecture? With Julie's fingers digging into her arm, Nelly shifted uncomfortably. "This must be a mistake," she said. "We are here to see the professor privately."

"Impossible. This is a university hospital and today's consultations are part of the lecture. Whatever the case may be, it is interesting enough to be included in the program."

"But . . . I was . . . we were . . . I hoped for something less public," Nelly stammered as the clock behind her back stroke the hour and Julie's hand began sliding along her sleeve.

The brunette dropped her files and caught the fainting girl.

"What do we have here, Dr. Putnam?" someone called.

Nelly turned. An imposing man in a double-breasted black coat and a tall hat bore steadily down the corridor, followed by a dozen acolytes.

"A case of fear, Professor," the young woman said while handing the limp Julie to a pair of nurses that rushed to her help. They began to carry her toward the infirmary.

"A unit of chloral, to calm the patient's nerves," the Professor said to the nurses, while his followers hovered around and the young woman bent down to pick up her scattered files. "Well, gentlemen, let us proceed to the lecture room!"

As the gathering moved apart, the medical eagles ranging behind their leader, Nelly was split with indecision. Julie would need her, but should she miss the opportunity to speak to the professor? Perhaps a private visit could be arranged after all.

"Professor! Please, Professor!"

All heads turned to her and several eyebrows knitted in disapproval. Charcot stopped, his sharp eyes boring into hers.

"Mademoiselle . . . ?"

"My name is Miss Woodridge," she said, her voice ringing too loud in the sudden silence. "I thought . . . If I may . . ."

"Woodridge," Charcot repeated. "Woodridge. Oh, you are the American lady whose maid has to be examined today." He turned to his entourage. "An extraordinary case of amnesia coupled with somnambulism. Experience has proved that somnambulists are excellent subjects and can reach the profound stage of hypnosis within a relatively short time. I intend to demonstrate the method today." He inclined his head to Nelly. "Charmed," he said. "Please give my regards to Monsieur d'Auzon. Tell him I'm grateful to him for bringing this case to my attention and that I'm hoping to see his Chinese medical texts in print very soon."

Monsieur d'Auzon? That must be Octave's friend Henri.

"Yes, of course," she said. "But Professor, I was hoping—"

Charcot silenced her by lifting his hand. "I regret, mademoiselle, but women are not allowed in the lecture room. We've made one exception for American ladies, but two could be mistaken for a rule."

A polite laughter followed his quip, which Nelly failed to understand. They were staring at the brunette, who was stacking her files.

"Dr. Putnam," Charcot said, "allow me to introduce Miss Woodridge, a fellow American, and probably another aspirant at medical science. Do me a favor and keep her company while she's waiting."

The young woman—was she really a doctor?—briefly nodded to Nelly and faced the amused men. "With all due respect, Professor, I'm in a hurry. I have to write twenty-seven patient reports."

Charcot frowned. "That is incorrect. You only have to write three. The rest are self-imposed. I'm concerned about your zeal, young lady. Take a break and socialize!"

He turned his back to her and resumed his progress to the lecture room.

"Well, I suppose that's that," Dr. Putnam sighed and led Nelly toward the infirmary. "Nobody says no to Professor Charcot. I'm sorry for being such poor company. You don't have to stare so hard, Miss Woodridge. It's true, I'm a female doctor. There are a few of us in the United States and none but myself in France. You seem uneasy with me. I'm Mary. What's your given name?"

"I'm sorry," Nelly said, utterly captivated. "My name is Cornelia, but I prefer Nelly. How does a woman become a doctor?"

The question pleased Mary. She smiled. "People usually ask why, not how. First, you need understanding parents. Family support is very important, for it is a source of strength in the battle with prejudice." She passed the stack of files from one hand to another and hooked her arm under Nelly's. "Tell me about the girl."

"She had a horrifying experience during the Commune uprising."

"Alas, there had been numerous tragedies."

"Do you think she can be helped?"

"I have assisted at a similar lecture. The case was somewhat different, but the hypnosis produced a satisfactory effect. I think there is a chance."

"How is it done?"

"No one really knows how it works. What is known is that some patients can be brought into a state of awareness during which memory is restored. What had been hidden in the deep recesses of the mind suddenly becomes accessible."

"She'll be cured then, will she not?" Nelly asked eagerly. "No more sleepwalking, no more fears. Isn't that right?"

Mary shook her head. "I'm afraid it's not that simple. First, she will have to come to terms with the horrors she has tried to suppress. That will take some time. A few months, perhaps a year. She may even become more distraught than usual."

"She'll have nightmares."

"Why, yes!" Mary's eyebrows lifted in surprise. "That's correct. The bad experience must be washed out of the system."

They reached the door of the infirmary. "You should wait here," Mary said. "Don't worry. The nurses know how to deal with frightened patients. Now that the professor has expressed interest in the case, things will go smoothly."

Nelly shook the offered hand. "It's been a privilege to meet you. I didn't know that women could study medicine. You still did not tell me how . . ."

Mary chuckled. "Oh, you really want to hear the whole story? I like inquisitive minds. Very well. A woman who wants to become a doctor studies exactly the same matters as men do – when she is allowed to study. That's the real bone of contention, especially here in France. The Americans merely believe that it is indelicate for a woman to study medicine. The French, on the other hand, consider it downright evil. Yet their medical training is the best.

"Despite the fact that I was already a fully trained physician, I spent two years knocking on doors, all the way up to the Ministry of Education. The important thing is not to lose hope, for if you don't, you are bound to find a crack in the wall. I found mine when the Medical School established a program for foreign physicians. Since they did not specify the sex of the students, they had no legal ground for refusing me. The door has since been closed to future female applicants. I consider myself to be born under a lucky star. Well, I really must go now. I still have to write those twenty-seven reports."

"Yes, I understand. It's just that you are such an interesting person . . ." Nelly gathered her breath, fully aware of her audacity. "I thought that, perhaps, we could meet again when you have more time."

Mary smiled and shook her head. "Regretfully, my time here is very limited."

"Of course!" Nelly said quickly. "Please, forgive me."

"I'm not uppity if that's what you think," Mary gently squeezed Nelly's arm. "I've been in France for six years. It's time to go home and marry my fiancé. See, I told you I was born under a lucky star." She giggled prettily, instantly dropping ten years of age. "Sincerely, it was nice to meet a fellow American. And remember, whatever your goals are, never give up hope!"

Chapter 17

Since they had spent the morning and a good part of the afternoon at the hospital, Nelly went shopping after she had deposited Julie at home. On her return, she found Octave's hat and his gloves in the hall. His umbrella stood in the holder by the entrance door. She dropped her own next to it and carried her purchases to the kitchen. On her way back, she stopped by Julie's room and gently opened the door. The curtains were drawn against the dim light of the rainy afternoon, barely illuminating the dark form curled up on the bed.

"Julie," she whispered, "you should change into your nightgown and get into bed."

"I'm not sick. Please, you promised—"

"I cannot help being worried. I brought Roquefort cheese, the kind you like. And beautiful juicy apples. They are not wrinkled at all. One wonders how they keep them in that state all winter—"

"Please, you promised!"

"Yes, of course." Nelly carefully closed the door.

Octave was asleep on the sitting room sofa, his face covered with a newspaper. She ignored him, merely passing into the bedroom to change. The slight draft caused by the sweep of her skirts lifted one corner of the newspaper. The gentle rustle woke him.

"Sorry," he said, rubbing the bridge of his nose. "I've had an exhausting day."

"So have I," she answered with a hand on the door handle.

"I sent you flowers at noon. Have they not been delivered?"

"They are in Julie's room. She needs them more than I do."

"Kitten . . ." he said tentatively.

She shook her head. "Let me change into dry clothes and we will talk seriously about a serious matter."

"Julie? How was it? Does she remember the facts?"

"She does," Nelly answered from the bedroom. "Although she feels as if all of it had happened to someone else. She's in her room trying to deal with it."

"Should I go and see her?"

"No, please don't! She doesn't want to see anyone, not even her aunt. The girl needs some time to sort out what happened to her, both then and today."

"How do you know her memory's back?"

"She told me that she would go and kiss Monsieur Goubert's hand for having saved her life."

"Ah. That's good."

Nelly distractedly patted her hair in front of the mirror. In the sitting room, Octave waited sagely. She found him sitting with his back hunched, legs apart, hands hanging limply between his knees.

"I behaved like a beast," he said.

She closed the bedroom door behind her and leaned against it, her arms wedged between the wood and the hollow of her back.

"I'm sorry," he answered her reproachful silence.

"You slapped me."

"You slapped me first, but I suppose I should have taken it like a man."

"You blackmailed me."

"Did I? Yes, so I did. I am a knave. That picture meant a lot to me. The clouds were coming and you kept stalling. I was angry. You don't know what light means in photography. It's everything."

She did not answer.

"The picture is superb," he said.

"I'm glad for you."

"You look like an angel on the verge of flying. It's almost eerie."

"Good."

"There's also bad news. The Salon's committee will not allow me to switch the entries. I've been busy trying to pull strings in all the right places but it's too late. The catalogs have been printed."

"I'm sorry for you."

"The good news is that I can still enter the Belgian Salon in June. It's not as grand as this one but still of a good size and it has an international exposure. How about you and I spending a few days in Brussels? I'm sure you would like that. Wouldn't you?"

He grinned like a naughty boy and combed back his hair. He knows how to melt my heart, she thought. Still, she resisted.

"Come, can't you spare a smile?" he coaxed.

"In the past two days, I've had time to think. Especially today."

She saw tension hardening his smile. He leaned back, searching the support of the sofa, and crossed his legs. "You are not going back to America, are you?"

The idea had been in her mind. America. Home. The sweet sound of English. Where would she go? Definitely not back to Butte. Hartford, Connecticut? Who would know her there after such a long absence? Her former schoolmates would be married and scattered about. The Misses Weinhardt? They would probably welcome her like two cackling hens, offer her a cup of tea faultlessly served in fine china and then say that she must leave as they did when her father died. Had she ever had a home? Not since her grandmother died and Father whisked her away to the boarding school.

"When I'm ready," she said. "Besides, there's Julie. She's just beginning to heal. I was told that it will take some time before she's back to normal."

"But . . . ? I suppose there is a 'but'."

"Yes, there is. I've decided to look for work. When I have enough money, I'll pay you what I owe you."

"I see."

"No, I don't think you do. In fact, I think that you are blind to other people's needs. All you care about is your work, your art and your reputation. I must spend your money because you don't want people to say that you are a miser. You force me to undress in front of strange men because it suits you. That slap on the face was the least of my injuries. You've been hurting both my feelings and my modesty."

"I've apologized, have I not? Had you looked into the flower basket, you'd have found a jeweler's box. Then you'd have realized the extent of my remorse."

"A golden plaster on my wounds? How convenient. Is money your answer to everything?"

"It keeps you warm and cozy, doesn't it?" Octave got up, crossed over to the cabinet, and poured himself a drink. "Care to join me?"

"No, thank you. Not on an empty stomach."

"Let me take you out to dinner."

"I cannot leave Julie alone today of all days. If you are hungry as well, there's liver pâté, blue cheese and fresh bread."

"That sounds good. To tell you the truth, I'm in no mood for a restaurant. I've seen too many people in the past two days."

"Yes, you do look tired."

In the kitchen, she sliced the pâté while Octave busied himself with a corkscrew. He popped the cork and sniffed it. "Hm, this will have to do. Are we eating here?"

"If you don't mind."

"Not at all. You must be tired as well."

"It's been an emotional day."

Nelly transferred the slices onto a serving plate and stretched her arms to reach a stack of coarse dishes on the upper shelf. It was a golden opportunity for Octave. His arms wrapped themselves around her waist as if they had always belonged there. "My sweet kitten," he whispered into her ear.

His breath disturbed the tendrils of hair at the nape of her neck, sending delicious shivers down her spine. "You've missed me as much as I've missed you," he said, his lips moving against her skin, melting down her resistance. "Admit it!"

She had missed the cradle of his arms and she hated herself for it. "Did you not say that you were tired?" she asked, wiggling out of his embrace.

"Never too tired for *that*."

"Let's eat."

He contented himself with the weakness in her voice and released her. To speed things up, he helped with setting the table.

"I'm so hungry, I could eat a horse," he said as he broke two pieces of bread, one for her, one for himself.

"I'm afraid you must content yourself with this," she put the serving plate on the table.

"From the Duchêne Frères?" he asked, before tasting the pâté.

"No, from the charcuterie around the corner."

"The Duchêne make the best liver pâté."

"It's raining. Duchêne's is on the boulevard Saint-Michel. Must you French always discuss every morsel you eat?"

"What's wrong with that? Food is important. Perfection is important as well. Would we have a fine civilization if no one strived for the best?"

"You are right as always."

"What's this nonsense about working?"

It was a poor choice of words. Instantly, Nelly bristled. "It's not nonsense! My decision stands and you will not talk me out of it."

"Of course I will. Leave work to the needy. You are being looked after and educated, just as I've promised. You are luckier than most."

"Then why do I feel that each day I sink lower and lower?"

"Because you are weighed down by silly notions of respectability."

"That's true," she admitted. "One doesn't throw out good and just values. I was brought up to be a wife and a mother. If I cannot be that, then I must make myself useful in other ways. Living on handouts from a man who is not my husband isn't good enough for me."

He bit into the bread with a thick layer of pâté spread on it. The crust gave way between his teeth, shedding crumbs down onto the plate.

"You are wrong," he said when he conquered the mouthful and washed it down with wine. "Married or not, women always take money from men. The fair sex was put on earth to pleasure men and to procreate. It's men's duty to provide for them. That's the way the world works."

"There are new ways. Better ways."

"Then by all means I want to hear of them."

"Today, I met a lady doctor."

"Are you talking about that Putnam woman?"

"You know her?"

"I know about her. It was a sad day for the profession when that virago was admitted to the Medical School. I cannot imagine anything more vulgar and demeaning for a woman."

"Vulgar? Demeaning? That's not what I saw. I saw a lady."

"A lady!" Octave rolled his eyes. "No true lady would ever consider such a calling. There is nothing more indelicate than the study of medicine. Oh, it does sound noble enough, I grant you that. Medicine comforts and heals. But is it a noble occupation? Not if you have to poke your finger up some poor devil's rear end. Ugh," he grimaced with disgust. "Not a suitable topic for the dinner table or anywhere else for that matter."

Nelly quietly pondered Octave's speech. "But isn't it indelicate for a woman to be treated by a man? If I had a private complaint I'd rather be examined by someone of my own sex."

He sighed. "This question has been debated *ad nauseam* in medical circles. The inevitable conclusion is that women are not physically nor psychologically equipped to sustain the pressure and demands that weigh upon the physician's shoulders. Their biological function makes them mentally unstable."

"There was nothing unstable about Miss Putnam," she objected weakly, overwhelmed by Octave's learned argument.

"She's most likely a product of rich, overly indulgent parents. A spoiled brat, if not an unnatural woman. And I emphasize the word unnatural because it is against nature when a woman usurps man's place."

He has an answer for everything, she thought, annoyed. Had she not met Mary Putnam in person, she would have believed him.

115

"And you," she asked sweetly, "did you find the pressures and demands of medicine too weighty for your shoulders?"

The arrow, aimed at his masculine pride, missed completely. Octave merely paused between two bites and shrugged.

"I'm, at best, a bad doctor," he admitted, taking not the slightest offense. "I did not choose medicine. It was thrust upon me, by way of filial duty. My grandfather was a military surgeon in the Great Army. Butcher would be a better word for his trade. He cut off limbs and patched bleeding wounds all over Europe. He even survived the retreat from Russia. In short, a hero. When the First Empire crumbled, he settled in his hometown and sent his first-born to Paris to study medicine. I, as the next in line, had my career chosen for me as soon as I was born. Tradition," he sighed, "what a trap!"

He reached for Nelly's hand. "Let's not quarrel, kitten," he pleaded. "I came here in the spirit of reconciliation. It's true that I behaved badly. I forced you into something you did not want to do. I trampled on your sensitivity. In your eyes, I was ill-mannered, even brutal—"

"Just in my eyes?" She tried to liberate her hand but he held it fast.

"Dearest kitten, I'm sorry you had to see me like that. Please, take into consideration that I was in a state of creative fever. You see, just as a birthing woman does not care about modesty, an artist in the act of creation may forget social graces. All that does not contribute to the result becomes unimportant. It has to be broken and discarded. Do you understand?"

"I'm trying to. All the same, how do you manage to stay in business if you behave so badly with your sitters?"

He laughed and finally released her hand. "My sitters? The paying ones? That's nothing but routine. There is only one rule to follow: make them look grander than they are. Transform a shopkeeper into a rich bourgeois, a bourgeoise into a duchess, a mediocre writer into a poet-laureate. In short, fulfill their dreams. That, dear kitten, is merely good photography. It's no more than a skill.

"Art begins with an idea. A hazy idea . . ." he reached toward the ceiling and seized a fistful of air, ". . . that threatens to disappear if you don't hold it tight." He squeezed his fist firmly. "But again, having an idea is not art. Art is the act of transition from the ethereal to the concrete form. A painting, a sculpture, a musical score. It's a struggle that does not always succeed, but when it does, one feels release and an immense satisfaction." He paused and added, "I suppose it's difficult for you to understand."

Nelly shook her head. "Back in Butte," she said, "each spring the prairie was covered with wild flowers. They were modest little things but they were fresh and colorful. Springs are short in Montana. As soon as the hot weather comes, the prairie is baked brown by the sun. I still had a box of paints from my school days and I decided to preserve the fragile beauty in painting to have something pretty to look at during the long winter months. But no matter how hard I tried, my flowers looked lifeless. I can only guess at the joy that I'd have felt had I succeeded, but I can understand the frustration of failure."

As she spoke, she realized that, for the first time, Octave paid full attention to her mind.

He smiled, repossessed her hand, and kissed it. "If you understand the need to create, then you understand more than most. You are an intelligent woman."

She blushed, genuinely pleased. "Thank you. That feels so much better than to hear how beautiful I am."

"Oh, but you are that as well," he said with a twinkle in his eye. "Let me show you how much!"

Chapter 18

"You want to be a shop girl?" Octave exclaimed, when Nelly had re-vealed her plans for the future. "Why not a barmaid or even a scullery maid? You can claim experience in that area!"

Checked by her cold stare, he reverted to negotiation. "Really, kitten, be reasonable. Twelve hours a day behind a counter! You'll be exhausted. What about your studies? Have you thought of that?"

She had, indeed. She could very well dispense with Mademoiselle de la Pelletière and her permanent disdain. She knew her irregular verbs, handled cutlery correctly and sat with her back stiff as a rod. She had even mastered the art of addressing letters and would not disgrace herself in the unlikely event that she should write to a bishop.

The argument ended in a stalemate. That night, Octave was leaving with a frown upon his brow. "I'll see what I can do about the situation," he said when he kissed her at the door. "I wish you'd reconsider. As far as I'm concerned, I believe this is nothing but a passing fancy."

Nelly swore to prove him wrong, and set out the next morning to do so. As the number of tourists visiting the post-war city was nowhere near the Empire boom, none of the fine shops along the boulevards expressed interest in hiring any additional English-speaking help. On her way home, she spotted a sign for a women's employment agency. She climbed to the third floor and sat in the waiting room along with five other postulants. In the embarrassed silence, which she could not explain by the need to work for a living, she was the target of hostile looks, even though she was dressed plainly as suited an applicant. The reason for the resentment became clear when the owner, a hunchback with unctuous manners, invited her to his office despite the fact that she had been the last to arrive.

"Do you think I can hope for a post with decent pay?" she asked.

"Certainly," he replied. "My agency supplies housekeepers and there's a constant demand for personable young women like you. In fact, you can choose from several positions. For instance, a gentleman from the Ministry of Agriculture with a suite of rooms near the Champ de Mars. The basic salary is forty francs a month with room and board. Of course, there should be extra rewards, depending on your employer's satisfaction. Such things vary from place to place."

"Actually," Nelly said, "I'm not interested in a room and board situation. I already have a place to live."

"No problem." The affable man flipped a couple of pages in his register. "Here we are. A widowed pharmacist, Avenue de l'Opéra. Sixty francs a month. However, after seeing you, he might agree to seventy or even eighty."

"What exactly would my duties be?" she asked with growing suspicion.

He smiled. "The usual. Seeing to the gentleman's comfort, his meals, his laundry, and whatever else he may require, including tucking him into bed."

"Tucking him into bed," she repeated frostily and rose. "Pardon me for wasting your valuable time, monsieur. This would not have happened had your agency sign announced the true nature of your business."

"That would be rather awkward, don't you agree?" He smiled again. "Most of the applicants already know. Those who don't, soon overcome their indignation. As to the true nature of my business, far from being disdained, my agency fulfills a pressing social need, mademoiselle. Few men earn enough to marry and support a family. Others prefer to stay single for various reasons. Now that you know this, you may return any time. I expect it to be soon. In your hunt for work, you'll be discouraged by long hours and miserable wages. What's more, some employers expect personal favors as a matter of course. Here, at least, the terms are clear from the beginning."

* * *

"You? Looking for work? But why?" Géraldine asked.

"To earn money, of course."

"Do you need to? It's so . . ." Géraldine searched for a word.

"Indelicate? Unladylike?" Nelly offered.

"Why, yes. I mean I thought—"

"—that I was rich? Well, I'm not."

"Oh!" Géraldine sucked in her breath. "Why did you not say so? I had no idea when I accepted your invitation to the restaurant."

Nelly already regretted her frankness. "I'm not destitute either. The fact is that I don't have to work. But I want to because I feel useless, especially after meeting a woman like Doctor Putnam."

"Doctor Putnam?"

Nelly told her friend about her experience at La Salpêtrière.

"No!" breathed Géraldine, her eyes wide open. "Are you sure? You must have misunderstood."

"It's true. Besides, Cousin Octave has heard about her."

"Really? What does he say?"

"He disapproves, of course."

"Of course." In the ensuing silence, Géraldine digested the facts. "Fancy that," she said at last. "A woman doctor. Who would have thought it possible? To be out there, with all those learned men and to be one with them! Of course, the poor girl has ruined all her chances to catch a husband. Men don't like bluestockings. A clever woman keeps her cleverness under a lock. It's a wife's duty to make her husband shine, not herself. That's what Mama says and I believe it to be true."

"Then you'll be surprised to hear that Dr. Putnam is returning to America to be married."

Géraldine sighed. "My dear, I don't know what to think anymore. It is all so confusing. Ah! Here's Julie with the coffee tray."

"Good afternoon, ma'am," Julie said, setting the tray on the table.

"She smiles!" Géraldine exclaimed. "Yes, of course, the visit to the hospital. How utterly amazing! Well, good afternoon, Julie. I'm glad for you."

"That's truly an astonishing improvement," she commented when Julie was gone. "I swear I thought the girl was retarded. That Professor Charcot is a miracle man. I wonder what else can be cured by hypnosis. Do you think it could turn a dull husband into a sparkling conversationalist? I'm joking, of course." She reached for the dessert plate Nelly was offering her. "So tell me about the work. Did you find any?"

"Not yet. I'll try again tomorrow."

"Let me come with you! I've nothing else to do. It could be fun."

Nelly shuddered at the thought of exposing Géraldine to the kind of experience she had at the agency. She was fishing for a believable excuse when the clock came to her rescue, striking four times. "Four o'clock!" she exclaimed. "Come, let's tease the schoolboys!"

She did not have to ask twice. Géraldine eagerly joined her at the window. They pretended to admire the view but, from the corner of the eye, they observed an approaching crocodile of students, headed by one attendant, and tailed by another. Stuffed into powder-blue uniforms with silver buttons, the teenage boys marched briskly along the quay, clearing their lungs of schoolroom dust. Their alert eyes were sweeping the surroundings for signs of female life; a sight they would soon be denied for another twenty-four hours. The two young women, so graciously displayed in the window, became an instant target for thirty eager gazes. Géraldine was delighted.

"This feels as good as a warm bath," she commented, her fingers playing with a lock of hair behind her ear. "One can pretend to be a queen reviewing a parade of loyal subjects. Then, at night, I can toy with the idea that my image comforts a lonely young heart in the darkness of an austere dormitory. In a way, we are the benefactors of these unfortunate boys."

"We are both very naughty and we know it."

"Oh, you!" Géraldine nudged Nelly with her elbow. They both giggled.

"Oh my! Dear God, who's that?"

"Where?"

"Over there, walking along the quay. Is that a man or a woman?"

"Oh, that," Nelly said. "It's the bearded gypsy woman. I saw her once before. She sells holy pictures and reads tarot."

"I once saw a bearded woman in a sideshow," said Géraldine. "Tarot, you said? Why don't we invite her in to give her a try? Just to have a closer look."

"Over my dead body. Why, she might have fleas! Remember the donkeys."

"You are such a spoil-sport, Nelly."

"There! Isn't that Bébert with a parcel under his arm? I wonder what he's up to."

Nelly was to know soon enough, for Bébert headed directly for their house and, minutes later, he rang at the door. "Monsieur Gaillard is sending this with all his respects," he said when she let him in.

Nelly put the parcel on the sitting room table and unwrapped the coarse brown paper. Inside, she found a thick stack of sheets covered with handwriting.

"This looks like a manuscript," said Géraldine. "Why would he send you such a thing?"

"Wait, there's a note attached to it." Nelly unfolded a sheet of paper and took a couple of steps away from the table to avoid her friend's prying eyes.

My adorable and utterly stubborn kitten, the note said. *Since you claim that you must work, I asked Henri to supply you with the task of copying his manuscript. At one franc a page, this should provide you with a reasonable fee while keeping you out of mischief. I kept hoping to see you tonight, but work has accumulated while I was busy with the Salon business. Since I'm to leave for Yvetot tomorrow, I will not be able to see you until next week. You shall be constantly in my thoughts during our short separation.*

A thousand passionate kisses, from your delectable lips down to the valley of bliss,
    Octave

Nelly could not help but to kiss the note. "Work, Géraldine, I've got work!"

* * *

Her jubilation did not last. The manuscript, written in an almost illegible hand, was a maze of erasures and additions with a number of separate notes glued to the margins. Nelly's spirit sank as she stared at the i-dots and t-crossings racing across the lines while leaving behind their respective letters, the deconstructed f's and g's, the economy of loops and absence of arches. Where would she find help in deciphering this? Octave would be gone and, as usual during the weekends, Géraldine would be expected to dance attendance on her husband. After a short deliberation, she dispatched Julie with an invitation to dinner.

"In my despair I've thought of you, Monsieur Goubert," she said over coffee. "You seem to be interested in all sorts of matters scientific. Perhaps you'd be able to read this illegible hand. One look at it, and I want to weep with frustration."

The music teacher leafed through the manuscript. "The Culture and Science of China by Henri d'Auzon," he read. "Volume I: Religion and Philosophy". How interesting, Miss Woodridge!"

"Yes, I've read thus far. But what about the body of the text?"

"I agree that it's a very hurried hand and you'll need some practice before you get used to it."

"Do you think it's possible?"

"But of course! Dear me, I've seen worse. At least, he keeps his lines straight and reasonably far apart. Also, the foreign words are written with care."

"And the pieces of scrap paper attached to some of the pages? Does it mean that the additional text should be included and, if so, where? It's such a jumble."

"I'm sure there is a logical order to it. We'll figure it out together."

"Monsieur Goubert, how can I thank you? You don't know what this means to me!"

* * *

"Copying a manuscript? You?" asked Mademoiselle incredulously. "Why would you do such a thing?"

"I'll be paid for it."

"I had no idea that your sort would entertain such an ambition. How careless of the author to entrust such an important work to you! Very well, what do you want from me?"

"It's very important that the spelling should be absolutely correct. I've copied the first few pages and I thought that you'd be kind enough to check them for errors. I'm willing to rewrite a whole page if there's but one mistake."

Mademoiselle puckered her lips. "Your zeal is surprising. I wonder how long it will last. Besides, correcting manuscripts does not enter into my agreement with Monsieur Gaillard. My task is to turn you into a lady. An impossible task, I must add."

Something snapped in Nelly. This sort of abuse had gone on for too long. "Correct me if I'm wrong, mademoiselle," she said as haughtily as her adversary, "but I have been your attentive student despite your lack of encouragement. Since you consider me a failure, we'll have to cease seeing each other. I'm sure you will solve the matter of your debt by other means."

* * *

By Monday morning, Nelly produced twelve perfect pages. The work had so far yielded three francs a day and there would be more as she gathered speed in deciphering the text. She cast a glance at the discarded sheets of the first draft. Cornered, Mademoiselle had applied herself to the corrections, but the red ink marks looked like vengeful stabs. There would never be a trace of friendly feelings in that quarter. She made a mental note to purchase a larger dictionary.

Around noon, Bébert rang the bell. He was laden with a wicker basket and a slightly wilted bouquet of late purple lilacs.

"From the master," he said to Julie who answered the door. "Home preserves from Yvetot."

"A wild game terrine, miss," Julie said to Nelly, who joined her in the kitchen. "A preserved goose, wild strawberry jam and a sponge cake. And there's a bottle of something."

"That's calvados, the apple brandy from Normandy. We should put it into the sitting room cabinet."

"Bébert said I'm to say to you that the lilacs are from the master's garden in Yvetot. How nice they smell!"

"They are lovely," Nelly buried her nose in the bouquet and smiled happily. All was well again.

Chapter 19

Blessé!—Qui que tu sois, ô jeune homme inconnu.
Toi qui me voyant seule et loin de ce qui m'aime...

The crystalline voice of Sarah Bernhardt carried across the darkened Odéon theatre, falling and rising with a nearly musical rhythm. The singsong technique of verse delivery, which Octave said was called the *mélopée*, lulled Nelly into a stupor. However, the fact that Octave was back, and as amorous as ever, would reconcile her with any kind of boredom.

"How lovely you are!" he said right in the door as he swept her into his arms and kissed her. That night, she was called the most regal names yet. Life was wonderful.

Puisque ton cœur subit une inflexible loi,
Sois aimé par ta mère et sois béni par moi!

She gently squeezed his hand and settled her head against his shoulder. He smelled of soap and Eau de Cologne and the red carnation in his buttonhole added its own spicy scent. How elegant, how handsome and manly he was! If only she did not have to share his attention with that skinny actress in a strawberry-blond wig. He was so taken with her that he did not even return Nelly's squeeze!

She yawned. Versified dramas were not her cup of tea. For a start, nobody in real life talked in verses. The Spanish court costumes were nice to look at, but the actors behaved without decorum, especially Mademoiselle Bernhardt. A real queen would dispense with such exaggerated writhing and flailing of arms.

The actress was one of Octave's steady clients and her portraits sold at a tremendous profit, especially the one where she sat draped over an armchair in a seductive snake-like pose that Octave had invented: an arm nonchalantly hanging over the backrest, her knees facing in the opposite direction. Mademoiselle de la Pelletière would highly disapprove of such a sitting position. Was it not ironic that Octave hired a teacher to erase her relaxed manners while he made money re-inventing them for this woman? Life was full of contradictions.

According to Octave, Mademoiselle Bernhardt was not skinny but diaphanous. Everything about her was fascinating: her marvelous diction, her extraordinary thespian talent and her success in this play by Victor Hugo, the greatest of all poets.

"Rumor has it that she has yielded to his genius in more ways than one," he said to Nelly before the performance began. "What a man! I wish I were as frisky when I'm seventy."

"He is seventy?" Nelly asked, scandalized. "She can be no older than thirty! Why would she sleep with him?"

"A woman can express her admiration in the most intimate manner," he said. "Why, Maître Hugo is a living national treasure! Don't tell me you've not heard of him."

"I don't read poetry. I mouth Racine, because Mademoiselle says it's good for my pronunciation but I don't have any interest in it."

"Racine is old-fashioned. Hugo is revolutionary. Besides, he's also a world-famous writer. Surely, you must have read Les Misérables in translation? No? How about The Hunchback of Notre Dame? Oh well, we'll have to do something about that."

How hard it is to be cultured, she thought as she watched the play. The tedium ended when a tiny, shaggy dog, no larger than a broom-head, entered the stage. For about five minutes, the tawny ball of hair busily sniffed the floor, oblivious to the stir it was causing. Like the rest of the audience, Nelly had to cover her mouth to stifle her giggles. Sarah and the male lead, unaware of the dog's presence, exchanged worried looks but struggled on with the dialogue. Then, in one of her dramatic gestures, the actress turned abruptly and swept over the dog with her heavy skirt. It rolled over with a yap of surprise, sprang back on its feet, and engaged in a frenzied barking.

The audience roared with laughter. Scared by the noise, the animal escaped into the wings. Sarah, in tune with her public, laughed as well and sent a kiss after the dog. Her lighthearted gesture provoked another gale of laughter.

"Let's go, and see Sarah," Octave said as the curtain went down for the intermission. "By tomorrow, the mutt will be a celebrity. Her portraits with the dog will sell like hot cakes. Come, I'll introduce you!"

Nelly followed him to the stage door. They left behind the blaze of gas chandeliers, the gilt and luxurious plush of the auditorium for the dim and badly ventilated corridors behind the stage, with their peculiar odor of grease paint and stale sweat.

"Evening, Monsieur Gaillard," a fireman greeted Octave from his post by the stage.

"Good evening. It seems that a new actor has joined the company."

The fireman's lips contorted with suppressed glee. "They're still trying to catch him," he said. "The director is heading for a stroke."

"Hah, Gaillard! Have you been watching the show tonight? What a disaster!" A short apoplectic man bore down on them, brandishing the whining and writhing dog by the scruff of the neck. "They found the beast down in the maintenance room. I'm going to have a word with Sarah right away."

He pushed past them, followed by a number of thrill-seekers who swept Nelly and Octave along with them. The red-faced man stopped in front of a door and drummed at it with his knuckles.

"Are you decent?" he shouted.

"Is that you, Chilly?" answered the famous voice. "Have they found Hamlet?"

"Yes to both questions."

"Come in!"

The director entered to be greeted with a shriek that brought yet more eavesdroppers to the door.

"How dare you to treat him so?" they heard Sarah shouting. "Oh, my poor darling! Put him down at once, you cruel man!"

"You are going to be fined, Sarah," the director's voice thundered. "What happened this evening is intolerable."

"You are intolerable. Do behave yourself, monsieur! Is it the dog's fault if you don't pay me enough?"

"I beg your pardon? What's the dog to do with it?"

"If you paid me what I'm worth, I could hire a footman to look after Hamlet."

"I'm paying you seven hundred francs a month. That's more than you've ever earned. Stop living beyond your means."

"What a horrible fellow you are! Had it not been for *Maître* Hugo, I'd quit on the spot."

"Ah, would you? And where would you go, madam? The Ambigu? The Gaîeté? Or perhaps the Vaudeville? What a step down from the heights of the Comédie Française! They were right to throw you out. You are insufferable!"

126

Something crashed in Sarah's room and shattered into small pieces. "I resigned! Do you hear me? Resigned!"

The eavesdroppers in the corridor stepped back to make room for the retreating director, who was brushing rice powder from his sleeve.

"Insufferable!" he shouted over his shoulder.

Sarah appeared in the door. "You have seen nothing yet! You shall regret this, Chilly!"

She was dressed in a silver brocade gown with a Medici collar. A small crown of paste diamonds perched on her reddish puff of hair, which, Nelly noticed, was not a wig after all. The tousled Hamlet, securely wrapped in her arms, his bulging griffon's eyes full of venom, accompanied the director's escape with vindictive barking.

"Shh, my love," Sarah kissed him. "I shall avenge you, I promise." She noticed Nelly and Octave standing alone in the corridor. The other spectators had stealthily dispersed moments earlier. "Oh, Gaillard, my dear Gaillard! I want you as a witness should it ever come to breaking my contract with the Odéon. I know I can count on you. You are an outsider and you don't have to fear Chilly like the others. You must tell everybody how badly he treated me."

"But, my dearest Sarah," Octave cooed, "you have nothing to fear. You are too precious. Monsieur de Chilly will never let you go."

"That's not what I mean," Sarah looked right and left, then her bony hand gripped Octave's arm, pulling him down to her level. "They want me back at the Comédie Française!" she whispered.

"No!"

"It's true. Perrin has written to me. He's offered me a full membership with pension."

"Don't do that. That fossilized government company is not the right place for you. You've been happy at the Odéon. We'd be crushed to see you go—"

"Oh, you!" she yelled suddenly. "You should be congratulating me. Instead, you are thinking of yourself."

"I never—"

"Yes, you are. You are afraid that if I move back to the Right Bank, I'd drop you for another photographer. And perhaps I should. Before you, I had been quite happy with Disdéri's work. And then there is Nadar!"

Octave frowned. "My dearest Sarah, you've hurt me profoundly. I have only your happiness at heart. The director has put you into a belligerent mood. Let's be civil to each other." He reached for Nelly's arm. "Allow me to introduce Miss Nelly Woodridge, an American, and a great admirer of yours."

127

Taken aback by Octave's lie, Nelly shook Sarah's hand without a word. Accustomed to admiration, the actress took her surprise for a silent tribute. She composed a mechanical smile on her face.

"How nice," she said. Her gaze shifted above Nelly's brow and her eyes sparked with genuine interest. "What fascinating hair! Would you mind?" she extended her hand.

"I beg your pardon?"

"Mademoiselle Bernhardt wants a closer look at your hair," Octave said with a subtle but decisive head jerk.

Nelly obediently bent her head forward.

"Amazing, truly amazing," Sarah flattened a lock between her fingers. "Such a wealth of shades! Everything from the palest ochre to the earthiest Sienna. A true Botticelli. Don't you think so, Gaillard?"

"Now that you mention it, yes, indeed," Octave went along. As always, color was not his department.

"I am getting ideas . . . an inspiration . . ."

Sarah was interrupted by the stage attendant knocking on doors. "Five minutes to the curtain! Five minutes to the curtain!" he shouted.

An assistant poked her head out of Sarah's dressing room.

"I'm coming, Madame Rose!" Sarah called to her.

"Friends?" Octave asked.

"But of course, stupid!" Sarah said amicably. She stood on her toes and planted kisses on both his cheeks. "You are the best."

Hamlet, caught between them, protested with a yelp.

"I've plans for your adorable little dog."

"Have you? How wonderful! Come tomorrow before five and we shall talk about it. Goodbye, Miss . . ."

"Woodridge," Nelly said helpfully.

"What did she say about my hair?" she asked Octave when they were on their way back to the balcony.

"Sarah is a talented painter and sculptor."

"There seems to be no end to her accomplishments."

"She may want to paint you."

"Really?" she said flatly.

He shook his head. "I don't understand. The fact of having been noticed by the most fascinating woman in Paris seems to annoy you. Another one would swoon with honor."

Not if the Fascinating Woman happens to kiss my lover, Nelly thought.

* * *

"I've done it! It's finished." Géraldine said.

"Done what?" Nelly asked distractedly as she closed her book. The unexpected visit interrupted her in the middle of *Les Misérables*, leaving her anxious for Cosette's safety.

"I've finished my first story. You don't know it yet but I've decided to be a female writer."

"Have you?"

"And why not?" Géraldine said defiantly. "There are women writers. For instance Marquise de Sévigné or Madame George Sand."

"Why the sudden decision?"

Géraldine settled at Nelly's side on the sofa. "Last Friday, you gave me a lot to think about," she began. "First was the fact that you were seeking work. Then you mentioned the female doctor. Last, but not the least, the manuscript was delivered. When I came home, my mind was a jumble. I could not sleep at night. I kept thinking about my empty life. Did I tell you that Babeau was a widower before he married me?—He was! His first wife died childless. Perhaps it was not her fault because, so far, there is no sign of a baby. What else is there to do with my life? My husband would never allow me to seek work outside. But, many times, I have been told that I was a born storyteller. When our little Dédé—that's a pet name for my baby brother Didier—well, when Dédé broke his leg, I told him a different story every day. He only had to point his finger at an object and I made it talk. Dédé wasn't the only listener. Everybody enjoyed my stories. Perhaps I'm conceited but I think I have a gift."

She fished in her reticule and removed a modest number of folded sheets. Nelly reached for the offering but Géraldine caught her wrist.

"First, you must promise not to tell anybody. Least of all Julie! She could tell her aunt, who could tell our concierge, who could tell Cécile, and Cécile could tell Babeau."

"What's wrong with writing?"

"Nothing, I'm sure, but I have to break it gently to my husband. He considers all artists Bohemians. I decided to wait until after Mama's visit. She could tip the balance the wrong way. If he forbids me to write, all will be lost. Believe me, dearest Nelly, now that I have found my voice, I will not give it up, ever! I'd rather kill myself."

"You are exaggerating."

"Indeed not!" Abruptly, Géraldine got up and began to pace the room. "I hate my life as it is. I miss home. I thought that Paris would bring me excitement. Instead, it has thrown me into the prison of marriage. You," she turned to Nelly, "are the only light in the unrelieved darkness."

Although she should feel flattered, Nelly experienced a flashback to her cold attic. "I say you are exaggerating," she said, irritated. "Unrelieved darkness, indeed! I could tell you more about despair than you'd ever care to hear—" She bit her tongue. There were things her friend did not need to know, neither now or ever.

Fortunately, Géraldine, focused on her own grievances, scarcely noticed. "I'm not exaggerating. Back home we lived thriftily but we were never sad. I'm hungry for joy. I crave smiles. I'm starved for hugs."

"Don't you and your husband—?"

"Yes, but it always leads to something else. And when it's over, he just turns his back to me—" Géraldine covered her mouth and blushed. "Pardon me," she said. "I got carried away. . . . Anyhow," she was all business now, "here it is. It is the story Dédé liked the best.— No! Don't read it now, please! Read it when you are alone and then tell me what you think of it."

Later that day, Nelly asked Octave to read the story. He laughed during the reading. "That friend of yours has a sense of humor," he said after he had finished. "Her writing needs a bit of polishing, but the story is very good."

Nelly nodded, pleased with his opinion that matched hers. Géraldine would be glad to hear it. As things turned out, she never did.

Chapter 20

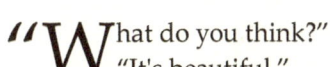

"What do you think?"

"It's beautiful."

Nelly sighed. The trouble with Julie was that she had no mind of her own. The girl was too young, too much in awe of her mistress, to express an opinion even if she had one. She cast a look at the pile of discarded clothing and sighed again. She needed the guidance of a woman with experience, someone who would understand the line between elegance and frivolity. She frowned at her reflection in the mirror.

"I'll wear this dusty-blue jacquard," she decided.

"Yes, Miss."

"Has the confectioner's boy been here?"

"Not yet."

"Why not? I said three o'clock at the latest."

"It's ten to three."

"Oh! So it is. Is everything ready in the kitchen?"

"I still have to make the butter shavings."

"Make sure that you change your apron, but not before you are finished with the butter.— The bell! It must be the boy. Go answer the door and then start grinding coffee."

Alone, Nelly turned in front of the mirror. The dusty-blue jacquard was the best choice. It was the simplest of Kitty de Chazelle's gowns, with hardly any frills on the underskirt. The bodice ended in a chaste scalloped opening at the neck. More scallops edged the overskirt, which puffed over a bustle and hung in soft, rounded folds where it touched the floor. Nelly turned, her eyes fixed on the train, enjoying the play of the fabric as it swept over the carpet. The scalloped hem added a lively touch to the movement, now disappearing

131

under a fold, now popping back in view. Why had she overlooked this gown? She should wear it more often.

The mantel clock in the sitting room struck once. A quarter past three! She sat at the dressing table and rummaged in the drawer. Her hand found an elegant leather box with the jeweler's name in a gold imprint on the lid. Inside, on white satin also stamped with gold, nestled a finely engraved ladies' watch, so silent that she had to hold it against her ear to hear the faint ticking. She ran the gold chain through her fingers with the same keen enjoyment of movement she had experienced with the scalloped edge of her skirt. With a brief pressure on the knob, the lid popped open revealing a mother-of-pearl dial. Inside the lid, engraved with a copperplate script were the words *A la vision en blanc*. To a Vision in White. What would this cryptic message mean when she was gone? Should the watch belong to her daughter, provided she had children, what thought would it bring forward? She hoped it would evoke a bridal gown rather than a vulgar morning wrap.

She clasped together the ends of the chain. *In fact, I'm wearing Octave's remorse around my neck,* she realized. Most of her jewels were connected with his misdeeds, like this watch after the fight at the studio. 'So that you shall never be late again.' How subtly he managed to shift the guilt onto her!

She was glad he was busy with the Salon, for she would loathe having him around this afternoon. He was cranky and liable to play some malicious joke on her guests. Instead of the coveted first prize, he had been awarded a paltry honorary mention for his *Greeting of Spring*. The photograph consisted of a carefully arranged procession of women and children dressed in flowing Greek robes and carrying flowering branches. They were walking a path along a body of still water, which reflected their silhouettes. It was a pleasant picture and was mentioned in the art section of several newspapers.

"The photograph is worth more than an honorable mention," Octave fumed. "It's politics, nothing but politics. I'm tired of being overlooked. But that will change, I promise you. As soon as the *Morning Breeze* hits the public eye, the name of Octave Gaillard will be firmly established as the leading light. In a way, it is a good thing that I could not exhibit it this year. Now I have time to plan my strategy. I have to rethink the Brussels Salon as well. Perhaps it was not such a good idea after all. Too soon, too far from the Parisian press."

In the meantime, he frequented all the official functions related to the Salon and she hardly saw him.

Nelly opened a second jeweler's box and held up the pearl earrings to dangle at her ears. Were they too dressy for an afternoon *collation*? On the other hand, the gown was so simple.

The earrings secured in place, she reached for the perfume bottle. She was about to dab a little behind each ear when her hand stopped in mid-air. No, no perfume after all. Too worldly. Next, she inspected her hands for ink stains. Traces of hard labor had disappeared a long time ago; she now had oval nails buffed to a shine.

She secured a lock of hair, stood up, and cast a last look at the mirror, which returned an image of a well-bred and poised young woman. No, she could not have done better. If there was a pebble of anxiety lodged in the pit of her stomach, she was the only one to know.

A crisp damask cloth covered the round walnut table in the sitting room. It was set with sparkling cutlery and china. A bouquet of tiger lilies in the center exhaled a pleasant perfume.

The clock told her that she had only ten minutes left and she had yet to check on the food. She rushed to the kitchen, where Julie crouched on the footstool, squeezing the coffee grinder between her knees and busily turning the handle. Nelly reached for her apron where it hung over the chair and tied it at her waist. She opened a baker's cardboard box to transfer its contents onto a serving tray lined with a paper lace. First a row of éclairs, followed by a line of miniature savarins, colorful fruit tarts in the middle, followed by the flans and, finally, the almond cakes. There was another plate dressed with slices of truffled galantine, purchased at the Duchêne Frères, surrounded by olives and gherkins on a bed of watercress. Brioches sat on a baking sheet, ready to be slipped into the oven for a brief warming.

The lavish spread, arranged on the sitting-room table, would not put a duchess to shame. There was also a bottle of sweet liquor in the cabinet but she'd wait to see how the visit progressed before offering alcohol.

Nelly straightened a fork and pushed aside one of the plates to make room for the coffee tray, the basket of brioches, and the butter, which were yet to come. *The butter!*

"Have you made the butter shavings?" she asked the maid.

"No, Miss."

"Oh Lord! And you've already put on your white apron!"

They raced back to the kitchen. Five minutes later, the bell peeled.

"They are here! Look at yourself, Julie!" Nelly exclaimed. "Your hands are greasy. Not on the apron, girl! Here—" she threw a kitchen towel at the maid.

They rushed back to the hall, Nelly carrying a small serving dish containing the butter shavings. She went on into the sitting room, while in the hall Julie was already greeting the guests. Nelly installed herself in the armchair and reached for her embroidery. A second later, she was up, hastily plucking at the apron ties. She managed to roll the garment into a ball and toss it into the bedroom through a crack in the door just as the guests entered.

At first, she thought that Géraldine brought the wrong mother as Madame Renaud could have easily given birth to her son-in-law. Like him, she was short and dark-haired. Unlike him, she was of a sunny disposition with alert eyes and a perpetual smile on her round face. The telltale needle holes in the smooth fabric, where trimmings had been ripped off to be replaced by others, indicated that her chocolate-brown dress had suffered many alterations to keep up with current fashion. The Alençon lace fichu adorning the bodice was doubtless an old family heirloom, passed from one generation to another. It was frail with age and unraveling at the edges despite the starch that was supposed to hold it together. Everything about the woman, from her worn hat to her carefully mended mittens, spoke of making do with whatever was available. Not surprising for a mother with five daughters to wed and two sons to educate. Nelly liked her at once.

Her surprise did not escape Madame Renaud. "Yes, Géraldine takes after her father," she said laughingly when they were seated on the sofa, her daughter clinging to her side. "He's a handsome man, isn't he, *mon chou*?"

"Yes, Mama. But for everything else I'm like you."

Her mother affectionately patted her hand. "That's not kind to your poor papa! He does miss you."

Géraldine's eyes misted over. "Oh, mama!"

"Come, come, no tears! What will Mademoiselle Woodridge think of such a display?"

"I think that your daughter is lucky," said Nelly, touched by their close relationship.

"Lucky?" Géraldine protested. "How can you say so? So far from my family!"

"So is Mademoiselle Woodridge, and she has no mother's breast to cry on. You have my deepest sympathy, mademoiselle. My daughter speaks about you in her letters and I could not wait to meet you. I'm pleased with what I see."

"Then call me Nelly, please."

"Gladly."

"The coffee will be here in a minute."

"How kind of you. But there is no need to rush. What a splendid view you enjoy!"

They walked to the window and Nelly opened it.

"Oh, Paris!" exclaimed Madame Renaud, leaning over the cast iron rail. "The first time I was here was on my honeymoon. Our families were shocked at the extravagant trip to Paris but believe me, girls, nothing is more precious than beautiful memories. They are jewels no one can take from you . . . I cannot believe how the city has changed! Where are the charming crooked streets I remember? I don't know whether I like the wide boulevards. The houses look the same for miles on end. It is all too regimented, too cold. And the traffic! The noise! Oh no, I'm not made for such a life. But you," she hooked her arms with the girls, "you are both young and adaptable. Nothing ever happens in our backwater. Remember that, Géraldine, and complain no more!"

There was such warmth, such earthy energy in the woman that Nelly did not mind the odor of naphthalene and whiff of mustiness that rose from her. She was the mother she never had. More than anything, she wanted her approval.

"Are those your parents?" Madame Renaud crossed over to the fireplace and inspected the photographs.

"Yes, madam."

"Your father is a nice looking prosperous gentleman. And your mother. Such a fine lady, Mademoiselle Nelly! When did she pass away?"

"When I was little," Nelly said, eager to add at least one touch of truth to the falsehood of the portraits. "I don't remember her at all."

"How little were you, when your mother died?"

Why was it so important? Why did Madame Renaud smile no more?

"I was six months old."

Madame Renaud's face hardened.

Géraldine eyed her anxiously. "Mama, are you feeling well?"

"No, as a matter of fact, I'm not. I think we should leave."

"But—"

"Immediately, Géraldine."

"Yes, mama."

"Would a glass of water help?" Nelly asked.

"No, thank you, Mademoiselle Woodridge. That will not be necessary."

Where had the warmth gone? Why the sudden distance? Anxious, Nelly saw them out.

"It must be something she has eaten," Géraldine murmured in the door while her mother was already waiting on the landing. "So sorry, Nelly. What a pity, that you should go into such lengths for nothing."

"Géraldine!"

135

"I'm coming, mama! . . . I hope that it's nothing serious and that she'll be fit for my birthday tomorrow. Come to lunch—"

"Géraldine, hurry up!"

"Yes, mama! . . . One o'clock sharp as agreed, all right?"

"All right."

"Géraldine!"

"I'm coming, mama."

"They are gone," Nelly said to the bewildered Julie, when she came to the sitting room carrying a coffee tray.

"Gone? Why?"

"I wish I knew."

Nelly did not sleep well that night. Twice, she got up and returned to the sitting room to study the photograph. As far as she could say, there was nothing wrong with it. A woman in an old-fashioned crinoline and a hat. She was just imagining things. Madame Renaud was simply taken ill, had to leave, and everything would be fine tomorrow. She blew out the candle and returned to bed.

* * *

"Madame is not at home," Cécile said.

"Not at home? What are you saying? I'm invited to lunch. See here?" Nelly showed an artfully wrapped gift.

"Madame is not at home."

"But—"

"Go back to the kitchen, Cécile! I'll take care of this," said a male voice. A hand shoved the maid aside and Monsieur Babeau appeared in the door.

"You are the American woman?" he asked.

"Why, yes. It's a pleasure to meet you at last, monsieur."

He ignored the proffered hand. "Madame Babeau is not at home. Neither now nor in the future. Do you understand?"

"No, I don't. What's the matter?" Nelly desperately needed to know even though she had already guessed that the truth would be merciless.

"Your impudence is equaled only by your depravity, Miss Whoever-you-are. Don't show up again, I warn you! I will not have my wife corrupted by the likes of you."

She took a step back. "Corrupted?" she breathed.

"Lying, running the streets like a tart, and God knows what else. Oh yes, fancying herself a writer! As you see, she's confessed everything. Or was there more?"

"No."

"Why should I believe a liar like you? If I ever see you around my wife, you'll regret it, I promise."

The door slammed in her face.

Nelly took a few wobbly steps down the stairs before she had to grab the handrail for support. She looked down into the stairwell. In a second, her life could be over. She imagined herself down on the mosaic floor, a pool of blood surrounding her broken body: a victim of the Babeaus of this world. Yet who would care? Géraldine? She had betrayed her. As for her husband, he would not give a damn. No, she would live and show them all!

The dog waited for her in the street. It was a creature of patched ancestry, big, dirty and as ugly as a devil. The short hair of its coat did little to hide its starved body.

"Shoo," she said.

The animal would not obey. It followed her as she wandered aimlessly through the streets of the Latin Quarter, delaying her return home.

"Shoo," she repeated, losing her patience. "Don't you think for one moment that you can follow me just because I gave you a croissant this morning!"

The animal listened to her, its head tilted to the side. Why had the dog-catcher not grabbed it yet? When he did, he would hang it until it was dead. There were strict rules for strays.

"Shoo! Shoo!" she waived her hand.

This time, the dog ran a few steps. She noticed that it was limping. When she turned to go, it was back behind her. They emerged on the quay where Nelly sat on the steps leading to the water, caring little for her fine dress. It was then that she realized she was still clutching the gift. She slid off the satin ribbon and tore at the paper. It was a box of marzipan fruits, similar to the one Géraldine had admired in the shop window before their trip to Champs Elysées. The donkeys, the goat milk, the Punch and Judy show, the fun they had had on their way home. It was all gone.

"There!" she threw a fistful of sweets on the pavement. The dog wolfed them down and pleaded for more. She threw another fistful.

Perhaps the scientists from the medical institutes would get it instead. Hanging would be a light sentence for wandering the streets as compared to vivisection. She could not believe her ears when Monsieur Goubert had explained the term to her. Cutting animals open before killing them? What awful world did she live in? What had the poor dog done to deserve such a terrible fate? It was just someone's reject. And so was she. Not just once, but many times. She felt sorry for both of them.

"Mademoiselle?" An elegant boulevardier bowed and lifted his hat. He opened his mouth to say more, but was given no opportunity. The dog, fearing for its meal, bared a formidable set of teeth, growled, and began barking. It had an amazing bark: deep, cavernous, and terrifying. The man jumped back, almost dropping his hat, and hastily retreated.

Nelly laughed and rose. "Come with me, my friend," she said to the dog. "You are hired."

Chapter 21

Célestine Cabrol drained the bottle until an indecent sound confirmed there was nothing left inside. There had not been much wine left when she found it propped against a bench on the quay, probably forgotten by some night revelers.

She tossed the bottle into the river. It broke the surface with a splash, disappeared briefly, and then popped up again to be carried away by the current. Swept away like all the good things in her life.

She sat down and rested her shoulders against the stone wall under the bridge. Later, after lunchtime, she would try her luck around the restaurants. God willing, she would be able to grab something edible from the garbage. However, that prospect was hours away. Right now, this place was as good as any. It protected her from the beating sunrays and the water exuded a refreshing coolness.

A *bateau-mouche* loaded with holidaymakers passed under the bridge, the tuff-tuff sound of the engine bouncing off the arch, the deep shade dimming the bright Sunday dresses of the women. The passengers were families with children or shop girls with their boyfriends, all of them brimming with anticipation of a beautiful day. They were going upstream to the Bois des Vincennes to spread their picnics on the grass.

Célestine closed her eyes and savored the image of a cold chicken, its tender skin roasted brown, served with fresh bread and a carafe of white wine, so cool that it made the glass sweat. She swallowed the saliva that had accumulated in her mouth.

A sound at her side alerted her that she was no longer alone. She turned her head to investigate the intruder and gasped. She had seen that unbelievable creature before but now she was allowed a closer look. The bearded gypsy woman, if she really was a woman, paid her no attention. She folded her portable vending stand, sat on it, and reached deep into some hidden pocket under her apron. Her grimy hand retrieved a package wrapped in a newspaper and a bottle of wine. She placed both down onto the pavement and, again, her hand rummaged in the depths of her skirts. A corkscrew appeared. Célestine watched enviously as the gypsy skillfully dealt with the cork and took a swig from the bottle. The gypsy sighed contentedly, put the bottle down, almost within Célestine's reach, and pulled at her skirts. Right above her boot, nested in a strap, Célestine glimpsed the handle of a knife. She cringed when the blade appeared.

She need not have worried. The gypsy used the knife to cut the string that held the newspaper in place. The package contained a scrumptious loaf of bread and a slab of cheese. With the newspaper neatly spread on her knees, the gypsy carved a large slice off the bread. When done, she attacked the cheese with the same calm determination. The bread crunched between her teeth. This was more than Célestine could stand.

"Say, that's a mighty large meal for one. Do you think you could share a bite?"

The gypsy finished the mouthful and tipped the bottle again. Just when Célestine ceased to hope, she cut another bread slice.

"Here."

"May the Virgin Mary bless you!" Célestine grabbed the bread.

"Take this," the gypsy brandished her knife.

"And bless you again," Célestine said happily, reaching for the cheese morsel spiked at the end of the blade.

She tore at the bread with her remaining teeth, stuffed it into her mouth, and then gnawed savagely at the cheese. Her jaws worked with a frantic speed and she swallowed the mouthful before it was properly chewed. Another bite, and another, to soothe her impatient stomach. After that, she slowed down to enjoy the taste.

"It's unseasonably hot for September," she said politely. After all, she owed the creature some kind of conversation.

Receiving no answer, she tried again, her gaze focused on the gypsy's bottle. "I don't say it has never happened before. In fifty-five—or was it fifty-seven?—the weather was hot well into October. I was young then," she added unnecessarily.

"Huh."

"I was pretty as well. Would you believe that I was pretty?"

"If you say so."

The gypsy tipped the bottle again. Noticing that Célestine was eyeing it eagerly, she passed it to her.

"Oh, bless you, bless you!" Célestine drank avidly, the wine running down the corners of her mouth. With a sigh of regret, she handed the bottle back.

"Keep it," the gypsy said.

"Thank you ever so much! God will pay you back twofold."

The gypsy studied her with a frown. "How long have you been hugging the bottle?" she asked.

"I'm not a boozer. Never used to be. It just helps me to forget. I'm a victim of circumstances."

"Aren't we all?"

It was more than true in the creature's case. Célestine eyed her with curiosity. "Are you a man or a woman?"

"What do you think?"

"I don't know." Her gaze went from the abundant beard to the swelling of the bodice. "Perhaps both?"

The gypsy laughed and shook her head.

"I don't want to embarrass you," Célestine said quickly. "I'm just curious."

"Everybody's curious."

"It must be hard. How old were you when the beard started to grow?"

"It's not a beard. It's facial hair. I was born with it."

"Oh. I didn't know there was a difference." Célestine remembered the bottle, took a sip, and followed it with another bite of cheese. "What happened to your nose?"

The gypsy's fingers stroked the deep gash, where a powerful blow had broken the bridge in half. "A jealous lover."

"You don't say."

"You think I'm too hideous to turn a man on? You'd be surprised."

"I said nothing of the sort. There's no accounting for taste."

"You can say that again. There are some that don't mind balling an old hag if the price's right and the alley dark enough."

Célestine took offense. "I never . . .! Oh, what the heck. Sometimes, hunger gets the better of me. I used to be pretty, you know! I had nice clothes and plenty of admirers. I watched the Emperor's wedding procession from a coach, wrapped in furs."

"Then what happened to you?"

"I married the wrong man."

"We all make mistakes."

A beggar, his face ravaged by drink, tottered toward them, attracted by the sight of food. The gypsy's stare barred his way. He paused and retraced his steps.

"I saw the advertisement on your case," Célestine said. "You read tarot?"

"For money."

"I just thought—"

"I don't need to look at the cards to know what's in store for you.'

"You don't?"

"The booze will get you if you don't catch the pox first."

The gypsy's harsh words hit Célestine like stones. "I haven't been drinking that long," she said. "But what else's there to do? Better go quickly." Defiantly, she drank some more.

"Can you cook?"

"Can I cook?" Célestine exclaimed. "What a question! You should've seen my galantine. A work of art. And my nun's farts! They melted on the tongue like snowflakes. The only thing I and my husband—may he rot in hell!—had in common was the love of food. I used to be round like a peach. Oh, how long since I've tasted a peach? A ripe fuzzy peach—"

"How do you make nun's farts?" the gypsy interrupted her.

"Why, you take flour—not ordinary flour, mind you, but the finest white kind—an egg yolk, butter, a squirt of rum, and a pinch of grated lemon zest, and work it into a dough with the help of milk. You roll the dough thin," Célestine closed her eyes, fondly remembering better times, "and cut it into small rectangles. Then you cut a slit in each rectangle and pull one end through it to make a sort of knot. Then it's into the frying grease and when the farts are still hot, you coat them with confectioner's sugar scented with vanilla—"

"You'd do," the gypsy said.

"—and you have a plate of the sweetest, the most delectable . . . What did you say?"

"I said you'd do. There's hope for you if you can stay away from the bottle."

"Hope?" Célestine asked, confused. "What's there to hope for?"

"Do you want to get off the street or not?"

"Do I? I'd do anything. Honest, I would!"

"Even to give up drinking?"

"In a second."

"Prove it."

Célestine's hands squeezed the bottle in a protective grip. It was far from empty. "What for?"

"The weather may be hot, but winter is coming. Think of that. You'll freeze to death in that coal cellar of yours."

A shiver ran along Célestine's spine. Suddenly, she was afraid. "What do you want from me? You seem to know an awful lot. How do you know that I live in a cellar?"

"You are covered with coal dust. It's etched in your skin. Besides, I saw you climb into the cellar through a broken window. Of course, as soon as the window gets fixed, you'll have to look for other accommodations."

Célestine sighed. "I'll deal with that when the day comes and not sooner. One thing at a time. It's hard to think ahead."

"That's because your brain is muddled with booze. Give it up, I say."

"Why? What is it to you?"

"All right, it's your life after all." The gypsy began to wrap the remaining food in the newspaper. "If you can't tell when luck is knocking at your door, I'm wasting my time with you. I'll find someone else."

"My God," Célestine said, "you are serious, aren't you? Is there really a chance for me?"

"It's up to you to decide."

"How?"

The gypsy nodded toward the bottle. After a brief hesitation, Célestine threw it into the water.

"What now?" she asked.

"There's an American woman I'm interested in. She needs a cook."

"Is that what I have thrown out the bottle for?" Célestine exclaimed. "Jesus, look at me!" she spread her tattered skirt. "Who in her right mind would allow me near her kitchen?"

"You can get scrubbed and deloused."

"Still, I have no letters of recommendation."

"You won't need any if you're smart."

"How's that?"

"She's got the habit of collecting strays. Play on her heartstrings and you'll get the job."

"So, I'm to go and say I want the post and then beg and cry?"

"It's not that simple. She doesn't know she needs a cook as yet. First, you'll have to implant the idea."

Célestine's face screwed with anger. "I was wrong to trust you. It has cost me half a bottle. Just my luck!"

"You were lucky to get the bottle in the first place."

This was fair enough. "You are right," Célestine admitted.

"Of course, I'm right!" the gypsy snapped. "If you listened to me instead of wailing every time I say something you don't like, we might get somewhere yet."

"Go on."

"The woman's got a dog, a stray she's adopted. She walks him every day. He's a fearsome bastard, but he's not vicious. He's greedy, though, and wouldn't hesitate to betray his mistress for a chicken wing. All you have to do is to pretend that the mutt is yours."

Célestine made a dismissive gesture. "It won't work. How can I pretend the dog's mine if he doesn't know me?"

"That can be easily arranged. You'll smear liver pâté on your hands and behind your ears and he'll be all over you."

"What if he bites me?"

"A cushy job in a cozy kitchen and plenty to eat for a start. Cowards need not apply."

Célestine mulled it over. "It's worth a try."

"It's your only chance. If you don't succeed, it's back into the gutter."

"I'll do it."

"Good. Here," the gypsy reached into a purse tied to her belt and retrieved a handful of coins, "buy yourself a respectable second-hand garb. Nothing fancy. Poor, mended, but clean. Go to the public bath and scrub yourself hard. I insist on that. No black moons behind the nails, got that?"

Célestine nodded.

"The rest is for food and nothing else," the gypsy said. "Especially not drink. I want to see you here tomorrow at the same time, presentable and sober. Make sure you've got that right."

Célestine counted the coins. Close to twelve francs! When did she last hold that much money? "What's in it for you? Why are you doing this?" she asked.

"Cushioning my own bed. That young woman has a high destiny coming to her. A very high destiny. A crown is close at hand."

"A crown?"

"The cards don't lie."

"A crown," repeated Célestine, awed.

"A thorny way leads to it. One false step and all will be lost. That's where I come in. She will need wise counsel. If you do exactly as I say, the rewards can be great for both of us."

Célestine swallowed. Visions of luxury, money, and power danced in her head. With a bit of luck, some of it could rub off on her. "I'll do exactly as you say," she said eagerly.

"Good. I'll tell you more when we meet again." The gypsy rose and fastened the straps of the stand around her shoulders. "Finish the bread and cheese but don't eat too much after that. The hungrier you look, the better. See you tomorrow."

She turned to go.

Célestine got up as well. "Aren't you going to ask my name?" she called after the gypsy.

"I don't need to. And I know where to find you."

Again, a shiver ran down Célestine's back. "What's yours then? What do I call you?"

"Nathaira. It means Lucky Star."

Célestine watched as the bearded creature climbed the stairs leading up to the quay.

"Lucky Star," she repeated with wonder, passing the coins from one hand to the other.

Chapter 22

Water exploded as the dog hurled himself into the river and swam eagerly after a stick thrown by a barefoot ragamuffin.

"That will be five sous for the shampoo and four sous for the flea treatment," the boy's mother told Nelly. "Any nail clipping this week?"

"He had it done last week," Nelly said.

The dog groomer rubbed her nose. "Oh yes, so he had. With so many dogs in between, one can't remember everything. Although this one I should," she added, nodding her head toward the embankment where the animal, already back after the rinse, shook himself, scattering drops of water in graceful spirals. "You two make quite a pair, if I may say so."

"I heard that opinion many times." Nelly opened her reticule and counted the coins.

"It's just that you two don't belong together," the woman persisted. "A fine lady like you should look for something smaller and prettier. I know a fellow who breeds Maltese. Now there's a dog for you. It looks like a silky white pillow and you could put a cute ribbon on its head to match your dress."

"Last week you tried to sell me a poodle," Nelly said, irritated. "My dog may not be handsome but I happen to like him."

She paid the woman and fastened a red leather collar around the dog's neck. Studded with steel spikes, it did nothing to sweeten his ferocious looks, quite the contrary. He waited patiently for his leash, but as soon as it was fastened to the collar, he started toward the steps, dragging his owner after him.

"He's becoming quite a handful," the woman called after Nelly. "As I said, a Maltese would suit you better!"

Ignoring her, they mounted the steps to the Quay du Louvre, where tourists and locals alike gave them a wide berth, and crossed the Pont des

Arts. The dog strutted ahead of Nelly, easing a badly mended fracture in his left hind leg. Past the bridge, he decided to follow an interesting smell to the rue Bonaparte. Nelly allowed him to go as he pleased. The city was theirs to explore at any pace they wished. She could pause to admire shop windows without being mistaken for a prostitute while her companion's nose read messages posted by the canine population of Paris. As for the black dress, it was back at the bottom of a trunk. She owed the dog an unprecedented freedom.

She stopped at the entrance of the School of Fine Arts and, twirling her parasol, read the advertisements with a growing interest. Dozens of models, both male and female, described themselves in glowing terms.

> Monsieur Bernardini, rue des Grands-Augustins, #43: Short but very muscular. A military type. Wears a beard but will consider shaving.

> Madame Lange, rue Dauphine, #14: A mature Venus.

> Mlle Castel-Vieux, rue du Four, #8. Tall and willowy. Poses draperies.
> Only 4 F for a 3-hour session.

Four francs for a three-hour session? Nelly calculated the time she had spent posing for Sarah Bernhardt and concluded that, so far, the actress owed her at least twenty francs. Not that she expected to see the money, as financial matters were never mentioned. Frequented by the rich and famous, Sarah's salon was a fishing pond of potential customers for Octave. Sarah would be very disappointed if Nelly decided not to sit for her, he said with an ominous frown. Nelly yielded, provided there would be no nudity. As for Sarah, she was the promising sort. Without being asked, she kept offering this and that. One of her sketches, Victor Hugo's autograph, a pair of Meissen figurines that Nelly admired. Perhaps, she even meant what she said, when she promised it. The trouble was that she immediately forgot her promises.

The rue Bonaparte led to the crowded boulevard Saint-Germain. The outdoor cafés were doing a brisk business, sheltering the thirsty Left Bank populace in the shade of canvas awnings. Thirsty herself, Nelly briefly entertained the idea of sitting down for a glass of grenadine. It was something she had not yet done on her own. Still, to be sitting alone in a café . . .

"Now look who's here," said a mocking voice from a terrace only a couple of yards away. "The Englishwoman!"

Nelly turned. She recognized the woman at once. "I would like to make it clear that I'm an American," she said loftily.

Loulou shrugged. "English or American, what's the difference? Don't we all have an *entente cordiale*? Come and join us!"

Nelly eyed her with wariness. When did Octave's feisty ex-mistress acquire such warm feelings toward her? Still, bad company was better than none. Alerted by a telegram, Julie had rushed to her ailing mother's bedside in Roubaix. Although the maid was never much of a talker, her absence accentuated Nelly's loneliness. "I don't know whether I should," she said half-heartedly.

"Oh, come on! No hard feelings, huh? It's water under the bridge. This is Gilda," Loulou introduced her companion.

Gilda was a sweaty, bovine blonde dressed in an apple-green gown that clashed with her reddish complexion. A small live lizard, attached by a silver chain, perched on her shoulder. She gave Nelly a limp handshake.

"Gilda's a dead bore," said Loulou. "She's—Jesus, what's that?" she noticed the dog. "Have you robbed a pound?"

"Don't worry, he's not vicious. Sit down, Schnitzel! Now there's a good dog."

With some scraping of chairs and adjustment of tables, a place was made for Nelly on the crowded terrace. The dog plopped down at her side and, tired by the heat, immediately went into a slumber.

"Schnitzel? Did I hear right? What a funny name for a dog," Loulou commented.

"Octave said he looked like a Prussian. He wanted to call him Bismarck, but I thought that it wouldn't be nice to the poor animal. Finally, we settled on Schnitzel."

"So you are still with Gaillard?" Loulou inquired.

"I am. And you? Are you still with that art critic?"

"Toussaint? Nah, that's over," Loulou waved her hand dismissively. "Who wants to waste time with a pen pusher? Say, you are paying for the round, aren't you? It's the custom here. The last one who joins the party. Isn't that so, Gilda?"

"Sure," said Gilda unconvincingly.

The purpose of the invitation became clear. The two had run out of money and needed a sap. Nelly did not mind. By the look of her, Loulou was down on her luck. She wore the same plum silk, probably the only good dress she owned. It had begun to discolor in the armpits. She was between lovers and the income from modeling was probably sporadic. The two Sèvres vases had cost her a professional falling-out with Octave, a fact that filled Nelly with satisfaction. She felt particularly smart and cool in her white cambric embroidered with rosebuds. Despite the heat, the small bunch of pink rosebuds tucked under her straw hat remained fresh thanks to a hidden vial of water: a trick she had learned from Sarah. She had good reason to feel generous.

"One must honor local customs," she said. "The round is on me."

"Good. Waiter! Two green fairies and . . . What is it going to be for you?"

"A grenadine."

"And a grenadine."

"And a bowl of water for the dog."

"Sure, we must not forget Madame's pretty puppy," Loulou cast an ironic look down at Schnitzel.

"What about the lizard," Nelly addressed Gilda. "What does it eat?"

"I dunno. I just got it."

"Well, you will have to feed it something or else it will die."

"That's what I keep telling her, the silly cow," Loulou said. "It's an advertisement," she explained to Nelly. "She's got nothing much going for her in the brains department and chubby is out of fashion. I told her to get something people would remember her by. Except that she forgot to ask how to care for it."

"I do believe that lizards eat insects," Nelly said.

"If that's true then the poor critter is as good as dead. I can't imagine fat Gilda catching flies!"

The very idea made Loulou hoot with laughter. Heads turned toward their table. Gilda remained impassive.

"Anyway," Loulou went on, "at least I don't need any gimmicks. I've got the profile, see?" she turned her head sideways. "See how my nose joins the forehead in a straight line? That's called the classical Greek profile."

Nelly admitted that she had seen such profiles at the Louvre museum. She mentioned the Venus de Milo.

"You're not stupid," Loulou said magnanimously. "So, you see, I don't need to advertise. Every time someone decides to paint an antique scene, I'm in it. We are art models," she added in case Nelly was stupid after all.

"I know. You pose in the nude, I believe." Annoyed with all the bragging, Nelly looked forward to seeing Loulou blush. She was wrong.

"Have you seen me in a painting? What did you think of my tits?" Loulou threw back her shoulders and wiggled her chest. "Fabulous, eh?"

Her shameless behavior did not escape the attention of the neighboring tables. The older guests merely raised their eyebrows, but students were less discreet. Snickering remarks and smacking sounds flew toward them. Loulou enjoyed the attention. Not so Nelly. She was furious with herself and ashamed to be seen in such company. Clearly, the woman was drunk.

149

Fortunately, the waiter came with the drinks. He dispatched Nelly's grenadine and the bowl of water for Schnitzel, and then turned his attention to a pair of sturdy glasses, each containing two inches of violently green liquid. Like her companions, Nelly found absinthe preparation fascinating. The conversation stopped while the waiter balanced a trowel-shaped slotted spoon on the rim. He perched a cube of sugar on top and slowly poured iced water over the construction. As the sugar-cube dissolved, the drink magically turned an opalescent yellow. The waiter gave it a swirl with the spoon and then worked on the other glass. Down, at Nelly's side, Schnitzel loudly lapped his water.

"Santé!" Loulou lifted her glass when the waiter was gone.

"Santé," repeated Gilda.

Nelly said nothing and quickly drained her glass.

"That was very nice," she said. She fumbled in her reticule looking for a coin.

"Going already?" Loulou inquired with a frown.

"Actually, I'm rather in a hurry."

"Are you?" Loulou's eyes narrowed to a slit. "Perhaps madam does not enjoy the present company? What do you think, Gilda?"

"What if she doesn't? Don't work yourself up, Loulou. It's not good in this heat. We've got the drinks so what does it matter?"

"It does matter! I don't like snooty foreigners who think they are better than us."

The *entente cordiale* seemed to be compromised. Fearing a scene, Nelly struggled to placate the drunken woman.

"It's not true," she said. "It's just that I have a headache."

"A headache? Is that why you've been making such a long face? Then we must cheer you up, mustn't we, Gilda? Laughter is the best medicine, just ask around. Isn't that so?" she addressed the grinning youngsters at the next table, who were unashamedly listening to the conversation. They supported Loulou's theory with appreciative nods.

"Indeed," one of them said, "a positive attitude is very beneficial to physical well-being."

"Just as I said," Loulou agreed, shifting her chair sideways to include her enlarged audience. "My poor American friend here suffers from a migraine and is in sore need of light entertainment. Fortunately, I remember a most amusing joke."

Nelly, too, shifted in her seat, her apprehension growing, while the young men leaned closer in anticipation.

"Sooo . . ." Loulou drawled, making sure she had everyone's undivided attention, "on a glorious spring day, Jacques and Pierre are strolling in the Bois de Boulogne when they see a couple kissing behind a bush." She folded her index fingers signaling quotation marks surrounding the word 'kissing'.

Someone chuckled while Nelly ground her teeth. *Oh Lord*, she prayed, *get me out of here as soon as possible!*

"'Aw,' Jacques says, 'how charming! Spring, blooms, love! Everything as it should be.' But his friend is horrified. 'Don't you see, Jacques, that the woman is dead? We must call the police!'"

Loulou pacified the murmur of disgust among the listeners by showing her palms. She paused, her malicious gaze gliding over her attentive audience, until it came to rest on Nelly.

"'Calm down, Pierre,' Jacques says, 'I know the woman, having kissed her myself. She's not dead. She's American!'"

An outburst of laughter followed the punch line. Loulou laughed the loudest, beating the table with her fist.

Nelly rose. The laughter died except for a few giggles here and there. Loulou stared at her defiantly and then exploded with another bout of hilarity.

A slap knocked her head to the side.

"What . . . ?" Loulou gasped, holding her burning cheek.

Nelly contemptuously threw the coin on the table and turned to go.

Loulou was on her feet instantly. "Oh no, you are not leaving like that, you stinking foreign bitch! We're not finished yet!"

Encouraged by catcalls from the students, who looked forward to an entertaining fight, she grabbed Nelly by the arm. It was then that Schnitzel, forgotten at the foot of the table, took charge of the situation and began to bark.

Loulou let go of Nelly's arm and jumped back, her face twisted with fright. With a slow stroke, Nelly removed invisible slime clinging to her sleeve. "Come, Schnitzel," she pulled at the leash.

She left with as much dignity as she could muster, ignoring a string of obscenities the enraged Loulou hurled after her. Outwardly calm, she was seething inside. The vulgarity of that woman!

As soon as the café was out of sight, she accelerated her pace. Ominous clouds began to gather in the sky and when they reached the Quay de la Tournelle, a sudden gust of wind announced the coming of a storm. They were nearing the entrance of the house when the first drops of rain hit the pavement. At that very moment, Schnitzel's sharp nose caught a scent so irresistible that he dragged his mistress past the door. He stopped briefly to lick something off the sidewalk, but before she could scold him he pulled at the leash again, this time yanking it out of her hand. On he went until he reached a gaunt old woman huddled in the neighboring door. Seeing the dog coming at her, the woman screamed with fright and crossed her arms in front of her.

"Schnitzel, come back!" Nelly shouted.

The dog ignored her. His tail wagging, he stood on his hind legs and licked the victim's hands. The woman crouched, trying to protect herself against the assault.

"Stop it! Come back!" Nelly pleaded with the dog.

"Médor? Médor, is that you?" the woman exclaimed. "It is you! My dog is back! My prayers have been answered! Thank you, dear God, thank you! Oh my darling Médor, we will never part again!" Shaking with dry sobs, she hugged the dog to her.

"Médor?" Nelly repeated.

She stood riveted to the sidewalk, unaware of the rain that was ruining her smart dress. It could not be. It must not be! She had taken it for granted that the dog was hers.

"Please, come upstairs with me," she said. "I'm sure we can come to an agreement."

Chapter 23

Célestine tasted the cold soup. It was a crude concoction of potatoes, carrots and limp leeks swimming in milk. Given the means, she could do infinitely better.

"I'm sorry there's nothing else," the American woman said. "My maid has gone for a few days and one does not feel like standing by the stove in this heat. Later, if you are still hungry, I can offer you some preserves."

"May the Virgin Mary bless you," Célestine said piously and shoveled in the soup. "Only yesterday, I passed out from hunger. People don't realize how lucky they are to have something solid in their stomach and a roof over their head. I myself had no idea until it happened to me."

"You mean you have nowhere to stay?"

"Not since last week. The landlord threw me out with only these clothes on my back. Oh, madam, you don't know how hard it is to sleep out in the open! One is never safe. And with this storm the weather may take a turn for the worse. How will I survive when the winter comes?"

She began to cry and this time she had no trouble summoning tears. After all, she was telling the truth, except that the landlord had chased her out four months ago. She was now reasonably clean and could not pretend to have lived in the street for more than a week.

"But isn't there a charity you can turn to?"

"There's the Public Assistance, to be sure. They give the poor one franc and a loaf of bread a day. Except that in order to benefit, one has to have a letter of recommendation from the parish. I hadn't lived at my last address long enough."

"What about your family and friends?"

Célestine shook her head sadly. "I've got only one living sister. She doesn't want to hear from me. Says that she has done enough and that I'm in this mess through my own fault. Saint-Geneviève up in heaven is my witness that one's own blood can be more heartless than a stranger! I'll have some of that preserve, if you don't mind. I haven't eaten in days."

"Of course," the woman said. She rose from the table and went to the pantry.

Célestine spread a generous helping of butter on a piece of bread and stuffed it into her mouth. Chewing hastily, she looked around her. The kitchen was just as the gypsy had said. Nice and cozy, especially with the rain pouring outside. She hated the idea of leaving such a fine place. If she had to go back to her former life, she would throw herself from a bridge. One can take only so much and no more.

She heard the woman coming back and quickly plunged her fingers into the butter dish. The dog, who had lost interest in her once he had licked her clean, came over and his slick tongue slurped the butter from her fingers. The greedy beast almost gave her a heart attack. As much as she anticipated the encounter, when she saw him coming at her, she nearly passed out.

She lifted her hand, forcing the dog to put his front paws on her lap. With her free arm, she hugged his body and when the woman entered, she found them close. She paused in the door with a sad expression in her eyes. That was a good sign. So far, they had avoided the issue of the dog's ownership and Célestine was not in a hurry.

Her hostess put two earthenware jars on the table. "I've brought pickles and a goose preserve," she said.

"A goose preserve? Oh, bless you, dear lady! The past is catching up with me. When was it last that I made a goose preserve? I'm a very good cook."

The woman did not swallow the hook. She opened the jars, filled a plate, and pushed it in front of Célestine. "Please, eat."

Her French was rather good with just a hint of an accent, not at all as Célestine expected. She had a healthy mistrust of foreigners, especially the English, whom she considered cold and not altogether human. It was said that they did not have the same feelings and emotions as the French. Perhaps it was different with the Americans. The woman sat at the table and watched her eat.

"As for friends," Célestine returned to the previous topic of conversation, "all I can say is that you lose them on your way down. It's as much your fault as theirs. One tends to avoid people who have known you in your better days. After a while, they don't even recognize you. Would you believe that I used to be pretty?"

"People do change as they become older."

"And how old do you think I am?" Célestine asked while secretly kicking the dog, who was begging for a morsel from her plate.

154

"I don't know. Sixty-five?"

"I'm forty-eight."

"Forty-eight?"

"That's what poverty does to people, dear lady. I used to be as pretty as you are."

Horror and disbelief spread on the woman's face. The emotions were much like her own when she had seen herself reflected in the mirror at the public baths after the layers of dirt and coal dust had gone. Her type of beauty was one that faded quickly after forty, and the four months in the gutter had devastated her looks. Her hair, once a shiny auburn, faded into yellowish gray. Her brown eyes lost their spark and looked smaller. In contrast, her upturned nose, insignificant when lodged between round cheeks, had become the most important feature in her face. A collection of wrinkles replaced her lips. All she had was her past.

"I see that you don't believe me, but I swear by Saint-Catherine that it's true! I was no stranger to jewels, furs, and elegant gowns. I kept a coach and a pair of horses. I had a maid and a valet. I had a smart apartment on the Chausée d'Antin and money in the bank. Where is it all gone? Where?"

Strangled by genuine grief, Célestine pushed the plate aside and cradled her head in her arms. Deep sobs shook her emaciated body, rage and sorrow squeezing her ribs and pulling them apart in powerful heaves. Something was pushed into her hand. Realizing that it was a handkerchief she accepted it eagerly. She blew her nose and dried her eyes.

"I'm sorry," she said.

"Please, don't apologize. About the dog . . ."

"The dog?" She had already forgotten the damn animal.

"I'll give you twenty francs for him."

"You can keep him. He's fine with you. But what about me? Your twenty francs will get me nowhere. In three weeks I'll be exactly where I am now."

"What do you want, then?"

"A job. I swear by Saint-Laurent, martyred on the grill, that I'm a good cook."

"But I don't need a cook. My maid is very competent in the kitchen."

"Can she make a galantine? Does she know how to prepare chocolate truffles or a truly tasty muslin sauce?"

"Why, I don't know. We cook simple food, and if we want something better, we go to a restaurant."

"Money wasted, I assure you. And you never know what goes into the dishes. There is nothing like good home cooking. It keeps the man tied to the house."

155

This seemed to produce some kind of effect, if only for a second or two, then the woman's face clouded again. "No, it's impossible," she said. "I cannot let you live here. For all I know, you could've been in jail. I don't even know your name."

"My name is Célestine Cabrol and I've never been to jail. This I swear on the highest authority of Our Lord and Savior, Jesus Christ."

"If you can cook as well as you say, then you will find a job elsewhere. I don't see why not."

"But there are too many cooks and I have never worked for anyone. I have no referrals. Please, dear lady, give me a chance!" Célestine went down on her knees. "Please, try me out!"

The woman's face drained of color. She rose and stepped back. "You must not do that. Please get up. Besides, it's no use."

Instead of obeying, Célestine collapsed on the floor. It was over. She cursed the gypsy for shining a ray of hope into her dark life - just enough light to reveal the human wreck she had become. Was she not happier two days ago, living from hour to hour like an animal, thinking of nothing but how to get the next meal? The worst of it was that she could no longer go back to that sort of semi-conscious existence.

"It's the bridge then," she said.

"What did you say?"

"Nothing." She allowed her to help her on her feet, but when the anxious woman brought forward a chair, she pushed her away. "I have to go now."

"Wait! I'll give you your money."

"Keep the money. I will not need it."

"What are you going to do?"

"None of your business."

"You cannot go like this."

"And who's going to stop me? You? Get your hands off me!"

Célestine was now in a hurry to her appointment with Death. The prospect appealed to her and she was surprised that she had kept putting it off for such a long time. Now that she was going to be free, she felt magnanimous.

"I forgive you. God bless you, girlie, and don't make the same mistakes I've made!"

"Listen," the woman said, her voice unsteady, "let's not be hasty. There's always a solution. Just sit down and let's talk. Please!"

* * *

The pots and pans on the stove bubbled and hissed, filling the kitchen with delicious aromas. Célestine opened the oven door and checked on the tripe stew. It was coming along nicely. Too bad she could not make it a day ahead.

The *tripe à la mode de Caen* always tasted best the next day when the flavors had matured. She poured in calvados and stirred the pot. Today, the master of the household would have his fill of his native Normandy. The paper-thin pancakes stuffed with a mixture of sole, flounder, oysters, and mussels had already generated praise. Now she was awaiting a report on the salt meadow mutton from the coast of Mont Saint-Michel. Aristide, her scoundrel of a husband, maintained that there was no better-flavored meat in the whole of France. She had browned the chops in Norman grease—part suet, part pork fat—and spooned a thick cream sauce over the dish.

She covered the stew and put it back into the oven. Just then, the door opened and Miss Woodridge came in, carrying the remains of the mutton dish. Célestine glanced at the serving plate. There was not much left. "He liked it, then," she concluded.

"Of course. And the duchess potatoes were excellent. What now?"

"There are two lime sorbets in the ice box, to refresh the palate. I'll get them for you."

Miss Woodridge sighed. "I can get by for a whole week for the price of this dinner. How much more food is coming after the stew?"

"Just a soufflé for dessert. Coffee and cognac afterwards, followed by fresh fruit."

"Where I come from," Miss Woodridge said, "we've never heard of a tripe stew. Tripe is something we throw to the dogs."

"A big mistake, Miss! In the right hands, it's a delicacy."

"Speaking of dogs, what have you done with Schnitzel?"

"He's down in the courtyard, tied to the tree. I can't have him under my feet. I'm a bit rusty and his begging distracts me," Célestine said. "I gave him a bone to chew on," she added quickly when she saw the frown.

"Well, I suppose that's all right for the time being. But don't leave him there for too long! It's getting dark."

"Amen," Célestine smirked when the door closed. Stupid dog, stupid American woman! Her own fate was being decided in the dining room and all she could think of was that lazy glutton.

She separated eggs and whisked the yolks with milk, then added the mixture to a *roux* of flour, sugar, butter, and vanilla. She gladly sat down with a whisk and a bowl of egg whites in her lap. It had been an exhausting day after an agonizing night in the windowless alcove. She could not sleep, tossing from side to side on the narrow cot, her feet catching one of the transatlantic trunks piled up all around her and reaching up to the ceiling. Her mind churned over frightening images of herself jumping off the bridge, water filling her lungs, Death slowly crushing her in his skeletal arms. She must have been mad to think of doing away with herself. As she got up to pour herself a drink of water for her parched throat, the dog woke up and growled. Frightened, she scurried back to bed, but her thirst grew stronger and she decided that she must have a drink no matter what. Armed with a shoe, she faced the growling animal.

"Shut up," she said and lifted the shoe above her head, ready to throw it at him.

To her surprise, the dog actually shut up and crawled under a chair with his tail between his legs.

"So, that's how it is," Célestine said, shaking with silent mirth. "You're a fraud! All brass outside and nothing but wind in the guts."

She went back to bed, pleased with her discovery, but soon began to worry again. Now that the woman was mollified, the next obstacle was the man. He was well off, she had been told, but she knew little else.

"The less I tell you, the better," the gypsy said. "I don't want you to blurt out a fact you're not supposed to know."

Célestine tested the egg whites by lifting the whisk. They formed a peak. Carefully, she folded them into the batter. She poked the fire, removed the stew from the oven, and placed the soufflé dish inside.

Alerted by the bell, she was spooning the stew onto a serving plate just as Miss Woodridge came back with the empty sorbet cups. When she left carrying the dish, Célestine realized she had forgotten to make the caramel sauce. Quickly, she stirred sugar in a heavy saucepan, watching it dissolve and bubble. Later on, after the dinner, she would collapse with fatigue. After what she had been through these past months, it was no wonder. Somehow, the pleasure she used to feel when preparing tasty dishes for Aristide—may he rot in hell!—was gone.

She wondered what Miss Woodridge's man looked like. Probably one of the square Norman peasants she encountered at the market, selling eggs, cream, cheese, or apples from their orchards. Well-dressed, of course, but a peasant nevertheless. Very likely an Empire profiteer. It was easy to make money then, if one had the right connections and, most of all, a good head on his shoulders, which her accursed husband had not.

The melted sugar was turning a deep amber color. She added cream and stirred the mixture smooth. She strained it into a bowl sitting on a bed of ice. By the time the soufflé was ready to serve, it would be reasonably cool.

She scratched her hair, hidden under a white mobcap, which belonged to the maid. So did the brown serge dress she was wearing. Her own clothes had been taken away the night before. She thought it was a security measure, but in the morning she learned that Miss Woodridge had tossed them out. She was made to bathe—again!—and wash her hair. Her poor scalp, already dried out by the delousing chemical in the public bath, itched horribly and sent down a shower of dandruff each time she scratched it.

She glanced at the kitchen clock above the door. Thirty minutes had passed since she had put the soufflé into the oven and no ring had alerted her for the next course. With the greatest care, she transferred the baked dish onto a round serving plate, poured the caramel sauce around it, and decorated the plate with fresh raspberries. She stepped back and admired the result. It looked grand. But where was Miss Woodridge? A soufflé simply could not wait.

Célestine consulted the clock and reached a decision. After removing her stained apron, she crossed herself for courage, and grabbed the dish. Down the corridor she went, past the smart bathroom that had taken her breath away—she had never seen such a luxury, even in her carriage-and-horses day—and on into unknown territory. She found the dining room easily as voices were filtering through the door. She flattened her ear against the keyhole.

"Of course the picture is yours to do with as you please," Miss Woodridge was saying. "That's not the point. The point is that someone could recognize me. Just remember what happened with that reporter from the Chicago Tribune."

"Frankly, kitten, you are exaggerating," a male voice answered. "That was back in March. If there had been any interest in the case, it had died long since. What are the chances that someone would recognize you in profile and with your head tilted back? Besides, why do you object now? When the photograph was taken, you knew very well that I had every intention of showing it in public."

"Back then, I was willing to take the risk for Julie."

"Am I less important than a maid?" the man asked. "Can't you humor me for once? You must admit that I've been very tolerant regarding your whims, including your propensity for bringing home dirt from the street. First the dog and now some old hag with a heart-rending tale."

"She's a good cook."

The man grumbled something Célestine's ear did not catch. "As for the picture," he added, "instead of whining, you should be glad for me. Do you have any idea what Sarah's patronage means to the project? One word from her and all Paris will come."

"Oh, it's to her advantage as well," Miss Woodridge said resignedly. "When is it to be?"

"Early December. I've booked a suite of rooms on the boulevard des Italiens. I hope I'll hear no more protests from you."

Célestine would have listened longer but the soufflé was developing wrinkles. She knocked, and composed an innocent face.

Later, she wondered how she had managed to hold onto the plate. There, sitting at the table, was Aristide reincarnated. Not so much in looks, although this one was a handsome devil as well, but in self-satisfaction and self-importance. She hated him on sight.

"This is Célestine, dear," said Miss Woodridge. "She's cooked this wonderful dinner."

"Good effort, indeed," said the man. He looked relieved by the interruption.

Célestine apologized profusely and explained her concern for the soufflé. With a trembling hand, she served the dessert on individual plates, and then humbly stood by the table, awaiting the verdict. The man plunged his fork into the frothy mass and tasted it carefully.

"Mhm . . . Very light. The sauce could be a little cooler but altogether it is a very satisfactory soufflé."

"Thank you, monsieur."

He ate two more forkfuls, and then leaned back against the chair and his gaze scanned Célestine from head to toe.

"So, Joséphine—"

"Célestine, monsieur. Célestine Cabrol."

"Célestine, then. Where did you learn to cook in the Norman style?"

"My husband was a well-known gourmet, monsieur. Food was his passion. His aim was to make a culinary tour of France without leaving Paris. He collected recipes from as far as Gascony and we recreated them in our kitchen. He intended to publish his findings in a book."

"An interesting concept. Miss Woodridge has told me your story, but I want to hear it from you. You said that your husband died in sixty-eight, is that so?"

"No, monsieur, in sixty-seven. June sixty-seven it was." She understood the game. He was trying to confuse her. "Charles-Aristide Cabrol was his name and he's buried in the Père Lachaise cemetery."

"How did he die?"

"He shot himself. Gambling debts." And other things she did not care to mention.

"What did you do after that?"

"The bailiffs came and took everything away. I moved into a cheap room in the Faubourg Saint-Antoine and my sister lent me six hundred francs for a peddler's license."

"A fruit cart, I believe."

"No, monsieur. I became a flower-seller. I had a fixed place on the corner of rue Saint-Antoine and Place de la Bastille. I was doing reasonably well. I had enough saved to withstand the war and the revolution."

"Really?"

"Well, only just. Like everyone else."

"And then?"

"Then the accident happened. It was nobody's fault. There was a fire somewhere and the din of the firefighters' wagon frightened a pair of horses. They tried to run away and the carriage crashed into my stand. I woke up in the hospital with broken ribs and a leg fracture. Then the pneumonia set in and I remained on my back for weeks. When the medical bills were paid, I had nothing left except debts. I sold my license, moved into a cheaper room, and then into an even cheaper one. Then I ended in the street. That's all, monsieur."

"And the dog?"

"The dog . . ." They were now on slippery ground but the gypsy had worked it all out. "I got him to guard my stand to keep the street urchins at bay. They used to steal my flowers when I had to take a break. I don't know what happened to him after the accident. Maybe someone took him in but did not treat him properly and the poor beast ran away."

"Miss Woodridge is very fond of that animal."

"Yes, monsieur."

"Do you agree that the dog is hers and that you will not lay any claims to it now or in the future?"

"I do agree. Does this mean that I'm hired?"

He reached for a small notebook, opened it, and poised a pencil above a page. "What was the number of your license and when exactly did you sell it? I'll check it out."

She told him and he wrote it down.

"If the information is correct, you will be allowed to stay. If not . . ." He let the untold menace dangle in the air.

"I've no fear. You'll find everything as I've said."

"I certainly hope so," he said. "In the meantime, Miss Woodridge will keep the kitchen door locked overnight. You may bring the coffee now."

Much later, after she scrubbed the dishes clean and restored the kitchen to its pristine order, Célestine collapsed on her cot and removed her shoes. Schnitzel came over and put his head on her lap.

She scratched him between the ears. "You are a clever critter, aren't you? Have you already figured out that I'll have something to say about the food? Well, don't set your hopes too high. From now on, I'll get the best leftovers, and that's the truth. Now beat it!"

She yawned and unhooked her bodice. It had been a long, tiring day but she had the job and something interesting to report to the gypsy. Nathaira, the Lucky Star. A lucky star indeed.

Chapter 24

"I'm convinced that I shall die young," Sarah said.

Protests rose from her assembled guests, while Nelly stiffened her lips to prevent a smile. Sarah never gave up performing. This audience included two dozen of her steadfast admirers admitted either for their influence in arts and public life or for the size of their bank accounts. The stage was Sarah's salon and the play, Sarah Painting.

The actress mixed paint on her palette, careful not to stain her outfit. A Worth design, it consisted of a pair of white satin pantaloons—an effective shock to newcomers—and a jacket of the same material with a froth of lace at the neck and cuffs. It had probably cost well over five hundred francs, which was the bottom price at the Maison Worth.

"I'm serious," Sarah said. She dabbed a few highlights on the canvas. "I feel death creeping closer and closer. It's calling me!" She turned to her guests, her painting brush pointing. "If you are my friends, if you truly love me, you must present me with a coffin of sculpted oak lined with white satin."

The devastatingly handsome boulevardier, Robert de Montesquiou, crossed a long leg over his knee. Today, he was accompanied by his latest flame, a supposedly talented and—as yet—unknown poet, whose long greasy hair added a touch of true Bohemia to the atmosphere.

"*Chérie,*" he said in his over-cultivated drawl, "would owning a coffin cheer you up? If so, I declare it a national emergency."

The company laughed and the chain-smoking novelist George Sand, long past her scandalous youth, lit her fifth cigarette. "My God, I think our girl is serious," she said in response to Sarah's mournful stare.

The guests were mainly men. Madame Guérard, Sarah's motherly companion, who was sitting in a corner with a piece of embroidery, and the lovely Sophie Croisette, one of Sarah's few friends at the Comédie Française, completed the female company. Nelly did not count as a person. By now, she was integrated in the decor like a piece of furniture. She felt uncomfortable, as her arm had grown stiff under the weight of a sheaf of corn. The prune-colored robe she wore had a large opening at the neck and constantly slipped down her shoulders, while the crown of grapes and vine leaves prickled her forehead. The painting was nearing completion and she was looking forward to her release.

The salon, a large elongated room divided in half by two steps, was stuffy due to Sarah's dread of open windows. Her solution for lack of fresh air was to drench the upholstery with heavy perfumes. Equally disconcerting, at least to Nelly, was Sarah's passion for hoarding. Curios and exotic objects cluttered the walls and every available surface. Showy embroidered Chinese dragons crawled across the oversized sofa fabric, while a live parrot perched among tropical foliage. A collection of vases and painted china was in constant danger of breakage by an ever-curious monkey.

The conversation shifted to Sarah's unhappy return to La Comédie Française. She had been fined six thousand francs for breaking her contract with Monsieur de Chilly and already regretted her hasty decision. Instead of her unique status at the Odéon, she now had to share her stardom with other great names.

"And now that I'm back with my honor intact, they treat me like a leper," she was complaining. "They are all a bunch of pompous prigs. Except for dear Sophie, who has always been a true friend. Sophie, tell them what happened yesterday in that solemn cavern they call the green room."

"Oh," said Mademoiselle Croisette, "that was a hoot! It's true that everybody is dreadfully serious even in the green room. When Sarah came in and said that it was a deadly boring place, she was told to leave her rough Odéon manners at the door."

"And I did say," Sarah interrupted her, "did I not, Sophie? I did say, 'Why, I believe I had! Had I kept them, I would have said that this place stinks!' "

Everybody laughed, mainly with relief that she had abandoned the subject of death.

Just as the laughter subsided, the maid came in. "*Maître* Hugo!" she announced.

The door admitted a vigorous elderly man with a close-cut bristling beard, a ruddy complexion and white hair topping a very large forehead. Those who were seated rose and surrounded him, eager to shake his hand. The women giggled with excitement. Sarah discarded her palette and rushed toward him with outstretched arms.

"Dear *Maître*, what a delightful surprise! What brings you here?"

He clasped her hands in his and offered his cheek for a kiss. "I was in the neighborhood and could not leave without calling on my Spanish queen. How are things at the House of Molière, dearest Sarah?"

Instantly, her face clouded and she asked whether he had heard any rumors.

"Nothing worth mentioning," he said. "Keep your head up, *chère amie*. I'm confident that the initial difficulties will subside and you shall triumph again. For all the prestige the company enjoys, it badly needs an injection of excitement and Monsieur Perrin has wisely chosen you. Am I right?" he turned to others.

Murmurs of approval confirmed his speech. Beaming, Sarah offered him refreshment. A cup of tea in hand, he noticed Nelly standing by the canvas.

"What have we here?" he asked.

"Ceres, the Goddess of Earth," Sarah said.

He approached the canvas and studied the painting at length. "It's clear to me that the Comédie Française is unwittingly employing a painter who also acts," he quipped and batted his eyelids as everybody laughed at his *bon mot*. "What made you choose a mythological subject?" he asked Sarah.

"I was inspired by my model's coloring. *Maître*, allow me to introduce Miss Woodridge, who has kindly consented to sit for me."

"*Enchantée*," Nelly croaked. Her throat had become suddenly dry in the proximity of such superior fame.

Maître Hugo took her hand, kissed it, and held it in his grip. "I see the abundance of harvest," he said. "Miss Woodridge's coloring is that of a sultry summer day. Her eyes hold the deep blue of a stormy sky and her hair is a subtle blend of rich soil and ripe wheat. She's also sculptural, as befits a goddess."

Who would not be charmed by such a flowery compliment? Nelly would have warmed to the man had it not been for his eyes glinting with rapacity and malice. Instinct told her that Victor Hugo was a prowling predator. Fortunately, the maid came in again and announced Marshal Canrobert. In the stir caused by the new arrival, Nelly was able to disengage her fingers from *Maître* Hugo's grip without giving offense.

The formidable warrior had been a steady fixture at the gatherings. This time, he was carrying a box. The greetings dispensed with, he offered it to his hostess.

"On my way here, I spotted a charming set of Chinese containers in the antique dealer's window," he said. "They shouted your name and I responded to the call. Add them to your collection, dear Sarah."

Sarah fussed about the present, opened the box and, soon after, four gaily-painted jars passed from hand to hand, generating suitable praise.

"The central medallions represent good luck symbols," the marshal explained. "I was told that the green dragon stands for a long life, the white tiger means good health, the red bird is success, and the yellow dragon a happy family life."

"Pardon me, monsieur," Nelly said, "but I'm afraid that you've been misled."

"How so?"

"The animals represent four of the Five Elements of Taoism. They stand for Wood, Metal, Fire, and Earth. There should also be a black tortoise, the symbol of water. Which means that . . . that the set is . . . incomplete . . ." Nelly's last words ended in a mere whisper because she was surrounded by frosty silence.

Canrobert's face flushed red. "If that's so, I shall return it immediately!" he boomed.

"You will do no such thing, *cher ami*," said Sarah quickly. "The jars are lovely and I'll keep them as a proof of your valued friendship." She turned to Nelly. "Thank you for your enlightening lecture, Miss Woodridge. As the daylight is fading, I shall tire you no longer."

Everyone began to talk at once, a string of banalities to mask the faux pas. The company split into chattering groups and Nelly retired behind a screen, swearing to herself that she would never open her mouth again. What a good thing that Octave was not around to witness the scene! She would never have heard the end of it. Hastily, she removed the robe and struggled into her corset. Her fingers groped for the strings at the back only to find that someone was already holding them.

"Allow me to help you, beauteous goddess."

She blocked her shriek of surprise in time. The last thing she wanted was yet another public embarrassment. How did *Maître* Hugo manage to creep behind the screen without anyone noticing?

The old reprobate giggled mischievously. "Don't be shy, nobody's looking," he whispered. He wrapped an arm around her waist, while his free hand crept into the opening of her chemise. "What are you doing tonight, Your Divinity?" he asked. "Why don't we ascend Olympus together?"

Her disbelief turned into anger. National treasure or not, she pushed him away. It was not her fault that his foot caught in the folds of the discarded robe and he fell on the screen, which went crashing down with a thunderous noise.

Even the most distinguished people look grotesque when they are astonished. For a couple of seconds that seemed like an hour, Nelly stared at the show of dropped jaws and bulging eyes. Then she remembered her half-nakedness, grabbed her clothes, and fled by the back door to the adjoining room, which happened to be Sarah's boudoir. She threw on her dress and was feverishly hooking up the bodice, when Sarah barged in.

"Have you lost your mind?" she asked, her voice an angry whisper. "So he was perhaps a little fresh with you, but that does not entitle you to excessive violence. Such barbaric manners have no place among civilized people."

"He's a dirty old man."

Sarah stepped close to her, so close that Nelly had to step back. "How dare you?" she hissed into her face. "How dare you speak thus of a genius! He's up in the sky," her hand pointed toward the ceiling, "soaring with eagles, while you are nothing, nothing at all . . . you . . . you pedestrian hen!"

This was too much for a day. "And this pedestrian hen says to hell with you all!" Nelly exploded. She spotted another door and ran through it. Her combs and hairpins remained back in the salon.

Once Nelly reached home, she fell into Célestine's comforting arms and sobbed the story to her. What would Octave say when he heard of the scandal she caused? Would Sarah be angry with him as well, to the point of taking her custom elsewhere?

Célestine led her to the sofa, stuffed a pillow under her head and dispatched Julie for a cold compress and a cup of chamomile infusion. She installed herself at Nelly's side and took her hand in hers.

"Don't fret about it," she said. "It was not your fault at all. That man has a reputation for womanizing that goes way back. Years ago, it may be twenty or more, when Louis Philippe was the king, Monsieur Hugo had an affair with a painter's wife. The husband had them followed and they were arrested *in flagrante*. Monsieur Hugo was then a great friend of His Majesty and had just been made a peer of France. You should've seen what the newspapers made of it! They talked of nothing else. Now that was something I'd call a true scandal. As for the actress, I wouldn't worry. The master strikes me as someone who's capable of looking after himself."

Nelly blew into a handkerchief and smiled through her tears. Dear, dear Célestine! What would she do without her soothing presence? She must buy her a set of dentures and a length of fabric for a new dress because the one she had on was already bursting at the seams. She seemed to gain weight every day.

They heard the main door opening.

"It's him," Célestine whispered. "Quick! Wipe your eyes and try to look calm. Don't tell him anything right now. Men are mellower after dinner."

As soon as Nelly saw Octave, she was sure that he already knew. "Good evening, dear," she piped.

He ignored her. "What's for dinner?" he asked Célestine.

The cook muttered something about mussels in wine sauce followed by a stew with mushrooms.

"Then why are you not in the kitchen?" Octave thundered. "You seem to spend more time in the sitting room than with your pots and pans. I hired a cook, not a lady's companion. Be gone!"

He waited until Célestine scurried away and then threw a loosely wrapped object on the table. "Your hat and hairpins. With Sarah's compliments. So, what do you have to say for yourself?"

"It was not my fault."

"Are you saying that having publicly embarrassed a Marshal of France was not your fault either?" He removed a bottle of liquor from the cabinet and poured a double dose into a glass.

"God, I needed that," he said after swallowing the drink. "What a day! As if the business was not bad enough, now that the days are getting shorter and there's no daylight to speak of. I left early, thinking that I would stop at Sarah's to see what's new and take you for an aperitif. Little did I know. The first thing I see when I turn into the rue de Rome is Victor Hugo, his nose buried in a bloodied handkerchief, climbing into his carriage. On the stairs, I encounter Clairin, Meyer, and de Montesquiou, choking with laughter. When I inquired about the source of their levity, I was told that Sarah would tell me all about it. And that she did! According to her, you are a walking disaster and I should keep you under lock and key."

He added that tongues were already wagging, and soon the story would be all over the town. The official version was that the *maître* was looking for a water closet, lost his way, and tripped in the dark. Of course, nobody would believe it. Only God knew what the rumor mill would make out of it. The distinguished laureate having been brutally attacked by an American Amazon!

"But that's an awful lie!" she exclaimed.

"That's of no consequence. Once a rumor gets going, there is no stopping it. It feeds on itself and grows."

She brushed moisture from her cheeks. "Are you not in the least concerned with what has been done to me?"

"Well, I didn't mean to be cruel, kitten," Octave said apologetically. He sat at her side, and squeezed her shoulders. "It's true that the old tomcat deserved it. Women keep falling into his arms and he considers himself irresistible. No, I don't approve of his behavior. Nevertheless, don't cross his path again. You've made a powerful enemy."

"Is Sarah mad at you because of me?" she asked. "Will she cancel her appearance at the exposition?"

"She was upset, but she knows better than that. After all, she'll take her cut in the sale of her portraits. On the contrary, I'm to portray her standing by the painting and display the photograph. We may as well cash in on the curious."

Later that night, Nelly wrote: *Dear diary, it takes a far more crooked brain than mine to understand the twists and turns of the world, but I'm learning!*

Chapter 25

"It looks like we are going to have snow," said Félicie Perrichon, glancing anxiously at the leaden sky suspended above the kitchen windows. "It means scraping the sidewalk, on top of my other duties. And today I still have to scrub the stairs. It's a hard life, Madame Célestine. Too much to do for an aging woman.—This coffee is so tasty I wouldn't mind another cup."

"It's the Dark Columbian," said Célestine, filling Félicie's cup. "The master will have nothing else."

Félicie eased her thin buttocks against the wooden seat. She really should go and wash the stairs if only she could gather enough will. It felt so good to idle by the crackling fire, sipping a cup of strong coffee and nibbling on walnut cake. Yet she could hardly contain her resentment. The old hag who had wandered in from the street had done well for herself in just a few short weeks. Look at her: new dress, dentures shining like piano keys and dispensing coffee and cake as if she were sitting in her own bloody salon! A cunning creature she was and no mistake. Disdaining the cot in the kitchen alcove, she had claimed Julie's room for herself on account of her age and Miss Woodridge agreed with her. However, there was nothing to be gained by making a sour face.

"There's something I wanted to ask you and it's not for Julie's ears, which is why I've sent her to the grocery," Célestine said.

"Is it about our Julie?"

"No, it's the Miss. She keeps a framed likeness of a fair-haired woman in the bottom drawer of her dresser. She showed it to me and asked me whether I could tell when the photograph was taken."

"And you could?"

"Without a doubt. That woman had a hat on with no veil at the back to cover her neck, so the picture couldn't have been older than eight years.

Remember when Madame Worth and Princess Metternich went to the races wearing those first high-perched hats and the back of their necks naked? Surely, you must have read about it in the papers? - Oh, you don't read newspapers. Well, they couldn't have been more criticized had they dared to smoke in public. That was in sixty-three and the reason I remember it so precisely is that it was the year my husband hired a cook from Provence. Actually, it wasn't until the empress herself sported a similar hat that everybody rushed out to buy them. And that was at least six months later. So I told that to Miss and she made a face and said 'Oh, that's why!' "

"She said, 'that's why'?"

"That's what she said. I would like to know what it was about. The reason I'm asking you is that you've known her longer. Do you have any idea what she meant by it?"

The concierge frowned, gathering her thoughts. "I think it has something to do with a former friend of hers," she said. "A certain Madame Babeau, who used to live in the neighborhood. She and Miss used to get on like a house afire and then, suddenly, there was a break. I haven't got much else to tell you for you know how hard it is to squeeze anything out of our Julie. A regular clam she is. But I remember that Miss took it very badly. She looked like a ghost for days."

"But what does it have to do with the photograph? Whose likeness is it?"

"Miss had told me that it was her mother's. She had the pictures of her parents displayed above the fireplace and then, around the time of the break, they vanished."

"Is that so? How interesting."

"What's even more so," the concierge said, exchanging resentment for the pleasure of gossip, "is that no one saw Madame Babeau after that except when she and her husband moved out at the end of their quarter lease. Clothilde Marceau, who is the concierge in that house, told me that they had to carry the poor woman down the stairs and into the moving wagon because she could no longer use her legs. There was a rumor that she wasn't right in her head. If that isn't odd, then what is?"

"That's very strange," Célestine agreed.

"An even stranger thing happened to our Julie the day before you arrived here. She received a telegram that her mother was gravely ill. She asked Miss for permission to go home—so scared she was, the poor child—but when she arrived to Roubaix, she found her mother in good health. No one sent a telegram from Roubaix, that's for sure. They live from hand to mouth. Where would they find money for such luxury? I forbade Julie to mention that to

Miss. Better to pretend that there was an illness than to make her think that we had orchestrated a deceit."

"That's terrible! Who would play such a cruel joke?" exclaimed Célestine a little too loudly. "Well, at least Julie had a short vacation. More cake?" She pushed the serving plate toward the concierge but Félicie's attention was already engaged elsewhere.

"Now look at that," she said. "I was right after all."

"What?"

"The snow. It's coming down thick. I'd better go and tackle the stairs. It was nice talking to you, Madame Célestine."

* * *

Nelly had not noticed the first snowflakes. She stared at the lovely square she had discovered by chance. By now she was used to awesome architecture but there was something unique and deeply attractive about the graceful arcades supporting identical four-story brick-and-stone pavilions, nine on each side of the square, all of them crowned with tall slate roofs. In all her forays into the city, she had never found a place of such serene beauty.

Schnitzel's frenzied barking spoiled the effect. A woman shrieked with fright and squeezed a whimpering lapdog in her arms.

"I beg your pardon," Nelly said, struggling with the leash. "Schnitzel, be quiet!"

"Such dangerous dogs should not be allowed in public places," said the woman's companion sternly. The pair left in a huff, exchanging disdainful remarks.

"An interesting specimen," said a deep voice in English.

Nelly turned. At first, all she could see was the man's broad chest enveloped in a worn overcoat. As her gaze traveled upwards, she discovered a smiling face lost in an incredible amount of light brown hair, which escaped from under a top hat, fanned over the shoulders and, on the face, sprouted into a beard two shades lighter. There was hardly any room left for a strong nose, topped with a pair of glasses. The amber eyes behind them somehow managed to look both sharp and warm.

"A puzzling amalgam of British breeds," the giant said. "The ears of an Airedale, the chest of a mastiff, the bark of a pit bull. Was the dog brought here from across the Channel?"

As if displeased with the recital of his various borrowed parts, Schnitzel bared his teeth and emitted a warning growl. The man shot him a stern look and extended a finger.

"Hush!" he ordered.

Schnitzel fell silent. For a brief moment, he considered his options and then retreated behind the shield of his mistress' skirts.

"And I would throw in an Irish setter for cowardice," the man added.

"Oh . . . I . . ." Nelly stammered, embarrassed to be found out. Schnitzel's lack of courage was a closely guarded secret, known, she hoped, only to Octave, who had turned it into a series of irritating jokes. "Are you a dog breeder?" she asked.

"No, I'm not. I saw you admiring the square."

"It's lovely. What is it called?"

"Place des Vosges."

"I have never seen anything so . . ." she searched for the right word.

"Harmonious? The secret of its beauty is based on mathematics. You see, the height of the façades is equal to their width and the height of the roofs is half that of the façades. When they completed the place, it used to be the finest in Paris."

"Are you a tourist guide?"

"No, I'm not. Am I boring you?"

"Not at all," she said quickly. "It's very interesting."

"Well then," he cupped her elbow and led her closer to the central park, "I should add that the square was built to hold the royal festivities. The wedding of Louis XIII and Anne of Austria was celebrated here." He made a broad gesture encompassing the whole. "Imagine splendid horses, dashing cavaliers, polished shields, feathers and jewels, silken banners, the roll of drums and the blare of trumpets. There were a hundred and fifty musicians, ten thousand cheering spectators and, to top it all off, a display of fireworks."

"Oh." Her imagination was working at full speed. "I wish I could have been here. Are you a historian?"

He smiled. "No, I'm not. I just happen to know such things." The snow was coming down wet and heavy. He flicked the white flakes from his beard. "I think we should part before we change into snowmen."

"A thick snow, indeed. Thank you for the interesting lecture, monsieur."

He reached for his hat. "My pleasure, entirely."

Something struck her as odd. "How did you know I spoke English? Because of my dog?"

"That, plus the fact that no elegant Frenchwoman would have the pluck to be seen with such a canine specimen. Original and admirable. I wish you a good day, madam."

Nelly felt exhilarated by the encounter. The friendly stranger had treated her without the syrupy gallantry with which other men addressed her. It was refreshing to be spoken to as a human being without the creeping undercurrent of sex. She glanced back at Schnitzel, strutting behind her. An amalgam of British breeds? How odd!

The brisk walk across the bridge had flushed her cheeks and stimulated her appetite. It was time for lunch. At the door, she did not have time to shake the snow from her fur-lined cape. Schnitzel, ravenous as well, charged up the stairs, dragging her along. They almost knocked over a pail of sudsy water as they brushed against the concierge, who stood by the rail, straining her neck upward.

"There seems to be some trouble upstairs," she said as they were passing. "A gentleman."

Nelly became aware of the raised voices on the floor above.

"The maid has told you that Miss Woodridge is not at home," Célestine was saying.

"And I repeat that I will not budge from here until I've spoken to her."

Nelly let go of the leash and Schnitzel, propelled by the vision of a lunch bowl, shot up the stairs past the irate visitor and into the door.

"Monsieur?" Nelly said.

"Are you Miss Woodridge?"

"I'm she. What can I do for you, Monsieur . . . ?"

"Bonnard. Charles Bonnard," the man said. "I'm here to discuss a serious matter."

Intimidated by his frowning face, she took the last steps warily. At least sixty, dressed in a dapper overcoat with a brown fur collar, the man did not look like a plain-clothes policeman. Yet he stared at her as if she had done something wrong.

"Let the gentleman in," she said to Célestine.

"Why did you want to see me?" she asked in the hall, as she passed her hat and cape to Julie.

"What I have to say is of a private nature," the boorish man said.

Nelly led him into the sitting room and indicated a chair. When they were seated across from each other, he took a careful look around. "A comfortable setup," he commented. "Still, it's not enough, is it?"

She grew impatient. "Kindly state your business, monsieur!"

"Don't act as if my name meant nothing to you."

"It means nothing to me, indeed."

The wrinkles on his forehead rearranged themselves into an expression of doubt. "I don't know what game you are playing, madam, but I'm here to tell you that it's over.—No! Don't say a word until I'm finished. I had you privately investigated and I know who you are. An opportunist of the lowest nature. But, as we speak, my son is on his way to South America and you'll never see him again."

"Your son?"

"Adolphe Bonnard, in case you don't remember. An impressionable seventeen-year old boy, whom you have ensnared and perverted."

"I never . . . Oh, my God!" she sucked in her breath.

"Ah! I see that you have recovered your memory."

"It was only a childish prank, monsieur."

"A childish prank that has ended in my son's emptying my safe and trying to run away with you."

"I beg your pardon?"

The visitor's face flushed red with anger. "I'm doing you a favor by dealing with the matter without the help of the police. There's no need to drag my good name through the mud as long as you promise not to answer my son's letters and not to encourage him in any way."

"But I never did!" Nelly exclaimed. "I've never answered his letters. That is, I never took them seriously. I'm deeply sorry for what has happened. It has never been my intention." She rubbed her palms together. "You see, I . . . we . . . a friend of mine . . . we used to tease the schoolboys from the window. But it was just for laughs, nothing serious. Then I got poems and some amorous scribbling—"

"Do you still have them?"

"I kept throwing them out. I did not even bother to open the last ones. Wait, I may still have one. I remember dropping it into the waste basket."

She sprang on her feet and rummaged among the debris. "Thank God, here it is," she retrieved an envelope from under orange peels. "As you see, it's still sealed."

Bonnard tore at the envelope and scanned the contents. "The fool! Young, silly, obsessed fool," he muttered. "Marriage . . . America . . . Meet me in Le Havre . . ."

"Impossible," Nelly said. "I already told you I never answered his letters. I thought that if I kept ignoring them they'd stop coming. I don't even know how your son got my name. He must have bribed the concierge."

He folded the missive and inserted it back into the envelope. "How much?" he asked. "Name your price for the letter. I don't intend to bargain."

"I don't want your money," Nelly said, offended. "I may not be respectable but I'm not that sort of a woman. I'm truly sorry for what happened. Please, take the letter. I'm giving it to you."

Bonnard remained silent for a while. "I was wrong," he said. "I believe that you are sincere." He pocketed the envelope and rose. "I apologize for having disturbed you, madam." He passed his hand across his sweating forehead. "I was very upset. You must understand that he's my only son. The last of my sons, the only future I have." He covered his eyes and fell back into the chair. His shoulders shook with silent sobs.

A wave of guilt washed over her. Now that he had broken down, she saw him for what he was: a bereaved father overwhelmed with anxiety. She went to the cabinet and poured a glass of calvados.

"Please drink this," she said, nudging him in the shoulder.

He shook his head, pulled a handkerchief from his pocket and dried his eyes.

"It will do you good," she urged.

After a short hesitation, he reached for the glass. "Thank you. I'm ashamed of this unexpected display of emotion." Again, his hand went to his forehead that glistened with perspiration.

"You should remove your coat."

"No. I will not bother you any longer," he said, rising. "You've been very patient."

"I must insist. If you go out now, you'll catch your death. Please take off your coat and allow yourself to cool down. Here," she extended her arm and waited.

He attempted a smile. "You don't take no for an answer," he said while handing her his overcoat.

Nelly folded the garment over a chair. "It's for your own good."

"You sound like my wife."

"I apologize. I did not mean to—"

"I'm not offended." He sat down, his back bent, hands resting on his knees. "She passed away last year."

"I'm sorry."

"The poor woman died of a broken heart. She never got over the death of our eldest son. Four children and none alive but Adolphe."

Nelly's heart went out to him. "Oh," she said. "How tragic!"

"That boy has always been a source of worry. He has a fragile nervous constitution. It comes from my wife's side of the family. He was to go to the Law School but it's not going to be. I own a shipping company up north in Dieppe, with offices in Africa and South America. I hope he'll do well in Rio de Janeiro. Work will make a man of him."

"I wish him well, monsieur."

"You've been very kind." He consulted his watch. "If I go now, I'll be able to catch the two o'clock train."

Nelly helped him into his coat and saw him to the door. He bent over her hand. "I came here with hostile feelings," he said, holding her fingers longer than necessary. "I leave reassured. You are not at all as I had imagined you, Miss Woodridge."

Chapter 26

"Lower!" Octave shouted at Bébert to make himself heard above the noise of hammering. "At eye-level, I said! What? You should know by now what the average eye-level is! — What is it?" He turned to a deliveryman, who had tapped his shoulder.

"It's the palm trees, governor. Where do you want them?"

Nelly drifted aimlessly through the gallery, stepping around empty cases, staying out of the way of the carpenter with his hammer and the charwoman sweeping up scattered wood shavings. She had come in the belief that she would be able to visit the exposition before the opening, unseen and undisturbed. Under the circumstances, she had to rely mostly on her imagination.

One of the rooms was entirely reserved for Sarah's portraits in her various theatrical incarnations and in her chic civil clothes: standing, sitting, reclining, smiling, brooding, dreaming, holding a bouquet of lilies, clutching a book of poems, embracing her dog, plucking the strings of a mandolin, sculpting, painting. Copies mounted on cardboard, as well as a choice of pretty frames, would be on sale in the reception room. The bulk of Octave's artwork was to cover the walls of the largest room, where a red velvet panel, fixed in the center of a wall, would showcase the *Morning Breeze.*

The photograph stood propped against the wall, ready to be hung. Of the largest cabinet size, it was amplified by a wide buff mat and a gilded frame. She had to admit that it was breathtaking. 'Like an angel on the verge of flying,' Octave had said. When she saw the picture for the first time, she was shocked by how much it revealed despite the opaque fabric of the wrap. Yet it was art and art required boldness.

"I've been calling you." Octave stood behind her, buttoning his overcoat. "Let's go! I'm starving."

They found a bistro on the boulevard des Italiens and ordered beef stewed in wine sauce, and crepes for dessert. Octave ate distractedly, his mind preoccupied with a multitude of details.

"Why don't you relax a little?" Nelly asked. "If you go on shoveling your lunch in like this, you'll get indigestion."

"I've to be back at two."

"It's barely quarter past one."

"If the sales counter is not delivered on time, I'll have to—"

"It is probably on its way." She put down her fork and stroked his hand. "Ease up and enjoy the meal."

"Easier said than done."

"We simply have to change the subject. Listen, I'll tell you something interesting. Did you know that Schnitzel could possibly be English?"

"How so?"

She told him about the encounter in the old square. "A most peculiar person," she added. "He talked like a professor and looked like a caveman. If there's ever been such a thing as a caveman with a pair of glasses," she giggled. "The hair! I've never seen such wild hair."

"Tall? Deep voice?"

"Yes, that's right! How do you know?"

Octave laughed and eased his back against the chair. "Why, that was Henri. Oh, the dark horse! I bet he knew who you were and was toying with you. It's hard to mistake you for another with Schnitzel at your side. And, of course, he had seen the *Morning Breeze*. Well, well, well," he chuckled. "Who would have thought it of good old Henri? Usually, he has no time for women. Curiosity, I suppose. As for the caveman, you'd be surprised. Henri d'Auzon, Count de Villermaine. He's inherited the title from his maternal uncle who died a bachelor."

"I always thought that aristocrats took good care of their appearance. Why doesn't he do something about his hair and that awful beard?"

"He calls it the socialist style and wears it mainly because it drives his father mad. They loathe each other."

"That's not very nice! Why?"

"Because General d'Auzon is a bonehead. The d'Auzons come from a line of military men and Henri has spoiled it by turning into a scholar. There's been a lot of friction as far as I can remember. But the worst thing—and Henri will never forgive his father for it—was that he made him marry a first cousin. Inbreeding can result in a disaster and, in this case, it did. My father delivered the child. He said he had never seen such a thing. The poor mite's blood seeped from all its pores. It looked like a piece of raw meat."

Nelly pushed away her plate of crepes. "How dreadful! Did the baby die?"

"It did, and so did the marriage. The wife turned to religion and Henri went as far away as he could. He was gone for almost ten years. First America, then the Far Orient."

"Have you known him for a long time?"

"Since I was about nine. The château is only two miles away from Yvetot and my father is the closest doctor. There was an epidemic of measles. We both fell ill, Henri and I. The recovery from measles seems endless as the patient has to stay in a darkened room because daylight hurts the eyes. A tough thing for a lonely boy. When Henri was about to climb the walls, my father suggested that since we were both the same age, we should keep each other company. I definitely liked the idea. Two weeks in a château, waited on hand and foot, and best of all, free of the smothering attentions of my sisters. It was then that we started to play chess and, amazingly, we're still at it. Actually, the chess is only a pretext. Henri is the closest thing I have to a brother." He reached for his watch. "What time is it? We should hurry up."

When they left the restaurant, it was snowing again. Nelly tightened her sable collar against the lashing wind.

"Have you come on foot?" Octave asked.

She nodded.

"I'll call a cab for you."

On the boulevard, he tried to stop a couple of vehicles, but none were free.

"You know, I have an idea," she said. "Do you think that your friend would come to dinner? Célestine could make something special."

"Henri?" Octave frowned and shook his head. "No, I don't think it's a good idea."

"Why not? I never thanked him for his help with Julie."

"I've already done it for you."

"But I also want to discuss the manuscript with him. It's strange that he's never asked to meet me."

"He approved the pages I had shown him. You're doing just fine. Enough of Henri!"

The harsh tone surprised her. "What's the matter with you? Are you jealous?"

"I'm pressed for time."

"Then go!" she snapped. "I don't need your assistance."

"Now, now, kitten. Let's not part like this," Octave wrapped an arm around her shoulder and kissed the tip of her nose. "I've been too busy, but that will change after the opening. In fact, I'll come tomorrow after the reception and spend the night. Look, here comes an empty cab."

* * *

Célestine greeted Nelly with a smug smile. "There's something for you in the sitting room. Let me show you."

"What a gorgeous bouquet!" Nelly exclaimed on the threshold.

"Two dozen hothouse lilacs, no less. I used to sell them at five francs a stem."

"But that's awfully expensive! It's nice of him but he shouldn't commit such follies."

"It doesn't look like Monsieur's doing, if you pardon my frankness," Célestine said. "There's a sealed envelope in the bouquet."

The envelope contained a calling card. Nelly's hand dropped with disappointment. "It's from the old gentleman who was here yesterday."

"The one with the shipping company?"

"Célestine! You were listening at the door."

"It was my duty, Miss. The man looked as if he wanted to tear you into pieces. I thought it wise to be on hand, just in case. What does he say?"

"Please accept this bouquet as a token of my appreciation for your integrity," Nelly read. "That's thoughtful."

"Thoughtful, thoughtful," Célestine grumbled. "At this price, it's cheap. I bet he'd have gone up to five hundred francs to get the letter. Why, even one thousand is too little for a letter that contains a promise of marriage."

"Célestine, you should be ashamed of yourself. You are so mercenary."

"Pardon me, Miss, but that's the wrong way to think. Money doesn't grow on trees. A woman in your position, with no ring on her finger, should grab as much as she can while young. It is all right to be magnanimous when one has money in the bank. If not, it's plain foolish."

"That's enough, Célestine."

Célestine shrugged and went to the door. She paused at the threshold. "Would Miss want to keep the bouquet in the sitting room?" she asked formally.

"Yes, why not?"

"It's none of my business, of course, but what will Miss say to Monsieur when he asks how she came by it?"

"Oh my, I didn't think of that."

Célestine smiled sweetly, curtseyed, and closed the door behind her.

* * *

181

"It's strange," Octave said, as he sat at the breakfast table. "I would have sworn I have caught a whiff of fresh lilacs on my way to the bathroom. Lilacs in December?"

"It's my new soap, monsieur," said Célestine quickly. "I keep it in my room."

"Why, Célestine, you are turning into a coquette," Octave said. "And a plump one at that! Since you've been here, you've shed ten years." He was in an excellent mood.

"Monsieur is too good."

"Is Julie back with the newspapers?"

"Not yet, but I'll send her here as soon as she's through the door. Will there be anything else?"

"I don't see the raspberry preserve."

"You had the last of it," Nelly said. "Remember?"

"So I had. Time to go home for provisions. It's all right, Célestine, you may go."

He spread a generous amount of black currant jelly on his brioche. "Over one hundred copies sold in the first two hours following the opening," he said, with his mouth full. "Close to three hundred by closing time. If this goes on, I'll break even within the first week and the other two will be clear profit."

"Which ones sell the best?" Nelly had heard it all when he came to her at midnight, tipsy and triumphant, following the reception at a restaurant, but she wanted to give him the opportunity to gloat again.

"The *Morning Breeze* by far. So much so, that it has made Sarah jealous. Did I tell you that a manufacturer expressed an interest in buying the negative? I'll not sell unless he guarantees five thousand copies and fifteen percent royalties. We are to discuss the details over dinner. That manufacturer, a certain Monsieur Quérat, seems to be very taken with your image. It's possible that he'll also buy Sarah's painting. In any case, Sarah told me that he's to see it in the afternoon. A busy beaver, this Quérat. Can you pass me the sugar?"

"Here."

"Come to think of it, should he buy Ceres, it would be the first sale of a painting based on a photograph. A newsworthy event."

"I'm glad for you." That her face and the rest of her could be reproduced five thousand times was news to her. Octave did not mention it last night. Should Honoré de Chazelle, the crook and murderer, ever come across the picture, he'd know where to find her. Revenge was a possibility. Had Octave thought of that?

"What is it, kitten? You don't look pleased."

"It's nothing." Let him enjoy his triumph. What were the chances that an outlaw in hiding would ever see the photograph? He was probably as far from France as he could get. It was time to shake off her fear.

"I know what it is! Come here," Octave patted his knee.

Nelly slid onto his lap and into his embrace. "You think that I don't appreciate your part in this, is that it?" he asked. "You are wrong, kitten. Your Octave knows that you've brought him luck. I'll show you how grateful I am, I promise. Let's—"

A timid cough interrupted him. "It's the newspapers, monsieur," said Julie, who entered unobserved. Nelly never thought that the day would come when she would want to strangle the girl. He had almost said it. *Let's get married.* At last!

"At last!" Octave exclaimed. "Have you brought Le Figaro?"

"Yes, monsieur."

"L'Intransigent? Le Gaulois? L'Echo de Paris?"

"They're all here." She passed him the bundle and left in a hurry.

"We'll talk later, kitten," Octave said. He pushed Nelly away and eagerly opened the first newspaper. The pages rustled furiously as he searched for the art column.

She resumed her seat with resignation and began to butter a brioche she had no desire to eat. It was just something to do.

"Listen to this! A decidedly new approach to photography. Monsieur Gaillard proves that the medium is not a mere reflection of reality . . ."

"That's wonderful." With a fork, Nelly carved a series of wavy lines in the butter.

He scanned the papers, one by one, quoting aloud choice bits. She turned the brioche and drew more lines across, creating a checkered pattern. It was not until the silence grew deadly that she realized something was wrong. She looked up from her artwork. Octave's face was livid.

"What is it, dear?"

He crushed the issue of Le Gaulois he had been reading. "This is the last straw," he said flatly. "I'll kill the bloody bastard."

The obscenity shocked her but what alarmed her most was his cold anger. His lips tightly pressed together, Octave rose from the table and untied the belt of his dressing gown.

"Where are you going?"

"Out."

"Why now? You haven't finished your breakfast."

"Leave me alone!"

She followed him into the bedroom. "Octave, what is it? You are making me nervous."

"I said leave me alone!"

For a while, she watched him helplessly as he dressed, then ran back to the table, and flattened the crumpled newspaper.

MORNING BREEZE THINLY DISGUISED PORNOGRAPHY
By Alfred Toussaint

Much had been said yesterday at the opening of Octave Gaillard's exposition of photographic work at the Gallery Serrault, boulevard des Italiens. The air vibrated with expressions such as "bold approach", "innovative use", and "dramatic lighting." Having heard it all before, we are no longer shocked by Photography posturing as Art. At the most, we feel a touch of ennui and a vague irritation - sentiments that are provoked by utter insipidness.

Mr. Gaillard's "*Morning Breeze*" is an exception as it introduces the element of sensuality, which allows the photographer to emerge from the sea of nothingness, if only to the level of his earlobes. That he has a remarkable skill in portraying the female body I cannot deny. For years, he has been specializing in nude studies as an affordable substitute for live models. Officially intended for painters and sculptors, the major overflow of Mr. Gaillard's production has been discreetly peddled under the street lamps and in the dark corners of cafés. No longer satisfied with obscure notoriety, the photographer has decided to make such filth public. To pay his due to decency, he dresses his model in cambric and lace while, cunningly, he allows the wind to reveal her nudity. Should a less perceptive visitor mistake the image for an expression of simple joie-de-vivre, Mr. Gaillard brings to attention a man's jacket with a wilted carnation in the buttonhole. It is regrettable that he did not go to the limit of his boldness where the title is concerned. I suggest "Mademoiselle Fifi Airing the Bedroom after a Steamy Night."

As for the rest of Mr. Gaillard's "art", it is largely forgettable, although I should mention the Sarah Bernhardt Gallery in the last room, where amateurs of La Divine will be satisfied to see her portrayed from every imaginable angle and, eventually, take her home wrapped in paper tissue tied with a ribbon.

Should my readers decide to visit this exposition, I advise strongly that they leave their daughters at home.

Shocked, Nelly did not even notice the bang of the main door when Octave left.

Chapter 27

Dear diary, it is three o'clock in the morning and this is my second sleepless night. It seems that I have been sentenced to finding neither appetite nor sleep again. I may as well couch my thoughts on your tolerant pages, for you are the only indulgence God is granting me at present.

Lately, I have not been paying much attention to my gradual descent into filth, but here I am, at the very bottom, and it was printed in the newspaper for everyone to see. I will skip over the day when Octave left me without any explanation or even a word of goodbye. I spent it locked up in a darkened bedroom. Yesterday, I heard excited murmurs in the sitting room. Shortly after, Célestine knocked vigorously at the door, saying that Monsieur Goubert was there, that he had important news, and—for the love of Jesus Our Savior—would I come out of my hiding at once?

I opened the door a crack. They stood there with grave faces. Monsieur Goubert told me that Octave had been grievously wounded. He handed me an evening edition and I saw the headline ART CRITIQUE LEADS TO DUEL. I attempted to read the small print but it started to dance before my eyes. The first thing that brought me back to reality was the sharp stench of smelling salts, which Célestine held under my nose. Despite many protests, I dressed and rushed to Octave's side.

I was shivering with cold fright when I entered the building, realizing that, shortly, I might hear the worst news ever. Was he still alive? Dear God in heaven, just let him live, I prayed.

As I passed the concierge's loge, Mother Laforge recognized me and barred my way. "What are you doing here?" she said. "You can't go up. His family's there."

I pushed her away and ran up the stairs while she followed on my heels, urging me to turn back. I plunged into the door of Octave's apartment and

185

closed it against her. The sitting room was full of people, at least ten of them, all grave and silent except for a sobbing young woman. An elderly couple stood in the bedroom door and I knew instantly that they were his parents.

"What's going on? Who are you, mademoiselle?" the father asked.

"A friend," I said. It is true that I hesitated slightly before identifying myself, which was enough for a young man in the Polytechnic School uniform to turn to the others and say, "Probably a mistress."

The mother covered her mouth in a shocked surprise. "Émile, I'm asking you to watch your mouth," she said indignantly. "There is an unmarried girl here."

"Is he alive?" I wanted to know. Everything else was unimportant.

The father said that his son would probably live, and would I, for the sake of decency, leave the premises at once.

Finding Henri d'Auzon was surprisingly simple. I had intended to search all the cafés in the rue Sommerard but the first one happened to be the place I was looking for. Yes, they knew Monsieur d'Auzon. The patron called an errand boy and asked him to remember where he had carried Monsieur d'Auzon's books a couple of weeks ago. A dignified valet opened the door. He gave me a once over and said that Monsieur was working and must not be disturbed under any pretext. I said that it was a question of life and death. He pondered that for a while and allowed me to wait in the salon, which reminded me somewhat of Sarah's, except that it was smaller, and the clutter consisted of books and exotic artifacts.

Henri d'Auzon wore a dressing gown over his shirt and pants. He asked what he could do for me and then, as he came closer, his smile vanished. "What happened?" he asked. "Have you been attacked?"

I touched my head and realized that half of my hastily knotted hair had collapsed and, consequently, my hat sat askew. I must have looked like a scarecrow. "You don't know about Octave?" I asked.

He said that he did not and would I please tell him, which I did. He sat down heavily, without saying a word. When he revived, he said that Octave knew exactly what he, d'Auzon, thought of duels and therefore did not tell him beforehand. Moreover, that it was an irony that such a moronic ritual was still performed in a country which prided itself in carrying the torch of enlightenment. Then he got up and rang for the valet to bring his jacket and overcoat. As he was dressing, he wanted to know more about the cause of the duel. I told him all, including the treatment I received from Octave's family. I trusted that he would not despise me as much as they did.

"Let's not concern ourselves with moral matters," he said. "I'll find out what's wrong with Octave and tell you."

He confided in me that he was catching up with a deadline and had no time to read newspapers. Except for that, we walked in silence the few blocks that separated us from the boulevard Saint-Germain. I waited for him in a café, drinking a cup of strong coffee and counting the minutes. He came back after half an hour, saying that he had to sit with the family and could not have possibly escaped any sooner.

"How is he?" I asked.

"Not as bad as the newspaper made it look. He's been shot just below the right shoulder. He's been weakened by the loss of blood."

I asked him whether he had been able to talk to Octave alone.

"Only for about five minutes."

"What did he say?"

"As regards you? He has left letters with a notary to be delivered in the event of his death. There is one for you as well, detailing the provisions he has made for you. I'm to tell you not to worry, that should infection set in and cut his life short, the letter contains the deeds to the apartment and a bank draft for five thousand francs."

He shook his head when I asked him whether Octave had offered any personal sentiment. "No, I'm afraid not. He tires easily and his parents kept looking in every once in a while."

I had to be content with that. As it turned out, I will not see him when his family is gone because his parents have decided to take him home when he is able to travel. I'm settling in for a long and agonizing wait.

Chapter 28

Octave was never far from her thoughts and the smallest detail would trigger a dull pain in Nelly's chest: finding his hair on the pillow, his handkerchief, discovered in the batch the laundress had delivered two days after the duel, a pair of kid gloves that missed a button. Once, when she stood by the bedroom window, she felt his arm around her waist. She knew it was only her imagination but the feeling was so real that her knees weakened with longing.

She worked long hours, grateful for the opportunity to occupy her mind. At eight hundred and five pages, the manuscript was nearing completion. Another thirty and she would be done. By now, she knew d'Auzon's hurried handwriting like her own - all the shortcuts of a mind racing ahead of the hand that transcribed ideas into words. Leaning over her work, she was dipping her pen into the inkwell when she heard the doorbell. Instantly, her back stiffened. Henri d'Auzon had promised that he would go to Yvetot at the earliest opportunity and inform her of Octave's progress. Could it be a message from him? If so, was it bad news? She sat frozen with apprehension, listening to Julie's steps, the sound of the main door opening, and the muffled sound of voices.

The visitor was a doe-eyed young fellow with curly hair, sporting a short beard that had probably originated from the desire to look older. With the visit of Monsieur Bonnard still fresh in her mind, she was on her guard.

"Monsieur?" she asked warily.

"Claude Savatier, mademoiselle."

"My maid said that you have a letter for me."

"Into your hands only."

She unfolded a sheet torn from a notebook.

Nelly, for the sake of our past friendship, please help me! Listen to what M. Savatier has to say. Yours, more desperate than ever,
  Géraldine Babeau.

"Please take off your coat, Monsieur Savatier."

"I will start at the beginning," Savatier said when they were seated. "I work as an advertising illustrator. Until a week ago, I was living in a student boarding house. We were three to a room and it was not exactly an environment where one could work in peace. With my first commission, I was able to rent a room, hoping for calm and privacy. It was not to be. My room used to be a part of a larger apartment and only a thin wall separates me from my neighbors, where strange things have been going on. It's not my business to meddle in a domestic dispute but this was repeated every day, at the same time, and with such regularity, that I found myself anticipating it. It was impossible not to listen and within a few days, I pieced together the facts. As unbelievable as it may sound, my neighbor has been finding pleasure in tormenting his invalid wife. As if that was not enough, when the man was not there, the unfortunate woman had to suffer at the hands of the maid, who treated her with hostility. I caught snippets of what was being said. The man called his wife the worst names. Once, she begged him for a wheelchair and he shouted at her that all she had to do was stand up and walk, or else go on crawling. I see that you are shocked and speechless."

"I'm shocked but not speechless," Nelly said, her hands squeezing the armrests of her chair. "Although, if I were to say what I think, you would find me rude. I believe every word you say because I know the man."

Encouraged, Savatier leaned forward. "Then you will understand that as the days went by, I became obsessed with the fate of the woman. I did not know what to do. I asked a friend, who is studying law. According to him, the husband is free to treat his wife as he pleases, providing he does not injure her permanently. As he was not physically threatening her life, the law has no reason to intervene. I decided to give my notice because the situation was robbing me of sleep and I could not concentrate on my work. I've found another room but before leaving I had to find out if I could help the woman in some small way. It was a matter of conscience. This morning, I chose a time when the husband was at work and the maid out shopping. The only way was to climb in from the outside. Fortunately, there was a fairly large cornice and, by gripping the masonry, I was able to reach the window. What I saw was far worse than I had imagined. The room was no larger than a closet. There was no furniture except for a mattress on the floor and a tray with the remains of breakfast. The poor woman sat wrapped in a blanket with her back propped against the wall."

"How did you get in?" Nelly asked. "Was the window open?"

"No, she let me in."

"Can she walk?"

"When she saw me, she hurled the coffee bowl against the window and broke the glass. 'Come in,' she said. 'Come in and kill me!' "

"Oh, Lord!" Nelly rubbed her forehead. "I have to find a way to get her out of there."

"It's been done. She's hiding in my room. I need to know whether you are willing to harbor Madame Babeau for some time. She says she trusts you and she needs a safe refuge until her parents come to Paris."

"Tell her that she can count on me."

"In that case," he said while reaching for his coat, "I'll bring her here today. It has to be done before the husband returns. My concierge knows that I'm moving tomorrow. I'll say that I've decided to move some of my stuff today. I've already borrowed a large wicker trunk that allows air in. All I have to do is to order a pushcart."

"I hope," Nelly said as she was letting him out, "that you have given thought to the fact that an invalid cannot vanish without help. Eventually, the suspicion may fall on you."

"Not necessarily. She assures me that her husband is convinced she can walk."

"Why would he think that? Did she tell you what happened to her? It wasn't an accident?"

Savatier shrugged. "That I don't know. There was no time for a long conversation. Once she understood that I was there to help, she immediately begged me to arrange an escape. A woman that desperate would not fake infirmity for the twisted pleasure of punishing her husband. Unless . . ." for the first time, Nelly saw him hesitating, ". . . unless I'm wrong. You are her friend, Miss Woodridge. Do you think she might be deranged?"

Nelly shook her head. "I haven't seen her for months. I don't know what happened between then and now. I heard that she was ailing while she still lived in the neighborhood, but that was all. I don't believe that she's mad but, if she is, her husband has driven her to it. It doesn't matter. Bring her. Bring her as soon as you can!"

* * *

Nelly poked the fire in the guest bedroom. "Are you sure you don't want to eat?" she asked.

Géraldine shook her head. "First I have to sort out how I feel. Half of me wants to cry while the other half laughs with relief."

"Here, let me comb your hair."

"No, I want to do it myself. It's a pleasure. I don't remember the last time I bathed and had my hair washed."

Nelly sat at her side. "Géraldine?"

"Yes?"

"Are you not going to tell me about the bruises?"

"It's nothing. Babeau kicked me last night. It no longer matters. Now that I'm free it does not matter at all."

"Why did he treat you like that?"

"He truly believes that I'm mad or set on driving him into insanity. The only reason I'm not in a lunatic asylum is that it would cost him money."

"Why does he believe it?"

"Because I'm insane."

"How can you say that?"

Géraldine let off combing and folded her arms into her lap. "It started shortly after Mama left. Babeau forbade me to leave the apartment until he was sure I had reformed. I wrote you a letter but Cécile never delivered it. Instead, she gave it to him. From then on, I lived in hell. He locked ink and pens in a drawer and kept the key in his pocket. He went so far as to drive nails into the window so that I could not open it and talk to you. He ordered Cécile to watch over me. When she went shopping, she locked me in the bedroom. The worst of it was that I could no longer bear his touch. I fought him with my fists whenever he approached me. Then one morning, I tried to get out of bed and could not. My legs had changed into cotton. He brought a doctor, who examined me and said that, physically, there was nothing wrong with me, that it was a mental condition called hysteria. My parents came. Mama cried. She said she could not help me since it was all in my head. Papa said that my husband deserved praise for trying to save me from a life of sin. I know they felt I've brought shame on the family. Babeau must have told them tremendous lies."

"But you are not mad. You think clearly even after such an ordeal."

Géraldine played with her comb. "I believe it has nothing to do with thinking. My legs are beyond my control. I tried, believe me, and I keep trying. I've learned to crawl and I can do it fast.—Don't cry, please! Are you not glad that we are together again? I know I am."

"Even now, when you know the truth about me?"

Géraldine took Nelly's hand in hers. "At the bottom of my heart, I've always known who you were, dear. At the same time, I was not willing to admit it. I wanted to believe you. It was exciting to have you for a friend. You've been leading such a free and glamorous life—"

"There is nothing glamorous about my life."

"— you had beautiful clothes, you were adventurous, you had seen the world, you were everything I was not. I wanted to be like you."

"Oh, Géraldine!" Nelly embraced her.

"Will you stop crying at last?" Géraldine admonished her. "Do you know what kept me from becoming a complete wreck even after we moved and he dumped me in that hole? I kept writing in my head. Every day, I was spinning stories. It's all up here," she pointed to her forehead, "word for word, enough to fill a book. And that was thanks to you. You know, I think I'll not wait until dinner after all. All of a sudden, I'm tremendously hungry."

Gladly, Nelly brought Géraldine a tray. It was a pleasure to watch her eat. Bathed, dressed in a pristine flannel nightgown, her drying hair gaining in volume, she began to look like her old self.

"Do you know that your hair is the color of moonlight?" Nelly asked.

Géraldine's lips quivered. "Oh, Nelly! I've not heard anything nice for ages . . ." She accepted a handkerchief and dried her eyes. "Are we not a pair?" she smiled through her tears. "Up and down like a see-saw!"

"And no wonder after such emotions," Nelly said. "I was dying with worry even though Monsieur Savatier made it sound so easy."

Géraldine's eyes lit up. "Is he not the bravest and the most noble of men?" she exclaimed. "God has sent him to me. It cannot be otherwise."

A light knock at the door and Julie entered, carrying a visit card. "Miss, a gentleman wants to see you."

Géraldine gasped and covered her mouth. "It cannot be Babeau, can it?" she asked.

Nelly reached for the card and glanced at the name. "No, it's someone I've been expecting." She nervously patted her hair. "I must go," she said to Géraldine. "And you, Julie, if ever a short black-bearded man shows up at the door, you must not let him in. Say that I'm out of town."

Henri d'Auzon waited for her in the sitting room, hands clasped behind his back.

"How is he?" Nelly asked as soon as she entered.

He smiled. "He'll live. He may even reach the end of his natural life span, provided he stays out of trouble."

"Has he written to me? Do you have a letter?"

"No, he cannot write for the moment. The bullet has damaged his shoulder. The whole area is still swollen and he's unable to move his right arm."

"But he'll recover from that, will he not?"

"There's a sizable hope that he will."

Nelly ceased wringing her hands. "I am so glad. Oh, forgive my manners! Please, sit down," she motioned to a chair.

Henri waited for her to take a seat before he sat down himself. "Octave has changed his plans for the future. He's charged me with finding you a more suitable accommodation."

She felt a deadly chill creeping into her extremities. "Why is this one no longer suitable?"

Henri cleared his throat and crossed his legs. "The fact is that tourism is expected to soar starting this spring and this apartment is a prime location. Octave will make a good income by returning it to the market. The agency that handles these matters has already made an inquiry as to its availability."

"I see."

"You have nothing to worry about. What I have in mind is a house with a garden. Not far from here, actually. It's located up the hill on the Mont de Sainte-Geneviève, close to the ancient Roman arena. Do you happen to know the area?"

She nodded. "I've strayed there while walking my dog."

"If you have no other plans tomorrow, I can take you there and show you around."

The doorbell rang furiously. Startled, Nelly gripped the edge of the table. The bell kept ringing until someone opened the main door. In the commotion that followed, she could hear Julie shouting, "No, monsieur, you can't go in! Miss is out of town! No! I'm telling you she's out of town!"

The door flew open and Babeau, his features that of an avenging God, entered the sitting room. He gave it a cursory look, wordlessly crossed over to the bedroom, and looked inside.

"Where is she?" he asked. "Where's my wife?"

"You have no right to break in like this!" Nelly protested.

"May I point out, monsieur, that your manners are somewhat lacking in delicacy?" Henri said.

"I'm performing a husband's duty, monsieur," Babeau said while repeatedly smacking his walking stick against his gloved hand. "My wife has run away and she might be here. In fact, I'm certain that she's here. With no money and only the dress on her back, she had nowhere to go but to this woman. Sadly, my wife is an accomplished liar, to say the least. Birds of a feather flock together. Yes, monsieur, birds of a feather!"

Henri rose to his full height. "Miss Woodridge, I expect you will raise no objection if I remove this man from the premises."

"There's no need to do that," Babeau said, while slowly backing toward the door. "I have a message for my wife," he addressed Nelly. "Tell her that I'll not be held responsible for any debts she may incur during her escapade. If she wants to separate, she'll have to learn your trade."

Babeau did not wait to be thrown out. The door banged shut behind him before Henri reached it.

"Well now, where were we?" Henri resumed his seat as if the unpleasant interlude had not happened. "Tomorrow then, if that suits you?"

* * *

"Thank God, that's over," said Nelly as she was tucking a blanket around Géraldine's legs. "He is only worrying about money. You'll be fine here."

"It's not over. Babeau is right about money. He knows that I have nothing to live on. I must support myself somehow until my parents decide what to do with me. Perhaps I could take in mending. What do you say? Could you ask around the neighborhood?"

Nelly patted Géraldine's knee. "Forget about mending. It pays nothing and it spoils the eyesight. Remember the manuscript?"

"Do I ever!"

"I'm just about finished with it. When I see Monsieur d'Auzon tomorrow, I'll ask whether he, or anyone of his acquaintance, has more work for me. If so, maybe we both can earn our living as copyists. It pays one franc a page and when you get used to it, you can make between ten and fifteen francs a day."

"Really? That's wonderful!"

"Isn't it? I count on it as an honorable means of living, especially now that . . ."

"What is it, Nelly? Why are you crying?"

"Oh, Géraldine, please hug me and hold me tight! I think that Octave is leaving me."

Chapter 29

Next morning, Nelly crossed the boulevard Saint-Germain and walked uphill along the rue de Monge. A heavy fog muffled the traffic sounds and conjured ghost-like forms from the vaporous curtain around her. She passed students on their way to college, their eyes still bleary from a night of carousing, and a number of shuffling maids laden with shopping baskets. A coal wagon startled her as it lumbered along. The stagnating air was pungent with rot and smoke.

She did not see Henri d'Auzon until she almost bumped into him near the entrance of the ancient arena.

"This is not the best type of weather for viewing the house," he commented, after they had exchanged greetings.

She followed him half a block up the street, where he turned into a vaulted passage that led to a nameless lane barely wide enough to accommodate a single carriage. A black cat shot across their path. An ominous sign, she thought.

"This is a private lane and the city does not provide illumination at night," Henri said, "but there are lanterns at the gate that can be fixed."

The gently down-sloping lane turned back in the direction of the arena and came to an abrupt halt at a forged iron gate. Behind it, she could see bare trees and shrubs blurred by the fog, but still no house.

Henri rummaged in both pockets of his overcoat and came up with a bunch of keys. One of them fitted into the padlock of the rusty chain which secured the gate. It took some effort on his part to swing the gate open. The metal protested with loud creaks and a rasp as it grated against the pavement.

"The hinges definitely need oiling," he said apologetically. "The house has been uninhabited for eleven years."

She glanced at the lanterns that topped the brick pillars on each side of the gate. Their glass panels were blind with soot and one of them was missing. It was enough to make one wonder what else needed to be fixed.

When they entered, her first impression was that of a sinister gnarled tangle. Unkempt for years, the garden had led a disorderly life. The rotting leaves shed by the trees in the fall concealed sprouts of ivy that had invaded the cobbled carriageway. Nelly had to stop to disengage her foot from the intertwined shoots. A recent thaw had contributed to the mess, the moisture causing muddy leaves to stick to the hem of her skirt.

Behind the bare branches discolored by milky haze loomed the façade of a house with a slate roof and tall chimneys. It, too, was covered with the ivy which seemed to reign supreme. Vines had crept up the walls, sealing the window shutters. They concealed the three semi-circular stone steps that led toward the main door. The two-story building, with third floor windows wedged into the roof, looked like a victim of strangulation.

The keys rattled as Henri searched for the one that would unlock the massive oak door. "The house was built some seventy years after those of the Place des Vosges," he explained. "It used to be what was called a pleasance, which means it served as a hide-out for gallant parties and secret rendezvous. The first owner was a man of the church with a mistress, a bevy of bastards and an understandable need for privacy. At that time, the property stood alone in the fields. The only structure older than the house is the wall over there," he pointed with his finger, "which belongs to a small sunken amphitheater built by the Romans. It provided ready-made protection on that side."

He found the key and inserted it in the lock. The door resisted and he had to ram it with his shoulder before it gave way with a noisy complaint.

At first, all she could see in the light provided by the opening were the dusty black and gray tiles of the floor, ending in darkness. She had an impression of space and, as her eyes grew accustomed to the obscurity, she realized that they were entering a vestibule with a stone staircase leading to the upper floor. Cold, stale air with a whiff of mold entered her nostrils.

She stood motionless while Henri opened the door and then tackled one of the two windows on each side. The shutters, imprisoned by ivy, did not give without a struggle. He conjured up a folding knife from his pocket to cut through the sprouts.

"Well, now," he said when he had won the battle with the shutters, "there should be a candle somewhere."

"There," Nelly pointed to a lantern standing by a wall.

"Capital!" Henri said. Again, he rummaged in his pockets. "I brought a box of matches, as we will need light for the tour. *A propos*," he said while lighting the stubble of a candle in the lantern, "I remember that there's a quantity of books I've not sorted out yet. I had intended to do it after my return to France but never got around to it. Too many other priorities."

"This house is yours?"

"Not any longer. I sold it to Octave two days ago." He frowned. "So far, I've not figured out what to do with the books. They will have to stay here for the time being, if you don't mind. Well, where shall we start?"

He hesitated between three doors, and then chose the one on the left, which led into a square room containing furniture covered with dustsheets and cobwebs. Henri lifted the lantern in order to extend the inadequate light.

"You will excuse me for not bothering with more shutters. It would slow us down. This is the drawing room. It belonged to the lady of the house, when there was one. The door over there connects it to the former dining room which was unfortunately turned into a laboratory. I say unfortunately because it contained valuable eighteenth-century wall paintings, which are now beyond repair. A maternal uncle, who left the house to me in his will, was a hermit with a taste for chemistry."

As he spoke, he led her through an unhinged double door into another dark room.

"Good Lord, what happened here?" she exclaimed.

"An explosion, which led to the instant demise of Uncle Guillaume. No one really knows what he had been working on in his last hours except that it involved acid and sulfur. The windows, or what is left of them, are boarded up with wood planks. If you want to use the room, you will have to replace the glass. I've sold the house as it is. Now, we will continue to what I think is the salon. Be careful not to bump against this door! It seems to remain erect only by the grace of God."

Speechless, she followed him into the salon, which featured more covered furniture. Henri pointed to the central door and said that it led back into the vestibule. The bedroom followed next. It contained a monumental poster bed with embroidered hangings loaded with more dust and cobwebs.

"There are more bedrooms upstairs," he said. "I don't know how many. Also, if you want to employ outside staff, there is lodging of some kind above the stable. Now we will go to the library, which is the last room on this floor."

Walking behind him, Nelly made a face. Employ outside staff? Who did he think she was? Mistress of a duke? Octave must have been out of his mind when he bought this smelly ruin.

"Where is the kitchen?" she asked.

197

Henri paused and scratched his nose. "To tell you the truth, I don't know. Probably in the basement, as usual."

"Is there running water? A bathroom? Gas for lighting?"

He smiled indulgently. "This house was built at a time when even kings had to do without indoor plumbing. But if you wish, it can be installed."

"Why did you sell it to Octave?" she wanted to know. "It's not far from where you live, and quiet enough for a writer." Quiet enough for a cemetery, she could have added.

He shrugged. "I like my bachelor life as it is, which means uncomplicated. I have no desire to be weighed down with repairs, additional staff, and all the ensuing household burdens. Besides, contrary to what you might think of writers, I find the distant street noise beneficial for my mind."

He cut short his explanations by opening the door of the library. "Mother of God!" he exclaimed.

Curious, she entered behind him and gasped when she took in a breath of a vicious stench.

"Mold," he said, lifting the lantern. "There is a leak somewhere."

The candlelight glided across shelves weighed with leather-bound books without finding the cause. Mumbling a curse, Henri disposed of the lantern, sprang for one of the windows, opened it, climbed on the sill, and inserted his knife between the shutters. In the light that streamed into the room, it was easy to discover the source of trouble. In a distant corner, the ceiling bore a moist stain that extended down the wall and disappeared behind a shelf.

"There must be a hole in the roof," Nelly said. "I wonder what it has done to the upper floors."

Henri did not pay the slightest attention to her. One by one, he grabbed the books from the warped shelves of the damaged section. "The first print of Molière's plays reduced to a gooey mess," he said with a sad pathos more suitable for the death of a loved one than for a book. "The original edition of Goethe's Iphigénie . . . The first French translation of Isaac Newton's Principia . . . They all came from Grandfather's library. Miss Woodridge, this is a tragedy of Greek proportions!"

"I'm sorry," she said, matching his mournful expression.

"I meant to give you the keys today," he said, "and be done with the task, but this has changed everything. I must save what is salvageable."

"Monsieur d'Auzon, frankly, I don't think I want to live here. Is there any way I could reach Octave?"

He shook his head. "I must advise you not to do it. Besides, he doesn't own the house any longer."

"Then who does?"

"It is yours."

"Mine?"

He paused to gather his breath. "It is Monsieur Gaillard's parting gift to you," he said. "Along with the draft for five thousand francs I mentioned earlier. The deeds to the house are at the notary's office. I'll give you the address. Miss Woodridge? Miss Woodridge, are you all right?"

Despite the misgivings, which had caused her a sleepless night, she had harbored hope. Now it was gone. Irretrievably gone. She spread her hands over her face.

"You are not going to faint, are you?" he said, alarmed, and grasped her shoulder.

She shook his hand off. "No, no, don't worry," she said. "I'm just absorbing the shock."

"Please, don't blame me. This mission is highly disagreeable to me. I don't know how to deal with this kind of situation. Believe me, had it not been for Octave's ill health—"

"No!" she interrupted him. "Don't apologize for your part in this. Did he . . . Did he tell you why?"

Henri clasped his hands behind his back. "He came too close to death," he said, slowly pacing back and forth. "After that, he had ample time to examine his past and conclude that he had behaved irresponsibly. He wants to turn the page and start anew, this time leading an exemplary life. I've no doubt that his parents had a hand in his conversion. He was reminded of the fact that the Gaillard name could have died foolishly because of the duel. There's going to be a wedding as soon as he's back on his feet."

"A wedding?"

He stopped his pacing and gave her a direct look. "You might as well know that he's been affianced for years."

She took that blow stoically. She would deal with the emotional devastation later. "Was she the young woman I saw crying in the sitting room?"

He paused, thinking. "No, that was Octave's youngest sister. Frankly, I don't see Amélie crying in public. She strikes me as inhumanly perfect."

"I see."

"Octave has charged me to tell you that he is acutely aware of the moral harm he has caused you and that he hopes you'll find it in your heart to forgive him."

"How soon does he want me to vacate the apartment?"

"There's no rush. The tourist season begins at Easter. There's plenty of time to complete the necessary repairs on this house and even install water and gas. And, Miss Woodridge . . ." he hesitated slightly, ". . .I want to express my gratitude to you for taking such bad tidings with calm."

"What did you expect? Tears and screams? A hysterical scene?"

"Something along that line," he admitted.

"I'll save such demonstrations for later. Now I simply want to leave."

"Your sincerity is touching. Do you want me to accompany you or do you prefer to be alone?"

"Alone. Which door leads out?"

"We are right next to the vestibule. That way . . ." he motioned.

"Thank you, monsieur. And please, do tell him . . ." she swallowed, ". . . tell him that I accept his gift only because I have no other choice."

"I will. As for the keys, I'll send them to you, along with instructions concerning the documents at the notary's."

She went only as far as the main door, and then retraced her steps. "Monsieur d'Auzon . . ."

He looked up from a book. "Yes, Miss Woodridge?"

"I forgot to thank you for what you have done for my maid. She's completely recovered."

"I'm pleased to hear that."

"Also, I'm very grateful for the manuscript. I'm almost done, and if you wish, you can have it back tomorrow."

"What manuscript?"

"*The Religion and Philosophy of China*. Don't you remember? Octave gave it to me for copying. Eight hundred and thirty-five pages at one franc each. I'm not pressing you for money, but if I'm to make a living . . ."

He stared at her, confused. "Why would I request a copy of a manuscript that had been published almost a year ago?"

"Published?"

"For your information, the *Religion and Philosophy* was published in January. I completed it while I was still in China. I'm now working on the final draft of *Alchemy and Medicine*."

"But I copied it page by page!"

"Then you've been fooled. I don't know how Octave came by the manuscript but I shall find out. This is outrageous! All I can say is that copying is done before the manuscript is presented to the publisher and the going rate is at the most thirty-five centimes a page."

By the time he finished the sentence, she was bent over the windowsill, vomiting her breakfast into the garden below. She wiped her mouth with a handkerchief.

Henri yanked the dustsheet from a chair. "Please, do sit down."

"No, I prefer not. I'd rather go."

He put his hands in his pockets. "Then I have nothing else to add except that I'm sorry you dislike the house. It was the best I could do under the circumstances. With two weeks past the deadline and with the publisher on my heels, I simply did not have time to scour the city for a house in Octave's price range." His anger grew as he spoke and his voice amplified into a thunder. "As for the manuscript," he went on, "Octave has clearly overstepped the line of our friendship. It's bad enough that I had to handle his breakup with his mistress, but I will not tolerate the fact that he commits misdeeds in my name."

A brief silence followed his outburst. He took in breath as if he wanted to say more and then shook his head. "Goodbye, Miss Woodridge," he said instead.

Chapter 30

Célestine expertly flipped an omelet over and shook the pan. "Cut the bread and then see if there are any pickles left," she ordered Julie. "Although what's the use of it I don't know. The breakfast came back untouched. The only one happy with the situation is the dog who's getting more than his due. Personally, I give up. I've been coaxing and pleading enough. And I'm cooking nothing for you because I'm pretty sure you are going to bring this back," she pointed at the sizzling eggs.

"One has to have the patience of a saint," she went on, reaching for a plate. "It's sad and irritating—yes, irritating!—to see her wasting away for a man like that. I knew from the very beginning that he wasn't for her. The other one, the ship owner, has money to burn, and if she played her cards right he could be a stepping-stone to better things. Did you see the bouquet of orchids he sent? An invitation for dinner came with it. Do you know what she said to me? She said, 'I'm not going that way, Célestine, and that's final.' If you ask me, that's stupid."

She plopped the omelet onto the dish. "At least she's going for my boarding house scheme. Already has that unhinged friend of hers as the first boarder, because the parents don't want her back. You know how it is in a small town, Julie. If the word gets around that she's left her husband, let alone that she's deranged, no one would marry her younger sisters. And I'll tell you something else, Julie. If it wasn't for my boarding house idea, we would both have walked, because Miss would have sold the house and returned to America. At least you and I are safe, thanks to my quick thinking. Except I don't know what it is going to take to shake her out of her misery. Did you hear the bell? I wonder who it is. On second thought, give me back the tray! I'll take it myself and see what's going on."

202

"It was God himself that has sent you here, monsieur," Célestine exclaimed after she read the card Henri d'Auzon offered her.

Henri, slightly unsettled by her enthusiasm, stared at her warily. "Have we met?" he asked.

"Célestine Cabrol, monsieur. I'm the cook here and a kind of confidante. I heard of your kindness. What a nice gentleman, I thought."

"My kindness?" Henri asked apprehensively. "Surely, this is a mistake."

If anything, he should be known as a knave. When he calmed down after his outburst, bad conscience began to gnaw at him for allowing a grief-stricken woman to walk home alone. It took him four days to gather enough courage for this visit.

"Monsieur is too modest," Célestine said. "Taking care of everything, being where needed. Such qualities are signs of a heart of gold. Oh," she sucked in her breath and joined her hands, "where are my manners? Please, come in and allow me to take your coat!" She peeled off his overcoat and grabbed his arm. "See that lunch tray over there?" she pointed to a console table.

"I do see it," Henri said, more and more puzzled.

"You seem to be a man of authority," Célestine said in an unctuous voice, "and we are at our wits end. Miss won't eat! In four days, she has only had a nibble or two of dry bread. If it goes on, she'll starve herself to death."

As Henri looked at her indecisively, pondering the best way of retreat, she lowered her voice to a whisper. "Talk to her, monsieur, I beg you! A couple of words from a man will carry more weight than our weak female pleas. I swear by Saint-Sebastian of the Arrows that I would not ask you were I not utterly desperate."

Henri cleared his throat. "Madame . . . Cabrol, is it? I only came here to talk business. A physician should solve a problem of this sort. I shall return at a more convenient time."

"And when would that be, monsieur?" Célestine pleaded, her grip on his sleeve tightening. "When she's six feet under? All I ask for are a few words. A small kindness. Five minutes of your time."

Henri gave up. The woman could talk a corpse into dancing at its own funeral. "Would you kindly release me?" he said. "I'll see what I can do."

"Thank you, monsieur, thank you!" Célestine exclaimed. "Make yourself comfortable in the sitting room and I'll bring her there in no time."

* * *

"Monsieur d'Auzon? What is he doing here?"

"He wants to talk business," Célestine said while throwing the shutters open. "Now get out of bed and let me brush your hair. It's a pity you cannot see yourself. What a sin to ruin one's looks in this way!"

Nelly squinted in the raw light. "For heaven's sake, Célestine, draw the curtains. My eyes hurt."

"You'll have to get used to it," the cook said mercilessly. "Now get up! There will be no more wallowing in self-pity."

"Oh, go away! I hate you."

Célestine yanked off the coverlet. "That's a risk a devoted servant has to take when the situation calls for it. Up, up, and take off that crumpled night-gown!"

Henri was anything but comfortable in the sitting room. Although the voices that filtered through the closed door were unintelligible, he guessed that Determination was fighting Apathy and that, shortly, he would have to play a benevolent uncle and dispense good advice. There seemed to be no end to the distasteful affair Gaillard had unloaded on him. He had had it with Octave. Ever since they were boys, the fellow had always managed to land him in trouble.

"Here she is!" the cook announced. She held the door open until her mistress entered. Henri found himself startled by her frail appearance. Where was the lively creature he had met in the Place des Vosges? This one was almost transparent.

He rose and bowed his head." Good afternoon, Miss Woodridge."

"Monsieur, I was told that you wish to discuss some business," Nelly said when Célestine had left and they were seated.

"I brought your keys," he said.

"Oh, yes, the keys. Thank you."

"And here," he reached into his breast pocket, "is the bank draft and the address of Maître Beliveau, the notary. I should have given it to you the last time we met but the circumstances were somewhat distracting."

He held an envelope out to her and, when she did not reach for it, he dropped it on the table.

"I'm sorry," she said.

"Sorry?"

"For taking up your time. I never wanted to be a nuisance. Last time, I did not realize how busy you were."

"Uh . . ." he mumbled. "Not your fault, really. Besides, I've negotiated an extension of three weeks. I . . . I hope that your nausea has subsided."

"I'm quite well, thank you."

He shifted in his seat. "You look very thin. Fasting is detrimental to one's health."

"I shall keep that in mind."

He felt immensely awkward and reached for a more comfortable subject. "I should inform you of what has been going on in your house. I've hired a man to keep fires blazing both in the library and in the rooms above in order to dry the walls. Since he has nothing else to do, I asked him to clear the garden and trim the ivy. The leak in the roof has been discovered and I'll have it repaired at my expense. As for the books, as soon as they are dry—"

"Monsieur d'Auzon," she interrupted him, "do you regret selling the house? I could find another place to live."

"Why do you ask? Do you dislike it as much as that?"

"I neither like nor dislike it. The fact is that it had belonged to your family and it seems to me that you've sold it in haste. Perhaps you've changed your mind."

"I appreciate your concern, mademoiselle, but I have no special attachment to that property. I had only visited it once, shortly after my uncle's death. However, you are free to do with it as you like. Once the walls are dry and the garden in shape, you can put it on the market and even realize a profit. May I ask what your plans are for the future?"

She shrugged. "Célestine suggests that I should start a boarding house."

"That seems to be a good idea."

"I don't know whether I'd be able to handle it. It means having to deal with strangers, and I don't feel up to it. I would rather live a private life. I had hoped to make a living by copying manuscripts but now . . ." she let the end of the sentence dangle in the air and covered her face.

Henri leaned toward her. "Let me be frank with you, Miss Woodridge. Copying is a very crowded market, especially here in the Latin Quarter. Every starving student seeks to make a few francs by this means. No one would consider hiring a woman with a foreign accent. The odds are clearly against you."

She nodded, lifted her head, and looked at him through the tears in her eyes. Tears! Let's have none of that, he thought and rose. "I should take my leave," he said. "I wish you good luck in any endeavor you decide to undertake."

"Thank you, monsieur. Do you want your manuscript back?"

"The manuscript. Yes, I would appreciate that, indeed."

He waited while she opened a drawer and removed a thick package wrapped in brown paper. "I must separate the original from the copy," she said and sniffled. "Excuse me, I need a handkerchief."

Impatient to be gone, Henri unwrapped the package while she disappeared into the bedroom. When she returned, he was sitting at the table, comparing two pages.

"This is incredible," he said without lifting his head. "You've managed to find your way through the maze of corrections, erasures, and additions while the copyists, who had to transcribe the text for the publisher, plagued me with questions. Did you have any training for this kind of work?"

"I had help at the beginning. It became easier as I went on."

He looked at her with awe. "How long have you been speaking French, Miss Woodridge?"

"Since I've been in France."

"Did you already know some French?"

"I had lessons at the boarding school."

He chuckled dismissively. "Boarding school French! We know what that means. Did anyone tell you that you've performed an extraordinary feat?"

"I have?"

"Your French is outstanding, both spoken and written. You have an unquestionable gift for languages. What's more, you have a very tidy hand. This," he tapped on the pages, "is top quality work and, if it were shown to interested people, you might get a serious commission."

"Is that true?" she asked, her eyes brightening, and color returning to her cheeks. She was standing somewhat taller.

He observed the transformation with a feeling of sadness. "If Octave were here, I'd whip him. When I think of the amount of hard work you have done for nothing—"

"It was not for nothing," she said quickly. "I'll consider it a learning experience."

"That's a good way to look at it," he agreed and smiled. "It's possible that Octave did you a service when he pinched the manuscript from a shelf in my study."

"Is that how it happened?"

"According to Joseph, my valet, he once came when I was not at home and insisted on waiting for me. After some ten minutes, he called out that he had changed his mind. He left before Joseph could see him to the door. It was sometime in June, am I correct?"

She nodded.

"My question is, why did he do it?"

She bent her head, working the handkerchief into a ball. "I badly wanted to earn a living. Octave was against it because it clashed with his principles. This was a means of keeping me busy. Now I understand why he bristled when I wanted to meet you." Her lips quivered. "I trusted him in so many ways."

"Don't think of it," he said quickly, fearing more tears. "Concentrate on the future. Here," he began to wrap both manuscripts, "I'll take the copy as well and see what can be done."

"I cannot express enough gratitude, monsieur. You've already done so much."

He dismissed the praise with his hand. "Do you, by any chance, have a string to secure the package?"

She turned on her heels, ran out of the room and came back with a length of used string. "It's full of knots," she apologized, "but it was all we could find on such short notice."

"That will do perfectly well."

With both hands pressed against her chest, she watched him eagerly as he tied the package. He could not help but smile.

"Let me tell you how you can express your gratitude," he said.

"How?"

"By showing more interest in your cook's efforts."

"Oh, I will," she said, nodding. "From now on, I will!"

Chapter 31

"Not now," snapped Géraldine. "Come back later! I must finish the story while it flows. Give me back my pen!"

"Enough is enough," Nelly said, while replacing the pen onto the holder and closing the lid of the inkstand. She sat at the paper-littered table, facing her friend. "All you have been doing since you came here is shutting yourself in your room and writing as if your life depended on it."

Géraldine's fingers drummed her impatience on the table surface. "It has to come out of my head and onto the paper before I forget it. I spent months shaping the stories without being able to set them in writing. Why don't you leave me alone? I feel best when I'm in my own world."

Nelly sighed. "Géraldine, you cannot avoid the real world forever. Come back to Earth! It can't be that hard."

"Who says it's hard? I just—"

"Let's put it this way," Nelly said firmly. "It's Christmas Eve. Célestine's got her hands full with the dinner, Julie is plucking the goose and I must make chestnut stuffing. It so happens that someone has to help with pitting the prunes. Guess who?"

Dissent was brewing in the kitchen where Julie sat in a corner with a goose between her knees, plucking the feathers, while Célestine chopped onion with more vigor than the task required.

"Some people I could name have no respect for tradition," the cook said provocatively as Nelly wheeled Géraldine through the door.

"Listen Célestine," Nelly said, while parking the wheelchair by the kitchen table, "as far as traditions go, I had to give up mine as well. In America, there's no midnight feast. If I can adjust, then you can too. It's unhealthy to eat a heavy dinner past midnight. By the time you'd get back from church, we'd be half-asleep. We'll eat at nine. That's late enough."

"Have it your way," Célestine grumbled. "As for me and Julie, we'll wait until after the midnight mass. Won't we, Julie?"

Julie ripped off the last fistful of feathers and closely studied the goose for any she might have overlooked. She would not be drawn into the dispute.

"I don't know why you are making such a case of the *réveillon*," Nelly said. "It will be just us and Monsieur Goubert. Thirteen desserts for five people is excess. I must've been brain-damaged when I allowed such an expense."

"That's for Jesus and his twelve apostles. They must not be denied. Nuts, raisins, almonds," Célestine counted on her fingers, "figs, dates, nougat, apples, pears, prunes, oranges, and three different tarts."

Nelly fanned herself. "I feel already stuffed just from listening to you. So what do you want us to do?"

Célestine distributed the tasks and they settled down to work. Potato peels dropped into the waste bucket, chestnut shells cracked, a knife rhythmically stroked the chopping board, accompanied with dull thumps from underneath the table, where Schnitzel wagged his tail, repeatedly hitting a chair leg.

"This is a truly magnificent goose," Célestine said appreciatively, while plunging her hand into the plump carcass and scooping out the innards. "I wouldn't be surprised to get at least eight pounds of fat out of it. Last Christmas, I could only dream of such a treat."

"And who knows what the next Christmas will be like," Nelly said gloomily. "Maybe we'll all spend it dreaming of roasted goose again."

"Speaking of dreams, you never know from one year to another," Géraldine added. "Last Christmas, I was readying my trousseau and dreaming of married life. I was the envy of my sisters. And here I am, a mere year later, with all my dreams gone."

"Jesus Christ and all the saints!" Célestine shrieked suddenly, frantically waving her stained hands. "Will someone get that dog out of here? He's tried to steal the goose liver. Get out! Out, I said! Will I ever have any peace with that thieving mongrel around?"

Fuming, she ordered Julie to lock Schnitzel in the bathroom and added that she would not mind if she drowned the beast in the bathtub.

"Now, Célestine," Nelly protested, "you sometimes behave as if the dog had never been yours. If I didn't know better, I'd think that you hate him."

The cook mumbled something unintelligible and resumed her work.

The doorbell rang.

Nelly glanced at Julie, who was brushing off the feathers clinging to her apron. "I'll see to it," she said.

She came back soon after, dragging a hesitant visitor by the sleeve. "Géraldine, look who's here!"

"Monsieur Savatier!" Forgetting her condition, Géraldine strained to rise and helplessly slumped back in the chair. "I'm glad, so glad," she said excitedly.

Abashed by four pairs of eyes boring into him, the young man advanced reluctantly into the kitchen. "I've only come to inquire . . ." he muttered and then, taking hold of himself, he bowed and extended his arm for a handshake. "Good afternoon, Madame Babeau. I hope you are well. Oh, no, please, you must not do that!" he exclaimed with embarrassment when Géraldine clasped his hand in both of hers and kissed it. His earlobes acquired a noticeable blush and the hand found a refuge behind his back.

"Thank you, thank you so much," said Géraldine, her eyes filling with tears.

"You are most welcome," he answered, while slowly backing toward the door. "Allow me to wish you all a Merry Christmas."

"Nelly, don't let him go! Not yet!"

Nelly smiled. "You've heard my friend, monsieur. I'm afraid we have to hold you captive for a while."

She whisked away a bowl filled with discarded chestnut shells that stood on a chair next to Géraldine's. Claude Savatier sat down obediently. A brief awkward silence descended on the room, filled only with the clatter of the roasting pan Célestine was readying for the goose. Géraldine, her hands folded in her lap, stared at the visitor with mute admiration. The bashful hero shifted in his seat, his ears still glowing red. Then everyone started talking at once.

"Have you—"

"How—"

"I'm pleased to—"

Their embarrassed laughter broke the ice. Nelly put a cup in front of the visitor and poured coffee.

"I'm glad you've come back now that things have settled down, Monsieur Savatier," she said. "Géraldine has often told me that she had not fully expressed her gratitude. We both thank you with all our hearts."

"Oh, but I didn't come for that!" Savatier said quickly. "I just wanted to know whether Madame Babeau was safe. I'm glad to see that she is." He turned to Géraldine. "I did not expect to meet you again, madam. I thought that by now you'd be in your parents' care."

An awkward pause followed his comment.

"Madame Babeau is not returning home," Nelly said. "Sugar? Cream?" she inquired.

"And you, Monsieur Savatier?" Géraldine asked. "How do you find your new lodgings?"

"Dark and miserable," he confided, stirring his coffee. "My landlady turns off the gas at half past nine o'clock. If I need light after that, I have to rely on candles. I think of moving again."

"Well, here's another lodger for your boarding house, Miss."

"Célestine!"

"What's wrong with asking? It's cheaper than running an ad in the newspaper."

"Are you taking in lodgers?" Savatier inquired.

"It's only a project."

"Miss Woodridge owns a house with a garden," Géraldine said eagerly.

"Correction, I own a ruin with a garden. It needs extensive renovations. I doubt Monsieur Savatier's willing to wait that long. But I wanted to ask you, where are you dining tonight, monsieur?"

"I'm to join a group of friends at a restaurant."

"Would they miss you terribly if you had dinner with us?"

"Miss Woodridge, you don't have to—"

"Oh, please, monsieur, do come!" Géraldine pleaded. "Madame Célestine is an excellent cook and we'll dine early. You still have time to join your friends before midnight."

"Well, if it's not too much of a bother, I'd be glad to," Savatier succumbed to the prospect of a home-cooked meal.

"It's settled then," Nelly said.

By eight thirty, fires blazed both in the sitting and dining rooms and the air was scented with incense and furniture polish, while fragrant cooking smells wafted in from the kitchen with Julie's frequent comings and goings. Chastised and fed on odds and ends, Schnitzel slumbered by the sitting room fireplace, one of his hind legs twitching as he pursued some prey in his dream. Fully seized by the Christmas spirit, Nelly had taken him to the market, where she acquired bunches of mistletoe which now decorated the dining table and both mantelpieces. Both she and Géraldine had spent nearly an hour dressing for dinner.

"It's like in the old times," Nelly commented.

"Except in the old times, I was able to dress myself. Oh, Nelly you cannot imagine how bad it feels to be such a dead weight to good people like you."

"Hush and put this on."

"The earrings? Why, they are superb! Are they genuine pearls? Why don't you wear them tonight?"

"It's your evening. I want you to look your best in Monsieur Savatier's honor. He deserves it."

Géraldine fastened the earrings and, looking in the mirror, she turned her head from side to side, admiring the result. "I feel like a princess."

"Then you must admit that there are good moments even in this imperfect world."

Monsieur Goubert arrived at quarter to nine. He was dressed in an old-fashioned frock coat with velvet lapels, a hunter-green vest, and a freshly laundered shirt adorned with a necktie of beige and ivory brocade, all of which showed wear at the edges and exuded a strong odor of mothballs. He sniffed the air, commented on the seductive aromas, and then repaired into the sitting room, where he sat at the piano to add music to the festive mood. It was to the sound of *Oh, Hear the Angel Voices* that Claude Savatier made his appearance, weighed down with a beribboned flower pot wrapped in tissue paper.

"The hellebore, also called the Christmas rose," he explained as both women admired the tiny white blossoms and glossy leaves.

He shook hands with Monsieur Goubert and his gaze strayed more than once to Géraldine, as if he wanted to pay her a compliment and couldn't find the pluck to do it. Nelly noticed that without a damsel in distress to rescue, he was lost in female company. Compared to his previous bravery, this kind of shyness was even more endearing.

Monsieur Goubert began the conversation while she was passing around a tray with glasses of aperitif. "I expect that you are from the provinces," he addressed the young man. "Do I detect a slight Auvergnat accent?"

"Indeed, I'm from Auvergne, monsieur. Clermont-Ferrand, to be exact."

"You are very far from home. It's sad that you cannot be with your family tonight. They must be thinking of you at this very moment."

Savatier shook his head. "I was brought up by an uncle who passed away."

"How long have you been here?" Nelly asked.

"A little over a year. With the small inheritance my uncle left me, I took lessons in drawing and engraving and now I'm slowly forging a career in Paris."

The aperitif finished, they entered the dining room. The first bottle of wine was uncorked and Julie served a plate of oysters on a bed of ice, accompanied by lemons and vinaigrette.

The company had worked their way through a series of canapés and hors d'oeuvres before the stuffed goose made its appearance, surrounded by a multitude of garnishes. Her back bent under the weight of the giant platter, Julie heaved it on the table, and a second bottle of wine was opened in its honor. Tongues unwound by degrees and faces glowed with the kind of well-being only a good meal can generate. Claude Savatier lost his natural shyness and, before dessert they were calling each other by first names, with the exception of the music teacher, who was too old and venerable for that sort of thing. At the end of the meal, Célestine was coaxed out of the kitchen to hear well-deserved praise for her culinary art.

"It was only a modest dinner," she said, reaching for a glass of wine. "You should see the *réveillons* I used to give. Up to eighteen courses. Guests would eat and drink all night long. Those were the times! Ah, life was good under the Empire."

"Only for those who could afford it," said Monsieur Goubert.

"At least the poor had something to look at," she replied. "None of the youngsters here can imagine what life was like in Paris. It was a continuous feast for the eyes. The rich were not ashamed to display their wealth then. The streets were full of sumptuous equipages and women were dressed in splendid toilettes and covered with jewels. Money poured in from around the world. Fortunes were made and spent and no one was preaching moderation. Say what you want about the Empire, but those were grand times that no dull republic can ever replace."

As no one could contest this, Monsieur Goubert proposed that they might move back to the sitting room to squeeze some Christmas cheer out of the piano.

They gathered around the piano, glasses of punch in hand, to sing *A Divine Child Is Born* followed by other French carols. When Monsieur Goubert showed signs of fatigue, Nelly replaced him at the keyboard, to play and sing *O Come, All Ye Faithful*.

"I don't understand a word, but it's beautiful all the same," Célestine said, squashing a tear in the corner of her eye.

"Let's have a rest," Nelly proposed. "I know what! Géraldine should read us one of her stories."

"Madame Babeau writes stories?" Monsieur Goubert asked. "What kind of stories are they?"

"They are just tales for children," Géraldine said modestly. "But I'd be glad to read one just to gauge your reaction."

Julie was dispatched to fetch the manuscript. Everyone settled down and Nelly introduced the story with a few piano chords.

"What is it called?" she asked over her shoulder.

"How Monsieur Fierce Danced the Gavotte."

"Hear, hear," Nelly improvised on the keyboard. "How Monsieur Fierce Danced the Gavotte, a tale written and read by Géraldine Babeau."

"That will be Renaud, if you please," Géraldine protested. "Isn't it enough that I have to bear that hateful name for the rest of my life? I shall not use it as a writer."

"Géraldine Renaud," Nelly corrected herself. "And now, everybody listen!"

It was a charming tale of mice having a ball while the cat was at home. Chuckles and outright guffaws accompanied the reading and when it was finished, everybody applauded heartily.

"Delightful! Utterly delightful," Claude said. "And to think that such talent might have gone to waste."

Géraldine beamed when they asked for more, but Célestine spoiled the happy moment by looking at the clock. "Good Lord! Ten minutes to midnight. Julie, get our shawls!"

The men rose as well. "Are you going to Notre Dame?" Monsieur Goubert asked Célestine.

"I wish! At this hour, there will be no standing room left. We're going only as far as the Saint-Julien-le-Pauvre. Miss, are you sure you don't want to come with us?"

"No, I'll stay with Géraldine," Nelly replied, glad to have a ready-made excuse. Ever since her moral downfall, she had been avoiding a direct confrontation with God.

There was a round of well-wishing and hand shaking as everybody was taking their leave.

"What a perfect *réveillon*," Nelly said when the door closed behind the company. "And now, let's make ourselves comfortable!"

They stripped down to their underwear and lounged in front of the fire, sharing an orange.

"Did you notice his eyes?" Géraldine asked.

"Are you talking about Claude?"

"Who else? He has such beautiful, velvety eyes. I also like the way he sometimes forgets himself and pronounces 's' as 'sh'. The Auvergnat accent is so cute!"

Nelly giggled. "Géraldine, you are falling in love!"

"Don't say that. For the love of God, don't say that!"

"Why not?"

"I'm a married woman and a cripple. That's enough said."

"Well, the first cannot be helped but as for your legs, I still hope that they can be fixed. I was thinking of Professor Charcot. He was able to cure Julie and he might do the same for you."

"I doubt it. Julie had something to remember. I haven't lost my memory, although I wish I had. I'd be happy to forget the nightmare that was my life with Babeau."

Nelly threw an orange peel into the fire and watched as the flames consumed it. "I wish I could wipe out certain memories as well."

"Are you still thinking of him?"

"Every day."

"Would you take him back if he walked through the door?"

"No. Yes. I don't know. I miss him terribly. Or maybe I just miss having a pair of arms around me."

Géraldine chewed pensively on an orange section. "You know, Babeau and Cécile did it. They made no secret of it. Maybe he thought he was punishing me, but I was glad it was her instead of me. I've never understood the appeal of the thing. On my wedding night, I cried myself to sleep. Why don't they tell us what to expect? In a way, I'm glad to be a cripple because I'll not have to do *that* again."

"Don't say that!" Nelly exclaimed. "It's the most beautiful thing in the world when you are with someone you love."

Géraldine spat a seed into her palm. "Now I will never find out, will I? I'm far more comfortable writing fiction than living a great love. Will you help me to find a publisher?"

"I'll do my best. I envy you, Géraldine."

"What's there to envy?"

"I wish I had a talent of some sort. Something that would give direction to my life. I feel useless."

Géraldine reached for her hand. "Nelly, you are not useless. You have the talent of making people around you happy."

"But I'm not happy myself."

"You will be if you put your mind to it. Find yourself another lover. I wouldn't recommend it in general, but it seems to be the right medicine for you."

Nelly shook her head. "No, one heartbreak is enough. Never again will I make a man the center of my universe."

"Behold the new ruthless Miss Woodridge!" Géraldine laughed. "Run and hide, gentlemen, because you haven't got the slightest chance of winning!"

"Right," Nelly yawned. "And on this high note, we should get ready for bed."

Chapter 32

Although 'rigolo' meant droll, there was nothing even remotely amusing in the atmosphere of the Café Rigolo. Célestine advanced cautiously through the narrow passage between the zinc counter occupying one side of the room and the row of tables covered with ripped oilcloth, where ageless men and women lingered in an absinthe-induced stupor. A stench of defeat floated in the smoke-filled air. Célestine hated coming here, always afraid to meet an old acquaintance. She was convinced that the gypsy had chosen this place to remind her where she came from and she resented it.

The *patronne*, a massive woman with a pasty face dotted with warts, acknowledged Célestine's presence with a nod and then jerked her head in the direction of the private room. It was nothing more than a wooden enclosure with a door and glass insets obscured by filthy cretonne hangings. Clutching her purse to her stomach for fear of being robbed, Célestine negotiated her way around a pair of drunks staggering in mutual support toward the exit and finally reached the door.

Nathaira was seated at the table with a half-empty carafe of wine in front of her. The paraphernalia of her trade were disposed at her side on a red plush sofa that had spent its better days in some gaudy brothel. Despite the broad daylight outside, the enclosure was so dark that it had to be illuminated by a gas sconce. When Célestine entered, the gypsy stretched her leg under the table and roughly pushed a chair with her foot.

"Sit down," she said. "You're late."

"Couldn't make it any sooner," Célestine said apologetically. "It depends not on me, as you know. And this time I had to be extra careful."

"Does it mean that you've brought the diary?"

"I have, but I cannot leave it with you. I already regret having mentioned it. If she ever finds out, I'll be in serious trouble. Besides, it's locked and I don't know where she keeps the key. Please, don't try anything funny like forcing the lock open."

The gypsy smirked. "Nonsense! What use would it be to me since you say that it's written in English? I don't know a word of the language. All I need is to touch the book and channel the thoughts into the crystal ball. Well?" she extended her hand.

Célestine opened her purse and removed a blue book secured with a leather strap. The gypsy took it from her and clasped it between her palms. She closed her eyes. "Yes, I can feel the vibrations," she said. "They are much stronger than those from the tarot cards."

"I hope it won't take long."

"That depends. Where is she and when do you expect her back?"

"She's all wrapped up in that house. She's gone there with the maid. I must be back before half past four if I want to get the dinner ready."

"Anything new and interesting?"

"Not much. She keeps refusing both the old man and the offer for modeling from Monsieur Quérat, the silly stubborn bitch. The Quérat's offer isn't much, but Monsieur Bonnard is willing to set her up in a modern house, with a carriage and a pair thrown in, plus fifteen hundred francs a month. Such a generous man! I'm losing patience, but what can I do? Instead, she's working on another manuscript. Something completely boring about industrial development. There's no money in it. When I think that we could be living in luxury, I feel like weeping."

"The renovations must be costly."

"You don't say!" Célestine was heating up. "Just the digging for gas and water and all the pipes that go with it will cost a fortune. Last Monday, she ordered the bathroom fixings. The tub, the water heater, tiles, the whole works. Twelve hundred francs for the unnecessary privilege of soaking in water! What's wrong with simple soap and a sponge, I ask you?"

Nathaira shook her head in commiseration. "You can't reason with the young. Let her do what she wants. When money's short, she'll come to heel."

"You think so?"

"Have I been wrong so far?"

"No, upon my soul, you have not! When you said there would be an interesting offer coming soon and Monsieur Quérat's offer came right the next day, I was so awed I had to cross myself. How do you do it?"

"It's a gift given only to gypsies."

Nathaira rummaged in a canvas bag and removed a round object wrapped in a black cloth. She unfolded the fabric, exposing a crystal ball which she put on top of the diary.

"Now go and wait for me outside!" she ordered.

Célestine's lips puckered with disappointment. "I cannot watch?"

"No. I need to achieve the deepest concentration. Go! Don't come back until I call you."

"You mean I should wait in the taproom? I don't like the company."

"Then go for a walk. Go shopping. What do I care? Just go!"

"I'll come back in an hour."

"Make it two."

"That long?"

"Time does not exist in the realm of supernatural powers."

The gypsy waved her hand toward the door, her eyes already fixed on the ball. Célestine hesitated for a moment and then obeyed.

As soon as she left, Nathaira sprang up and stuck the back of a chair under the door handle. Back at the table, she carelessly wrapped the crystal ball and discarded it into the canvas bag. She reached under her headscarf, removed a hairpin, and inserted one end into the tiny lock of the diary. With a couple of deft twists, the leather strap yielded. The gypsy smiled with satisfaction and settled back for an interesting read.

* * *

Did Henri d'Auzon realize how comical he looked sitting on a horse? Nelly could not contain a chuckle when she saw him riding past a crew of diggers in the garden. Julie dropped her brush into a pail of water and joined her at the window. She, too, covered her mouth to stifle a giggle. The horse was of a normal size yet the bulk of the rider managed to reduce it to the dimension of a pony.

Nelly removed her coarse canvas apron and stepped out to greet the visitor.

Henri dismounted. "Nice afternoon, isn't it?" he said, shaking her hand.

"Yes, the weather is outstanding for this time of the year," she answered. "We are lucky in that there's no frost, otherwise the digging could not have started so soon. Everything is in such a state of disarray," she said, rolling down the sleeves of an old dress. "Excuse my appearance, I did not expect visitors."

"This is not a social call, Miss Woodridge, only a business visit. About the fumigation, remember?"

"I'm glad you've come in person. I did not dare to do it without your approval. Come in, please."

He followed her into the house, which resonated with hammering coming from unseen parts. The vestibule was crammed with chairs, console tables, chests of drawers and dismantled beds, most of them freshly scrubbed and polished. The scent of furniture wax and a sharp odor of vinegar mingled with a persistent undertone of mold.

"We are doing what we can but it's not enough," Nelly said when they entered the library. "The stench will not go away. There is nothing more persistent then the smell of mold. I asked around and someone advised me that fumigation with juniper would help. We'd have to remove all the books from the shelves. I prefer that you know this before we embark on the task."

Henri clasped his hands behind his back, his favorite posture, she noticed. "I have no problem with that," he said. "In fact, it would be a good opportunity to sort out the books for indexing. Since I've finished the manuscript, there's no better time than now. I'm only too grateful that you are willing to harbor the library for a while."

"It can stay here as long as you want. This is all new to me. I didn't know that a single person could own so many books. I wish I could read them all."

"Be my guest."

"Would you recommend something?"

He went to the shelves and studied the titles. "Here," he said and handed her a book. "Candide, by Voltaire. I think you'll enjoy it. I'll take care of the rest, starting tomorrow," he said. "It will probably take a couple of days to empty the shelves and sort out the books."

"If I help you, it will take less."

He looked at her inquiringly. "From what I've seen, you've been taking a very energetic approach to restoring the house. Does it mean that you no longer consider selling it?"

She smiled. "It has grown on me. Very slowly, I must say, but with each visit, I discover something new and lovely. I cannot wait to move here. Of course," she sighed, "there is much to do. Between this and the new manuscript, I've been keeping so busy that I no longer have time to feel sorry for myself. And it's all thanks to you. No," she waved her hand when he opened his mouth to answer. "Please, let me say it. You are the finest human being I've ever met, Monsieur d'Auzon, and God bless you! There—" Moved by a sudden impulse, she stretched on her toes, pulled his head down, and planted a kiss on his cheek.

For a couple of heartbeats, Henri stood motionless, his eyes wide open and arms apart as if indicating that he had nothing to do with such an unexpected outburst. Then a wide grin lit up his face.

"Henri," he said. "Would you mind calling me Henri?"

"Not at all!" She was happy that he did not look the least offended. "I had known about Henri long before I met Monsieur d'Auzon."

"And I had heard about Nelly long before I met Miss Woodridge."

"It somehow sounds more natural."

"Very natural, indeed."

"I'm honored to have you for a friend, Henri."

"The feeling is shared, Nelly."

They found nothing more to say and laughed. Then they grew silent. He shortened the awkward moment by pulling out his watch.

"Well, I'd better be going," he said. "I'll see you tomorrow."

Nelly wrapped a shawl around her shoulders and saw him outside. She watched, tongue in cheek, as Henri inserted a foot in the stirrup and swung his long leg over the horse's back.

He gathered the reins. "By the way, I've just remembered another interesting feature of this house. There is a secret entrance in the ancient wall. One of the keys, I don't know which one, is supposed to fit into the lock. One day, when you have nothing better to do, you may want to go and look for it."

"I will do that. Well, goodbye then, *Henri*."

"Goodbye, *Nelly*."

With a palm shielding a smile, her whole being bathing in a warm feeling, she stood in the door until he disappeared through the gate.

* * *

"So?" Célestine asked, anxiously looking for the diary.

It was there, on the table, apparently untouched. With a sigh of relief, she put it back into her purse.

"So?" she repeated.

Nathaira, who was snacking on smoked oysters, pushed the plate toward her. "Want some?"

When Célestine shook her head, she leaned back and crossed her arms. "I had extraordinarily fruitful revelations. You must bring the diary again. It's a superior filter for divination."

"Really? What did you see? Tell me!"

"The crown will come through Monsieur Quérat's offer. Make sure that she accepts it."

Célestine made a long face. "But I already told you that she won't hear of it. She's done with posing for the camera."

"She'll come around when the time is right."

"I don't know. As I said, she's quite stubborn. How long will the offer last? There are scores of models that would leap at the opportunity."

"I've a strong feeling that he will ask her again."

"Perhaps she would change her mind if I told her about you."

Nathaira frowned. "Keep your mouth shut until I tell you," she ordered. "And one more thing. I saw the image of a man with a dark past." She shielded her eyes with her palm and took a deep breath. "I see him again. A tall hairy fellow. A scientist of some sort."

"Why, that's Monsieur d'Auzon!" Célestine exclaimed. "What about him?"

"There's something brewing between the two."

"She and d'Auzon? I doubt he has any serious money. Why, the man can't even afford a barber."

The gypsy made a dismissive gesture. "When did that ever stop feelings? She has a passionate nature and that's the source of all her troubles. She shouldn't allow men into her life until the right one comes along."

"And who would that be?"

"Don't be impatient. The future is revealed slowly. The images are hazy at first but they sharpen with time. All I see so far is a figure of world-wide importance."

Célestine frowned pensively. "Is that so? Well, well, well . . ."

"I'll see you next week," Nathaira said.

Chapter 33

Nelly removed her gloves and contemplated the dark smudges on her wrists. "I never thought that handling books could be such a dirty job."

"It's the dust," Henri said. "Books seem to eat it up. Did I not warn you?" He cocked his head to the side, appraising her. "You look like a giant duster."

"And you are not the picture of fashion either!" she fired back.

"This is my lucky pullover," he lovingly patted the fraying garment. "Good quality seaman's stuff. It has seen three oceans."

She giggled. "And your boots have made the tour of the world."

He brought a foot forward, studying the worn out leather. "Nicely seasoned, are they not? Very comfortable."

"Henri . . ." she drew a deep breath. "I hope you realize that you need a haircut."

He lifted an eyebrow. "Are you trying to reform me?"

"You cannot blame me. It's a female urge." She wiggled her fingers. "Every time I look at you, my hands are itching."

"I see. If I spruce up, would you take me for a stroll along the quays? I don't look any worse than your usual company," he aimed his thumb at the window.

In the darkening garden, disturbed by construction, she could barely discern Schnitzel under a bush, earnestly working on his own digging project.

She pursed her lips. "That's arguable. I don't even know how you look under all that forest on your face. When have you last seen a barber?"

He shrugged. "I don't remember. Joseph usually takes care of me."

"Usually? How often is that?"

"Well, when I let him."

"Henri, please let me do it!" She rubbed her palms together, begging. "I'll give you a very good haircut, I promise. Back home I was a barber to all my cousins."

"Hmm," he pondered the offer. "That will cost you. A dinner with me, right now. It will give you the opportunity to convince me that you possess necessary skills for the operation."

"Where do you want us to go, dressed like this?"

"I know an Italian trattoria near the Sorbonne. There are bare tables and candles stuck into empty Chianti bottles, but they serve the best veal *parmigiana* in town. The aroma itself is edible."

"Could we get civilized before dinner? First the haircut and then—"

"I'm hungry. Dinner first, haircut after. The negotiation is closed."

The food was everything Henri had promised and the trattoria was not as dingy as Nelly expected. Halfway through the dinner, the chef, flushed from the kitchen heat, made his entrance to the dining room. In a powerful baritone voice, he rendered a Rossini aria to the enthusiastic applause of the patrons. A mandolin took over after the amateur singer's production. Nelly's cheeks were already glowing from the effects of the wine when the waiter brought a second carafe of Chianti.

"Why science?" Henri repeated when she wanted to know what led him to choosing a scholarly career instead of becoming a military hero. "Because building up knowledge is what truly brings us to a higher level. As far as other needs are concerned, we are no different from animals. I believe," he said, his fingers playing with the glass, "that without creating intellectual values, without exploration and discovery, we would forever go round in circles, each of us being but a grain in the absurd mill of life and death. As for heroes," he frowned, "there are two kinds. There are those who brave danger for the sake of personal glory, and they are the stuff of which legends are made, even though they accomplish nothing useful.

"The other kind quietly sacrifice themselves for the benefit of all. Just before I left China, I had the privilege of meeting one. He is Père David, a French Jesuit, who has dedicated his life to the discovery of unknown species of Asian fauna. Out of curiosity, I accompanied him on one of his expeditions and only then did I realize what we owe to men like him. It was the most grueling and dangerous journey I've ever undertaken. A memorable adventure for myself, but a way of life for him. He does it for no other reason than to offer a lasting heritage to humanity. But enough of scholarly matters." He replenished her glass. "Tell me about yourself."

Nelly told him her story, part of which he already knew from Octave. He had an intense way of listening as if she was telling him her deepest secrets and, indeed, after a while she was pouring out her soul.

"Religion," he said when she confided in him her dread of entering a church for fear of instant punishment, "is a tool invented for coping with the trials of life and the finality of death. Like all human inventions, it is both beneficial and hurtful. It provides guidance, solace and hope, but it becomes an ugly weapon when it divides people and brings on violence and personal suffering. God is another matter. It's impossible to understand such an immense entity embracing the universe, let alone to be sure of its intentions. Anybody who claims to know God's mind is guilty of arrogance. The only rule you should abide by goes back thousands of years and it wraps up all moral concepts into one neat package. Do not do to others what you do not want them to do to you."

"Confucius, the Golden Rule," she said, glad to display the knowledge she had gathered from his manuscript.

He nodded. "It's simple common sense. In light of that you must ask, who do I harm by my behavior, by the so-called sin of free love?"

"If I harm nobody, why is it considered wrong?"

"Because it undermines social rules. Without rules, there's chaos. You are paying for overstepping the boundaries, but you can decide how much you allow society to tax you. You can either suffer the tortures of guilt and be miserable or take a stand and learn to live on the margin. Luckily, it's easier in Paris than anywhere else."

Nelly savored the moment. No one had ever spoken to her of spiritual matters with such clarity and without condescension. Her mind was ready to cultivate new ideas and, with the help of the wine, she felt that she could charge the world head on.

They left the trattoria in a mellow mood and descended to the boulevard Saint-Michel. Schnitzel lazily trailed behind them. The sidewalks teemed with post-dinner strollers taking advantage of the unseasonable weather. Nelly became acutely conscious of the old patched skirt beneath her hip-length jacket. It had not mattered in the dimness of the cheap restaurant, but it became embarrassing under the gas lamps and in the abundant light coming from cafés and shop windows. Her gaze strayed to Henri's beard. That beard! She would make short work of it soon enough.

"Did you hear me?" Henri was asking.

"Sorry," she said. "What did you say?"

Before he could repeat the question, Schnitzel dashed past them and made a beeline for a giant white poodle. Despite its aristocratic looks and a pink collar sparkling with gemstones, the poodle greeted Schnitzel warmly and graciously allowed him to sniff its butt.

"No, Duchess! Don't be nasty!" the owner tugged sharply at the leash.

Nelly's fingers dug into Henri's sleeve at the sound of a familiar voice. "Oh, my God!" she breathed.

"I know that ghastly dog!" Loulou exclaimed. "Shoushou, do something about it!" she addressed her companion, a dapper gentleman with closely cropped gray hair beneath a shiny top hat.

"Oh my God," Henri echoed and began to steer Nelly to a crossing, but "Shoushou" had already spotted him.

"Henri."

"Father."

General d'Auzon inspected his offspring with visible disgust. "The ladies will excuse us," he said in the deep rumbling voice his son had inherited. "Private business matters." He seized Henri by the arm and led him aside.

"I can't believe what I see," Loulou said. "That ape's the general's son? I heard that Gaillard has finally dumped you. Some replacement you've got there!"

"Monsieur d'Auzon is a friend and he's worth ten Octaves."

Loulou made a face. "Would that be in gold? Not by the looks of him."

"There are other values you know nothing about."

Loulou shook her head and clicked her tongue. "You don't say! And what, pray, might they be?"

"How do kindness and a great mind sound to you?" Nelly said but her high-minded speech fell flat, for Henri and his father were engaged in what appeared to be a hostile argument.

"Good for you!" Loulou said. "Personally, I don't give a shit for lofty ideas. See that?" she drew apart her chinchilla-trimmed velvet cape displaying a diamond necklace. "If you think it's a fake, try again! Twenty thousand francs! How does that sound for a kindness, huh? And my getup is a genuine Worth." She pinched her skirt and fingered the fabric. "So you're welcome to all the great minds in Paris, but this girl is going to stick with solid money. And by the way," she added smugly, "I can promise you that when I'm done with the old monkey, there'll be nothing left for your big ape. Even my dog's collar will be worth more than him."

She turned her head, searching for her poodle, and gasped. Her horrified shriek brought everyone's attention to Schnitzel and Duchess locked in an intimate embrace.

And screw you too, Nelly thought.

The disagreeable encounter knocked the good mood out of them. They walked the last stretch of the boulevard in heavy silence, Nelly clinging to Henri's arm, he with his hands stuck deep into the pockets of his unbuttoned overcoat, and Schnitzel trotting in front of them. It was not until they turned the corner on the quay that Nelly spoke.

"How tall are you, Henri?"

"One hundred and ninety-seven centimeters."

"Uh?"

"Six foot five inches, if you prefer. Why do you ask?"

"I was just wondering. Your father's rather a short man."

"He's not my father," he said gruffly. "I was begotten by a footman."

"That's not true."

"No, it is not, but that's what we both like to think."

"How sad when father and son don't get along."

A long silence followed.

"He's cutting me out of his will," Henri said.

"Good Lord! Why?"

"Apparently, not paying him my respects during Christmas was the last straw. He's summoning his lawyers tomorrow and wants me to think about it. It's supposed to put me through mental torture."

She stopped and stroked his arm. "Henri, I'm sorry. If you want to go home, I'll understand."

"No," he said, bringing the lapels of his coat together as if suffering from cold. "Under the circumstances, I prefer to take advantage of the free haircut."

"Oh, dear! Is it that serious? Listen, if you are ever forced to leave your lodgings, I'd be happy to offer you room and board."

He laughed and kissed her hand. "How sweet of you, dear Nelly! Please don't worry about me. I'm a man of independent means. Father is deluding himself if he thinks he can hurt me."

"So she's back at last?" Célestine asked. "She should have told me that she'd be late. The dinner's all dried up."

Julie shook her head. "Miss said there'll be no dinner. They've already eaten."

"They?"

"Monsieur d'Auzon's here as well."

"Is he? What for?"

"I don't know. Miss has requested a pair of bed sheets."

"What?" Célestine clasped her hand around her throat and then quickly crossed herself. "Mother of God, the gypsy was right again!"

"Who?"

"Never mind!"

Henri put on his glasses and bent down to inspect a pile of hair on the sheet spread under his chair. "Is that all mine?"

"All of it." Nelly shook her skirt, littering the sheet with more cuttings.

"In that case, what's left?"

"Plenty." She whisked off the second sheet that protected his shoulders. "Stop touching your head! I've just combed it neatly. There's a mirror in the bedroom. I can guarantee you that you'll not recognize yourself."

He followed her into the bedroom and peered at himself in the mirror.

"Well? What do you think?" she asked, waiting for a compliment.

He turned his head from side to side. "I think that, thanks to you, I'll have to reintroduce myself to my acquaintances."

"You look handsome. Say it."

"You are merely admiring your handiwork."

"And is it any wonder? Look how it flatters your high forehead," she stretched out her hand and combed the hair back. "And how the short beard defines the outline of your face," she drew her fingers along his jaw. "All your attractive features have been hidden under a—"

"Please!" he said and caught her wrist.

They stood motionless, staring into each other's eyes. In the charged silence, she could distinctly hear the clock ticking away in the sitting room. Finally, he released her wrist.

"I'll go now," he said softly.

"Don't," she said.

"We had too much wine, I think."

"Don't talk!"

"Are you sure of what you're doing?"

For an answer, she grabbed at his pullover. The next few moments turned into a flurry of discarded clothes. The bed creaked as they fell into it.

"Am I too heavy?" he asked, propping himself on his elbows. "Am I crushing you?"

"I want to be crushed within an inch of my life," she said huskily and pulled him down by his short hair.

Something cold dampening her forehead brought her back from a dark oblivion.

"What happened?" she asked.

227

"You passed out." Henri dropped the wet handkerchief and reached for a carafe. "How do you feel?"

"A little dizzy."

He poured a glass of water. "Drink this."

Nelly drank thirstily and then slumped back against the pillow.

"Does this happen to you every time?" he asked.

"No, never before. It must be the corset. We didn't have time to take it off." She patted her stomach and abruptly sat up. "What have you done to it?"

"I've cut through the laces," Henri said sheepishly.

"But there are hooks at the front."

"Too many of them. Too small for my fingers. I was seriously worried."

She smiled. "I'm all right now. Come back to bed!"

He joined her under the cover and stroked her shoulder. "So, where do we go from here?"

"*You* tell *me*."

He propped his head on his palm. "I don't know. I've never been seduced before."

"Seduced? Is that how you see it?"

"Do you have any idea what goes on in a man's head when he has a woman's hands all over his face? I had to endure that torture for the best part of an hour."

She pouted. "Sorry for being such a nuisance!"

"Seriously, I've the impression that I've somehow talked my way into your bed. I'm afraid that you'll end up regretting it."

"I will not!" she protested. "I can think of nobody I'd rather be with than you." She sat up, anxious. "Henri, are you trying to get yourself out of the situation? Is something wrong? Don't you find me attractive?"

Henri pulled her down and kissed her. "You are a delight to every sense. But the fact is that although I'm technically a bachelor, I'm still legally married and will remain so for the rest of my life. I'm chained to a woman I've not seen for years."

"I know. It doesn't matter. I'm no longer the marrying kind. I want nothing from you, Henri. You are kind, you are as reliable as a rock, and you make me feel good about myself. That's more than enough."

"Friends, then?"

"Yes, friends. A special kind of friends."

She settled against his shoulder. Henri kissed the top of her head. "Friends," he repeated, squeezing her against him. "You enchanting witch!"

She ran her palm across his chest, from shoulder to shoulder, and giggled.

"What?"

"I thought your chest would be all hair. Instead, there is just a small patch in the middle."

"Is that a problem?"

"I like it the way it is. I like all of you. Do you . . ." she hesitated, "Is there anyone else?"

"Another woman? No, up until now, I've found the fair sex too much trouble. You made me reconsider."

"You mean you've been completely chaste? How did you manage that?"

"Sublimation."

"What's that?"

"It means that you draw on your sexual energy and redirect it to other pursuits."

"How interesting!"

He chuckled. "It doesn't work any longer, as you may have already noticed. And, besides, it's wrong."

"Is it?"

"Yes. Celibacy is the greatest sin against nature. From now on, I intend to be virtuous."

Nelly laughed.

"I mean it!" he said and reached for her, this time without haste.

Chapter 34

Nelly woke up late, slowly remembering what had happened, and stroked the empty space at her side. She stretched voluptuously. The restlessness she felt in the past few weeks, the insidious hunger building up in her and impossible to satiate by food, was gone. Henri's embrace was a stronghold where she would always find a safe refuge. She knew that there would be neither angry scenes nor disappointing surprises between them. No lies, no stashed-away fiancées. Their future held no constraining ties—after Géraldine's disastrous experience, matrimony no longer seemed an attractive state—just a simple friendly relationship. She felt complete.

Unusual comings and goings in the sitting room caught her attention. She wrapped herself in a dressing gown and opened the door.

Standing in the middle of the room, Célestine issued orders to a procession of delivery boys. Giant flower baskets containing fragrant red roses were being placed on the furniture and on the floor. Nelly rubbed her eyes and stared open-mouthed at the scarlet invasion.

"Morning, Miss," Célestine greeted her. "That's ten and two more in the dining room."

"What's going on?"

Célestine shrugged and handed her an envelope. "Why ask me? I thought you'd know after last night."

Nelly frowned. Henri? Was it possible?

The boys lingered in the door.

"Give them something," she said.

Célestine distributed a few coins into eager palms, while Nelly tore at the envelope. "Oh, for heaven sake," she said angrily, "it's him again!"

"Monsieur Bonnard? That's more likely. So he's escalating the courtship."

"He knows I want none of this. What more can I do to make him understand? This is insane!"

Célestine winked knowingly and poked her forehead. "The old age demon! There are no bigger fools than old men falling in love. You could ruin him if you put your mind to it."

"But I don't want to ruin anybody!"

Célestine sighed, disapproving.

"He sends me another invitation to dinner," Nelly said, "and a carriage to pick me up. You'll go in my place and tell him that I want him out of my life for good. And get rid of this," she waved her hand around, "before we die of asphyxiation!"

* * *

Henri had left saying that he would meet her at the house. Nelly busied herself with the rest of the books, spreading them on the floor, spines up, a row upon row of little tents, ready for the fumigation. By three o'clock, she felt both hurt and worried. When a carriage and a pair rattled down the driveway and a man dressed in black stepped out, she knew that something was very wrong. Were it not for his height, she would have not recognized the distinguished stranger. Without the lush beard, his face appeared unusually lean and serious.

"I did not sleep a wink last night," he said after they kissed. "Father is dead."

She gasped. "Dead? He looked fine yesterday. What happened?"

"A stroke. In his mistress's bed. The woman got hysterical and managed to create a stir before a doctor sedated her. I'm not sure the affair will not leak into the press."

"Oh, dear." She disliked Loulou but she would not wish that kind of trouble even on an enemy. "When were you told?"

"As soon as I got home. Plain-clothes police, very discreet, thank God. All the same, secretly transporting a corpse across the town was something I didn't bargain for. However, that's Father. Troubles to the very end."

His expression belied his cynical words.

"You look like you need a hug," she said softly.

He pressed her against him. "More than one. So good to see you. Unfortunately, I'll be gone for a week or so. The funeral and related matters."

"Yes, of course. How did your mother take the news?"

"She's been gone for years."

"Gone?"

"Gone, as in deceased."

"Oh! I'm sorry."

231

"I have seen you and I must be going now. There's much to do."

"Let me get my shawl."

Outside, she hooked her arm through his. They walked slowly to prolong the parting.

"Will the funeral be in Paris?"

"No, I'm taking the body back to Normandy. There'll be a special train for the mourners. It's not a simple matter."

Nelly became aware of the liveried coachman observing them. It was a private carriage, not a hired one. She lowered her voice. "When do you think I'll see you?"

"I'll write to you." Henri stopped and put his hands on her shoulders. "In the meantime, there's something I want you to consider. The Society of Arts and Sciences has arranged a series of lectures for me, abroad. Vienna, Prague, Warsaw, and St. Petersburg. I would like you to come with me. A little romp across the continent for the two of us."

"Henri, that would be wonderful! But how could I leave all this unfinished?" she waved her hand around, encompassing the house and the garden.

"Shhh," he put his finger over her lips. "Just think about it, all right?"

A glacial gust of wind lifted a cloud of dirt from a pile of rubble and blew it across the driveway. "I think the warm spell is over," she said and buttoned up his overcoat. "Take good care of yourself! I'll miss you."

"I'll let you know when I'm back." He scooped her hands in his and kissed them. "Well, I cannot think of anything else to say, except that you are the loveliest friend I ever had and that I cannot wait to be back to pursue this particular . . . friendship. Are you sure you want to call it that?"

"Yes, Henri, I'm sure. The word love has left a bitter taste in my mouth."

If he was disappointed, he did not show it. "You lead the dance," he said. "Goodbye then," he kissed her on both cheeks, as he would an old aunt, and walked to the carriage. He looked over his shoulder. "All the same, think about it!"

"I will," she promised although she was not sure whether he meant the lecture tour or the nature of their relationship.

* * *

Claude added his last domino to the game on the dining room table. "There," he said. "The victory is mine!"

"More tea?" Nelly asked.

"It's nearly ten o'clock. I should be going."

Géraldine's lips puckered with disappointment. "Already?"

"I'm a humble working man. Up at six in the morning. The client wants to see what I've been up to and I still have to add a few touches to my presentation. But," he lifted his index finger, "before I go I have something for you, Géraldine," he pointed to the buffet, where a mysterious marbled folder had been waiting all evening long.

Géraldine wheeled her chair closer, reached for the folder, and excitedly tugged at the black ribbons that secured it. When she saw the contents, her palm went up to her mouth and she squealed with pleasure. "Nelly! Come and see this! It's wonderful!"

It was a lithograph of dancing mice, dressed in fantasy costumes.

"How cute!" Nelly said.

"Cute?" Géraldine protested. "It's absolutely and utterly charming. And it's so fitting! Exactly as I had imagined the scene. Claude, you are a genius!"

"I thought that illustrations could boost your chances of having your stories published," he said.

"Oh, Claude!" Géraldine extended her arms to him.

Nelly observed the two with a feeling of sadness. How different her friend's life would have been had she met Claude only a year sooner! That they had a natural affinity was clear from the way they kept their heads together whenever they were left to themselves. She did not know what their conversations were about, but she could not help but wonder where it was all heading. Unquestionably, Claude had turned Géraldine into his personal project, but how long would his devotion last? Young men had strong natural needs and this relationship could hardly be fulfilled. She feared the heartbreak that loomed in the future.

She heard the main door opening. "That would be Célestine. Will you excuse me? I have to talk to her."

"Take your time," Géraldine said breezily. "I'll see Claude out."

"It's ten o'clock! Where have you been for so long?" Nelly asked, while Célestine divested herself of her finery. She had insisted on borrowing a stylish cape and a smart hat for her mission. Nelly impatiently pushed her into the sitting room and closed the door. "You were supposed to give him my message and that was that."

"Monsieur Bonnard invited me to dine with him. I could not refuse," Célestine said defensively. "What harm is there in indulging myself a little? Do you know how long it's been since I last went to a restaurant? I, who was used to that kind of life in the good old days? Surely, you wouldn't be heartless to the point of begrudging me an innocent pleasure?"

Nelly sighed. "I'm not heartless. Just tell me that the man will not bother me again. That's all I want to hear."

"Miss, do you know how much he's worth?" Célestine said earnestly. "Sixty million! Just imagine the pile! The life you could lead if you were smart, and such a small price to pay for it! Have a look at this," she reached into her reticule and removed a flat leather box. She opened it and displayed a stunning sapphire necklace. "A proof of his good will and an example of things to come. There's a pair of matching earrings waiting for you at his hotel."

Nelly scrutinized her with a frown. "Célestine, have you been negotiating with him behind my back? Did he pay you to soften me up?"

"Pay me? No, Miss. I swear by Saint-Clothilde, the martyred queen—"

"Leave your saints alone! You'll take that thing back tomorrow." Nelly turned and headed for the bedroom.

Célestine followed in her wake. "Listen to me!" she pleaded. "I have your future in mind. He's rich enough to set you up for life. Besotted old men are easy to handle. I could see to it that you would not put a foot wrong. I'd have everything on paper, signed and notarized, before you as much as lift the bed sheet to let him in. No more worry about money, ever. Isn't it a better prospect than running a boarding house?"

Nelly stretched her arm. "Give me that necklace, Célestine."

Célestine obeyed eagerly. "You will not regret this, Miss. Your own carriage, the best jewels, an opera box, trips to spas, you name it! And you can have young lovers as well, if they are discreet. That's how things are done."

"Go to bed," Nelly said evenly. "Tomorrow, I'll return the necklace myself since I can no longer trust you in this matter."

Célestine gasped for breath. "Miss!" she wailed. "I beg you to think it over. Look at me! In my better days, I had enough money in the bank to retire in comfort. But was I content with that? No, I foolishly fell in love and dreamt of a respectable life. At my age and with all the experience I had! It was simply inexcusable. You know better than anybody the price I paid for it. How do you think I feel when I see you throwing your chance away?"

"Go to bed," Nelly repeated.

* * *

"Marry you?" she asked, not sure she had heard correctly.

"I spent the night in deep reflection," Bonnard said solemnly. "This morning, I went to church to seek divine guidance. I'm now absolutely certain that this is the right thing to do. I'm ready to erase your past and restore you to a respectable status. You can no longer doubt the depth of my feelings for you."

Nelly took in the gilt, plush, and rare woods of the hotel lobby furnishings, the thick carpet of the marble staircase, the hum of quiet conversations, the discreet but readily available hotel personnel: all the comings and goings of the well-oiled machinery of expensive hospitality. This could be her world if Célestine had her way. Except what would the future hold when the novelty wore off?

Her eyes scanned Bonnard's face like an unknown landscape. One by one, she made the inventory of his features, the few wisps of gray hair carefully combed to conceal an advancing baldness, the bushy eyebrows, the pockets under his eyes, the deep ridges flanking his mouth. Only the humble expression in his eyes prevented her from yanking her wrist out of his grip and fleeing. Instead, she attempted to reason with him.

She wiggled her hand free. "Have you given any thought to your son?" she asked. "Could you, as a father, do something so utterly reprehensible and then look him straight in the eye?"

"My remaining son has been a great disappointment to me," Bonnard defended himself, "and my family life has been a tragedy. Yet I was a good husband and a caring father. I'm in reasonable health and not too old to start a new family. I hope for a child or two to brighten my old age. Here," he pressed the jewelry box into her hands. "Consider this necklace a wedding gift. I chose sapphires because they match the color of your eyes. Such beguiling eyes! Marry me and I solemnly swear that you will lack for nothing, including the respect that is due to my spouse."

"Respect," Nelly said sardonically. "What an attractive currency!" She rose to her feet, dropping the box into his lap. "Except that I don't need to be rescued. Good bye, Monsieur Bonnard."

She swept around and headed for the exit.

Bonnard followed in her wake. "Don't make any hasty decisions," he urged as the liveried porter sprang to open the door. "Take time to think it over! I'm a patient man."

Chapter 35

Professor Charcot opened a file and studied the contents, while Nelly's gaze roamed over his study. The room held nothing special that would distinguish it from other medical cabinets other than a series of disquieting photographs. This gallery was a far cry from Octave's luscious beauties. Faces twisted in spasm mingled with those where expression was wiped out as if the soul had already left the body. She was deciding what disturbed her more—eyes staring in terror directly into the camera or turned up, exposing the whiteness of the eyeball—when the professor spoke.

"The fact is that I cannot treat this patient unless I receive an authorization from her legal guardian. As I understand it," he retrieved Nelly's letter from the file, scanning the contents, "the guardianship is being disputed between her husband and her parents. Until the issue is settled, the law considers the husband to be legally in charge. Nothing can be done without his permission."

"But that's simply awful!" Nelly exclaimed. "I believe the husband to be the cause of her illness. All he has ever done was to make it even worse by inhumane treatment."

Charcot lifted his hand as a barrier to her outburst. "Law must be respected but there are discreet paths around it. Although, at the present, I cannot treat the patient officially, I can give you my advice in a strictly private way."

"Oh." She settled in her chair, hands in her lap, attentive. "Is she curable?"

"Only with patience. Do not expect a fast cure, as with your maid. Partial amnesia caused by a single traumatic incident is an altogether different problem. What we have here is a young, energetic woman of vivid imagination who had been trapped in a stifling environment. Boredom is rampant among women of her class, especially when there are no children to occupy their time. The easiest way out is an interesting ailment. Vapors, migraines, female troubles, and a general weakness are the most common problems. Add to it an insensitive and domineering husband and the set up for a tragedy is complete. There is more to it, of course, but I'm not sure whether you have full knowledge of the intimate nature of marriage, Miss Woodridge."

She nodded.

"Good, then we can speak frankly. The conspiracy of silence preceding the wedding night has created more emotional cripples and sexual dysfunctions than is generally admitted. Usually, the young bride is kept in complete ignorance and the groom is overexcited by weeks or months of courtship. As a result, the act resembles a rape rather than an expression of love. Often, the price is frigidity. I'm not sure whether I'm making myself clear."

"She told me that she could not stand her husband's touch. She kept fighting him off."

"You said in your letter that she discovered her infirmity when she woke up in the morning, is that so?"

"She told me that."

"Then I would not be surprised if the night before she had lost one of those fights. She may or may not remember the fact, but conjugal rape was probably the trigger. What we have to find now is whether the paralysis is a true ailment or an imposture."

"An imposture? Oh no, I don't think so!"

"Many of the cases are simulations. It only takes sustained vigilance to catch the patient doing what she is not supposed to do and the play-acting is over. Of course, some of the imaginary illnesses may turn into genuine ones if drawn out too long. Have you seen her legs? Are they fleshy or are the muscles wasted?'

"Her legs are very thin. They are bluish and swollen around the ankles."

"What's the quality of her sleep? Does she complain of nightmares?"

"She told me she often dreams of falling into an abyss."

He made a note of both answers. "What are her activities during the day?" he asked next.

"As I mentioned in my letter, she writes children's stories. They are not sad, quite the contrary, and I think writing makes her happy. What worries me though is that she does it feverishly and, if left to herself, she would pause only for sleep." Nelly leaned forward. "Tell me, Professor, isn't that what is called sublimation? A redirection of sexual energy?"

Charcot gave her a slightly amused look. "You are a most surprising young person, Miss Woodridge. Yes, there is that. Sublimation usually takes the shape of religious fervor or any other socially accepted behavior. When talent is there, it can also be expressed creatively."

"Is it not dangerous when done in excess?"

"Yes, there's a danger of intellectual exhaustion. You must moderate this trait by introducing other activities. Be kind but firm. If possible, one outing a day, if only sitting on a balcony, would be beneficial."

"She has that, Professor. We take her for a stroll in the wheelchair, whenever the weather allows it. Monsieur Savatier comes with us. Géraldine worships him."

"Is he the young man you mentioned in your letter?"

"Yes, that's him. He's been very helpful."

"Are they in physical contact?"

"What do you mean?" she asked half-indignantly.

"Do they happen to touch occasionally? A hand on the shoulder, that sort of thing. If so, does she shrink away from him?"

"Shrink away?" She chuckled. "He is the one that carries her down the stairs when we go out. I'd say that Géraldine is not displeased to feel his arms around her."

"Hmm . . ." Charcot joined his hands. "That sounds promising. I would encourage the friendship as long as it stays within acceptable limits. Well," he straightened his back, "let's wrap this up. I believe this case to be genuine, although one has to allow a margin for error. By genuine, I mean that this young woman has persuaded herself that she cannot walk. Reasoning with her will not help. It will actually strengthen the patient's conviction. The cure has to come from within herself. Once she has been isolated from the environment which had brought on her condition—and that has already been achieved—the protective wall she has constructed in her mind will gradually crumble. Patience is the best option."

"Is there no way to speed up the recovery with hypnosis?"

"Not at this point. First, there is no guarantee that she would respond to it. Only twenty percent of patients can be induced into a hypnotic state. Even so, should she be one of the number, her legs would be too weak to support her. To begin with, we must rebuild the atrophied muscles by daily exercise. I will send you a nurse, who will teach you how to manipulate the legs to improve blood circulation, loosen up the joints, and renew the muscle mass. The rest is a matter of patience."

The sound of Nelly's clattering heels disturbed the stillness of La Salpêtrière chapel and bounced off the high dome above. She knelt before the altar and bent her head until it touched her clasped hands.

"God Almighty," she whispered, "I've not come to see you for a long time because I've been afraid of you. Right now, I don't know where I stand with my faith. I don't even know whether you are too busy with running the universe to pay attention to every single human being on Earth, but if I have your ear, I most humbly beg you to help Géraldine. Please, give her strength and the will to heal herself. Thank you."

She crossed herself and rose, only to fall to her knees once more. "While I'm here, Lord, I also want to thank you for all the good people in my life. Thank you for Julie, Claude, Monsieur Goubert and Géraldine. I'm not sure about Célestine because she's corrupted, but she had suffered a great deal. Please, guide her steps! I even thank you for Octave. He had many faults, but he taught me that physical love is a wonderful thing. But, most of all, thank you for Henri!"

Chapter 36

Coming to the Gare Saint-Lazare, where she had first stepped onto Parisian soil, brought back a string of memories. Nelly had the impression that she had lived several lives in that short span. Rewinding time back to the narrow world of her old dreams, hopes and shallow aspirations made her realize how little all of it weighed when balanced against the freedom of being her own mistress.

She purchased a platform ticket and passed through the passenger gate into the vast echoing hall, where several trains were being readied for departure. An employee directed her to the platform where the train from Le Havre was expected in ten minutes. Only ten minutes to end the ten days of waiting since Henri had left. All she'd had from him were brief notes either from Normandy or from some place in the province of Poitou. Disentangling the twisted ends of his finances was the reason he gave for his comings and goings between the north and the west of the country. He wrote to her that his father's last will dated from nine years ago and it favored a nephew. General d'Auzon's mind was made up the day he understood that Henri and his wife's separation was a permanent fact. His threat to disinherit Henri was merely a playful stab. Henri's choice of words sent shivers down her back. What had gone on between those two, for a father to do this to his only son?

Strolling back and forth, Nelly repeatedly passed the same people, all of them waiting for the train. A little girl, well past her bedtime, dropped her lollipop on the ground and wept with frustration. Her mother returned Nelly's sympathetic smile and wiped the child's sticky mouth with a handkerchief.

A distant rumble caused sudden animation. The porters extinguished their cigarettes, half-finished butts found a temporary refuge behind ears, and caps were steadied at the prescribed angle. Necks stretched and heads craned in the direction of the incoming train.

With a grand show of screeching brakes, the engine came to a halt. In the tumult of opening doors, shouts of recognition, and the exchange of greetings, she quickly spotted Henri, who stood head and shoulders above the crowd. He waved, and weaved his way toward her.

"At last," he said and clasped her to him. They made their way toward the exit, Henri's arm wrapped around her shoulders.

In the hall, he turned to Joseph, who followed them, trailed by a porter carrying the luggage. "Don't expect me early tonight," he said to him.

"Bien, monsieur."

"In fact," Henri tightened his arm around Nelly's shoulders, "don't be surprised if you don't see me at all."

"Bien, monsieur."

"Nice to see you, Joseph," Nelly said.

The valet bowed stiffly, his face a perfect blank.

"He doesn't like me much, does he?" she asked when they were alone.

"Nothing personal, I'm sure," Henri said. "Joseph's greatest dread is finding stray lace stockings stuffed behind sofa pillows and face powder spilled on the carpet. His previous employer was a man about town, much versed in gallantry. A new outfit?" he asked, stroking her sleeve. "You look lovely. Say, would you mind if we stopped at the railway restaurant? I'm starving."

"I've a dinner waiting for you."

"Let's turn it into a midnight snack. Right now, I need a bite or two to keep me going. Besides, I doubt that we'll find time for a serious talk once we are alone. Do I detect a spark in your eye or am I too presumptuous?"

"I've missed you, Henri."

"I have too, love. I was counting the hours. The things I wanted to write to you and never dared!"

They found a vacant table covered with a fresh white tablecloth. Nelly nibbled at a roll, while they waited for a roasted chicken. Henri had already eaten two rolls generously spread with butter.

"Everything was a mess," he said. "I must admit that I was guilty of negligence. Years ago, I left my estate in Poitou in my father's care and was content with cashing my quarterly bank drafts. The old rascal sucked most of the profits into his lands and thought he would get away with it. I had to sort it out with my cousin. Pages and pages of ledgers and bank statements. At least we've avoided a costly lawsuit."

"I thought that the inheritance went to your cousin."

"Yes, Father's part of it. The one in Poitou came to me with the title when my uncle died. I don't grudge my cousin's good fortune. He has a family and I'm unlikely to ever produce a legitimate heir. We've done some financial compensating and real estate shifting. I've ended up with Father's townhouse in the Faubourg Saint-Honoré and joint ownership of a sugar refinery. That, in addition to the land in Poitou. I'm afraid my carefree days are over. What? Why are you making a face?"

"When I think I offered you a room in my boarding house!"

"I assure you that the gesture was truly appreciated. Listen, Nelly, the reason why I'm telling you all this is that I want to talk about our future. Where do you see us a year from now? In ten years?"

She shrugged. "I hope that we will remain friends as long as possible. Forever, if you want."

"Is that all?"

"What else do you need? Or, rather, what else can there be?"

"Yes, what else can there be . . ."

"Henri, let's not think about it now." She leaned over the table and squeezed his hand. "You are here and that's all that matters."

"I'm leaving next week."

"What? Again?"

"The lecture tour. I'm committed. Please, come with me!"

"You know that I'm to move in four days."

"I do. It's not a big hassle. What does it take? A day or two?"

"I've already booked guests. An Australian family is coming the first week in May."

"Cancel the booking."

"Cancel my first booking? A nice start in business! What would the agency think? "

He entwined his fingers with hers. "Please!"

"Henri, I've put a lot of hard work into the house. And what about Géraldine? She needs me every day. You have your commitments and I have mine. Why should there be a difference?"

"Why indeed." He fell into a sulky silence and gave way to his vexation by pushing his fork and knife around. The arrival of a waiter who set plates on the table ended the silent spell.

"I could hire a nurse for your friend," he offered.

"Please, Henri, give up! You know that I'd love to go with you, but I simply cannot. Let's talk about something else."

"Forgive me. If you want to change the topic, I have news for you." He put down his fork and knife. "I've been debating with myself whether or not to tell you, but I think that you ought to know. Octave got married yesterday."

Nelly did not anticipate the searing pain that shot through her like a lightning.

"You are still in love with him, it's plain to see," Henri said.

She rallied immediately and gave him a reassuring smile. "Don't mistake surprise for sorrow. I should've expected it, should I have not? Did you go to the wedding?"

"No. Octave's no longer my friend. And, please, don't pretend to eat when you've lost your appetite. I understand that you need time to get over him, and I'm willing to take whatever you are able to give me at present."

"Henri, it's over." She reached for his hand. "It's you and I from now on. You must believe me."

He kissed her fingers tenderly. "I believe you."

"We have only a week. Why don't we make the most of it?" she said.

"You are right. Waiter! The bill, please."

* * *

Nelly tied the belt of her peignoir, a sleek satin garment softly hugging her body. This time, there would be no corset to constrain her breathing. She sat at the dressing table and dabbed perfume behind her earlobes. As she was reaching for a hairbrush, she heard the door opening.

"It will only take a minute," she said.

"Kitten, my own kitten . . ."

The brush clattered on the floor. She turned. Octave stood in the door, or rather hung onto it, trying to keep balance on his unsteady legs. His clothes were rumpled, the unbuttoned end of his shirt collar poking into his unshaven chin.

Nelly sprang to her feet and backed into the dressing table, while Octave advanced into the room and collapsed on the bed. Shocked, she stood still for a few seconds, before she darted out and kept running until she reached the bathroom.

Henri, naked to the waist, was rubbing himself with a towel. She closed the door and leaned her back against it.

"What is it?" he asked. "You look as if you've seen a ghost."

"He's here!"

"Who?"

"Octave!"

"What? Why?"

243

"I have no idea. He's dead drunk. By the sight of him, he's been drinking all day long."

"How the hell did he get in?"

"He's kept his keys."

Henri dropped the towel, reached for his shirt, and was buttoning it while they rushed back into the bedroom.

He gripped Octave's shoulder and shook him. "Wake up! Do you hear me? Wake up! — Into the bathroom with him," he said, when there was no reaction.

He heaved the limp body over his shoulder.

"At least you could've removed his clothes," Nelly protested, when Henri dumped his load into the bathtub and turned on the water faucet.

"I don't intend to pamper him."

It did not take long for the cold water to do its job. The drunk revived and his bewildered eyes focused on Henri. "Where am I?" he asked.

"Where you have no business to be. Why aren't you with your wife?"

"Amélie?" Octave stroked his wet face. Suddenly, his memory returned. "Amélie's pregnant!"

"Well, congratulations."

"Not by me, she's not! Four months gone with a child . . . afraid to tell anybody . . . and I had to find out on my wedding night!"

Nelly bit her hand to stop an explosion of hysterical laughter, while Octave covered his face and his shoulders shook with grief.

"I treated her like a china doll . . ." he complained between sobs. "I worshipped her . . . respected her virginity . . ."

"Your mistake," Henri said. "All you have given her were nearly three years of small-town wooing while you were living it up in the capital."

Octave finally noticed his surroundings. He looked at Nelly and then back at Henri. "What are you doing here, you bastard?" he asked as he tried to scramble out of the bathtub. He stumbled and his fingers clawed at Henri's arm for support. His knuckles were raw.

"Easy now, easy!" Henri helped him out. "What happened to your hands? Have you been in a fight?"

Octave brought his hands in front of his eyes and frowned. "I've broken everything."

"What did you break?"

"Everything in the studio. Everything!"

"Oh, *merde*," Henri said.

"And I'm going to kill Cousin Émile as soon as I find the swine."

"Is he the father?"

"Not for long. I'll kill him."

"You will do no such thing," Henri said. "Your family would never survive the scandal. I'll tell you what you are going to do. You are going back to your wife. She'll have more children and, eventually, some of them will be yours."

"You think I'm not serious? You think that? I'll show you!" Octave furiously patted his jacket. His hand plunged into a pocket and reappeared clutching a revolver.

"I'm afraid this is not going to be easy," Henri said to Nelly and aimed his fist at Octave's jaw. He scooped up the body before it hit the floor.

"Out of the way!" he barked at the wide-eyed Célestine and Julie, who blocked the door.

"Go to the kitchen, both of you," Nelly said, "and stay there. I'll ring if I need anything. Wait!" She bent down and picked up the revolver. "Hide this somewhere!"

In the sitting room, Henri put Octave on the sofa. "Let's get him out of those wet things before he catches cold on top of his other troubles. Poor fellow, it must be hard on him. The least I can do is to wake up his concierge and ask for a change of clothes. Do you see his keys somewhere?"

Nelly found them still stuck in the door lock. When she returned, Henri had stripped Octave down to his shirt and underpants, and kept slapping his cheeks until he got a result.

"Now, listen," he said when Octave stirred and opened his eyes. "I'm going to your place and get you dry clothes. I won't be long. Do you understand?"

Octave nodded. Henri turned to Nelly. "See that he gets some coffee. The stronger, the better. I'll hire a cab and get him out of here as soon as possible. However, I would prefer that he make it down the stairs on his own feet rather than on my back. Can I count on you?"

"I'll keep him awake. Come back soon."

"Coffee," Nelly said to Célestine. "I need a quantity of strong coffee." She sat down, her elbow against the kitchen table, and buried her face in her palms.

"Serves him right," Célestine said, busying herself with the coffeepot. "After what he did to you."

"I did not invite your comments."

"It's true though. See what you've wasted your time on, while there are men like Monsieur Bonnard. He wrote again, I saw his letter torn into pieces in the wastebasket. Such devotion! This would never happen in his household."

Nelly's palm hit the table. "Shut up! Julie, go and see whether Madame Babeau needs anything. Tell her not to worry about the noise. Everything's all right. When you are both done, you'll go to bed and I don't want to hear a single word. Especially not from you, Célestine!"

Nelly was surprised not to see Octave on the sofa. The blanket she had spread over him before she left for the kitchen lay in a heap on the floor. Through the open door, she could hear him moving about in the bedroom, muttering to himself. She put the tray on the table and went to investigate. He had flung his wet underwear over a chair and, naked, was rummaging in the closet. He did not look off balance and she could but marvel at his recuperative powers. When he turned, she saw a pink scar where the bullet had entered.

"Where the hell is it?" he asked.

"What are you looking for?"

"My dressing gown. What have you done with it?"

"It's somewhere at the bottom."

He found the rumpled garment and put it on. "You and Henri! How long has it been going on?" he asked while tying the belt.

"We're not going to talk about it. I brought you a pot of coffee, but don't make yourself at home."

"Coffee. Yes, I could do with a cup."

He followed her into the sitting room and accepted a steaming cup. "It's too hot," he complained after the first sip.

Holding the cup, he went to the cabinet and poured in a trickle of water from a carafe. He sat down in a chair and drained all in one drought. "More please!"

Nelly stood with her arms crossed, while he emptied the second helping. "Well now," she said, taking the cup from him and putting it on the table, "what about Amélie the Perfect?"

"Go ahead. Kick me when I'm down." Octave's back curved as he propped his elbows on his knees, his fingers running back and forth through his tousled hair.

"No, I shouldn't," she said. "In fact, I find little pleasure in all this. But, it seems there's justice after all. I loved you so much I would've given my life for you. Now my heart is dead. I doubt I'll ever love again the way I loved you, without thinking and with no restraint whatsoever. How I wish I could! Henri deserves no less."

"I've been a bloody fool," Octave said. He lifted his head and there was moisture in his eyes. "Deep inside, I loved you too, and now that I know it, we'll start over. Everything will be different, I swear it! Let Henri go and give me a second chance."

"Don't you come near me," she stepped back when he rose and extended his arms to her. "You should have told me this ages ago! Now it's too late."

He gripped her waist tightly. "I'll show you that it's never too late, my sweet kitten."

"No!" She pressed her palms against his chest. "Don't ever call me that, do you hear me? I'm nobody's kitten." She aimed a kick at his shin. "Let go!"

Octave winced with pain and loosened his grip only to swiftly immobilize her arms by grabbing at the peignoir and pulling it down to her elbows. Nelly kicked at him again but this time without success, as he managed to spin her around and lift her off her feet. He carried her over to the bedroom and dumped her onto the mattress, pinning her shoulders down the moment she landed and weighing down her legs with his knee. They remained still for a while, both breathing hard.

"I hate you," she hissed.

"Shhh, just begin to remember! Remember this?" he kissed the base of her neck and ran his tongue up to her ear. "And this?" he caught her earlobe between his teeth, and pulled gently. "See, you do remember!" he whispered when she shivered and her head rolled to the side. "Your body remembers me. What else did we used to do? See if you remember this . . ." still holding her shoulder down with one hand, he untied her belt and pulled the peignoir apart. His palm ran across her breasts, down between her legs and back again, first with a feather-light touch, then with a gentle pressure, until she moaned.

"It keeps coming back, doesn't it? Don't look away! Look at me!"

"I hate you!" she repeated.

"No, you don't. You want me to go on, you little slut, you want me inside you and that's exactly what you are going to get!"

After a short exertion, Octave groaned with release and rolled to the side. "I'm sorry I could not wait for you. Drinking doesn't agree with me. Next time—"

"There will be no next time. Never!"

"What do you mean? We're back together. It has been sealed right here and now. Are you crying or what? It couldn't have been that bad."

"Jesus . . ." Nelly curled her back forward and brought her knees up to her face, "Jesus Christ!"

"Oh, come on!"

"Don't touch me! I hate you and I hate myself even more. How can I look Henri in the face?"

"Leave Henri to me. I've more right to you than he does."

She slapped his hand away. "I said, don't touch me!" She got out of bed, her shaking fingers clumsily retying her peignoir. "It was rape, nothing less. Rape!"

"You are angry because you missed the finale, that's all."

"Damn you to hell!"

"Exactly as I said. Angry."

He caught up with her in the sitting room. "Listen, stop the hysterics! I've done nothing you did not want me to do. You are overwrought. Go and get some sleep and I'll talk to Henri."

Nelly opened her mouth to protest when they heard the click of the main door and she panicked. Quickly, she gripped his arms. "This has not happened, do you hear me? Act as if nothing has happened. Please!"

"Nothing has happened?" Octave shouted. "Surely, you are joking! Don't make me angrier than I am already!" He brought her arms behind and twisted them, forcing her to turn her back to him. He swept her around until they both faced the door. "Now here's Henri and I'm sure he wants to know what's going on. Don't you Henri? So, you have been lusting after her hot little body? She cannot control it, I'm afraid. Now she has second thoughts but you should have seen her five minutes ago. A genuine she-devil! I don't think you can handle her, my friend. She would melt down your cold intellect in no time."

Henri said nothing. He walked to the table and took his time putting down the leather travel bag he was carrying. It looked as if he was simply going to leave and Octave relaxed his hold on Nelly. The rest happened in a flash. Gripping Octave by the throat with one hand, Henri backed him into the cabinet. A glass panel shattered on impact. A fist, hitting his stomach, brought Octave down to his knees.

"As for the two of us," he addressed Nelly, "I've made the mistake of taking it far more seriously than you. Goodbye, Nelly. I'll try not to think of you when I'm in Saint-Petersburg."

She ran after him. "Henri! Please! I know that I don't deserve you, but . . ."

Henri paused only to remove her hand from his sleeve. "Damn right, you don't deserve me."

"Let me explain! I did not want this. I swear I did not. You must believe me!"

"I believe only once."

"Please, Henri! Henri!!!"

The door shut behind him. Nelly pressed her forehead against it and gave way to tears. Behind her, Octave was slowly getting on his feet.

She turned in a fury, swiftly crossed the room, and seized the leather bag. With a shake, she emptied the contents over his head and flung the bag on top.

"Get out!" she yelled. "Get out!!!"

Chapter 37

Dear diary, more and more I turn to you in sadness rather than in joy. I've reached an important decision. I'm going to marry Charles Bonnard.

Géraldine is appalled by my choice. Célestine, of course, is overjoyed. Between the three of us, I'm the one with a clear head. I know this is the right thing to do. After Henri and Octave left and I sat in a bathtub trying to soak off my shame, I saw the error of my ways. There was some truth in what Octave said. Nothing would have happened had I been able to control my body. I could have fought him harder and I did not. I could have screamed for help, but I was silent.

Henri was wrong about God. Reading cynical freethinkers like Voltaire has spoiled his mind. God sees and hears everything and He has been displeased with me. What angered Him the most, I'm sure, was that instead of coming to His house as a supplicant asking for forgiveness, I thanked Him for my sinful life. God does not want me to live in sin and that's why He has sent me Mr. Bonnard and others before him. I had scorned all His choices but now I'll obey. If He wants me to marry the old man and breed little shipping magnates, then He must have his reasons. I don't say I understand them, but then who can understand divine mind? In that, at least, Henri was right.

Therefore, I shall not listen to Géraldine's arguments. She said that if I don't want to pursue this kind of life, all I have to do is to renounce the dubious pleasures of flesh and give my entire mind to business. But how can I trust myself? What if another man catches my fancy and I'm not able to resist my evil urges? No, I want to become a virtuous person and marriage will be my shield. Mr. Bonnard offered me redemption and, finally, I'm grabbing at it with both hands.

Charles (I've yet to get used to calling him thus) got my letter yesterday in the morning and by five in the afternoon he was in Paris. He said that he would have the marriage contract prepared and ready when I visit him in Dieppe tomorrow, to take stock of my future home. I'm to see his townhouse and his country estate in the Calvados region after which I'll sign my name to the contract and we'll be officially affianced. In three weeks I shall be a married woman!

The only problem is Géraldine. Even though I promised her the best care in my new home, she refuses to leave Paris. Now, that her stories have been accepted for publication, she feels that it is in her best interest to stay in the capital. I know that it's all about Claude, who is already more important to her than I am. We had a heated argument over it. I would loathe losing her because she is as a sister to me and I know I'll need her desperately to get through my new beginnings. I'm not sure whether the Dieppe society will accept me. I may earn their scorn as a gold digger, which God knows I'm not, although I don't disdain material comfort. But Géraldine is digging her heels in, saying that she still does not believe that I'm serious. She's wrong.

I've already begun burning bridges between the past and the future. We've moved into my house two days before the expected date, despite the fact that the dining room was not wallpapered and the new paint on the doors was tacky to the touch. Tonight, as soon as Charles left, I wrote to the agency, canceling the Australian guests and withdrawing the house from the listings. The forged iron sign above the gate cannot be removed, but it only says 'La Plaisance' in arched letters and does not mention the nature of the business. But the one that says 'Family Pension La Plaisance' is no longer hanging in the passage and pointing into the lane. It is stored in the stable, face turned to the wall, and will remain there until it turns into dust—much like my desire for independence.

Chapter 38

Célestine could not believe it had really happened and yet the train was actually moving away while the two of them stood in the middle of nowhere, growing more lonely with each turn of the wheels. In the meadows, on both sides of the rails, cows chewed at the tender spring grass, their black and white coats smeared with mud. Mud was everywhere, as far as the eye could see - and one could see far in the flat Norman countryside. The heavy sky held a promise of more rain. On the horizon, here and there, the clouds had already broken under the weight of the rain that was pouring down in grayish fringes.

"Why?" Célestine asked. "Why on earth? Why?"

"I cannot do it. I just can't." Nelly said.

"But did you have to pull at the emergency brake and throw the luggage out? Couldn't you simply wait till the next stop?"

"I was not thinking."

"Damn right, you weren't! You are mad! Mad like that friend of yours. It must be contagious. A fifty francs fine, and people looking at us as if we were a pair of lunatics. "

"I'm sorry."

"Sorry! Now, that's a great consolation to me. And what, pray, are we to do next? Carry the luggage on our backs?"

"There are only three pieces. I'll carry two. See that church steeple over there, behind the trees? That will be a village. There must be some kind of transport available."

"They are not just trees. It's a forest and maybe it's full of savage peasants. Dressed as we are, we might be robbed and killed. Saint Virgin of the Lourdes! What have I done to deserve this?"

"Oh, shut up, or I'll leave you here!" Nelly picked up two travel bags and started across the meadow toward the forest.

Célestine, seething with genuine hatred, had no other choice than to follow down the gravel embankment and onto the slippery grass. The hem of her skirt soaked up moisture and her shoes grew heavier as they gathered mud. A couple of cows observed her laborious progress and one of them decided to step closer. Célestine stopped and looked around with apprehension. Her new jacket was made of burgundy wool, and there could be a bull somewhere. Wasn't it said that bulls were partial to red? She could end up trampled to death. Wouldn't that be the limit? And all because of that damned American slut. 'I just can't do it.' Like hell she couldn't! What had she been doing until now? Hoisting up tents in bed she was, and being paid for it too. She didn't get the house by winning it in cards, did she? Bonnard's millions would more than make up for thin hair and bags under the eyes. She, herself, would happily slip between the sheets if he wanted her. No such luck. Men did not look at old women. They looked through them as if they were transparent. The bitch didn't know it—could not begin to understand it—but one day she would, and then it would be too late to be sorry.

There was no bull, thank God. Célestine put a foot forward and slipped on fresh cow dung, landing painfully on the suitcase she was carrying. She dragged herself on her feet and the sight of her muddied gloves brought tears to her eyes. That morning, she had squeezed her thickening waist into a new corset and dressed with the utmost care. She had wanted to impress Monsieur Bonnard's staff with a dignified bearing, suitable for the future housekeeper. She would have been perfect for the promised post. Had she not had experience in issuing orders and supervising her own staff? In the good old days . . .

The fall was the last drop to overflow her cup of bitterness. She sat heavily on the suitcase and gave way to grief. Tears flowed down her cheeks, carrying away aborted aspirations and all the hard persuasion she had exerted to reach her goal. Her mistress, who had heard her fall, had put down the luggage and was retracing her steps. *Go away*, Célestine thought, *go away or else I'll squeeze your throat with both hands and end up a murderess!*

"Célestine, are you all right?"

What a stupid question! No, she was not all right and it was plain to see. She allowed herself to be pulled onto her feet.

"My hip hurts. It must be bruised."

"I'm sorry."

Sorry! Sorry you should be, sorry you will be, you brainless creature! Célestine blew her nose and righted her hat. She gathered her purse, her umbrella, and the valise. Back to the kitchen she was to go. And what a kitchen! A basement with small windows beneath the vaulted ceiling. A dungeon! What pleasure could there be in a modern stove if she could not see what was happening outside? She'd miss all the comings and goings in the Quay de la Tournelle courtyard. There would be no pleasurable gossip with the concierge, no distraction from her duties, just turning out breakfast, lunch and dinner for a bunch of strangers, day in, day out. She had over seven hundred francs put aside, hidden in her mattress. Some of her own savings, five hundred from Bonnard for talking her mistress into seeing his courtship with a favorable eye, plus what she got for the flower baskets she had managed to sell back to the dealers. She still had acquaintances in the Les Halles market. If she wasn't to lord it over a millionaire's staff, going back into business for herself was the best option. With what she already had and her salary of forty-five francs a month, she would be able to open a flower shop within a year. With some clever cheating on the cost of food, which was the privilege of every cook with a stupid mistress, she would achieve her goal even sooner. The American was soft and careless. She treated servants like family and never locked up provisions. In the past, when she'd had a staff herself, she had kept the keys of the larder and had taken stock of everything, knowing well what servants were like, the whole cheating and thieving lot of them.

More mud on the narrow path through the forest and then a clearing with a crumbling farmhouse. Hens and pigs rummaged in a dunghill, the courtyard reeked of piss, and curious faces peered at them from behind the windows.

"Let me handle this," Célestine said when the dumb faces went on staring and no one responded to their call.

Resolutely, she approached the door and knocked at it with the handle of her umbrella. It took several hard knocks, before the door opened a crack.

"My good woman," Célestine said to the wizened old peasant who stood in the shadow behind the door, "we are stranded and we need some sort of transport to the nearest town. Where can we hire a horse cart?"

She had to repeat the question before the peasant answered in her thick local brogue. The farmer was not at home, no one was, except herself and the youngest children.

"Where can we find him?"

The woman stepped over the threshold and pointed toward the fields skirting the village, where, diminished by distance, half a dozen workers bent their backs over the soil. Célestine sighed. More negotiations ahead.

An hour later, they were both seated at the back of an ox-drawn cart, their legs hanging down, with the luggage piled behind them and competing for space with dirty potato bags. Célestine hooked her arm around the side of the cart for fear of falling off during the bumpy ride. In her free hand she clutched an open umbrella, but the rain that had finally begun to fall had already soaked the front of her skirt.

"That's another two francs on top of the fine," she said testily. "Nice going! Spending as if there was no end to your money. And thirty centimes had to come out of my own pocket! We are lucky we've our return tickets because I don't know how we'd have managed without them."

"I'll pay you back," Nelly said.

"Frankly, I start to wonder with what money. If I'm not mistaken, the bill for the eight new mattresses and the bedding is still to be paid. That's a big expense. Do you have enough in the bank?"

"We'll get by. I still have the copying and Claude and Géraldine will chip in with their rent."

"Scraping the bottom of the barrel, that's what you're proposing to do. When I think of the life we could be leading if it weren't for your crazy mood swings! Think of the millions that are waiting for you at the terminus in Dieppe! We can still take the next train and say we missed the first one. Think, I beg you! Think!"

"For the last time, shut up!" Nelly snapped. "I'm getting tired of your ceaseless nagging. My mind is made up and if you don't like it, you are free to go. You are not irreplaceable."

Célestine swallowed. She had gone too far. "That's what a body gets for deep devotion!" she exclaimed. "Irreplaceable? How do you replace maternal love? You are the daughter I never had. Can you reproach me for worrying about your future? Why, my heart's breaking, when I see how little you appreciate my sincere feelings!"

"Oh, stop crying, for heaven's sake! It's not the end of the world. I'm going to list the house with another agency. We have the advantage of offering English spoken and there will be no shortage of foreign tourists. And I'll see if I could do some modeling."

"You mean you'll go and see Monsieur Quérat?"

"I will."

Fate. It was futile to go head on against fate, the gypsy said. "This marriage will not take place," she predicted. "Both the tarot and the crystal ball speak against it. If your mistress accepts the proposal, something irreparable will happen. Don't go against what's written in the Book of Life or you'll regret it bitterly."

True, she had scorned the advice. But could she be blamed for being a down-to-earth person seeing the millions far more clearly than some hazy image?

The ox-cart left them in front of a small railway station four miles down the road. Célestine, whose bladder was bursting, went immediately in search of the privy. Only on her way back did she notice the sinister agitation that filled the passenger hall. A newspaper copy circulated from hand to hand amidst loud comments.

"What's happening?" she asked Nelly.

"They say that last night there was a murder on the train."

"On this very line," said a man nearby.

"Who was murdered?" Célestine asked him.

"An important fellow from Dieppe. A shipping company owner."

Nelly passed her palm across her livid face. "Oh, God," she whispered. "Oh, God!"

Célestine, trembling from head to foot, knew better. God had nothing to do with this. There were dark forces at work, terrible, unstoppable dark forces and, if she tried again to mess with destiny, she could be next.

Chapter 39

The omnibus advanced slowly in the dense traffic as everyone who had time on their hands decided to enjoy the heady spring air. Crowded sidewalk cafés with guests basking in the sunshine and shops invitingly spilling their merchandise into the street passed before Nelly's eyes, but two smudges left behind by a child's hands on a window panel above the opposite bench held her attention. The imprints varied in intensity depending on the changing light. Almost invisible in the shade, on a light background they appeared as a milky film where the little palms and chubby fingers had pressed against the glass.

She imagined a three-year old kneeling on the bench and eagerly observing the passing scenery. The child in her imagination was as insubstantial as the prints on the glass, a colorless silhouette with no features and no name. Something like this was growing inside her. She suspected that she had not yet fully grasped the immense responsibility motherhood was bringing upon her. Never again would she be only Cornelia Jane McKay or whatever name she chose to go by. For the rest of her life, she would be someone's mother. The fact filled her with both awe and panic. Lately, she often felt like running away from the intruder in her womb, who was turning her into a primitive being concerned only with the most basic urges: eat, sleep, and throw up. Free love. What a joke! Nothing was free.

She sat in a corner near the entrance, where there was some exchange of air, but even that precaution was not enough. With her newly sharpened sense of smell, she felt nauseated by the odor of cold tobacco and stale wine hanging around the man who sat at her side. When he got out at the corner of the rue Castiglione and was replaced by a maid with a basket, the situation worsened. The basket, resting on the maid's lap, contained a fish loosely wrapped in newspaper, the slimy tail protruding over the rim only inches from Nelly's nostrils. The stench was insufferable. She pressed her hand under her nose and breathed through her mouth, making each breath as shallow as possible.

She wished she could escape onto the roof, but that would not be safe. Only men could climb the steep steps. Why did women make their life difficult by dressing so uncomfortably? Why the constraining corsets, tight bodices, bulky petticoats, trailing skirts and high heels? Men strode with confidence in pants and comfortable shoes, and that was why they ruled the world, while women had interesting ailments and babies. She felt a growing anger at being trapped in a female body.

She had to tell someone about the baby and her first choice was Célestine. She expected loud exclamations and ready advice, but Célestine had changed since the journey that was never completed. She expressed no surprise and merely asked how many periods Nelly had missed.

"Only two? A Christmas child then," she commented and went on tallying the kitchen expenses. Usually expansive and free with her opinions, she seemed prone to an unexplainable lethargy. She hardly looked at the newspapers, which were describing the railway murder, discussing travelers' security and asking questions. Why did the robber empty the victim's valet but left behind an expensive watch? Had he genuinely overlooked it, or was the robbery a cover up for a political murder? The victim had been known as a staunch Bonapartist sympathizer. Although she had feared it then, Nelly was never bothered with police inquiries. Her letter, which Bonnard said would always be close to his heart, had probably disappeared with his pocketbook.

The omnibus crossed the rue Royale with its luxury shops and entered the rue du Faubourg Saint-Honoré. Where did she hear that name recently? Henri. Did he not say that his father's townhouse was somewhere in these parts? Now he would live in this grand neighborhood. Henri d'Auzon, Count de Villermaine. Suddenly, she became fully aware of the wide social gap that separated them. Her eyes misted over as they invariably did when she thought of him. He left a painful void in her life, and each time she remembered the hurt in his eyes she experienced a stab of shame.

Octave sent her a letter, a concoction of remorse, apologies and promises. She tore it to pieces and stuffed them into an envelope together with a note. *I've kept your revolver. If you come near me, I'll shoot you.* That was before she discovered she was pregnant. Now, she would never be entirely done with him. There would be the child. Should it be his, it could pursue her with Octave's puppy eyes and his endearing smile. It could be malicious, unscrupulous, and manipulative, and she would have to love it because she would be its mother. God, have you not punished me enough? Please, let the child be Henri's!

"*Rue d'Anjou!*" the conductor called. It was her stop.

The Quérat-Beaulieu Agency shared the mezzanine of a six-story building with a law office and an export-import company. It consisted of a suite of rooms, the first of which was occupied by two clerks and an office boy. On the walls hung a number of coded photographs representing a wide choice of subjects: still life, racing horses, landscapes and buildings, religious themes, fashionable beauties, famous people and infamous criminals. Nelly recognized some from seeing them sold in stationery shops and market stalls or hawked in the street. The place was cleaner than a hospital room and reeked of disinfectant. The office boy busied himself with a duster, sweeping the already dust-free surfaces, while the two clerks bent over their paperwork. One of them lifted his head and asked her business.

"Miss Woodridge to see Monsieur Quérat."

"Yes, of course. Kindly wait here."

He crossed the room to a door, opened it, and talked to someone in a hushed voice. He returned followed by a rotund man with the florid complexion of a dedicated gourmand. His salt and pepper hair was neatly parted in the middle and a pair of mutton chop whiskers enlarged the already round face. He extended a hand with an onyx ring on the middle finger and clasped hers in a handshake.

"Welcome to Quérat-Beaulieu, Miss Woodridge. I'm Monsieur Tassin. I run the agency in Monsieur Quérat's absence."

"But I have an appointment with him."

"He's in his office. Although he suffers from a rare medical condition and seldom deals with visitors, he's made an exception for you."

He led her through his office, its walls hung with photographs that were less innocent than the ones in the reception room. Nelly recognized several of Octave's nude studies. She did not have time for a closer look as Tassin had already reached a door with padded leather panels and motioned to her to hurry.

"A word of warning," he said. "The patron is going through a bad period. Not only has he difficulty breathing, but his eye trouble has returned. His eyes are very sensitive to bright light. Don't be surprised by what you see. As for the smell of disinfectant, Monsieur Quérat has recently subscribed to Doctor Pasteur's newfangled theory of dangerous microbes. Don't offer him a handshake."

Quérat's office contained neither drapes nor carpets and the window shutters were tightly closed. A lamp softly illuminated the room, creating a halo behind a figure seated at an oversized oak desk. A table flanked by a pair of leather armchairs stood at some distance from the desk. Again Nelly smelled carbolic acid, this time mingling with a faint odor of camphor.

Tassin introduced them. The man behind the desk nodded and motioned toward one of the chairs. The rasping sound of his laborious breathing filled the silence as Nelly sat down, trying not to stare. A white linen mask protected the man's nose and mouth and she could barely discern his eyes behind a pair of green-tinted glasses.

"Glad to meet you at last," Quérat said. The muffled words came out quickly to fit between two painstaking intakes of air.

"My pleasure, monsieur."

Why would anyone in his condition drag himself into his office instead of staying in bed? Perhaps the business was on its last legs as well. She must be cautious and get everything in writing.

As if he had read her mind, Quérat patted a folder in front of him. "I have your contract ready ... for signing," he said. "Monsieur Tassin will ... explain what I have in mind ... for you."

"I must emphasize again that I will not pose in the nude," she said.

"We are well aware of your wishes," Tassin said, bringing the folder to her. "The nudity clause is contained in paragraph five. At no time will we ask you to bare your body below the armpits and above the ankles. We've already discussed it with the Maison Worth, where your costumes will be designed. In fact, I've here a sketch to give you an idea of the kind of work we expect from you." He sat down, opened the folder, and handed her a drawing. "The Queen of Sheba," he explained.

The costume was stunning. Although drawn in black and white with shades of gray, it managed to convey the sheen of silk and the glitter of jewelry. It consisted of an elaborate jeweled headdress and a flowing white robe with a striped mantle, which fastened to the shoulders by two gem-studded brooches. Other jewelry included a heavy, barbaric necklace, a pair of disc-shaped earrings, and a number of rings and bracelets.

"This is the first one of a series of famous queens, beginning with antiquity," Tassin explained. "We feel that the public is tired of war deprivations and the general lack of luster. Time has come to give them a dose of luxury. We're aiming specifically at the female market. What do you think is the main element lacking in women's life, Miss Woodridge?"

"Freedom?" she hazarded a guess.

"The correct answer is power. We want women to look at the pictures and imagine themselves beautiful, fabulously rich and, most of all, wielding absolute power. We want them to contemplate the magnificent costumes and imagine the life they would lead had they been born to rule. A harmless but seductive fantasy."

"Am I to model for more than one queen?"

"All of them."

"All? Wouldn't they soon tire of one face?"

Tassin shook his head. "Think back when you were a little girl. Did you have a doll?"

She nodded.

"You enjoyed dressing it in different costumes, did you not? Did you not look forward to seeing it in a new outfit, anticipating the thrilling effect of change? What was your doll's name?"

"Mary Ann."

"Now, you'll become a doll yourself. You too will have a name. The one Monsieur Quérat has chosen for you has already been made public by Sarah Bernhardt's painting."

"Ceres?"

"Exactly. By associating you with La Divine's fame, we'll have an advantageous start for the series."

This was heady stuff. "Wouldn't Mademoiselle Bernhardt object?"

Tassin shrugged. "Mythological names are in the public domain. She has no legal ground for objection."

They were distracted by Quérat suddenly gasping for breath. His hand went to a tray at his side, filled with medicine bottles, accidentally knocking some of them down. Nelly let out a cry of distress.

Tassin lurched to his feet. "This is worse than usual!" he exclaimed.

While Quérat clawed at his chest, he reached for one of the bottles and let a few drops of liquid fall onto a folded handkerchief, which he pressed against the mask. Almost immediately, a strong odor of camphor hit Nelly's nostrils. After a while, the man's breathing improved.

"You should have a nurse with you at all times, *patron*," Tassin said, "or else one of these episodes could be your last."

Quérat shrugged and waved him away angrily. Tassin returned to his chair. While his back was turned to his boss, he glanced at Nelly with a tight-lipped smile, the like of which adults exchange when confronted with a child's tantrum. The incident created an atmosphere of intimacy and Nelly felt her spine relaxing.

261

"Let's discuss the financial aspect of your contract," Tassin proposed. "Rather than remunerate each pose individually, we propose to retain you for a weekly salary of one hundred francs."

"How much?" she asked, thinking that she heard him wrongly.

"One hundred francs a week. However, for this price the agency would expect you to fulfill certain obligations. While you are under contract, you will pose for the Quérat-Beaumont Agency exclusively and, indeed, you are not to engage in any sort of activity that could jeopardize the public image we are attempting to create. What you must, can and cannot do will remain at the discretion of the agency."

She hesitated. "Pardon me, but I've the impression that I'm to be turned into a slave."

Tassin smiled. "That's hardly the case, Miss Woodridge. The agency is merely protecting its investment. Monsieur Quérat has to advance a considerable sum for costumes, props, fees of portraiture, and the manufacture of copies."

"How many weeks do you have in mind?"

"We'd like to leave it open. The contract guarantees you a trial period of six weeks. If the project turns out to be a success, as we hope it will, we may extend your contract indefinitely," he looked at his boss for confirmation and received an encouraging nod. "At that point, we may discuss a salary increase."

Nelly signed without asking further questions. On her way out she noticed the *Morning Breeze* hanging on the wall among a collection of oil paintings of stormy landscapes. It was the only photograph in Monsieur Quérat's office.

Chapter 40

"I still think it's vandalism," Claude said from the ladder he was perched on. "I don't know who painted the murals, but it's clearly Fragonard's influence. With time and patience, the stains could be cleaned and the missing parts filled in."

"Time, patience, and *money*! I have none of the three," Nelly said heatedly. "Should I tell you how much I paid for the new table and twelve chairs? There was not a single piece of furniture in this room that was not damaged in the explosion."

Claude shrugged and took from her a length of wallpaper. Climbing to the top, he stretched his arms and pressed the sticky side along a penciled line. "You still have time to stop the sacrilege," he persisted.

"Claude, please! I cannot have satyrs chasing nude nymphs around the dining room. This is supposed to be a respectable boarding house."

"You win. Pass me the brush."

She stepped up two rungs and handed him a brush. With sweeping strokes, Claude smoothed the upper section, chasing out air bubbles from the center toward the sides.

"Adieu, art! Bonjour, middle-class hypocrisy," he said mockingly.

That did it. With her nerves stretched to the point of breaking, tears appeared in her eyes and rolled down her cheeks. She sank to the foot of the ladder, her back against the wall, and buried her face in her apron. To be called a vandal and a hypocrite, while all she wanted was to make a decent living, was too much to bear.

"Nelly?" Claude climbed down the ladder, squatted at her side and put his arm around her shoulders. "Oh, come on! I didn't mean to hurt you."

"I'm doing my best, you know!" she sobbed. "I cannot please everyone. It's just not possible."

"Here, here . . ." he gave her shoulders a brief squeeze and pressed a handkerchief into her hand. "Let it out if you must."

She obeyed and had a good cry. "I'm sorry," she said after she had blown her nose. "Usually, I'm not like this. It's just that lately everything seems to be so difficult."

"It's your condition."

"Géraldine told you?"

"I needed an explanation for your moodiness."

"Claude . . ."

"What?"

"What is it like to be illegitimate?"

"Géraldine told you?"

"She knows that I worry about the child. Tell me, was it hard?"

He rubbed his thigh, thinking of an answer. "Honestly?" he asked.

"Honestly. I need to know."

"It's not good. You grow up noticing that sometimes the grownups are whispering when you are around. Then a schoolmate calls you a bastard and soon you hear it from all sides. You punch and kick. You win some of the fights but mainly you lose, because the enemies are too many. You make some friends but you feel humbly grateful for their friendship and that, in turn, makes you angry. Sometimes even with those who genuinely love you."

"How awful!"

"You wanted the truth. Now look," he patted her shoulder, "mine was a small town experience. It's different in Paris. There is no better place to bring up illegitimate offspring. If I'm to believe the statistics, there are eighteen thousand born each year. People don't stick their noses into their neighbors' business, mainly because they hardly know them. Your child will be fine, I promise."

"I so want to believe you."

"Let me tell you this. Had I been born without the stain of illegitimacy, I'd have stayed at home, run my uncle's little bookstore and dabbled at painting on Sundays. In time, I would have married a narrow-minded local girl and spent the rest of my life wondering what I could have accomplished, had I possessed enough guts to pack up and move to Paris. I begin to think that being what I am is a blessing in disguise. It makes one try harder to be successful. Most people who leave the safety of home feel they have to prove something. Just think of it! Would you be here had you been satisfied with the hand Fate had dealt you?"

"You are right. I wouldn't."

"You see, you are a fighter. So stop worrying and keep fighting! Besides," he got up and pulled her to her feet, "if we want to finish today, we cannot keep chatting forever."

Whistling a merry tune, he returned to the ladder.

Nelly went back to the table and dipped a brush in a pail of paste. She began to spread it over another length of wallpaper, while her mind mulled over Claude's speech. He was a collection of contrasts. Despite his boyish looks, he was surprisingly mature. He had physical strength no one would have expected in his slim body. He was disciplined and purposeful, yet harbored a dose of idealism bordering on self-sacrifice. She could not fully understand him. But did it really matter? She was glad their paths had crossed and grateful for his helpful nature. Whenever something needed fixing, whether it was a broken service bell or a door that would not close properly, Claude would look at it with a frown and find a way to make it work. Today, although it was Sunday and the beguiling scents of spring poured in through the open windows, he had refused an invitation to a boating party. Instead, he was helping her, knowing that, with all the bills still to be paid, she could ill afford professional service. No wonder Géraldine adored him. But what exactly did he feel for her? She could not help but worry about the issue. Now that they had reached a new degree of intimacy, she felt a nagging urge to set the record straight.

"Claude?"

"Yes?"

"What exactly is between you and Géraldine?"

"Why do you ask?"

"I only want what's best for her."

"So do I!" he said with a flash of annoyance.

"You shouldn't fill her head with notions of platonic love if you don't mean it."

Claude did not answer. Instead, he stepped down, and busied himself with the lower section of the cut, taking his time to smooth it. Finally, when she no longer expected it, he spoke.

"I don't want to scare her off," he said to the wall and then, turning and looking at her directly, "You were not there. You have no idea what she went through."

"She told me all I need to know. It's time she began to heal and your attitude doesn't help."

"What am I doing wrong?" he asked, genuinely surprised.

"You are making her too comfortable. It's as if you wanted her to remain dependent."

She did not know it until she said it, but now the truth was staring her straight in the face. She saw it in his eyes.

"That's not true!" he protested.

"You're afraid that once she starts walking, you'll lose her. That will not happen."

"I'm only trying to be patient. I keep hoping that with time—"

"There's no better time than now. I've been exercising her legs twice a day. They cannot get any stronger. She could be up and walking this very minute. All she needs is a good reason to try."

"Then what do you suggest?"

She shrugged. "Honestly, I don't know what should be done. But I think I know what you should not be doing: that is, saying that you love her the way she is."

"Come back when you have a better idea."

"Oh, I certainly will. I've written to Professor Charcot and I hope he'll see me soon."

"Have you finished?"

She looked at him, hurt, before she realized that he meant the next cut of wallpaper. One way or another, he wanted her to drop the issue and she had run out of ammunition.

* * *

On Tuesday, Nelly delivered the finished manuscript, picked up the tassels she had ordered for the dining room curtains, inspected the house from top to bottom, went to Maison Worth to be measured for her costumes and hired a cab to get to the railway station on time. The cab got caught in the traffic jam caused by an accident. She paid the driver and went the remaining two blocks on foot.

Claude was waiting for her in front of the railway station, a cardboard sign stuck under his arm.

"I'm awfully sorry!" she said. "It took longer than I expected. How do I look?"

"Out of breath."

"Are the carriages waiting?"

"Calm down, everything's fine. The train from Calais has just been announced."

"Oh, thank God," she let out a sigh of relief and fanned her face. "I really appreciate your help."

She re-pinned her hat as she followed him inside. Already, a trickle of passengers was passing through the arrival gate. Claude lifted the sign over his head. *The Fullerton Family*, it said. The trickle thickened into a stream of travelers, flowing around moving islands of luggage. Faces and clothes showed signs of weariness from the Channel crossing and hours of confinement on the train. The English tourists were easy to spot by their no-nonsense flannels and tweeds, while the color-loving American women looked like tired parrots. A few such parties passed by, showing no interest in the sign, when a sharp female voice cut through the blurred noise.

"Daddy, look! It says Fullerton. That's us!"

A young woman in a mustard-yellow outfit with trimmings matching her red hair, which, in turn, was topped by an emerald-green hat, pushed her way through to Claude and Nelly, separating an English couple in her haste.

"I say!" the man protested.

She paid him no attention. "Are you from the Pension La Plaisance?" she asked Claude. "I'm Poppy Fullerton. *Je parle français. Voici mes parents et ma soeur!*" she made a vague gesture indicating practically everyone behind her back.

In a series of smooth movements, Claude folded the sign, stuck it in his pocket, lifted his hat, and kissed Poppy's hand. His social skills had vastly improved since Christmas. Poppy let out a yelp of delighted surprise, followed by a light giggle, which revealed a gap between the upper front teeth.

"I'm Mrs. Woodridge," Nelly said. "Welcome to Paris!"

"You really speak English! I'm so glad!" Poppy enthusiastically pumped her hand. "Mommy and Daddy have been a little worried because they cannot utter a word of French. —Over here!" she called to the party that began to gather around.

There were six of them. Mr. and Mrs. Fullerton, followed by a pale-faced, solemn brunette with a nervous tic to her mouth, who turned out to be Poppy's sister Hyacinth, and two maids named Mabel and Janet. While the overseas trunks were being strapped on the roof and the back of two waiting carriages, Poppy single-handedly undertook the distribution of seats. She herded her parents and Hyacinth into the first carriage and decided that since she could speak French, she would ride in the second one with Monsieur Savatier, Janet and Mabel. Nelly, fighting to keep a serious face, joined the Fullertons in the first carriage. The moment it moved forward, Hyacinth's face crumbled and she dissolved in tears.

"Oh, Mommy," she sobbed. "I can't bear it any longer! I shall never survive the embarrassment. Judge Pinkham is a friend of Bobby's father. Poppy does it on purpose, I swear she does. Already, she has ruined my engagement ball and now she's mortally offended Mrs. Pinkham. I'll never speak to her again as long as I live! Ooh . . ." she whined, nesting her face in her hands.

Mrs. Fullerton reached for her daughter's hand. "Shhh, darling," she cooed, "let's not have a public display! Mrs. Woodridge is not interested in our little problems."

Hyacinth straightened up at once. "You call it a little problem? Mrs. Woodridge will soon realize herself that my sister is certifiable. Now she's set upon ruining Daddy's political career and nobody is doing anything about it. And it's your fault, Mommy, for inviting the Pinkhams to share our train compartment. You should've known what Poppy's like! Ooh . . ." She collapsed against the backrest, giving way to another bout of weeping.

Nelly discreetly acknowledged Mrs. Fullerton's silent plea for patience, while wondering what Poppy might have said or done to unleash such a storm.

"You must excuse our Hyacinth, Mrs. Woodridge. She has a talent for exaggeration," Mr. Fullerton said, while unfolding a good-sized handkerchief. "Give her this," he passed it to his wife. "Those lacy ones you women carry around don't hold any water."

"Do you have any children yourself, Mrs. Woodridge?" his wife asked.

"Alas, not yet."

Mrs. Fullerton sighed. "How sweet they are when they are little and what a worry when they grow up!" She assessed Nelly ponderously. "Pardon me, dear, but you seem to be too young to be in charge of a family pension. When shall we meet Mr. Woodridge?"

Nelly was ready for that. "I'm older than I look. As for my husband, he is currently traveling in China," she said, fingering Géraldine's wedding band under her glove.

"In China?" Mrs. Fullerton exclaimed incredulously.

"In what capacity?" inquired Mr. Fullerton.

"Scientific research, sir. He is collecting and translating ancient manuscripts."

"A scholar? How interesting!"

"His travels have been funded by the Society of Arts and Sciences."

The Fullertons looked suitably impressed.

"And the young man, is he a relation of yours?"

"Monsieur Savatier is my husband's brother from a second marriage. As you see, I'm not without protection during my husband's absence."

Should Mrs. Fullerton continue with her cross-examination, Nelly had cooked up similar convincing details. After all, she was a graduate from Octave's School of Skillful Deception. For instance, there was Henri's library to sustain her claim to a scholarly husband. Everything would be fine, provided Julie didn't forget herself and call her Miss.

"Did you have a pleasant stay in London?" she changed the subject.

"London is most unsanitary," Mr. Fullerton said. "The air contains a quantity of soot and the river Thames is an open sewer. The monuments are impressive, but the popular districts show a regrettable lack of care. I would not recommend the city from a hygienic point of view."

"Nor would I recommend our hotel!" Mrs. Fullerton chimed in. "For the price they charge, one would expect excellent service and bug-free beds. I was not impressed with the English. The personnel seemed to look down on us and, at the same time, they expected to be paid for answering every simple question. As I said to my husband, no more hotels! You really do provide a fully equipped bathroom, don't you, Mrs. Woodridge?"

Nelly assured her that the bathroom was fitted with every necessity, and there were no bugs in her beds. Meanwhile, Hyacinth nursed her hurt feelings and Mr. Fullerton sharply observed the street life. When the carriage paused briefly at the crossing of boulevard de Strasbourg and boulevard Saint-Denis, his attention was attracted by the white-marble interior of a butcher shop, where meat cuts were neatly displayed among tropical foliage or suspended from gleaming steel hooks. Gilded mirrors on the back wall reflected the immaculate white aprons of the sales clerks behind the counters.

"Are there other spotless butcher shops like this one?" he asked.

"All the butcher shops are kept spotless. They are regularly inspected by the city and fined if found dirty."

"Fascinating." Mr. Fullerton conjured up a thick notebook from his pocket and scribbled something on a new page.

Hyacinth stopped sulking and began to pay attention to her surroundings. "Daddy, look at the wide streets! Six lines of traffic and all of it going so fast! How can one go around on foot without being run over? Mommy, look!" she pointed at a sidewalk café, "There are men and *women* sitting out in the street and *drinking!*"

"Where?" Mrs. Fullerton leaned toward the window. Just at that moment, a messenger wagon, preceded by an ear-deafening trumpet blare, passed at a high speed only inches in front of her nose.

"Upon my word!" she jerked her head back. "I'll not feel safe until we are back home. I'm sure, Hyacinth, that you could've had a beautiful wedding dress made in Baltimore without dragging the whole family through the ordeal of travel."

"But it wouldn't be a Worth, Mommy."

"Travel broadens the mind," Mr. Fullerton interjected.

"My mind is as broad as it ever will be," his wife said. "It doesn't have to include tolerance for wickedness. Men and women drinking in the street! I wonder what other vice is waiting for us here."

All of a sudden, Nelly felt exhausted with life in general and these people in particular. Bouts of exhaustion were not new to her ever since she discovered her condition, and they were always demoralizing. Mrs. Fullerton seemed to be a paragon of virtue. The mere act of lying to her required energy Nelly could hardly spare. How much easier it would be to tell the truth! Look here, she yearned to say, I have spent a fortune to provide you with good accommodation and my private life does not concern you. Unfortunately, truth was a luxury she could not afford. The recoil of disgust and the indignation her presence stirred among Octave's relatives were still etched in her mind.

"Are you all right, Mrs. Woodridge?" Mrs. Fullerton asked. "Suddenly, you look very pale."

The carriage was crossing the Pont de Change. "A passing headache," she said lightly. "If you look to your left, you will see the Conciergerie, where Queen Marie-Antoinette was held prisoner during the first revolution. Above the roofs are the towers of Notre Dame."

The Fullertons obediently turned their heads and let out little ah's and oh's of approbation.

Stop fretting! Everything will be fine. Nelly relaxed against her seat and felt blood flowing back into her cheeks.

Chapter 41

Dearest diary, I have neglected you for some time despite the fact that pouring my thoughts onto your pages has always had a soothing effect on my nerves. Had I more time for myself, I would have turned to you as soon as I learned the latest bad news, but the arrival of the Fullertons, followed by an accumulation of petty problems, drained my energy. Each night I have collapsed into bed and fallen asleep as soon as my head touched the pillow, which was actually a blessing because the fatigue freed me from ruminating over the situation and giving it far more importance than it deserved.

The floor of Monsieur Tassin's office heaved under my feet and I almost disgraced myself by fainting when I heard that Octave was the photographer assigned to the job. Looking back, I know I should have expected it, considering that he'd had previous dealings with the agency. When the blow came, I reacted like a harpy. On the verge of hysteria, I threatened to break my contract at once unless the agency agreed to pair me with someone else. Monsieur Tassin immediately lost his unctuous manners and told me that had I read my contract attentively, especially the last paragraph, I would have discovered that I was liable to a substantial fine if I did not fulfill my obligations.

"Surely," he said, "you don't want to become involved in a lawsuit you are bound to lose."

As I sat at his desk, mulling it over, he added in a conciliatory tone that Octave, with all his theatrical experience, was by far the best man for the job and that signing him up had required an effort because he, too, was not happy with the situation. Then he said that instead of dwelling in the past, I should consider the financial advantages of my contract. His hand went to the envelope containing my first weekly salary and his sausage-like fingers pushed it toward me.

My fighting mood fizzled out like damp fireworks. I kept thinking of the money inside the envelope as well as all the problems that awaited me at home, the most urgent of which was to hire more help. Julie was run off her feet acting as a maid of all work, while the Fullertons proved to be both demanding and time-consuming. I felt I was standing in the middle of a bog with the prospect of mud clinging to my feet no matter where I decided to step next. I put my pride aside and reached for the envelope.

On my way home, I purposely turned my mind to practical matters, and especially to the trials of running a boarding house without a shred of experience. From day one, I had to act like a captain of a leaking ship. While nothing went irreparably wrong, a number of small crises kept me on my toes. The first concerned the bathroom, of which I'm justifiably proud, as such a convenience is an exceptional luxury. This I pointed out to the Fullertons during the tour of La Plaisance. They approved of the pretty tiles, the shiny brass faucets shaped like dolphin heads, the zinc bathtub and the ceramic sink, but looked with some puzzlement at the bidet. Although I explained its use in the most delicate terms, Mrs. Fullerton was deeply shocked. She called it a French abomination and requested that it should be removed immediately, as the mere sight of it would offend the sensibility of her daughters. I had some difficulty in explaining that the contraption could not be removed as it was fixed to the floor and the plumbing would have to be seriously altered. A compromise was reached when I found a small table that fitted over the 'abomination' and covered it with a fringed Spanish shawl reaching down to the floor. In the future, foreign guests must be told that the bidet serves for washing feet.

Apart from the plumbing issue upstairs, another crisis was brewing down in the kitchen. Instead of keeping to their room under the eaves when not needed, the two Fullerton's maids expected to be shown into a servant parlor. There was something of the sort next to the kitchen, but the room was crammed with dusty odds and ends I had not sorted out yet. With all the work inside and outside the house, I did not give it the smallest thought. Yet the maids could not remain upstairs during the day, as they would not be able to hear the service bell. All I could offer them were two chairs by the kitchen table, where they sat with their knitting and drove Célestine to distraction with their 'English chitchat'.

"This can't go on," she protested. "I refuse to have those two biddies in my kitchen outside of meal times. I don't understand what they are saying, but I know they keep talking about me. It makes me self-conscious and I keep dropping things and spoiling the food. Isn't it enough that I have to be a cook and a scullery maid rolled into one, now that Julie's too busy upstairs?"

In the end, I spent the night emptying the servant's parlor, while poor Julie scrubbed the floor and dealt with the worst cobwebs. We restored it to some degree of comfort. Still, it needed further refurbishing, including a rug to protect feet from the cold flagstone floor. Where will the expenses stop?

I owe an increasing debt to Claude because Poppy is set on taxing his patience more than anyone else's. I would be inclined to sympathize with her desire for a fulfilling career, but her stubborn attitude and an utter lack of diplomacy repel me. From what I have gathered so far, I suspect that her parents agreed to the overseas trip mainly to keep her away from Baltimore, where her reputation had suffered some unspecified damage. She is determined to become a painter and, when she learned that Claude himself was an artist, she was elated. She appointed him her guide, or rather general factotum, completely disregarding the fact that he has to work for his living. At her demand, he accompanied the whole family on an extended tour of the Louvre, where the Fullertons, except for Poppy, endured a large dose of tedium. They find it difficult to reconcile their conflicting interests. Mrs. Fullerton and Hyacinth are mainly bent on shopping, while Mr. Fullerton, whose ambition is to be elected into the municipal council of Baltimore, intends to apply his time in Paris to the study of the serious matters of urbanism and public hygiene.

The trip to the Louvre had dire consequences. When the party emerged from within, Poppy consulted her city map and took her bearings. She proposed that they should round off the day by treating themselves to dinner at the best of restaurants which, according to her guidebook, was the Véfour. She met with half-hearted resistance, following which she seized Claude by the arm and took the lead. After a short hesitation, her parents and sister simply tagged along. As Claude told us later, their faces fell when they were presented with thirty-page menus. Everyone turned to him for help. Being used to modest restaurants, he felt painfully out of his element. He did what he judged his best by turning the matter over to the waiter and approving his suggestions. The dishes started to come, each more sumptuous than the last, accompanied with a choice of wines. Two hours later, when they worked their way to coffee and desserts, they began to experience mild physical discomfort. When the bill arrived, the discomfort was temporarily forgotten as Mr. Fullerton stared in wordless astonishment at the total. He passed it to his wife, who gasped audibly. There followed an exchange of words, whereupon Poppy turned to Claude, showing him the bill.

"Monsieur Savatier, my parents want to know whether such robbery is fully justifiable. Please, say it is, so that we can get out of here with a minimum of fuss."

Poor Claude! He still has not got over the guilt. But the worst was yet to come. By the time the party reached home, the Fullertons felt more and more out of sorts. Mrs. Fullerton was the first to develop a full-fledged liver crisis, which is the solemn term the French use for monstrous indigestion. At midnight, the house was ablaze with lights and the maids rushed up and down the stairs, while the Fullertons moaned and groaned in their beds, clutching now at their ribs, now at their bellies, inside which raged an unaccustomed collection of rich food and various vintage wines. A doctor was fetched, principally to lend support to my reassurances that death was not imminent.

At three in the morning, when the worst was over, I rolled into bed next to Géraldine.

"Poor dear, isn't it today that you are to meet with Octave?" she asked anxiously. "Do you feel up to it?"

"I don't know and I don't care," I answered, already half-asleep. Truer words were never spoken!

Chapter 42

Octave was seated at his desk, comparing prices in two chemical supplies catalogs, when Bébert ushered Nelly into the office and closed the door behind her. On her way through the shop, she had become aware of furtive glances and an exchange of sly smiles among the staff. She suspected that Bébert's ear would be pressed against the keyhole.

Octave flipped a page and studiously scribbled something on a notepad. Finally, he lifted his head and looked her up and down. "You look awful," he said. "Been carousing all night long?"

With only four hours of sleep, followed by the usual morning sickness, she indeed looked drawn. She had hoped for frosty politeness, but the opening remark proved that he was in a combative mood. Old anger welled up in her. She smiled and struggled to sound cool.

"You, on the other hand, are looking much better than when I last saw you. Fatherhood suits you."

It was a direct hit. He flinched as if she had poked a raw wound. "You bitch!"

"Just remember what I wrote to you. If you ever lay a finger on me again—"

He sprang to his feet. "As if I would!" he hissed with contempt. "Rest assured, that I'll never dirty my hands with you again, you ungrateful baggage! You seem not to remember that when I first met you, you were nothing but a greasy kitchen slut. Where would you be without me? I pampered you, I educated you, I worked my fingers to the bone to provide for you. In a weak moment, I even offered you my heart. And how did you reward me? By bewitching my best friend. I'll never forget that, you harlot!"

As the abuse poured out of him, she experienced a conscious catharsis. The bitter resentment that had been blocking her chest began to melt and when he spewed out the final insult, it was gone. She no longer felt love or hatred toward him, only an immense relief as she realized that he had lost his power over her. Impatient to be done with him, she magnanimously glossed over the details. They no longer mattered.

"You are right," she said.

"What?"

"Everything you said is true."

Poised for a fight, her lack of resistance threw him off balance. His Adam's apple flicked up and down as he swallowed.

"I want my revolver back," he said peevishly.

"That cannot be done."

"How so?"

"I intend to keep it until I'm sure you really mean me no harm."

"It's my property."

"So sue me."

Once more, his eyes flashed with anger and he raised his arm to slap her face.

"Suit yourself," she said invitingly. "I expect nothing else from you."

He expelled the air from his lungs and let his arm drop. "Go and get dressed," he ordered.

* * *

Géraldine's pen descended over the numbers aligned in the account book, her lips moving silently. She dipped the tip in the inkwell and wrote a cipher at the bottom of the column. She discarded the pen in the holder, yawned, stretched her back and turned her attention to the open window. By the length of the shadows cast by the trees in the garden, it was about two o'clock. Except for the chirping of the sparrows, an uneasy calm reigned over La Plaisance after the excitement of the previous night. Something stirred at her feet. Schnitzel, who had been snoozing under the desk, rose and shook himself. He let out a whimper followed by a single bark.

"What is it?" she asked. "Is your Mama coming home?"

Soon she could hear the click-clack of heels herself. She wheeled her chair close to the window and caught the flash of an ivory silk parasol behind a magnolia bush before Nelly emerged in full view on the driveway. There was a spring to her step that had been absent since her breakup with Henri and the dreadful business with Charles Bonnard. She noticed her friend and waved. Impatiently, Géraldine motioned her in.

When she entered the library, Nelly had to deal with Schnitzel's greeting ritual. "Good boy, yes, good boy," she patted his head. "Next time I'll take you with me, I promise. Now, get your paws off my skirt!" She turned to Géraldine. "How's everything? Did they have their lunch?"

"Only tea and dry biscuits. Poppy and Mr. Fullerton went out. Mrs. Fullerton and Hyacinth are still convalescing. Claude is in his room, catching up with his work. He had his lunch on a tray. By the way, did he tell you that Poppy made him promise that he would help her apply for a copyist permit at the Louvre? What next? I think he should hide until the Fullertons are gone."

"That will not be for another three weeks. I'm sure things will settle down."

"I hope so. So, how was it?"

"Better than I expected," Nelly said, removing her hat. "I'm starving. Have you eaten?"

"No, I was working on the accounts."

"How are we doing?"

"Walking on a tight rope. The hundred francs are nearly gone. Today, I paid the collector from Bon Marché for the dining room china and Célestine wants another twenty francs for groceries. Did you not say that you had something coming for the manuscript? Because if not, we are going to be seriously short of cash. You should ask the Fullertons for an advance."

"Not after what happened yesterday."

"That was not your fault."

"Of course not, but it would be bad timing considering the state they are in. Besides, I don't want to appear too eager. I'd better go after the manuscript money."

Géraldine sighed and juggled a couple of imaginary balls.

"At least, I've solved the staff problem," Nelly said. "Someone is coming tomorrow. A boy I know."

"You have hired a male maid?"

"It's just for the summer. He's someone I trust. He used to be kitchen help in the restaurant I worked in. The owner died suddenly and he's out of a job. I bumped into him at the studio. About a year ago, Octave had promised him to take him on as an apprentice but not until he's fourteen. Believe me, it is a stroke of luck. Zidore is a darling and a good worker."

"You know best. Now will you please tell me what happened at the studio?"

"First let's get a tray from the kitchen and make ourselves comfortable in the bedroom. I need to put my feet up."

"Cold chicken and potato salad." Nelly put the tray on Géraldine's knees and began to undress. "You would not believe what's happening down in the kitchen. Célestine is learning to knit! They seem to get along at last, she and the maids. A true *entente cordiale*."

"How do they speak?"

"Hand signals, mostly." Nelly unhooked the front of her stays and sighed with relief. With her shoes off, she sat on the bed, cross-legged, and spread a napkin on her lap. She reached for her plate. "Everything seems to be falling into place," she said, biting into a chicken leg.

"Well, that's enough of an introduction," Géraldine said impatiently. "Get to the point!"

"I'm over Octave at last."

"You don't say."

"Completely! Well, he'll always be here," Nelly touched her forehead, "but I have finally kicked him out of my heart."

"It's about time," Géraldine said. "How did he behave?"

"Awful at first. We had an ugly scene in the office. I think he needs the contract as much as I do, otherwise he would not consider working with me. I had a good look around the studio and there was a quantity of new equipment. That spell of madness must have cost him a lot of money."

"What about his wife?"

Nelly shrugged. "We did not talk of that. As soon as we were working, he behaved as if we had never met. It was 'Miss Woodridge, would you kindly do this' and 'would you kindly do that'. Very icy. No shouting, no swearing. One would think we were at a social tea. It only shows that one can make good pictures while keeping the creative fever at a civilized level."

"So, things are looking up."

Nelly dug into the potato salad with her fork. "I believe so. I think I'm going to like it. Everybody treats me like a princess. I've my own dresser. She's Madame Odille from the Odéon. She did my makeup and my hair and she helped me with the costume. It was rather complicated, but it looked fabulous. Today, I even had my own slave."

"You are joking!"

"I am not! Picture this—" Nelly paused to swallow and discarded her plate to free both hands, "I'm sitting on a throne with gilded lion carvings, among a heap of treasures. They must have scoured all the theatres in Paris for fake gold dishes, strings of pearls and gems. Just think of Ali Baba's cave. I'm leaning back like this, one elbow on the armrest, and my foot is pressed against the shoulder of a prostrated Negro slave. Nude, except for a loincloth!"

"No!"

"His skin was oiled to better show his muscles and believe me, dear, they were spec-ta-cu-lar! His name is Monsieur Narcisse and he is from Martinique, which is an island somewhere in the Caribbean. He'll lend a truly exotic touch to the picture. So there I sat, with my bejeweled sandal on Monsieur Narcisse's broad back and Octave told me to look disdainful. I looked directly at him from under my eyelids and I did not have to pretend. Later, everybody said that I'm a natural."

"And what's next?"

"Cleopatra, followed by the Empress Theodora. That's the Byzantine period, I was told. Jewels, jewels, and more jewels! Monsieur Worth is very knowledgeable regarding the historical details. After that, I don't know. The only thing I'm sure of is that it will not last. As soon as they find out that I'm expecting, it will be over. I might as well enjoy myself while it lasts."

Nelly scraped her plate for another forkful of salad. They ate in silence, while the worrisome Specter of the Future passed between them.

Dropping the plate back on the tray, Nelly yawned. "I can hardly keep awake. I looked so tired that Madame Odille had to camouflage the circles under my eyes. I wish I could sleep for an entire week, but a nap will have to do. Can you hold the fort for a couple more hours? Provided there's not another crisis . . ."

Nelly fell asleep so fast that Géraldine would have sworn she had fainted.

Chapter 43

According to Poppy's guidebook, the Mabille Garden—despite its naughty reputation—was a marvel of urban landscaping and night illumination. According to Poppy again, visiting Paris without seeing the Mabille Garden was akin to having been in London without having seen Westminster Cathedral. Although the comparison was somewhat lame, Poppy had gathered support for the project and her mother's opposition got outvoted. Obeying Mrs. Fullerton's firm request, the party was seated as far as possible from the two hundred and fifty-foot wide dancing circle, where an orchestra of fifty played the overture from *Orpheus in the Underworld*. The cheerful music drifted across the tables and mingled with the murmur of conversation, punctuated by discreet outbursts of laughter. For the moment, nothing much was happening and newcomers had the leisure to admire the myriad lights, including a mammoth chandelier hanging from the ceiling of the orchestra stand. Halfway between the platform and the outer edge of the dancing circle towered twelve iron replicas of palm trees, some twenty feet tall, their leaves bearing a multitude of luminous glass coconuts. A double row of gas jets blazed along the arches surrounding the circle, with a giant chandelier in the center of each arch. As the darkness deepened on this warm May evening, the garden, with its artfully illuminated fountains, bushes, and flowerbeds, turned into a magic land.

Mr. Fullerton scribbled into his notebook, while Hyacinth eavesdropped on a nearby table. "Our neighbors are Englishmen and their wives," she reported. "They look very proper."

"Everybody looks proper," Poppy commented. "If something very improper doesn't happen soon, I'll be inclined to think that we're in the wrong place."

"Poppy!"

"Have a little sense of humor, Mommy! I think I shall have a strawberry cream soda. What are you having, Monsieur Savatier?"

"Are you all right?" Nelly asked Géraldine, who sat at her side, still recuperating from the attention she had stirred up as her wheelchair was being pushed through the narrow space between the tables. They were all here at Mrs. Fullerton's invitation. Believing that there was strength in numbers, she had recruited the natives for this risky expedition into the territory of sin.

"It was worth it, I suppose," Géraldine said.

"Don't you like it here? Perhaps the real thing doesn't come up to your expectations?"

"No, it's fine, I assure you. Very beautiful."

"Something's wrong, I can tell."

Géraldine bit her lips. "Don't you think that Poppy is rather forward?" she said bitterly. "Look how she's appropriated Claude! How dare she? Does everything have to be her way? And he goes along with it!"

"Like the others, he finds it easier to swim with the current rather than against it. Don't be cross! When she's gone, everything will be back to normal."

"That's the only comforting thought. And what's eating you?"

"Do I look like something's eating me?"

"As a matter of fact you do. Ever since dinner."

"I'm just a little tired."

It was not true. In reality, Nelly felt edgy. Her state of mind had been triggered by a banal conversation at the dinner table. She had asked Hyacinth about the progress of her wedding gown, whereupon Hyacinth launched into a long monologue concerning watered silk, tulle, lace insets, appliqué, and seed pearl embroidery. When she paused for breath, Mrs. Fullerton addressed her husband.

"By the way, dear, I did not tell you whom we met at Worth's. None other than Clemence Lippincott! Remember the Lippincotts? We met them last year at my sister's ball. A bean canning fortune. Their daughter Prunella, the one with the slight lisp, is to be married to Lord . . . uh, I didn't quite catch his name. I hope that they had the fellow thoroughly investigated or the child could end up like that poor heiress who was murdered. Cooper was her name. A dreadful story."

"Indeed, I remember it well," Mr. Fullerton said. "A clever crime. Had it not been for the maid—"

"I don't believe that the maid was not an accomplice. She was seen in Paris long after the crime wearing an expensive dress. You did not happen to meet her by any chance, Mrs. Woodridge?"

Nelly's heart skipped a beat. "Why me?"

"Well, I suppose that occasionally you meet Americans who live in Paris, do you not?"

"There are thousands of Americans living in Paris. One cannot possibly meet them all."

"That many? On the other hand, I doubt that the woman would be bold enough to show her face among honest people. Very likely, she's hiding where nobody knows her and enjoying her part of the spoils."

The episode ruined Nelly's evening. When, at nine o'clock precisely, the orchestra struck a lively polka and the dancing began, she watched half-heartedly, wishing she could go home to bed and pull the covers over her head. Since such blessed relief was not close at hand, all she could do was to sip her lemonade and fight off insidious recollections of happier times. Last year, she was here with Octave on Bastille Day. After dinner and an evening stroll along the boulevards decked with national flags and tricolor bunting, they ended here on a whim. They drank wine, held hands, kissed, laughed, applauded the daring dancers, and joined in a waltz. At midnight, the sky exploded with fireworks. They stood among the cheering crowd, Octave's arm hugging her waist, her side snug against his as if their bodies had been molded for the very purpose. It was one of those moments of which perfection was made.

The energetic polka, a mere warm up, yielded to a wild gallopade.

"Upon my heart," Mrs. Fullerton exclaimed, "I've never seen such furious dancing! If two pairs were to collide, there would be a heap of bodies on the floor in a matter of seconds."

The dancers separated, the women gathering up their skirts, spinning around and diving under their partners kicking legs. The vivacity of movement revealed frilled petticoats, multicolored stockings and even an occasional flash of lacy drawers.

"Well, Mommy, aren't you glad we came? You wouldn't see anything like this in stuffy Baltimore!" Poppy enthused.

"I should hope not," her mother said, in a sanctimonious tone that barely hid her fascination with the lively spectacle. On the floor, the action evolved to yet a higher degree of daring. Several circles formed around the more agile dancers, now mostly hidden from view. Occasionally, a female foot in a dainty slipper would appear above the throng of spectators, aim at a hat, and send it spinning to the floor. One particular leg, encased in a red and white-striped stocking, was scoring success after success. The music stopped for a drum roll, followed by a triumphant clash of tympani and wild cheers as yet another tall hat left its owner's head. The ever-thickening crowd exploded in final applause and two men hoisted the mysterious dancer on their shoulders. "Bravo! Vive Manon le Cannon!" the audience shouted. Nelly experienced her second shock of the evening. The disheveled brunette in a bright green dress, laughing and lifting her arms in acknowledgement of the general admiration, was none other than her former neighbor Marie.

Poppy, who had been watching, standing on her toes, clapped enthusiastically. "Was it not terrific?" she shouted above the tumult. "Except that one can scarcely see from here. I'm going to have a closer look at the next dance."

"I forbid you to even think of it!" her mother said.

"Why not? I promise not to do anything wild. Monsieur Savatier could—"

"Poppy, sit down!" her father ordered.

Poppy's face reddened with anger. "It's always been the same with you all! The moment I start enjoying myself, you make long faces. If you think I'll sit here like a stuffed doll all evening long, you are mistaken. I feel like throwing darts."

She turned on her heel, and soon melted into the crowd strolling along the amusement stands.

"Oh Lord, she's in one of her states," Mrs. Fullerton said. "She will not listen to anybody. Mrs. Woodridge, would you please ask Monsieur Savatier to keep an eye on her? At the moment, he's the only one who can do no wrong, in her eyes."

Nelly translated the request. Géraldine's lips tightened when Claude rose to follow in Poppy's wake.

"Next thing I know, they'll both be on the dance floor," Hyacinth predicted.

"Claude would do no such thing," Nelly protested. "He's a responsible man."

"You don't know my sister. She is—Oh, no!" Hyacinth's eyes widened. Quickly, she spread her fan in front of her face. "Nobody move! Don't look! Please, don't look!"

"What is it, Hyacinth? What do you see?" Mrs. Fullerton asked anxiously.

"To our left. The table under the tree. The Pinkhams!"

Like the others, Nelly could not help but follow Hyacinth's alarmed gaze. Four tables away, a middle-aged couple were taking their seats.

"If they see our daughters, we shall be the talk of Baltimore," Mrs. Fullerton said in a strangled voice.

"Mommy, it must not happen!" Hyacinth wailed. "We must leave before they see us. If word reaches Bobby's ears that his fiancée was seen in such a naughty place—"

"Nonsense," her father said. "They are not facing in our direction. The best thing is to sit it out quietly. In any case, we cannot leave until Poppy and Monsieur Savatier come back."

Hyacinth's eyes widened. "They must not come back! They would pass directly by the Pinkhams' table. This is a nightmare. They must be stopped somehow."

"I told you we should not have come, but you girls wore me down with all your pleading."

"It was Poppy's idea, Mommy."

"As always."

"Like her women's liberation speech at my engagement ball."

"We shall not go into that, Hyacinth. We'd better think of how to get you out of here without the Pinkhams noticing it."

"What on earth are they talking about?" Géraldine asked.

"I'll tell you later," Nelly said. "Right now, I must launch a rescue mission."

Neither Claude nor the bothersome Poppy were to be found by the amusement stands. Nelly inspected the grottoes and the dimly lit promenade. She even peered behind bushes, disturbing kissing couples. With a sinking heart, she was retracing her steps toward the dancing ring, when she saw Claude quietly standing by a fountain.

"Why aren't you looking for Poppy?" she asked, a little cross with his inactivity.

"I've already found her."

"Where is she? Did you lose her again?"

"No, I'm waiting for her. She went to the powder room."

"Ah. Well, that's fine then," Nelly said, relieved. "Now listen! There's an emergency. I'll fetch Poppy while you return to the table. There are some acquaintances nearby, who must not see the Fullerton girls. Once you are there, the parents will go and meet those people and while they are busy greeting each other, Hyacinth will sneak out. Meanwhile, you must take care of Géraldine. We'll all meet at the cab station outside the gate."

In the noisy powder room, Nelly encountered a crush of bodies massed in front of the mirrors. The air was thick with perfume and the sharp odor of sweaty armpits. Minor damages to appearance sustained in the dancing ring mêlée were being patched up, missing hairpins replaced, powder and rouge re-applied. Standing by and lapping up the cocktail of excitement, bawdy jokes, vicious comments, and peals of laughter, was Poppy.

"Now, this is what I call local color," she said when Nelly elbowed her way to her side.

"There's no time for local color," Nelly said and explained the situation.

Poppy laughed. "So Mommy and Daddy are sacrificing themselves for our sake? I relish the picture of mutual embarrassment. Life is far from dull if you shake it occasionally and see what falls out of the folds."

Nelly was about to answer, when a slap landed on her back. "Amity Moncarelli! It is you! I thought I heard English. My, look at you! Back in the saddle, aren't we?" Marie, still flushed from her exertion, seized Nelly's hand and inspected her palm. "No calluses, no kitchen grease, and dressed like a fashion plate! Caught someone better than the cook, I gather. Well, more power to you!"

"Hello, Marie," Nelly said in a small voice.

"Manon, don't you remember? Manon! I still have that peacock-blue gown of yours. How come you've never come to see me? Haven't done badly myself. Have you seen me dancing? Pretty good, eh? I'm here every night, paid by the management. And who's that with you?"

"I'm Miss Fullerton," Poppy introduced herself.

"From America as well? Stick to your friend, *ma belle*! She knows her way around Paris by now. Ain't I right?"

"We have to go," Nelly said, feeling nauseous. "We're expected."

"I bet you are," Marie smirked. "Better put some color on your cheeks first, though. You look a bit sickly to me."

"A former neighbor," Nelly explained, when they left the powder room.

"How interesting." Poppy sounded like her father. She had his serious look as well.

* * *

"Nelly, I'm telling you, she's after Claude," Géraldine complained the next morning. "Why does nobody see it but me?"

"She's only a capricious child."

"A child? She's at least eighteen!"

"Some mature later than others. Concentrate on your exercises."

"Oh, what good is there to it? I'm just laying here like a bag of potatoes, while you are doing all the work."

"One thing I will not allow is for you to lose hope." Nelly doggedly pulled at Géraldine's leg. "Knee up, knee down!"

A knock at the bedroom door interrupted the dispute.

"Who is it?" Nelly called.

"It's Poppy," said a familiar voice.

"Her again!" Géraldine whispered furiously. "It makes me sick just to look at her insolent face. Don't let her come in here!"

Nelly crossed to the door and opened it a crack. "What is it, Miss Poppy? I thought you went to Versailles with your family."

"I pleaded a headache," Poppy said. "I need to talk to you."

"Now? I'm in the middle of something."

"It's important."

"Well, what is it then?"

"It cannot be discussed standing at the door."

Nelly entered the salon and motioned toward the sofa. "Will this do?" she asked.

"Quite. Thank you."

"Now then," Nelly said, when they were seated, "what can I do for you?"

"I need to know how things stand between you and Monsieur Savatier."

"I beg your pardon?"

"Let's not play games, Mrs. Woodridge! I don't think you are what you claim to be. That woman in the Mabille Garden has opened my eyes. I think I can safely say that Mr. Woodridge is pure invention. I checked at random the books in your library and they belong to someone called de Villermaine. There was an *ex libris* glued in each one with the name and a coat of arms."

"You intolerable brat! How dare you spy in my house?"

"Don't be angry with me. I mean no harm, although I can tell you that we would not stay here one minute longer if Mommy knew that you were a liar with loose morals. I don't take offense at such things. In fact, the situation suits me just fine."

"What is it you want from me?"

Poppy crossed her legs and clasped her knee. "I have serious goals, Mrs. Woodridge. Unfortunately, they are not what my parents think are suitable goals for my sex. It is expected of me to marry someday and to be no more than a wife with a hobby of painting. I abhor the very idea! I don't want to spend my life in social visits and charity work. Such pastimes are adequate for simpletons like Hyacinth. I'm my own person and I want the same freedom as is allowed to men. I want to settle in Paris and study painting. It's been my wish for the past three years and I've worked hard toward it. Isn't my French proof enough?"

"Your French is very good," Nelly had to admit, even though she felt an urge to slap the girl's cheek, which was something her parents should have done long ago.

"I took lessons from a native Frenchwoman. I also had lessons in drawing and painting. I'm talented, Mrs. Woodridge. My art teacher has told my parents that if I had serious training, I would become as good as any male painter. That scared them off, especially Mommy. They hope that my passion for painting is just a passing fancy. It is not, I assure you, and I would do anything to have my way. When I am twenty-one, they cannot hold me down any longer. But that's seventeen months away. I cannot wait that long. And then, I had this wonderful idea!"

By now, Nelly knew Poppy well enough to be wary of her ideas. "Has that wonderful idea of yours something to do with Monsieur Savatier?"

"Indeed, it has. Tell me, is he your lover?"

"That's an insulting question!"

"What's insulting about it? He is reasonably good-looking and he can hardly be your brother-in-law since you have no husband. I've my sources and know everything there is to know about men and women, and I want you to know that I'm not interested in him in that way."

"What exactly do you want, and how does it concern me?"

"I intend to ask him to marry me, and I don't want any misunderstanding between us. Mine is nothing but a business proposition. All I need is his name and I'm willing to pay for it. You see, the day I marry, I'll be given my part of Grandmother's jewels. They are worth no less than thirty thousand dollars. Once I'm married, no one can tell me what to do. I'll go my way and Monsieur Savatier his. No strings attached. Later, he can divorce me and marry you or whatever. He could use better clothes and I mean to be generous far beyond that. I was thinking of one thousand dollars payable as soon as I sell my jewelry."

Nelly stood up. "Frankly," she said, "I think that you are beyond outrageous. You silly girl! Do you think that your parents would allow you to marry on a whim?"

"We could elope. The jewels are in trust for me and I'll get them under any circumstances, have no fear!"

"Miss Poppy, I have confidence in Monsieur Savatier's good judgment, which is why I will not tell your long-suffering parents about your disgusting little scheme. For your information, divorce is not allowed in France and I doubt that any thinking man would saddle himself with you for life. You have some growing up to do and I pray that seventeen months will be enough. Now, you must excuse me. I've better things to do."

"I was wrong to confide in you," Poppy said heatedly. "You are no better than the others. Is it my fault that the world is made the way it is? I happen to love my parents, but they don't understand me. Nobody understands me. But I will prevail. I will!"

She ran out of the salon, banging the door behind her.

In the bedroom, Géraldine waited with her back propped against the bedpost, her face distorted with anguish.

"It was about Claude, wasn't it? I heard his name mentioned several times."

"Don't pay attention to her. Let's go on with the exercise."

"Don't treat me like that! I've the right to know."

"She is just a spoiled rich brat, who thinks she can buy herself a bogus husband," Nelly said. Seizing Géraldine's foot between her hands, she began rotating the ankle.

"She wants him. I knew it! Now you believe me. If only I could move, I'd show her!—Oh, stop it!" Géraldine yanked her foot out of Nelly's grip. "What's the use? I'll be forever a cripple."

"Géraldine! Did you see what you've done?"

"What?"

"Your leg! You kicked me with your leg!"

"Let me see . . . It's true. I can move my toes. Look!"

"Try to move the other leg."

"It works! Oh, my God, it works!"

Nelly shut her eyes and clasped her hands so tightly that her knuckles whitened. "God bless Poppy Fullerton!" she said.

Chapter 44

Dear diary, a chapter in my life has been definitely closed. This afternoon, as I was coming back from yet another photographic session, I encountered a mover's wagon in front of my house. It was full of crates, and as I came closer, I saw a pair of workmen carrying another crate through the entrance door. Leaning out of the library window, Géraldine was watching them with a frown. When she saw me, she disappeared instantly and, soon after, she was running down the driveway to meet me. Learning to walk again took weeks, but she runs a lot nowadays, as if she has to make up for all the time she wasted in the wheelchair.

"Here," she said, handing me a document. "The clerk from the moving company gave it to me."

Henri's request was couched on paper with an engraved count's coronet, which lent it an air of official gravity. It empowered the carrier to remove the entire contents of the library. As I scanned the impersonal words written in the familiar hand, a feeling of loss and a profound sadness came over me. I remember that, involuntarily, my hand went to my stomach, where a little bulge had recently started to show. For Henri it was all over, as the letter testified. The date was preceded with the words 'In Paris'. He was back in town, but as remote as if he dwelled on a different planet. With the books gone, the last link between us has been severed and I trust that, by now, I'm hardened enough not to give way to useless tears.

The Fullertons are gone, having taken a somewhat subdued Poppy with them. "Not in a million years," Claude said when I told him about her wish to marry him. An Argentinean family is now living with us. They are here to see their son Manuel through his first weeks in Paris. The young man must improve his French before he begins his first term at the Sorbonne. His family is returning home but Manuel will stay as a permanent boarder.

Zidore has grown at least three inches since I last saw him and needed to be outfitted from head to toe. As I was cutting his hair, he told me that Widow Koenig died on Christmas Eve, choking on a fish bone. Her Alsatian son-in-law tried to run the restaurant but failed miserably. The boy has settled down for the summer with us. Although he does not say as much, I know that he is looking forward to his fourteenth birthday and the excitement of being apprenticed to a photographer. I don't want to disillusion him but I know for a fact that he is in for a rough ride. Only today, I had a talk with Bébert, and he too is looking forward to a change in status. As he will become a junior assistant, he plans to buy a hat to replace his cap and expects to be called Monsieur Albert. He also intends to pass down a few cuffs on the ear to the new apprentice. He became very indignant when I told him that I'm taking a personal interest in Zidore's well-being and expect him to be treated kindly. Bébert thinks he has earned the right to be unfair.

I'm cultivating Bébert because he is an excellent source of gossip. This I discovered by sheer luck when I met him in the street while it was raining. He was hurrying back to the studio from some errand and looked so drenched that I took pity on him. I bought him a glass of spiced wine in a nearby café. As it turned out, it was a good investment. He rewarded me with details of Octave's private life, which—I have to confess here to my morbid curiosity—I was dying to know. Warming his hands on the glass, Bébert told me that he was just returning from his weekly trip to the rue des Médicis, where he carried an envelope containing the household money. Although he deals mainly with the maid, he recently glimpsed the new Madame Gaillard. She is very beautiful, very sad, and very pregnant. The apartment he knows well, having been sent there with a message while it was being hastily readied prior to the wedding. The front windows face the Luxembourg Garden and the apartment contains a sunlit nursery, which—and here Bébert assumed the worldly posture of a man-about-town, accompanied with a knowing smile— was a wise precaution, as Madame Gaillard seems to have taken to child-bearing with undue haste. At that point, Bébert finished the last of his wine and expressed a desire to taste a glass of absinthe. I felt like smacking him but that would have effectively dried up the flow of interesting information. I granted his wish, and learned that Octave has kept his bachelor apartment across the street from the studio and has often been seen coming out of there in the morning, which proves that he does not see his wife much, if at all. What's more, he is going through mistresses at an alarming rate and, in Bébert's expert opinion, his taste in women has deteriorated. The present one is the seventeen-year old granddaughter of his concierge and has absolutely no class. As Bébert did not mention any hint of a scandal, I assume that

Octave has managed to keep his marital problems under wraps. The damage he had done in the studio was reported as vandalism and the police are still looking for the culprits. I wish them good luck!

All those sordid details made me feel nauseated. As Bébert's speech became noticeably slurred, I sent him back into the rain, hoping that the natural shower would restore his wits before he reached the studio.

Things are happening there as well. The latest buzz is about Sarah, who has got her wish. Her friends have chipped in and actually bought her a massive coffin and she liked it so much that she staged her own funeral in Octave's studio. I would not believe it had I not seen the photograph. She lies in the coffin with her hair spread loose on the pillow, dressed in a white robe and holding a couple of palm branches in her crossed arms. The very image of a tragic virgin! Madame Odille told me that although not for sale, the copies are already circulating among insiders, and rumor has it that Sarah had the coffin moved from the studio to her bedroom and frequently sleeps in it. It will not take long for the newspapers to get hold of her latest eccentricity, which I suspect is precisely Sarah's aim.

Having people gossiping and pointing their fingers at me would not be my idea of success and I doubt I could handle it. I'm definitely shy of the public eye and that is why I have been having second thoughts regarding my present work. The first series of queens was published last week. They were introduced by an advertisement in several newspapers, which was craftily disguised as a flattering critique. I have saved a clipping. The author, signing only as 'our correspondent', praises the laudable efforts of the Quérat-Beaumont Agency in bringing easily digestible history to the general public, whose knowledge of the past is often rudimentary. He goes on to say that the Maison Worth has spared no effort in faithfully reproducing the splendor of historical costumes. He refers to me as 'Ceres, the fascinating young model first introduced to the public by Sarah Bernhardt'. There is no mention of the *Morning Breeze* (very good as far as I'm concerned!) and I'm sure that this must have put Octave's nose out of joint. On the other hand, Sarah is probably pleased with yet another free ride in the press.

Even though it all seems above board and the pictures are truly beautiful, I found it somewhat unnerving to see my face staring at me from several stationers' windows. Ceres as Cleopatra, the Queen of Egypt. Ceres as Boadicea, the Warring Queen of the Celts. If truth had its way, the titles printed on the pictures should be something like 'Cornelia McKay as the Queen of the Deceivers'. I should not have signed the permanent contract with the agency, but the conditions were so seductive that I could not resist. Three months of copying would not equal the money I earn in a week. All the same, when my thickening waist is finally noticed, everyone will be seriously angry with me. The moment of truth hangs over my head like a thunder-cloud.

Chapter 45

Shouts, laughter and the splashing of water echoed along the banks of the Marne in Bougival. From where she sat in the shade, Nelly stared enviously at the inviting river teeming with swimmers and pleasure boats, their bright colors enlivened by the hot August sun. The slightly muddy odor of water held an irresistible attraction.

"I'm dying for a cucumber salad," she said longingly.

Géraldine waved away a buzzing drone. "Cheeky little beast!" she said. "Cucumber salad, is it? For once, your cravings keep up with the season. Oh, but it's hot! I think I'll go for another dip after lunch. Are you sure you don't want to give it a try? I've packed up your bathing costume just in case."

"Don't do this to me," Nelly said. "I'm dying both for a cucumber salad and a dip in the river. Unfortunately, wet fabric is too revealing."

Géraldine took a swig from a bottle of tepid lemonade. "Who do you think you are still fooling?" she asked.

"Octave for one. He remarked the other day that I was becoming chubby and that I should watch what I eat. He couldn't figure out why we are to hop from the medieval queens to Empress Josephine. He thought that there was a screw loose at the agency. If they haven't already told him, he'll definitely be enlightened when he sees me in that skimpy dress tomorrow. I'm not looking forward to the session. I so hate to discuss private matters with him."

"He'll get over it," Géraldine said dismissively. "The agency did."

Relying on one face alone, the agency had in fact little choice. The matter of pregnancy was handled with surprisingly little fuss, thanks to Nelly's dresser who suggested switching the fashion periods and focusing on the most revealing costumes first. Later, the heavy wide forms characterizing the Renaissance would easily conceal a larger belly.

"Madame Odille is a genius for suggesting the switch. I must send her a gift. That mocha Indian shawl that I don't wear anyway would do. What do you think?"

"Good idea. Women like her are an asset in your camp."

A ball shot from the river and bounced on the grass. Géraldine caught it and threw it back. Manuel shouted his thanks.

"Go and join the boys," Nelly said.

Géraldine shook her head. "They must be hungry. I'm going to spread out the lunch. That way my back will be turned when they get out of the water. I never know where to hang my eyes. Whoever invented the jersey bathing suit for men must have done it on purpose."

Nelly kept a serious face. "I don't follow your line of thinking," she said slyly.

"Well," Géraldine grimaced, "those horizontal stripes make the distortion even more noticeable. You know," she blushed, "the bulge . . ."

"Ah! Yes, that is indeed a problem," Nelly exclaimed, fanning herself. "How unsightly!"

Géraldine's flushed cheeks acquired a deeper shade of red. "You are being flippant!" she reproached and then lowered her voice. "Have you noticed Claude's?"

"Noticed what? His eyebrows?—Ouch! What was that for?"

Géraldine smacked Nelly's hand again. "You are impossible!" she giggled nervously. She leaned closer. "Do you think it's normal?" she whispered. "I mean the size of it. Compared to Babeau or even to Manuel, it seems rather . . . you know . . ."

"Somewhat inflated?"

"So you've looked."

"Couldn't miss it. That young man is full of surprises."

"You!"

"Stop slapping my wrist! Frankly, I don't think it's the sultry weather alone that makes you all flustered."

Géraldine flicked off a stray lock of hair clinging to her moist forehead. "I'm sure I don't know what you mean. I should go and see what's in the picnic basket."

She rose and meticulously pulled at the pantaloons of her bathing suit, making sure that they covered her calves.

Nelly cupped her hands around her mouth. "Manuel! Claude! Lunch is being served!"

She watched, amused, as the male half of the party noisily emerged from the water, scattering droplets around, while Géraldine quickly turned her back to them and busied herself with the basket. The first to reach the picnic site was the ever-hungry Schnitzel, closely followed by Manuel and, finally, Claude.

"Are we having Madame Célestine's duck pâté?" Manuel inquired, energetically toweling his hair. "There was quite a bit left at dinner."

"No, Célestine decided against it. It spoils quickly in the heat," Nelly said. "We are having egg salad with vinaigrette, I believe. And a black currant tart."

Cross-legged, they sat around the checkered tablecloth and tucked into the bounty, sharing bread and an assortment of cheese and fruit. They had worked up a ravenous appetite and the food disappeared quickly. Replete, they stretched out on the grass to give their stomachs a rest before attacking the dessert.

"Ah, *la douce France*," Manuel said, wiggling his toes and lighting up a cigar. "You French seem to live mainly for pleasure. And yet, under the veneer of frivolity, I detect precise thinking and not a small amount of calculation. Your trains run on time and you are not given to exaggerated spirituality. I suspect that the principal current in this country is pragmatism."

Claude laughed and poked him in the ribs. "That's a sharp observation for someone whose main interest is food."

Manuel patted his stomach, where a little padding had taken hold. In his middle years, he would pile on weight like his father. "Did I also mention," he said peevishly, "that despite the fact that France is considered the cradle of diplomacy, its inhabitants are singularly lacking in tact?"

"Oh, but that's not true," Géraldine protested. "I'm surprised that you see us in this light."

Nelly shook her head. "I must side with Manuel in this. I was brought up with the maxim that if you cannot say something nice, you must say nothing at all. Ever since I came to France, I've been steadily losing control of my tongue. Nowadays, I'm more likely to say what I think."

"Are you saying that we French are having a corrupting influence on you?"

"I'm not sure. Let's say that courtesy is the oil that prevents people from chafing against each other but, on the other hand, sincerity helps to forge deeper bonds."

"Beautifully said. I guess the most difficult part is to balance both," Claude said.

"Which brings us back to diplomacy." Manuel puffed at his cigar. "A thoroughly fascinating subject. Actually, I intend to pursue a political career."

"In that case, you are studying in the right country," Nelly said. "Here, political squabbles are the national sport."

"Oh really?" Géraldine said sharply. "I hope you see nothing wrong with that. Our forefathers fought for liberty, equality, and fraternity."

"Except that poor Fraternity got lost somewhere in the chaos."

"Mesdames, mesdames," Claude chided them, "no heated discussions, please! My esteemed friend and I want to digest quietly, and you two go at it like tricoteuses."

"Tricoteuses?" Manuel repeated. "I've never heard that expression. What does it mean?"

"They were harridans who used to bring their knitting to the guillotine to keep their hands busy while they enjoyed the spectacle."

"Harridans, did you say?" Géraldine said frostily.

"Harridans?" Nelly echoed. "What do you say to that, my dear Géraldine?"

"I say, dearest Nelly, that Claude ought to pay for his insolence. Let's show him what harridans can do. Into the water with him!"

They both pounced on Claude, dragged him to his feet and pushed him toward the shore. Laughing, Manuel followed them as Claude put on a mock struggle while he was being propelled toward the water. At that very moment, the prow of a small rowing boat emerged from the deep shade cast by the overhanging branches of a tree. Schnitzel, who had joined the struggling party, adding his sonorous bark to the general exuberance, suddenly lost interest in the horseplay. He ran past them and excitedly pranced in the shallow water toward the boat. A female scream interrupted the mock fight.

A plump young woman pressed her hand to her over-developed bosom to calm down after the shock. She was dressed in a canary-yellow blouse with a quantity of looped lime-green ribbons and a crimson polka dot skirt with an exaggerated bustle. Her garish outfit was too new and too overdone for a Sunday romp outdoors. Nelly instantly knew what Bébert meant by no class. Octave, handling the oars, was dressed casually in white canvas pants and a sleeveless jersey top. As the boat glided by in the sudden silence, punctuated only by the dog's barking, he acknowledged the party on the riverbank by doffing his straw boater.

Nelly sighed. "Of all the Parisians in Bougival," she said after the boat had passed, "we had to meet Octave!"

"Well, really!" Géraldine commented. "He's into milkmaids now. I'd say that he's in his dotage."

"And who was that unfortunate gentleman you are enjoying tearing apart?" Manuel asked.

"No one of importance," Nelly said. "Who wants a piece of black currant tart?"

* * *

"How could they wear such indecent dresses and not be arrested for public outrage?" Nelly pulled at the flimsy white fabric of the high-waisted gown in a futile attempt to conceal her half-exposed breasts. "Even my most impudent nightgown comes nowhere close to this."

"It was the fashion then," Madame Odille said. "They admired Greek statues and tried to imitate them regardless of the weather. In winter, they simply added flesh-colored tights. Many a fashionable lady died of pneumonia caused by cold drafts."

"We women are so silly, when it comes to fashion," Nelly said. "Oh, but I cannot stand looking at myself," she wrapped her arms over her stomach. "How can I face the camera like this? It's so obvious that I'm expecting!"

"We'll arrange a shawl over it. Now, let's put on the wig and, after that, you are to go to the office. His Lordship wants to talk to you before he starts on the picture."

Octave, hands in his pockets, was standing by the window observing the activity on the boulevard. He did not turn immediately when Nelly entered.

"What I see," he addressed the window, "is a far cry from the bucolic scene I witnessed yesterday. No bacchantes, no satyrs in the throes of lust. Just a boring everyday routine."

"Please spare me the introduction," she said. "Have a good eyeful and say whatever you like. I don't care."

He turned and scrutinized her changed figure. "It's no longer a surprise. Tassin has filled me in on your interesting condition. So, which one of the two young bucks knocked you up? Or perhaps both?"

"If that's all you have to say, I prefer to go."

"Right, I concede that what you do with your life is no longer any concern of mine. Let's get down to business. I've something of interest to show you. It was sent to me via Maison Worth. Sit down," he motioned to a chair by his desk, "and have a look at this!"

She reached for the photograph he was handing her. It was a shot of a skillful painting: a woman languidly reclining on a sofa, her face caught in profile.

"Why, it's me in the dress I'm wearing right now," she exclaimed. "Who-ever has painted me from memory is a genius."

"Genius is the right word. The painting is by Ingres, who was the most celebrated artist of his time and, at the present, it hangs in the Louvre. Today, we have to reproduce it to the last detail."

"Is this . . . ?"

". . . the Empress Josephine," he nodded. "When I first met you, I had a vague feeling I had seen you before. I just did not make the connection. Obviously, Quérat did and that's why he wanted you and no one else."

"How is this possible?" she asked, studying the picture. "How can two women who have nothing in common look so much alike?"

Octave shrugged. "An inexplicable quirk of nature. Besides, the resemblance works only in profile. You have lighter coloring and fuller lips. However, I'm curious to see how the agency intends to play the card. Well, we'd better start while the light is good," he said.

When she rose, his attention returned to the mound of her stomach. "How far are you gone? Four months?"

"Why do you ask?"

"Solely professional interest. I want to know what's in store for the future."

"Five months and some. You really are not much of a doctor, are you?"

He was shocked into silence and she could almost hear the clicking of his brain as he counted back.

"Well, I'll leave you to your arithmetic," she said grandly and swept out of the room.

* * *

An hour later, Empress Josephine left the studio dressed as ordinary Miss Woodridge in her corset and bustle, her bulky petticoat and her white dress embroidered with rosebuds, the bodice of which had been enlarged with discreet panels at the sides. She paused in the door to tie a light shawl across her elbows and opened her parasol.

She started briskly homeward, the floating ribbons of her hat flying in her wake. As she was passing a noisy sidewalk café, scarcely noticing the patrons seated at the round tables, she heard her name called and saw Octave rising from his chair.

"I've been waiting for you," he said.

"I cannot imagine why. We said goodbye barely fifteen minutes ago."

"Come and sit down!"

"Why? I have to go home."

"Give me five minutes, will you? This is important."

He led her back to the table.

"Well, what is it?" she asked when they were seated.

"Let *me* ask the questions! I have the right to know."

298

"The right to know what, exactly?" She knew well what he meant, but was wickedly savoring his intense curiosity. It had not occurred to her that he would care so blatantly.

"Whose child is it? Mine or Henri's?"

She shrugged. "All I know is that it's mine."

"That's impossible. A woman always knows. You must have a feeling, an intuition—"

"What nonsense. Thanks to you, I may never know. I did not ask for this. It's your fault entirely."

He ran his fingers through his hair and she noticed that he had forgotten his hat. He was too much a man about town to go anywhere without it intentionally.

"Listen," he said, "can we get over this guilt hurdle and talk sensibly? May I order for you? What will you have?"

"A grenadine with ice."

He clicked his fingers at the waiter and placed the order. Then he turned back to her and stared at her in silence. She suffered his intense scrutiny until it became unbearable.

"If you don't say something immediately, I'll assume that this interrogation is over," she said crossly.

"God, you are beautiful!"

She sighed. "What do you want?"

"Come back to me."

"You have a wife who is about to give birth."

"My marriage is a sham. I'm keeping up the pretense only to protect the reputation of my family."

"You've made your choice and now you have to stick with it. Besides, I cannot guarantee that the child is yours."

"But you cannot say that it is not. That's more than the one who will be bearing my name."

"It could be Henri's. It probably is."

"Does he know about this?"

"No."

"That's good."

"What's good about it?"

"He's not a family man. He lives only for his books. Don't you remember how easily he gave you up?"

She lapsed into silence and ran her finger along a marble vein in the tabletop. "I don't love you anymore," she said.

He shook his head and clasped his hand over hers. "We had something unique, Nelly. Don't say that the flame cannot be rekindled."

She was glad the waiter came with her grenadine and Octave loosened his grip. She folded her hands in her lap.

"I grew up without my parents," she said, "and I know how important it is for a child to have both a mother and a father. If you want to acknowledge my baby and be a father to her, I can only be glad. As for the two of us, that's over and done with. You can do without me, seeing that you had no trouble finding a replacement."

"That witless chick who was with me yesterday? She means nothing to me. A man looks for consolation wherever he can. I'd give her up in a flash."

"Don't bother on my account. I've already made a life for myself and I don't intend to change it."

"Made a life for yourself?" he said bitterly. "Will you ever admit my part in it? Were I not a generous man, you wouldn't live as comfortably as you do. I've provided for you and I intend to provide for the child. No one can say that Octave Gaillard shrinks away from responsibility."

She frowned. "Yes, you have your own code of honor despite the fact that the rest of your mind is rotten. You don't realize it because of the way you men have been brought up. You can lie to us and cheat on us and discard us on a whim, and think all is well as long as you provide." She grabbed her parasol and rose with the firm intention of leaving.

"It's her, I'm telling you it's her! It's Ceres! — Pardon me, madam, are you Ceres?"

Nelly found herself surrounded by several young women accompanied by soldiers. The high-spirited group was on their way to some pleasurable outing. One of the girls produced a flat object wrapped in tissue paper.

"My boyfriend bought me your picture," she said, unwrapping the paper. "Would you mind signing it for me? — Marcel," she turned to her soldier, "do you have an ink pencil?"

After Marcel ineffectively explored his blue tunic and the pockets of his red trousers, Octave offered his own pencil.

"Please, write 'to Mireille' and add something nice," the girl instructed Nelly, who sat down and complied with her wish.

"To Mireille with affection, Ceres," Mireille read aloud. "Thank you ever so much! Now I'll have something to put in a frame - when I get a frame," she cast a significant glance at her boyfriend.

The group was gone, leaving Nelly the center of attention among the café guests.

"I must go," she said, returning the pencil.

"Keep it. You may need it again. As for the two of us—"

"I don't want to talk about it anymore. Goodbye!" she said and left him there to stew in disappointment.

Chapter 46

"Géraldine, wake up!"

"What? ... What is it?" Géraldine sat up, disoriented in the darkness.

"You've been having another wild dream," Nelly complained.

"Did I wake you up again?"

"Not only that. As you kept rolling from side to side, your elbow hit my stomach."

"Jesus, I'm sorry!"

"Listen, I've been putting up with this for quite a while and it has to stop. I'll not have my baby pummeled because of you and Claude and your silly games."

"What are you talking about?"

"It's what *you* are talking about in your sleep. '*Oh Claude, chéri!*'" Nelly moaned, "'*Oh! Please, hold me!*' That sort of thing."

Géraldine sucked in her breath. "I had no idea! Do you want me to move to another room?"

"How about Claude's? His bed is large enough for two."

"Nelly!"

"Don't you 'Nelly' me! You've both been dying to do it. It's been a pity, watching you. I begin to fear for my dining room china. Like last night, when you were passing him the butter and he accidentally touched your hand. You dropped the plate as if it had burnt your fingers and then you avoided looking at each other for the rest of the meal. Even Manuel noticed. Please, be done with it so that we can all live in peace!"

"How can you talk like that," Géraldine said indignantly. "You are wrong if you think that Claude and I would defile our beautiful relationship with base animal sex. He's never so much as kissed me."

"That's because he does not dare. He's afraid that if you are not ready, you'd turn against him. Besides, I think he's still a virgin."

"He is pure. I must climb up to his level instead of dragging him down as you suggest."

Nelly plumped up the pillows and shifted to ease her back. "Did it ever occur to you that he desperately wants to be dragged down? Besides, what kind of language is that? Sex is the most natural thing in the world. In fact, celibacy is the greatest sin against nature."

"Who said that?"

"Never mind who said that. It's common sense. Why do you think we have all those urges? It is nature's way to make us do certain things. And if we don't, we do other, much sillier things. I know about the books."

"What books?" Géraldine asked in a small voice.

"Oh come! You know exactly what I mean. The books hidden in the last drawer of the writing desk. Boccaccio's Decameron, the illustrated Art of Love by Ovidius and Marquis de Sade's Justine. You are a little thief, Géraldine."

"I did not intend to steal them. The movers came so suddenly that I didn't have time to return them to the shelves. I was too embarrassed to mention it."

"No wonder you think of sex as something dirty if you read de Sade. He was a pervert."

"So you have read it as well?"

"I browsed through it because I was worried about you. Don't get mixed up with such ideas, I beg you! Think of what you've been through just recently. I don't want to see you in a wheelchair ever again."

"Oh, Nelly, those books gave me such a headache!"

"Listen," Nelly groped in the dark and entwined her fingers with Géraldine's, "stop filtering your feelings through your brain. Use your heart! Do you love Claude?"

"You know I do."

"Then go to him and reward his patience."

For a few minutes silence reigned over the room. Then Géraldine threw off the cover. She found her way to the dressing table and lit a lamp.

"What are you doing?" Nelly asked.

"I have to brush my hair."

"Do you mean to go now, in the middle of the night?"

"That's exactly what I mean. It's now or never."

Nelly giggled, propped herself on her elbows, and watched as Géraldine hastily brushed her hair and dabbed Eau de Cologne on her throat.

"Wait!" she said. "Are you not forgetting something?"

"What?"

"Remember what I told you about the sponge. You don't want to end up like me."

"What if I do? Would that be such a bad thing?"

When the door shut behind her friend, Nelly stretched and stroked her stomach. "I guess from now on, it's just you and me, Pumpkin," she whispered.

* * *

The mirror returned a satisfactory image. No one could tell that she was six months gone with child. The loose wrap-like jackets the fashion dictated were Nelly's salvation. As soon, as the weather grew cooler, she would be able to replace the mixed bouquet she always held on her lap with a fur-lined mantle and a muff.

Although it took some practice to be paraded in an open carriage, she rather enjoyed her outings to the Bois de Boulogne, courtesy of the Quérat-Beaulieu agency. The very first time she was petrified with stage fright. Now, if a street urchin in the crowd would shout, "Here goes Ceres! Ain't she a looker?" she would merely smile and respond with a gracious wave. She was paid handsomely for being friendly. "Friendly but distant," was the assignment she received from Tassin.

The agency readily acknowledged the fact that her boarding-house business was incompatible with her public image and adjusted her salary. Of the guests, only Manuel remained. He did not say as much, but she knew that he would no longer recommend her house to his mother and sisters. Some things were best left unsaid.

She reached for her gloves and the parasol Julie was handing her and went through the vestibule, where she glimpsed Claude and Géraldine at the top of the stairs.

"We are leaving," Nelly called while passing by.

Outside, Zidore, arrayed in a livery, waited by the open carriage, while Schnitzel, the spikes of his collar polished to a high shine, was already comfortably installed inside. As soon as the landau moved, he would stand up, his front paws on the backrest, and enjoy the ride to the fullest.

"Bonjour, miss," Père Caullier greeted her from the driver's box. "No need for a parasol. Have you seen the clouds? I think we'll barely make it to the Bois with the roof down."

Nelly looked up, scanning the sky. "You may be right."

"Well, get in then," Père Caullier said. "Are you alone today? Is your girlfriend not coming with us?"

Nelly turned her head. "She was coming right down. I don't know what's keeping her. Or rather I do!"

She retraced her steps, only to find Claude and Géraldine hugging in the vestibule.

"Oh, for heaven's sake," she exclaimed. "Will you cease and desist, you maniacs? She's not leaving for another planet!"

"It's not what you think," Claude said, a little breathless. "We are celebrating. Tell her, sweetheart!"

"Claude's finally signed the contract to illustrate my book," Géraldine said.

"Is that true? I'm so glad for both of you. That calls for champagne tonight. My treat."

"That's very kind, but no thanks," Claude said. "I'm paying. I find myself unexpectedly affluent."

"He has negotiated an advance," Géraldine explained. "We've been making plans. I'll tell you about it."

They settled in the landau, spreading their skirts, while Zidore climbed up next to the driver, where he would perch stiffly with his arms folded as befitted a 'tiger'. The expression had something to do with the yellow and black-striped vests boys like him wore. For this essential service he was paid fifty centimes a ride by the agency. He, too, considered himself affluent.

The coachman cracked his whip and the two matching grays moved forward.

"Well now," Nelly turned to her friend. "Tell me what you have cooked up, you and Claude."

"It's about the rooms above the stable. You don't have any use for them in the future, do you?"

"Not unless I buy a carriage and pair myself. Then, of course, I would have to house a coachman."

"Are you going to?"

"I was only joking. How long do you think this bounty will last?"

"You never know. You thought you'd have to quit months ago and here you are, still going strong."

"Knock on wood!" Nelly said. "Should I become permanently rich, all I'd buy as a mode of transport would be a dog cart I could drive myself. So what is it about the rooms?"

"If you really, and I mean really, have no plans for them, Claude and I thought that the wall between the two could be knocked down and part of the roof replaced by glass."

"A studio for Claude?"

"A cozy place for both of us. Claude needs better light for his work and I could put my desk in a corner and do my writing there. Imagine a quiet winter day with heavy flakes of snow falling down and settling on the garden, the fire crackling in the stove, and the two of us both busy and snug in our little world."

"Sounds a bit costly."

"I got an advance too. If we pooled our resources, we could manage to pay for the essentials and do the rest of the work ourselves. Claude is able to knock down the wall all by himself. And," Géraldine added, "we could make the studio into a permanent house for Demoiselle. That would please Schnitzel no end."

Nelly laughed. "Now that's a fine offer! Whose idea was that? Yours or Claude's?"

Demoiselle was a fearless tabby kitten, brought by Zidore as a gift for her. She made Schnitzel's life miserable by chewing at his ears, chasing his tail, and otherwise disturbing his siestas.

"It was just an idea," Géraldine shrugged. "No need to draw false conclusions."

"In any case, I'm sold."

They launched into a discussion focused mainly on Géraldine's future projects. Her uncommonly fast success was due to the winning combination of extraordinary imagination and a light-hearted style. She drew her characters from life, complete with their tics and quirks, and molded them into the humorous heroes of her stories. Nelly had instantly recognized Célestine as a scheming coffeepot trying to seize power in the kitchen. Schnitzel became the king of an edible castle, struggling between his voracious appetite and the need to keep a roof over his head. The obsessive squirrel, who washed and polished her nuts and denounced her neighbors' sloth, was uncomfortably much like herself. No one was allowed to escape Géraldine's sharp pen.

"I've lost my family, together with my right to respectability," Géraldine said, "but it was all worth it. Even though Claude and I can never marry, we're determined to live happily ever after, and the rest of the world can go and hang itself." She squeezed Nelly's hand. "I only hope that one day I'll be able to repay you in some significant way."

"Géraldine—"

"No, listen to me! Maybe you are right and this stuff," Géraldine motioned around, encompassing the smart carriage, "will not last much longer. I do worry about you and this precarious career of yours, but rest assured that, should it all come to nothing, you still have us."

"I know," Nelly said and returned the squeeze.

They sank into the maroon upholstery of the seats and enjoyed the motion of the carriage. They had a mission to accomplish and Nelly hoped the weather would co-operate, giving them at least enough time to reach the Bois, where she and Géraldine would take refreshment at the Swiss Chalet, while Père Caullier would join the coterie of other coachmen waiting for their fashionable masters. A glass in hand, puffing at their pipes or cigarettes, they would exchange the latest gossip and spread useful tidbits of information, which would eventually reach the sharp ears of the social columnists who were snooping around. This time, Père Caullier had a pearl of gossip to impart. The Austrian Empress, currently considered the most beautiful woman in the world, and herself an avid collector of pretty faces—she was said to possess a collection of ten thousand photographs—liked the first series of Powerful Queens of the Past and her office had ordered the whole set. The information was an invaluable free advertisement, especially as it was to coincide with the release of the latest pictures.

Despite the change in the photographic schedule, the agency managed to maintain the flow of historical periods intact. The growing numbers of collectors were shortly to be treated to the sinister Catherine de Médicis in her starched ruffle and to Elizabeth of England in a heavy gown laden with pearl embroidery and an enormous fan-shaped collar. After a frantic shooting schedule, Nelly's work at the studio was done. Her next assignment was to sit for a poster advertising scented toilette water. There her thick waist would not matter as the artist could edit out her pregnancy. In the remaining short time before she would have to disappear from circulation, she was to promote herself by public appearances, swathed in concealing clothes.

At the top of the Champs Élysées the landau turned toward the Bois. An unusual number of carriages were stationed in front of the Swiss Chalet. Nelly recognized the stately phaeton of Princess Mathilde, the only member of the Bonaparte family allowed to live in France, side by side with the elegant carriage of Cora Pearl, one of The Guard, as the top courtesans catering to grand dukes and petty royalty called themselves. As the landau came to a halt, the restaurant door opened and a cluster of journalists surrounding a bearded man spilled out. Schnitzel's ears straightened. He sniffed the air and leaped out with a joyous bark.

* * *

"What followed was simply incredible," Géraldine said. "Wasn't it, Nelly?"

Manuel put down his knife and fork, although an irresistible aroma was emanating from the grilled trout on his plate.

307

"Well, go on," he urged Géraldine. "We are all ears!"

"It was Jules Verne, the famous writer! When he saw Schnitzel, his jaw dropped and he exclaimed, 'I don't believe what I see! This must be a nightmare!' "

Both Claude and Manuel chuckled as Géraldine related the story. According to *Maître* Verne, the stray dog had wandered aboard his yacht *Nautilus* in Plymouth without anyone noticing, which was an incredible feat in itself. He was not found until the yacht left the harbor, and since the tide did not allow for an immediate return, he had to be kept on. Somewhere between England and France the dog managed to devour a bar of Marseilles soap that had appealed to him because it was made of olive oil. As the yacht neared the mouth of the Seine close to Le Havre, he became sick. The plan was to take him to the harbor authorities in Honfleur, but the animal looked so weak that Maître Verne relented and even contemplated adopting it.

"But, gentlemen," the celebrated novelist was heard saying to the members of the press, "the brain is a larger organ than the heart. When it was discovered that this voracious beast had devastated my entire reserve of smoked Scottish salmon, I had it dumped mercilessly on the quay and hoped never to see it again. And here it is," he pointed at Schnitzel, who wagged his tail and seemed to be grinning, "over a year later and obviously expecting more salmon. Not only is it alive and well and in Paris, but it seems to be thriving!"

As further inquiries revealed, the canine traveler was not only thriving, he was leading a princely life, enjoying elegant carriage rides in the company of his present owner, a rising star in the firmament of Parisian life — the beautiful and intriguing model Ceres.

"That was Père Caullier's contribution to the story," Nelly commented. "I know he expects a hefty tip from the agency for having seized the opportunity. Now everyone wants to delve into Schnitzel's past. The questions I have had to answer! Some journalists followed us here. That's why you found the gate locked. Even Zidore was offered a bribe, if he would tell all he knows. I hope he'll remember where his loyalty belongs. Such fuss over a dog is unseemly."

"It's simply an entertaining story and you cannot blame the press for liking it," Claude said.

Manuel resumed his interrupted dinner. "I don't see why you are so skittish about the whole thing. Most people would be elated at seeing their name in print, especially in such a good light."

"Nelly does not want anyone digging into her private life," Géraldine said.

"You are right, Manuel," Nelly said, quickly curtailing the subject before it should get out of hand. "Something bothers me though," she went on. "Célestine said that she lost Schnitzel after her accident and that happened before *Maître* Verne picked him up in England. The more I think of it, the less sense it makes."

Célestine, summoned from her kitchen, stared blankly at the company.

"Well," Nelly said, "what do you think of that? How can you explain that the dog was not in France when you had supposedly lost him?"

The cook stood silent, her hands plucking at her apron.

"Célestine?"

"I don't know. Maybe Monsieur Verne made a mistake. Maybe it was a different dog. A look-alike."

"A different dog? How many dogs look like Schnitzel?"

"I don't know," Célestine repeated and her face crumbled. "I cannot talk. I must not. It's all black magic. I cannot help it and I cannot stop it. All I've ever done, Miss, was for your own good!" She turned abruptly and hurried out of the dining room, leaving them perplexed.

Manuel cleared his throat. "A slight madness should not constitute a reason for dismissing a good cook," he said hopefully.

"Let's sleep on it," Nelly said.

Chapter 47

A brief fight broke out in the taproom of the Café Rigolo. A dull thump on the side of the enclosure as someone's body landed against the wall interrupted the conversation inside. The *patronne*'s sharp voice screamed insults. Eventually, as peace was restored, the sounds returned to their normal level.

Inside the cubicle, the mood was somber.

"You've landed me in big trouble," Célestine said.

Nathaira shrugged. "The dog's been useful in many ways. It's a slight problem, I'll grant you that, but one has to take the good with the bad."

"A slight problem, you say? With the story being published in all the newspapers and myself hardly sleeping for fear of being dismissed? The fact is that she doesn't trust me anymore, and I'm sure she'll get rid of me eventually. I know I would!"

Nathaira eased her back against the red plush of the sofa while her hand twirled the stem of her wineglass. The gaslight on the wall behind her sent playful reflections through the ruby liquid.

"What do you want from me?" she asked.

"I know you have powers and that you can make things happen. I need time to get my finances together before I strike out on my own. I don't believe anymore in that crown business getting her up in the world. She's got a score of crowns but they're all made of paste. There's nothing in it for me and I want out. Just give me the chance to get through the winter and I'll be fine. Here," she opened her reticule, "I've brought the diary. Be so good as to cast a spell on it so that she'll forget about the dog business. Make her trust me again for a while. You owe me that at least."

"I'm disappointed in you," Nathaira said gruffly. "All this was just the first step to bigger and better things."

"You keep saying that, but you've never told me who is that man of worldwide importance that you've been dangling before my nose. For all I know, he exists only in your imagination," Célestine countered. "Not that I doubt your good intent," she added quickly, conscious of the precarious position she was in.

The gypsy reached for one of the two bottles standing on the table between them and poured wine into an empty glass. She pushed the drink invitingly toward her guest.

"No offense," Célestine said, "but I'm in no mood for drinking. Besides, they don't put much effort into washing the glasses here."

"You've acquired dainty manners. I remember the time when you drank from abandoned bottles and found nothing wrong with it."

"That was then and this is now."

Nathaira smiled but there was a dangerous gleam in her stare. "So you want me to cast a spell? I'd be careful if I were you. There are all kinds of spells. Displeased as I am, I could accidentally cast the wrong one."

This was a barely veiled threat. Célestine shivered with fear and clutched the reticule, to protect the diary inside. "I never meant to displease you," she said in an unsteady voice. "Perish the thought! I just find it hard to work in the dark. If only I knew more, I'd be willing to go on, because I know you are always right. I've no doubt about it, none whatsoever."

"I'm not sure I can trust you with such an important matter."

"I swear by Saint-Catherine, martyred on the wheel, that I'm worthy of your trust."

The gypsy folded her arms and scrutinized Célestine with her dark eyes. She seemed to reach a decision. "What I'm going to tell you must never leave this room, do you understand?"

"Yes, of course. Absolutely."

"The Emperor of the French."

"Louis Napoleon?"

"The very same."

"But he's in exile."

"Not for long. Forces are gathering to bring him back. I read tarot for a military man who consults me before taking decisions."

Célestine's mouth dropped open and she forcibly expelled air from her lungs.

"I'm sure it no longer surprises you," Nathaira went on, "that I don't want such a piece of news leaking out before its time. This is akin to a state secret."

"God in Heaven and all the Saints!" Célestine exclaimed, astonished. "Are we going to have the Empire back?"

"It's been written in the Book of Fate to which I have access through my superior powers."

Célestine clasped her hands and pressed them against her mouth. She was elated by the news. The Empire was coming back with all its excesses and its crumbs of luxury to be scattered to those who dealt in the pleasure trade.

"And her? What will become of her?" she whispered excitedly. Her imagination kicked in. "Don't tell me the rest. I know! Now I know where it will end. He cannot keep his hands off women, the old goat. Everyone knows that. Mistress of the emperor! No one would be able to resist the lure, not even her. Good heavens, what a fortune! Remember the Englishwoman? Howard was her name. She gave him a bastard and ended up with the title of countess and a château in the country. Before that, there was that lowly washerwoman he was allowed to keep while the king held him in prison. She had two boys by him, both made counts after he seized power. And to think I wanted out of this scheme! I most humbly apologize for my lack of faith."

"Let's drink to that," Nathaira said.

Célestine reached for her glass. "To a bright future!"

"To palaces and titles!"

They drained their glasses.

"And now go, and worry no more," the gypsy said.

When the door closed behind Célestine, Nathaira laughed silently. Playing chess with live pieces was delightfully addictive. There was more to come. To celebrate the exquisite moment, she poured another glass for herself and moistened her lips in it. In the nick of time she remembered what was in the bottle. She spat on the floor and quickly rubbed her mouth against her sleeve.

* * *

Célestine's funeral was a simple nine-grade package costing only twenty-eight francs and another five for tips. That was all they found in the drawer where she kept her money. It was not until Julie was asked to turn up the mattress in Célestine's bed and noticed a roughly sewn slit on the side that the stash of hundreds of francs was discovered.

The cook had collapsed in the street. Witnesses said that she had thrashed about her as if in the throes of madness and vomited copiously. Fearing it could be an attack of cholera, no one was willing to approach her. When the ambulance men picked her up, she was barely conscious. Before she lapsed into a coma, she managed to shout what they took for her name: Nathaira. They found no identification papers on her and when she died several hours later in the hospital, her body was taken to the morgue, where it was registered under the name of Nathaira. Her death certificate indicated gastric fever combined with a stroke.

Claude and Manuel took it upon themselves to launch a search when the cook went missing. Of the dire news they brought back, the greatest shock to Nelly was the diary recovered with other personal effects from the morgue. That, and the money in the mattress, caused her great emotional upset.

"Black magic! Did she not mention black magic? What did I ever do for her to treat me so?" Nelly sought refuge in her friend's arms.

"Shhh," Géraldine comforted her. "You're too smart to believe in such old woman's lore."

"She did believe in it and that's what matters. Where did the money come from? Who paid her for betraying me and why? Does it mean that I can trust no one? I'm scared, Géraldine. I'm scared!"

* * *

"Nathaira? What a strange name," Monsieur Goubert said, when the mourners gathered for a cold buffet after the funeral, which Nelly refused to attend. "I've never heard such a name."

"I have," said Félicie Perrichon, reaching for a brioche from the tray her niece was offering around. Two others were already stuffed in her voluminous reticule along with slices of ham wrapped in a handkerchief. "It was the name of the bearded gypsy woman, who used to come to the neighborhood. She read tarot for me and predicted a great fortune for Miss Woodridge."

Whatever conversation there was ceased as all turned to her. Pleased to be the center of attention, the concierge went on relating what she knew. She confided that the gypsy came several times, offering a tarot reading, and always managed to steer the conversation to the American tenant. The visits stopped when Célestine Cabrol came to work for Miss Woodridge.

"Although one should not speak ill of the dead, I ought to say that I've never liked that crafty creature," she said in the way of conclusion. "You should've seen her when she first came! A toothless bag of bones she was, and greedy with that! Did you notice how fat she looked in the coffin? No wonder she suffered a stroke with all that weight she had put on."

The doorbell interrupted the conversation and Julie went to answer the door. Octave entered, shook hands with his acquaintances and introduced himself to Claude, Géraldine and Manuel.

"An unfortunate demise," he commented. "I'm here to express my sympathy and inquire whether Miss Woodridge needs anything." He accepted a glass of wine and, as soon as the conversation broke into several topics, he addressed Géraldine, lowering his voice. "Where is she? I wish to see her."

313

"Not now," she replied. "She's too upset to discuss anything concerning the funeral."

"I'm convinced that at this hour, and in her condition, Nelly needs a man at her side."

"She has steadfast friends to fill that gap."

Octave frowned. "Am I to be prevented from seeing her? If so, you are assuming too much responsibility."

Claude, who had been observing the exchange, joined them and protectively cupped his hand under Géraldine's elbow. "Any problems?" he asked.

* * *

"You've done well," Nelly said when she heard Géraldine's report. She sat on the balcony, basking in the weak autumn sun and playing with the kitten in her lap.

Géraldine joined her on the wicker settee. "He left in a huff," she said. "Why is he behaving as if he had rights to you?"

Nelly examined the scratches on her wrist and put the kitten down on the tiled floor, where it immediately started to pursue a stranded ant. "It's his way of making up for his mistakes," she said.

"Could it be that he's developed a conscience?"

Nelly took in a deep breath as if to say something of importance, but let it out in a sigh instead.

Géraldine frowned. "Well, don't let him practice it on you. What is it, dear?" she asked, when she saw Nelly's face crumble.

"Oh, Géraldine, I feel so lonely! I miss Henri. I miss him so much that it hurts."

Chapter 48

My poor violated diary, I had the firm intention never to return to your pages, but as days have turned into weeks, I had to acknowledge my need for you. Why blame you for revealing my most intimate thoughts, while the fault is with me alone for not being able to judge character and for assuming that all people could be salvaged if given the opportunity? Now, that the pain of betrayal has lost its sharpness, I intend to carry on as usual.

Actually, to carry on as usual is impossible. Things have changed drastically after the Schnitzel episode. The same day Célestine died—although I did not know it yet—we set off to the Bois de Boulogne. The traffic on the boulevards slowed down the carriage and, while we were waiting at a crossing, a crowd surrounded us. At first, people simply pointed their fingers and waved in a friendly manner, but then an adventurous young man hoisted himself on the step and patted Schnitzel on the head. Many felt encouraged to follow his example and as other arms reached into the landau, the dog got frightened and snapped at them. While I caught him in my arms, Géraldine called to the coachman to hurry, but the way was already blocked. Other carriages stopped, their occupants wanting to see what was going on. Loud comments flew back and forth. Although no one meant to harm us, the intense scrutiny to which we were subjected filled me with genuine dread. Never before had I been caught in the focus of public attention without a means of escape, and never before had I experienced such a paralyzing fear. I vaguely remember a policeman coming forward and ordering people to disperse, then the landau slowly gaining speed and turning into a side street, where we paused long enough to raise the roof. Throughout the entire ordeal I sat with a smile chiseled on my face, but as soon as we were free I collapsed into Géraldine's arms. That was our last expedition to the Bois. I wrote to Monsieur Quérat that no amount of money would make me reconsider. Some people are not made for this kind of exposure and I'm definitely one of them.

In response to my letter, in which I also stated my wish to be released from the contract, Monsieur Tassin came in person to remonstrate with me. Clearly, he said, I was being hypersensitive due to my delicate state, and Monsieur Quérat, in his infinite generosity, decided to suspend me with pay until the end of my pregnancy. Far from him to judge me—were we not all sinners each in our own way?—but the time had come for me to acknowledge the agency's good will with regard to my shameful situation, and to show due loyalty. All that was asked of me, at the present, was to pose for a couple of commercial posters and then take a paid vacation.

"In all my long experience," Tassin said, "I've never heard of such a generous offer. On top of that, Monsieur Quérat is willing to alter the contract to your advantage. I'm speaking of a percentage on the sale of your pictures. And since I've already mentioned your delicate state, let us dwell on it for a while. You are about to bring into the world a child with limited prospects. Unless you take protective steps, it will grow up in shame and be able to marry no one but another social outcast. Money is the supreme cure for such ills and, in this case, adoption is the answer."

When I protested, saying that I would never give my child away, he smiled and shook his head. Did I not know, he asked, that there were families in financial distress that would be more than willing to sell their respectable name for the opportunity to see their debts settled? The adoption would happen only on paper.

"With enough money," he went on, "and if you fancy such a luxury, you can purchase a genuine title for your child. You, I should think, being an intelligent and practical woman, would settle for something more pedestrian and well within your means. Ten thousand francs is the bottom price. I can give you the name of an agency that handles these subtle matters," he reached into his breast pocket and removed a folded document, "but first, I want you to have a look at the draft of your next contract. Let us study the figures and calculate how long it would take for you to accumulate the sum, provided that you are interested in your child's future."

What mother would not be interested in her child's future? I studied the figures and ended by signing the improved contract. In any case, it was too late to do otherwise. Fame has already sunk its teeth into my flesh. As I cannot go out without being recognized, I have reverted to my widow disguise. Instead of a protection, Schnitzel has become a liability. He has the run of the garden and Zidore takes him out for walks after dark, but I was wrong in thinking that, by hiding him, the attention would go away. It is now stylish to be seen with a scary dog. As a newspaper reported, there has been a rush on the municipal pound and all large mongrels are guaranteed to find a comfortable home. As a result, the boulevards feature fashionable beauties accompanied by hideous beasts—the uglier the better!—and spiked dog collars are at a premium. But the height of popular fashion is to have one's hair colored 'à la Ceres', which means horribly streaked with bleach. It appears (here I quote another newspaper) that recently the dance halls have been overrun by young women whose ambition is to look like a skunk.

That I should be linked with such a ridiculous fashion is a source of irritation to me. It is true that Mother Nature has given me unusual hair, but she has done it in a subtle way, or so I like to think! Claude has taken to hiding his newspaper because the articles upset me terribly. Do I have to take all the blame for causing women to bleach their hair or even for inciting them to independence? Does it really make me less feminine?

And the mail keeps coming. It began in the early days, when the first pictures were published. A trickle at first, it has grown into a stream. Hundreds of letters arrive at the agency. To find me, interested parties pick up the information printed on the back of the pictures, although recently I have received a batch addressed simply to 'Ceres, Paris'. To date, I have received 68 offers of marriage and 813 lecherous letters. There are men who seem to be perversely excited by the image of a woman in a position of power, and who offer me money for the delight of being punished. It is so sad, so very, very sad.

Géraldine now filters all the mail. She puts aside inoffensive correspondence and we read it after dinner. To some, I'm a bad example of unnatural ambition. What would the world ruled by women come to? A woman's place is in her home and her happiness in the joys of motherhood. The bulk of the correspondence contains nothing but shallowness and incredible naïveté. My female admirers want to know with whom I'm in love, what color I like, what fabric is this or that gown made of, or where to obtain a particular lace. Some address me as 'Your Majesty' and one fool asked me how I managed to be queen of so many countries.

A brighter note in the correspondence is the letters from animal lovers, who praise me for adopting a stray dog. The League Against Vivisection has invited me to become an active member. I plan to do so as soon as I regain my figure. Sarah, amused and moved by Schnitzel's story, has suppressed her grudge against me. Since we are both animal lovers, she wrote, we should bury the hatchet and resume our former friendship. She cordially invited me to bring Schnitzel to an afternoon tea. I'm wary of her advances. As far as I know, we have never been true friends and I never felt at ease in her circle.

I said as much to Octave, who delivered her letter in person. He never misses an opportunity to wiggle his way back into my life. He has stopped pestering me about us getting together again. Instead, he has adopted the attitude of concerned friend. A woman of single status needs as many protectors as she can get, he said, especially a woman that is soon to become a mother. His wife has given birth to a boy, but Octave says that he will never forgive her for her abject treachery and that his heart already belongs to the child I'm carrying. I had to remind him of Henri and his part in the equation. He dismissed my remark with a wave of hand. He says he feels that the child is his.

I don't know what to make of it. Is he telling the truth? Has he really reformed? He seems to be unhappy enough. Should I deny my child the chance of having a father?

Manuel is no longer living here. As my cooking comes nowhere close to Célestine's art, he packed his things and rented a room above a good restaurant. I wish him well but I'm glad he is gone. Claude and Géraldine, both busy with the construction of the studio, don't seem to mind simple meals and with Zidore helping in exchange for his keep I don't have to hire another cook. Only now do I realize that in addition to betraying me, Célestine had been doctoring the kitchen accounts. With the salary savings, and without spending money on elaborate meals, I can do without Manuel's financial contribution. Now that there are no longer strangers in my house, it has truly become a home. God knows that I need a safe haven with all that is happening outside!

Chapter 49

A bleak November light penetrated the basement windows under the vaulted ceiling of the kitchen. Nelly tasted the thick potato soup simmering on the stove and threw in a pinch of salt. The steady drum of Claude's fingers on the table accompanied the clink of metal on wood as Julie set out spoons and the butter knife.

"It's nearly two o'clock. I'm not waiting for her any longer," Nelly said. "Julie, get the ladle!"

She poured the soup into a tureen and carried it to the table. As the weather cooled off, the kitchen became the gathering place of the reduced household. Instead of heating the large dining room, they found it more convenient to eat by the fire on which food was cooked. Claude and Géraldine, both racing against time, usually showed up looking their worst, he in a blue worker's blouse and pants that needed mending at the knee, she in Nelly's old kitchen dress. They both ate ravenously whatever she served them and, as soon as the meal was over, they returned to the construction site. Today was different.

"She's never been so late," Claude said. "She left early to be there as soon as the office opened. I should've gone with her. She had to carry home a large sum of money."

"I'm sure she's spending some of it as we speak," Nelly soothed his anxiety. "Let's eat."

The three of them were finishing their lunch in uneasy silence when they heard the clatter of footsteps down the staircase. Relief softened Claude's features as the door opened and Géraldine came in.

"Are you all right?" he asked.

"Why shouldn't I be? I'm sorry for being late, but there've been some difficulties."

"Difficulties?"

"Nothing to worry about," she said, turning her back to them to warm her hands by the stove. "Only some changes to one of the stories. I'll have to work on it for a couple of days. Oh . . . and . . . uh . . . the account clerk is sick, but I'll get my money as soon as he's back at work and the books are balanced."

"Claude's been worried," Nelly said.

"I said I was sorry."

"It's all right," Claude said. "Come and eat your lunch. You must be starving."

"Starving? I haven't been hungrier in my entire life." Géraldine sat at the table and reached for the ladle. She poured just enough soup to cover the bottom of her plate and made a great show of eating it.

"Are you feeling well?"

Géraldine paused and looked at Claude. "Of course, I feel well. Why do you ask?"

"You look very pale."

"It's the light," Géraldine said. "Everybody looks pale in this kind of light. It's drizzling outside."

"Julie," Claude said, "do I look pale?"

Julie scrutinized him. "No, monsieur."

Géraldine shrugged. "It's nothing, I assure you. By the way, Nelly, the posters for the *Eau de toilette* are up. I saw nearly a dozen of them on my way. You look very slim amidst all those violets."

"What violets?"

"Don't you know? What exactly did they tell you at the agency?"

"Nothing precise. I just went to pose for a few sketches and that was all."

"Well then, it's called The Time of Violets and the artist has done a very good job. Perhaps they will send you a sample of the product."

The clang of the gate bell interrupted the conversation.

"That would be the Bon Marché collector for the last installment," Nelly said. "There's an envelope on the desk upstairs. Give it to him, Julie, and don't forget to ask for a receipt."

She was leaning over the table and cutting a wedge of Cantal cheese, when Julie came back. "It wasn't the collector," she said placidly and then delivered a thunderbolt. "It was Monsieur d'Auzon."

Nelly nicked her thumb but did not feel the pain. "Henri?" she asked. "Are you sure?"

"Well, Miss, I may be stupid but I'm not blind," Julie said tartly. A year under Célestine's guidance had resulted in some of the cook's mannerisms rubbing off on her. "I left him waiting in the salon."

"There's no fire there. It's as cold as an icebox."

"I had to put him somewhere. Have I done something wrong?"

"No, of course not," Nelly rubbed her face, leaving a smudge of blood on her cheek. "Did you dust there this morning?"

"Calm down," Géraldine said. "Julie, get a bottle of iodine and a clean rag!"

"What am I to do?" Nelly panicked. "I cannot see him like this. I've nothing to wear and my hair needs washing. And look at me! I'm larger than an elephant!"

"As for that, it will be no surprise to him," Géraldine said.

"No surprise? He's not set his eyes on me since—"

"Nelly, I wrote to him."

"What?"

"I could not bear watching you pine after him. Did you not say so yourself? You said you wished he were here. Don't you shake your head at me! You said it the day of Célestine's funeral. I had to do something. You've been lonely and vulnerable to all sorts of mistakes. I did it because I felt that you two should have a second chance, especially as there's a child on the way."

Wordlessly, Nelly collapsed on a chair.

"You shouldn't have interfered," Claude said.

"Interfered!" Géraldine exclaimed. "I did what I thought was right, especially with you-know-who hanging around her and biding his time. Don't you see that he behaves as if he owned her? I don't want her to fall for him a second time. All I did was to let d'Auzon know that he was to be a father and that if he was a gentleman, he should be at her side. I've kept it secret because if he happened to ignore my letter, it would be a bitter pill for Nelly to swallow. But he's shown up, which means that he knows what's right."

During Géraldine's speech, Nelly stared at the table in front of her, holding her bleeding finger. "I lied," she said in a flat voice. "I did not break up with him. He broke up with me because he caught me with Octave. And now you can all despise me!"

Géraldine pressed her hands against her cheeks. "Jesus Christ, I've made a complete fool of myself!"

"Is that all you can think of?" Nelly shouted, furious. "You've insulted the finest man under the sun and made it look like a clumsy conspiracy. One thing you can bet on is that he's not here to tell me that all is forgiven."

Claude gulped down the last of his wine, rose from the table, and knotted a wool scarf around his neck.

"Where are you going?" Géraldine snapped at him. "Are you deserting me? Don't you see that we have a crisis?"

"It has nothing to do with me," he said. "You acted on your own and you'll fix the damage on your own. I've work to finish before nightfall."

"He's right," Nelly said. "I cannot face Henri after this. You will."

"So everything is my fault, is it?" Géraldine raised her voice as well. "Pardon me if I thought we were family. I'm disappointed in you, I really am. To do a thing like that, to keep such an important fact to yourself only shows your lack of faith in me."

Nelly opened her mouth to answer, but all she could manage was a sob. She covered her face with her hands.

Claude squeezed her shoulder. "It will be all right," he said softly. "It will be all right," he repeated in a harsher voice, frowning at Géraldine.

A few seconds went by, during which Géraldine resisted his accusing stare and that of Julie, who stood by the cupboard, clutching a bottle of iodine in one hand and a handkerchief in the other.

"Well, don't you two look at me like that," Géraldine said at last. "I'm going to speak to him."

* * *

A fire was made up in the salon, where Julie had polished the furniture to a high sheen and placed three armchairs at an equal distance from each other. Nelly inspected the setup and dragged the chairs back and forth several times as if the few inches could make any difference in what she perceived would be a trial before judge and jury. In any case, it was something to do.

She had spent the afternoon washing her hair and rummaging in her wardrobe for something to wear over her fat clothes. A light cashmere shawl, large enough to cover her shoulders and hips, won the contest. That, and a starched lace collar, was the only improvement to her appearance she could manage.

The door opened, letting in Zidore with a bouquet of white chrysanthemums slightly past their prime.

"They had nothing better?" she asked.

"It's a large bouquet. I bargained it down from three to one eighty."

She could have gotten a far better deal for the price but this was not the moment to be choosy. Her mind was on something else.

"How was your day?" she asked innocently.

"Fine," the boy said. "I was helping with the lighting."

"Nothing unusual?"

Zidore blushed. "There were pretty ladies in the studio."

Most likely with next to nothing on, she thought. But that, too, was unimportant. "Nothing else?" she pressed on.

"Now that you mention it, Monsieur Gaillard asked me whether a very tall gentleman had been visiting here more than once. I said I had not seen him at all."

"Ah," Nelly said. "That's fine. Now run along and have your dessert and cocoa!"

So Octave got Henri's message. He would be coming tonight 'to discuss the situation'. Just what Henri meant by discussing the situation was difficult to predict. She had to rely on Géraldine's report that he had listened to her explanations, taken a few moments to think it over, and then proposed a meeting at eight o'clock. What he thought of the whole thing Géraldine could not say because he did not move a single muscle in his face during the visit.

The ancient grandfather clock rattled and struck a quarter to eight. With an unsteady hand, she arranged the bouquet in a vase. Remembering the last encounter between the two men, she was worried about the meeting. Would there be another violent confrontation? And what would Henri say to her? Or worse, what would she say to him?

A doorbell interrupted her fretting. Nelly glanced at the clock. Whoever it was, was a full ten minutes ahead of time. The prospect of being alone with either of her visitors filled her with dread. As fast as her bulk allowed, she hurried into the vestibule.

"Wait!" she motioned to Julie, who was already approaching the main door. Quickly, she mounted to the floor above. She sat on the last step, hidden behind the balustrade where she could not be seen unless the visitor lifted his head.

It was Octave. Julie took his hat and coat, and ushered him into the salon. There was some verbal exchange which Nelly did not hear clearly, and soon after, Julie reappeared, closing the door behind her. She crossed the hall and joined Nelly upstairs.

"He was surprised not to see you," she whispered. "He wants to talk to you before the other one shows up."

Nelly shook her head. "No, let him wait! Better yet, go back and offer him a glass of vermouth. Say that I'll be there shortly."

A few minutes passed, interrupted only by Julie's coming and going, then the salon door opened. Quickly, Nelly ducked her head.

Octave was calling her name but she did not budge. She could tell that he was looking for her by the sound of doors opening and closing. She heard him mumbling an excuse as he poked his head into the library and disturbed

Géraldine, who was working there. That he might carry his search to the upper floor was a distinct possibility, but Julie reappeared in time to assure him that her mistress was on her way. He gave up and went back into the salon.

The silence returned. She began to fear that Henri would be fashionably late, but a few minutes later the bell rang again and Julie opened the main door. Through the opening in the balustrade, Nelly had a limited view of the hall below. Henri appeared in her field of vision, and she inspected him carefully as he passed. Had he reverted to his careless appearance, she would have relaxed, but there was nothing warm and fuzzy about him now. His hair and beard were cropped closer than ever and he was dressed with studied elegance. She had the impression that General d'Auzon's spirit had remained behind and invaded his son's body. A shiver ran along her spine. She did not know exactly what she expected from him—a spark of his former feelings?—but it was not going to happen. Not with this forbidding Henri.

When she heard the click of the door, followed by Julie's steps fading away, Nelly rose and smoothed her skirt. As she approached the salon, she overheard the men's voices. By the tone of the conversation, it was probably small talk. She inhaled and exhaled deeply to calm her beating heart, and opened the door.

Octave was standing by the fireplace, one hand in his pocket, the other one on the carved mantelpiece. If it was a calculated pose, it was meant to project a master-of-the-hearth status. Henri, who was already seated, rose when she entered.

"Here you are at last! Where have you been?" Octave asked.

She did not answer him because her attention was focused on Henri. At the distance, she could not judge the expression in his eyes. There was a tension in the air caused by words waiting to be said. As she advanced into the room, Henri pressed his lips together, in what could—if one were inclined to optimism—be interpreted as a smile.

"Good evening, Nelly," he said and extended his hand.

"Good evening," she repeated and offered hers.

He kissed it lightly. "How are you?" he asked.

"She's very well," Octave jumped in. "I've been looking after her. A heartening picture of fertility, isn't she, Henri? So, what's the program for this get-together? An auction?"

Was that the opening of hostilities? She had been wrong to ignore him. Nothing would make him angrier. "Good evening, Octave," she said and busied herself with the vermouth decanter.

324

Henri resumed his seat. "We're here to discuss an important matter and we will do it calmly," he addressed Octave. "I'll allow no room for resentment or provocation. We're both familiar with Descartes and Voltaire, so we are able to make use of rational thought."

"To Voltaire and Descartes!" Octave proposed a toast with his glass.

"Why don't you sit down?" Nelly asked him.

"I prefer to stretch my legs," he said.

Henri frowned. "I wish you would stop hovering. Sit down, for heaven's sake!"

During the couple of seconds they glared at each other in a contest of wills, Nelly had a flash of illumination. She pictured both as they must have looked twenty years ago, in short pants, arguing over some trivial matter. The image was so vivid and so comical, that it did away with her anxiety. Men were just grown up boys. Why had she never thought of them in this manner? She burst out in a loud giggle.

"I'm sorry," she said, when both looked first at her and then at each other as if to assess the degree of her foolishness.

"Here's someone who takes the matter lightly," Octave said gloomily but he finally sat down.

A short pause followed.

"Why was I not told?" Henri asked.

"We did not think that you'd be interested," Octave said.

"We?" Nelly repeated, her merriment turning into irritation. "*You* thought Henri would not be interested. Whether *I* thought he would not be interested is a separate matter. I've done my own thinking and I don't want it lumped together with yours."

"Very well, then," Henri said. "What was the outcome of your thinking?"

"I thought that you would not be interested."

Octave let out a snort and a chuckle.

"You've both been wrong," Henri said. "The possibility of a child of mine living unprotected is unacceptable to me."

Octave shrugged. "You need not be concerned. I've already offered Nelly my protection and I've been carrying it out since the day I became aware of her condition. I'm perfectly capable of seeing to her needs, and that of the child."

"Nelly," Henri said, "let's make one thing clear. Your friend told me the date of your expected delivery and I've done calculations of my own. It seems that our brief relationship falls within the time of conception. If you are certain that it is not so, and that the child is Octave's, then say it now before we take this any further."

She entwined her fingers. "I cannot say whose child it is. It's true that it could be yours."

"In that case," Henri turned to Octave, "I demand that you tone down your involvement until we have more evidence."

"What specific evidence do you have in mind?" Octave asked.

"The child itself, naturally."

"A resemblance?" Nelly asked. "But what if it looks like me?"

Henri shook his head. "Nature has its own way with progeny. If not in looks, there's resemblance in mannerisms and proclivities. We will look for those."

"But that could take years." she said.

"Possibly. In the meantime, I've opened a bank account for you and you will draw on it for half of the child's needs. Octave may reimburse me if later the offspring turns out to be his."

"Well, there you have it, Nelly," Octave said. "All cooked up and served cold. You must have noticed that I had offered to recognize the child be it mine or not. And I'll do it without dragging my feet."

"You will do no such thing," Henri said, his brows joining in a frown.

Octave smiled provocatively. He leaned back in his chair and crossed his legs.

Henri rose. "Octave, I want your solemn promise that you will not alter the birth register without my consent."

Octave was on his feet immediately. "Don't you pull your height on me," he said menacingly. "Sober, I can stand up to you any time."

"If you think that I'll become physical, you are wrong," Henri replied. "I'm done with primitive conflict-solving."

Octave took a step forward. "Oh? And what is it then? Suppose I don't give you any promise. Suppose I recognize the child without your consent. What will you do?"

"Then I'll sue you."

"A paternity suit? That's ridiculous! You know very well that they're forbidden by law."

"It's true that a woman cannot sue a man for paternity. But the law doesn't say that a man cannot sue another man."

"You must be mad. Do you want a scandal? That's exactly the kind of juicy story newspapers are looking for."

It was Henri's turn to take a step forward. "I want justice for the child. If you cannot live with a scandal, then don't push me in that direction."

"Enough!" Nelly shouted and plunged between them. She shoved her hands into their chests, first Octave's, and then Henri's.

"You, sit down! And you too!"

It was her wrath rather than her rough handling that made them obey her. She remained standing, glaring at them accusingly.

"This," she said, spreading both hands on her stomach, "is a baby. A baby, not a pawn in some silly chess game. And must I remind you that it is also *my* baby? How is it that nobody has asked my opinion? Or do you think that because I'm a woman, I've no right to decide what's best for my child?"

She shamed them into silence. When nobody answered, she resumed her seat. "As a mother," she said, "it would be irresponsible of me not to accept custodial help from either of you. Later, after you two make up your mind as to who's the father, you'll sort it out between you. But I will not bring up my child in shame if I have the means of making it legitimate."

Now she had their undivided attention. She told them about Tassin's scheme.

"Absolutely not! I forbid it." Octave said.

"And so do I," said Henri. "That's completely out of the question."

Taken aback by such an unexpected alliance against her, Nelly braced her elbows against the armrests of her chair. "Oh? Why is that?"

"Because you would lose legal rights to your child," Henri said.

"But people like that will not be interested in the child. They'll take their money and I'll not have to meet them ever again."

"Nelly," Octave leaned toward her, "neither of us doubts that you want the best for the baby but this is not the way to go about it. Have you thought of what would happen if—God forbid!—you were to die before the child grows up?"

"No, I haven't," she admitted.

"Well, think of it!" Henri chimed in. "No matter how well-intentioned we might be, none of us would have the legal leverage to protect the child against abuse. A bogus adoption has its risks. In addition to their financial reward, those people would want caution money deposited in the bank to cover the child's upkeep and education should something happen to you. You'd not be there to see whether it would be used as intended. On top of that, they would have the power to decide where and with whom the child would live, whether or not it would be properly educated, and even whom he or she may marry. Every little detail would be left to their discretion, including the quantity of food."

She stared at him in horror. "You mean that they could let it starve?"

Henri shrugged. "With people unscrupulous enough to sell their name for profit we have to consider that as well."

"Most likely," Octave added, "they would send the child into the care of some crass peasants who do this for a living. It would grow up crawling in dirt and sharing food with dogs and pigs."

She pressed her hands against her ears to hear no more. "Stop! You've scared me enough. I promise I'll not do it."

"Good," Henri said. "Finally, we've agreed on something."

* * *

Around midnight, Géraldine had thrown the last log into the dying fire. Now, an hour later, the air was becoming chilly. She rubbed her hands together to ease the cramp in her fingers. At the same time, she reread the page she had just written and a satisfied smirk appeared on her tired face. She put the finished page on top of a growing stack and reached for a new sheet of paper.

A light knock at the door sent her into a panic. With lightning speed, she shoved the manuscript into the desk drawer and replaced it with another. The door had already opened, revealing Nelly, bundled up in a thick flannel dressing gown. She was carrying a tray.

Géraldine let out a sigh of relief. "I thought it was Claude," she said.

"I could not sleep," Nelly said. "I went to the kitchen to prepare a cup of herb tea and on my way I noticed a light under the door. So I brought you some as well."

"You are a sweetheart! Exactly what I needed to revive my circulation."

Nelly put the tray on the desk. "It's late. You should be in bed," she said while pouring the tea.

"And so should you."

"As I said, I couldn't sleep. Do you want honey in your tea?"

"By all means. So, what's churning in that head of yours and robbing you of sleep?"

Nelly scooped up Demoiselle, who had been sleeping on a padded chair by the desk, and sat down. She stirred the tea in her cup. "I've been replaying in my mind what happened today. Or, considering the hour, yesterday. The things they said, the way they behaved. First, they almost fought, then they united against me and, finally, they left together, apparently to hone the finer details of the matter."

Géraldine chuckled. "To hone the finer details?"

"That's Octave's way of talking, of course. I've been tossing it around and I've come to the conclusion that there's something going on under the surface."

"Meaning?"

Nelly blew to cool her tea and took a careful sip. "It's no longer about me or the baby. It's about them. From what I know about their past, they used to

328

be very close and I'm the jinx who had split them apart. All that look-at-me-what-a-good-boy-I-am behavior is Octave's way of getting back at Henri. And Henri is falling into the trap. Perhaps knowingly—I'm not sure on that point. The fact is that they've missed each other and that now they have something to fight over, which is a good excuse to stay in touch. It's better to be enemies than nothing at all. Still, I'm glad you wrote to Henri. He had the right to know."

"To tell you the truth, I did it mainly for my own comfort. Every time I snuggle against Claude I think of you, alone in that large bed. It takes away from my own happiness."

"I won't be alone for long. The baby's coming soon."

"That's not what I meant. You need a good man to put his arms around you. It's a necessity. I didn't understand it until Claude came into my life. Do you think you and Henri could patch it up, despite everything?"

Nelly shook her head. "He was cold and detached. I've injured him too deeply." She let her gaze roam around the room, seeking a less painful topic. It fell on twelve fat canvas bags, stored in a corner. "Something has to be done about the mail. No one has gone through it for weeks."

Géraldine glanced over her shoulder. "The price of fame. I'll do it as soon as I have more time."

"No, it's not your business, after all. Claude was right, you look sickly. Is something wrong?"

Géraldine hesitated shortly, before dropping her face into her hands. "It's Babeau. He showed up at the redaction with a court order and seized my money. Since our separation is not yet legalized, it belongs to him."

"That's not possible! You worked for it. It's yours."

"Wait, that's not all. It was the same at the publisher's. I ran there as soon as I left the redactor. All my future royalties are blocked as well. If they pay me as much as a centime, he'll sue."

"What a monster!"

"It's the law that's monstrous, and he makes good use of it. It's his chance to recover some money in case he loses the court case and has to return the dowry. I wish my parents had the good sense to leave him alone."

Demoiselle, uncomfortable in Nelly's lap, and tired of being ignored, clawed her way up and jumped on the desk. Géraldine reached for the kitten and cradled it in her arms.

"He cannot sit on your royalties forever," Nelly said. "As soon as the separation becomes legal—"

"Yes, but in the meantime, my six hundred francs for the magazine articles are gone. Claude cannot face the builder's bill by himself. I'm so choked up with rage, that I could kill Babeau. But don't you worry! I'll cut him out of my life so swiftly he'll not see the knife coming."

Nelly gasped. "Please don't do anything without thinking it over," she begged. "You should discuss it with Claude."

"No. This is my own fight and what I'm doing is not pretty. I don't want Claude to know this dark side of me. As for thinking it over, believe me, I have. I know how Babeau's mind works and I intend to apply pressure at his weakest point."

"But—"

"There are no buts."

Nelly fell silent. The quiet was broken by the sound of footsteps approaching the library. Claude opened the door and paused on the threshold, a dressing gown carelessly tied over a nightshirt.

"What are you two doing here at this time of the night?" he asked, rubbing sleep out of his eyes.

"Girl talk," Géraldine said.

"At half past two in the morning? Where's your common sense?"

"We were wrapping up and just about to go to bed."

"I'm glad to hear that. I wish you good night, Nelly. And if the other one is not in her warm bed within five minutes, I'll be back."

"Yes, my revered master," said Géraldine half-mockingly, half-fondly, when the door closed behind him.

Nelly rose. "Whatever you do, I hope it will meet with success," she said.

"Thank you," Géraldine planted a kiss onto her cheek. "Good night, then."

Alone in the library, Géraldine opened the desk drawer and removed the hidden pages. Clutching them in her hand, she wheeled the ladder to one of the empty bookcases and climbed to the top. She stashed the manuscript onto the highest shelf, well out of sight. No one, not even Julie with her duster, would find it there.

Chapter 50

"No one told me," Nelly said. She folded the copy of the newspaper and returned it to Octave.

"Keep it for your collection of clippings."

She dropped the paper on the floor, rose from her chair, and paced the salon, from the blazing fire in the hearth to the windows behind which wet snowflakes fell at a slow pace, the first of the season.

"When is this farce going to stop?" she asked.

Octave shrugged. "Not until they milk it for all it's worth."

"Damn Quérat and Tassin and their greedy minds! And to think that I knew nothing of this!"

"Thanks to your overprotective friends."

"Claude and Géraldine mean well. Articles of lesser importance had upset me in the past."

"This time, they were wrong not to tell you. Soon, you may have the press knocking at your door. I'm surprised that no one has, so far."

She paused in front of the floor-length window, biting her lips. Outside, the snow was melting as soon as it touched the ground, darkening the uneven slate tiles of the balcony, the water accumulating in puddles.

"Is there anything I can do to extricate myself from Quérat's claws?"

Octave caught up with her and enveloped her shoulders with his arm. "First of all, do me a favor and sit down." He guided her to the sofa. "There. That's better. How's the baby doing?"

"Impatient and squirming around. It seems to me that I've been carrying it forever. And now this! I've been branded as an attention-seeking schemer just because they want to boost the sales. If I protest, who will believe me, now that I have a share in the profits?"

Octave sat at her side and stroked her stomach. "Calm down! Take care of yourself and the baby and let me handle the agency. I'll need your permission to hire a lawyer on your behalf. You must also entrust me with your copy of the contract. With a little luck, we'll find a loophole that will set you free."

"Will I ever be free now that I'm notorious? What's worse, they've hurt the memory of my mother. She was a respectable, married woman who had never set foot in France. How dare they suggest that she was a whore? For this alone I could bring the agency to justice."

"But, of course, you will not. Not unless you want to expose your real name and revive your involvement with the de Chazelle murder. What could invite more attention than that? Besides, what proof do you have that this was Quérat's doing? My advice to you is to keep quiet and let it blow over. It's too risky to leave Paris so close to your confinement but as soon as the baby is born and you are fit to travel, I'll take you both to Normandy to a secluded house by the sea, with fresh air for the child and complete anonymity. In a year or two, nobody will remember the name of Ceres."

He fell silent, allowing his offer to sink in. As soon as she nodded her consent, he took his ease against the sofa, stretching his legs toward the fire and crossing his ankles.

"A sound decision," he said, plunging his hands into his pockets. "Now, as for the press, should one of those hounds ring the bell, you will be ill. Let's make it a contagious disease. Typhoid fever for instance. That will keep them at arm's length."

Nelly wrought her hands, cracking her knuckles. "Normandy. I know no one there."

"That's the very thing, is it not? If you think that you'd miss Madame Babeau's company, ask her to move there with you. Let her prove that she's as good a friend as you think."

"I could never do that. She's practically married to Claude."

"As long as you know where her priorities are."

"And Henri?"

Octave abandoned his comfortable position. "Henri!" he hissed. "As far as I know, he's remained in Paris. So why is it that I'm here to sort out your troubles and he's not? If the truth breaks out about your true identity, it's no longer fame that you will be facing, but infamy. And you, my dear, possess neither Sarah's talent nor her savoir-faire to thrive on public attention. You are too thin-skinned to resist the blows."

He was right. "Wait," she said and rose. "I'll find the contract for you."

* * *

The garden was exhaling a raw breath of rotting leaves. The sleet had subsided and the snow caught in the trees and shrubs dripped from the branches. Nelly pulled the warm shawl closer over her shoulders as she walked the path that led to the new studio. Only yesterday, they had celebrated the finished project with cake and sweet liquor. The exhilaration seemed far away, as if years had passed instead of hours.

She climbed the stairs and found Géraldine on her knees, scrubbing the floor clean of the dirt left behind by the workers. Fire cracked in the new stove, a black barrel-like contraption standing on three curved legs and connected by a long fluepipe to the chimney. The room still smelled sharply of the caulk paste used for fixing the numerous glass panels. Even under the leaden sky, the light was strong and pervasive. So far, the only furniture consisted of two chairs and a tabletop propped on a couple of trestles. Nelly paused on the threshold, listening to the grating of the brush and waiting for Géraldine to look up from her work.

"You had your first snow. Was it as you expected?" she asked.

Géraldine grinned. "A satisfactory test run. Wait until the studio's properly furnished! There will be no cozier place in the world."

"Julie could've helped you with the floor. All you have to do is ask."

"She's your maid, not mine. Besides, I enjoy this. I feel like a bride readying her new home. What brings you here? Has Claude got worse?"

"Worse? Not as far as I know. Last time I heard of him, and that was from you, he was sweating out his cold."

"Good. Making him stay in bed's been an awesome task. Men are impossible when sick. What is it? You look terribly serious."

Nelly unfolded the newspaper she brought with her. "What do you know of this?"

Géraldine frowned and dropped the brush into the pail. "*The Echo de Paris*? How did you get your hands on it?"

"Octave."

"The cad! He cannot leave well enough alone, can he? Well, since I'm already on my knees, I'm in the proper position to greet Your Imperial Highness."

"This is not funny! If you knew, you should've told me."

"To what purpose? What can you do about it except to fret? Soon, you'll be too busy to care. That's where your mind should focus, on the baby."

Géraldine got up, rubbing her hands on her apron. "Come and sit down!" she said tersely, advancing a chair toward Nelly. She sat on the table, her feet dangling several inches above the floor. "We discussed it with Claude. He says that it's not the first time that a rising celebrity has been given a lofty background. The article's nothing but a puff of smoke. Chances are that no one will take it seriously. There are no facts and no names, only suggestions and innuendoes. Give it to me and let's go over it once more!"

The paper rustled as Géraldine searched for the relevant lines. "Listen to this . . . The rumor that has been circulating for some time links the elusive Ceres with the banished Bonapartes. Indeed, upon close examination, her profile seems to be an exact copy of that of the Empress Josephine, while her eyes bear the stamp of the great lady's grandson. Bets have been taken on which one of the squadron of light-footed international beauties who circled the throne at the beginning of the Second Empire was the mother of the present star. However, let us not delve too deeply into details that could cause a great deal of embarrassment to the interested party, who presently enjoys the hospitality of our stiff-lipped British friends. Suffice it to say that Ceres wears her royal costumes with a natural grace seldom found in common people." Géraldine looked up from her reading. "As I said, no facts. And no lasting consequences either. Trust me on that."

"All the same, I wish I could sue the rumor-mongers. I know exactly who they are. But that would make it even worse."

"Definitely. All you can do is sit tight and admit no callers. I've already instructed Julie on that matter."

Nelly smiled. Somehow, in her casual way, Géraldine had managed to take the edge off her anger. "What you are saying is that I'm the victim of a conspiracy in my own house."

"Yes, indeed. The men who have been ringing at the gate were not salesmen. Any other complaints?"

"None. In fact, your advice is identical to Octave's."

"Sooo . . ." Géraldine shifted on the table and folded a leg under her, "what other advice did he dispense?"

"An extended stay in Normandy. Complete seclusion in a secret place."

"I see that he's got it all mapped out. If what you think of their rivalry is right, that would put Henri out of the game. Are you sure Octave's not the one who has started the rumor, just to snatch you under his wing?"

"My God! It cannot be."

"I wouldn't put it past him."

"If that's true, three can play as well as two. I'll use him the same way he uses me. He volunteered to hire a lawyer on my behalf. That's one expense I'll not have to pay. As for the rest, I'll shape my future according to my will, not his."

"That's my girl!" Géraldine clapped her hands. "It pays to act hard. Take your cue from me. I pushed Babeau's back against the wall and made him part with my money in a hurry. He'll never bother me again, the swine!"

"You still haven't told me how you managed that."

"I sent him a copy of my latest manuscript and set an appointment in town," Géraldine said. "He came on the dot, sweating like a pig, his pocketbook bulging with my six hundred francs. He knew that I meant business." When Nelly stared at her without comprehension, she laughed. "A private memoir by Géraldine Babeau," she said. "All the dirty stuff he did to me."

"You did not!"

"Oh, but I did! In graphic detail. The vilest pornography I could manage. I let Babeau know that since he intended to live off the fruit of my labors, I had given it my best effort. And would his superiors each appreciate a free copy?"

Nelly's hand shot to her mouth. "I'm a little afraid of you."

"Why should you be? I only treat my enemies harshly. And, honestly, I prefer children's stories by far. I want your promise that this will stay between us. I'd probably die of shame should someone catch a whiff of my secret literary career. Besides, it's going up in flames as we speak," she motioned toward the stove. "I've just got the news that he had the court order revoked."

"I shall not tell a living soul. How could I? In fact, how could you? Where did you learn to write like that?"

"Marquis de Sade, of course. There's no such thing as a useless education."

* * *

At the end of the afternoon, a sudden wind swept the sky clean, just in time to unveil a spectacular crimson sunset. Later, the rosy light so unexpectedly pouring into the kitchen acquired an important status. It was the last thing Nelly remembered with extraordinary clarity. Everything else came back in hazy fragments. She marveled at the pinkish glow that coated the worktable. She became fully aware of the grain of the wood, the smooth texture of the dough she was kneading and the particles of flour dust suspended in the air. The movement of her hands slowed until it came to a full stop. Standing still, she felt weariness creeping over her and reaching for her brain. A squeak of the range door followed by the grating of the poker, as Julie worked on rekindling the fire, jerked her back into reality. She turned the dough a few more times, plunging her fingers into its yielding mass and then stopped again, overcome by exhaustion.

"I don't know what's wrong with me," she said, "but all of a sudden I'm dropping with fatigue."

"It's the turn of the weather," Julie said. "My grandma used to be like that. When the weather changed real quick, it would knock her right off her feet. Please, go to bed and I'll finish the dinner."

"I don't think I can make it upstairs."

She crossed the room to a far corner where a gingham curtain hid Zidore's cot and his meager possessions. She landed heavily on the mattress and fell into a shallow, uncomfortable sleep, half-aware of the comings and goings in the room. Géraldine came in to fetch Claude's tea, then Zidore, back from the studio, brought in Schnitzel from the garden. She felt the dog's damp nose delicately stamping her cheek, heard the click and clang of the kitchen implements and shreds of conversation.

". . . dead tired . . ."

". . . coming down with something? That would make two . . ."

She was standing in the vastness of the Montana prairie, watching the tall grass yield to the wind, except that there was no wind and, on closer inspection, the grass was giant human hair that smelled of frying grease. She felt nauseated by the discovery.

"Nelly . . ." a hand ran across her forehead. She opened her eyes. It was Géraldine.

"The dinner's ready."

Food? The idea of food was disgusting. The crackling of grease, the smell of it . . . "Leave me alone!"

"It will get cold."

"I said leave me alone!" She shut her eyelids tight.

"Miss . . ."

"Whatever she's got, it is not a fever. Her breathing is normal. Let her sleep, Julie."

Your Mommy died. Drowned in the river, poor soul. Let us say a prayer for her so that the Lord may welcome her in heaven. Yes, Grandmother. Will I go to heaven as well? Only if you behave as a God-fearing Christian. But do you, Ceres? Do you? You shall never meet your mother.

"Miss . . ."

A bad dream, nothing but a bad dream.

"Miss, you've been sleeping for hours!"

She sat up, rubbing her eyes. A lamp spread a pool of light on the table, where Zidore slept sitting on a chair, cradling his head in his arms.

"I've kept your dinner in the oven," Julie said.

The revulsion came back with full force. Why was everyone forcing food on her? If she stayed here, she would suffocate.

"I need air," she said, her voice rasping in her dry throat.

At the sink, she filled a glass with water and gulped it down. The baby had shifted while she slept. She felt an unusually strong pressure at the bottom of her pelvis, which added to her irritation.

"You must eat something."

"Shut up, Julie."

"May I go to bed now?" asked Zidore.

Once she was outside, the irritation ebbed out. The moon, a fraction short of full, bathed the garden with a silvery glow. Her breath misted but she felt no cold. Her mind adjusted to the tranquility of her surroundings and in no time at all she reached a state of quiet elation as the ground glided under her feet. After reaching the end of the driveway, she turned and retraced her steps. A silhouette was racing to meet her.

"Miss! Miss! You forgot your wrap. Put it on!"

A wrap? What for? "Go back! I want to be alone."

"But Miss . . ."

She pushed the importunate girl aside and resumed her walk. It was important to be on the go, at one with the pace of life. She left the driveway, and plunged under the trees, deeply appreciating the pattern of black lace created by the moonlight filtering through the branches. Reaching a wild patch, the site of her future vegetable garden, she stopped to ponder the rhythm of nature. She, too, was a part of the grand scheme of nature. Like the earth herself, she was in the process of giving life.

"I'm giving life," she said aloud.

"Not here, at any rate!"

That was Géraldine, a thick shawl hastily thrown over her nightgown. And Claude with a blanket.

Chapter 51

Dearest diary, I'm the proud mother of a completely healthy baby girl! I have no clear recollection of all I said and did. I can hardly believe certain assertions. Did I really take myself for Mother Earth? How ludicrous! It is only Géraldine's way of teasing me, the same as when she told me that I had given birth to Poppy Fullerton. That was when she handed me a screaming bundle, saying that it had Poppy's temper and would I please feed it to stop the racket. The little mouth greedily latched onto my breast and as my thinking adjusted to the silence, I realized that Géraldine's remark was an allusion to my daughter's red hair. Poppy Fullerton, what rubbish! My daughter — My daughter! Two wonderful words I'll never tire of repeating! — is the sweetest thing in the world, when dry and replete. I still find it difficult to think of her as a separate human being. She has been part of me for such a long time that I feel incomplete when she is not in my arms. Yet she is no longer a shapeless lump in my belly. When I touch her little hands with their fully formed fingernails, I cannot but marvel that such perfection is of my own doing.

I owe a large debt to Julie and Géraldine, for whom the night was particularly stressful, and to Claude, who, despite his cold, braved the icy streets to alert the midwife. As for Zidore, he did not enjoy his bed for long. At daybreak, Géraldine dispatched him to town to deliver the news, first to the Faubourg Saint-Honoré and then to the boulevard Saint-Germain, with the result that Octave and Henri almost collided with each other at the gate.

They had to wait until Madame Bergeron, the midwife, allowed them into my bedroom. She had helped me into my prettiest nightgown, brushed my hair and tied it up with a ribbon, plumped up the pillows, smoothed the covers and generally made the room look as cozy as possible. She is a very orderly woman and I'm glad of my choice, especially as she had assured me that discretion was the mainstay of her trade. ("You'd be surprised at how many secrets we midwives harbor," she said.) Octave turned her into an instant enemy.

"What's this?" he barked when she proudly brought the neatly wrapped baby to the visitors.

She was taken aback by the tone of his voice, as was I, because until then everything had gone as smoothly as possible, both he and Henri complimenting me on my looks and the child sleeping like an angel.

"Why, it's a little girl," she said. "Isn't she a darling?"

"I'm fully aware of who she is," Octave said. "What I object to is the sight of a newborn swaddled like an Egyptian mummy. Are you trying to strangle her?"

Madame Bergeron protested that she followed an age-old wisdom according to which the tight wrapping insured the growth of straight limbs; that, until now, no one had dared to question her savoir-faire and that she had a flawless reputation, he only had to ask around.

To which Octave replied that such views belonged to the age of dinosaurs. He made a move for the baby but the midwife stepped out of reach. I don't know whether it would have resulted in some kind of physical altercation had not Henri put an end to it. During the exchange, he stood still, scratching the stubble of his beard, but now he stepped between them. He said to Madame Bergeron that he appreciated her concern and that he had no doubt that she was a well-meaning professional. However, as much as he respected her long experience, the progress of science ought to be taken into consideration. She surrendered the baby without further ado, gave me a look heavy with pity and left the room.

"Now, then," Henri said, handing the bundle over to Octave, "let's see what we have here."

I felt disappointed with him for sounding like a tax excise inspector and I was annoyed with Octave for having alienated the excellent Madame Bergeron. By then, I was spoiled by the oh's and ah's of admiration at the first sight of my wonderful daughter and I expected at least as much from them.

Octave put the baby on the bed, untied the pretty bow, and handed an end of the swaddling band to Henri. In no time at all, the baby was stripped bare. Although still sleeping, she immediately brought her little fists toward her chest and bent her knees.

"A superb specimen of the human race," Henri said. He gently poked her cheek with his finger, while Octave tickled the red crop on her head.

The sight of them bending over the baby with such awe and tenderness went directly to my heart. Instantly, I forgot my earlier annoyance, I forgot the past. A wave of warmth washed over me and I wanted to stop time so that I could savor the blissful moment when I loved them both without reservation.

"Do you have any red-haired relatives?" Octave asked Henri.

"Not that I know of. And you?"

"None. But this kind of hereditary feature can skip a couple of generations. Besides, the more I look at the chin, the more familiar it seems. It's definitely a Gaillard chin."

I said that the chin was too small to look like anything and Henri agreed, saying that it was far too early to decide what belonged to whom. The baby woke up and began to cry.

"My, my," Henri said and picked her up. "What a mighty voice in such a tiny body! Look, her back fits into my palm!"

"Put her down at once," Octave ordered. "Obviously, you've never held a newborn." He demonstrated how to hold the baby correctly by supporting her head. "I had training in obstetrics," he reminded us.

"So you had," Henri said. He put his hands behind his back and looked so contrite that I wanted to hug him.

Octave, looking pleased with himself, wrapped her loosely in a blanket and handed her, still crying, to me. "What are you going to call her?" he asked.

"Florence," I said.

"Laurence?"

"Florence," I shouted. The only way to have an intelligible conversation was to put little Florence to my breast and so I did. Henri blushed and remarked that she had a healthy appetite. I invited him to sit on the bed, because my neck hurt from looking up at him. Octave, not to be left out, sat on the other side.

"Florence sounds nice," he said.

"A beautiful name," said Henri.

"My mother's," said I. And then, looking at them sitting so close to each other, I added, "Henriette Octavie."

"What was that?"

"A sudden inspiration. Florence Henriette Octavie. That will be her full name."

Octave frowned and asked why not Florence Octavie Henriette.

"Alphabetical order," Henri said. "And it sounds more rhythmical."

"I beg to differ! Florence Octavie Henriette sounds fine to me and I was first."

"Here we go again!" Henri snapped at him. "Would it kill you to be second at anything?"

"Please, do be nice to each other," I said, unhappy to see the rare harmony go. "I so wish you were friends again! Can't you make an effort?"

They apologized, but the spell was broken and after a few clumsy attempts at civilized conversation they looked relieved when I said that I was tired and needed rest. When they left I felt lonelier than ever.

Later that day, I received two dozen pink roses from Octave and two dozen cream-colored ones from Henri. The next day, Octave sent me a sapphire ring, followed by a gold bracelet from Henri. Although flowers and jewelry are not unusual gifts for a new mother, the timing of it, on the same day and within less than an hour of each other, was a trifle odd. When two identical prams were delivered to my door in a single afternoon, I suspected supernatural powers.

"There's no sorcery in that," Géraldine said after Claude tested the suspension and declared the prams the finest pieces of engineering. "What it proves is that they think alike. They just happened to choose the most expensive model on the market."

I must admit that I have developed an unhealthy preoccupation with the supernatural. It began the first night after the birth. As I laid in my bed, straining my ears for Florence's gentle breathing, I was overcome by an irrational fear for her safety. Perhaps it was the dead quiet of the night and the knowledge that we were alone on the entire floor, but my mind began to conjure up steps in the dark, shadows moving across the walls, and malevolent currents of air converging on the crib. It occurred to me that it could be the ghost of Henri's uncle Guillaume, who had perished in the explosion. Perhaps the baby was a Villermaine after all and the spirit had taken an ancestral interest in her. I lit a candle and my dread subsided when I saw Florence sleeping peacefully. In the morning, I chided myself for being such a fool. Nevertheless, I still carry with me a remnant of that apprehension and each time something out of the ordinary happens, the anxiety sends it soaring. Of course, I must not succumb to such ridiculous feelings but it is a difficult fight, when combined with the dream.

Ever since I learned what Julie's aunt had revealed at Célestine's funeral, that horrible creature, the gypsy, has visited me in my sleep several times. Each time, I'm walking along a road and I see her standing at a distance, waiting. I'm both afraid and insatiably curious, but no matter how desperately I try to come closer to get a better look at her, the distance remains unchanged. Upon waking up, the first time the dream occurred, I tried to remember how the gypsy looked when I saw her from my window on the Quay de la Tournelle.

There was the beard, of course. As for the rest, I think her face was disfigured in some way. I wish I had paid more attention to her, but how was I to know that she was Célestine's associate in some shady scheme?

My baby has been officially registered as Florence Henriette Octavie McKay, the illegitimate daughter of Cornelia Jane McKay, spinster, and of father unknown. Later, when either Octave or Henri decide to assume the paternity, the father's name will be filled in, but since both are married, all little Florence will gain will be the unenviable status of child of an adulterous relationship. Although I had known all this beforehand, it struck me hard when I read the copy of the registration certificate. There it was, black on white, forever. My poor darling Flo, what's in store for you? What can I do to make your life bearable? How can I protect you against scorn and humiliation?

Chapter 52

At five o'clock in the afternoon, the weak winter light was surrendering to darkness. The street lamps were being lit, lights sparkled in the shop windows and the cozy interiors of cafés and restaurants lured chilled shoppers. The approach of the New Year's celebration kept the sidewalks teaming with Parisians in search of gifts for the *étrennes*. On the smart boulevards of the Right Bank, where the carriage and wagon traffic was particularly heavy, pedestrians accumulated at the crossings, waiting for the opportunity to make it safely to the other side.

Henri dodged a hurrying delivery boy burdened with several parcels. He paused in his walk, unbuttoned his overcoat and reached into the watch pocket. The watch told him that it was too early for dinner. He intended to spend the evening at Madame Gollet's. The lady ran an unpretentious salon where she gathered a collection of minds busy with absorbing projects. Tonight, the attention would most likely center on the anthropologist Dupuis-Lacroix, back from his second study of the Tuareg tribes in the Sahara. After a long spell in the sleepy agricultural Poitou, Henri absorbed such events like a dry sponge.

The question was what to do with the remaining time before dinner. He could enjoy a walk had it not been for the constant reminder of Nelly's face. There she was again, just ten yards away, glued on one of the round poster columns that dotted the boulevards, and this time she was peddling honey. *The Imperial Delight*, said the ornate letters. Surrounded by flying bees, she was portrayed holding an open glass jar and carrying a finger dipped in honey to her pursed lips.

Honey from Malmaison
—Superior Taste—
Available at select stores

The symbolism of this was obvious to anybody familiar with history. Malmaison used to be the residence of Empress Josephine. The bees represented diligence and industry, an emblem chosen by Napoleon I. Combined with the violets of the previous poster, another symbol of the Bonaparte dynasty, this translated into a political campaign, a fact that could not go unnoticed. That Nelly allowed her resemblance to the empress to be exploited on such a large scale, and that she probably reveled in it, was a source of disappointment to him. But then, she had already disappointed him in a far more personal way.

Henri turned his back on the enterprising Miss Woodridge. The lights in the café behind him had just come on, revealing one of the dazzling interiors with a vast expanse of mirrors, elaborate cornices, gilded moldings and tropical plants. His gloved hand explored the edges of a small package in his overcoat pocket as his gaze lit on an unoccupied table. Time for an aperitif together with a read.

From the conversations going on around him, he soon figured out that the café was a gathering place for budding financiers, which was not surprising considering that the Bourse was only a block away. The table next to his had been transformed into an office, its sole occupant busy checking a stack of forms and transferring the data from one onto another. Further back, a trio of brightly dressed young women, two brunettes and one blonde, their glances darting around the room, nursed their drinks, hoping to be noticed and taken out to dinner.

"Monsieur?"

"A glass of madeira."

The waiter gone, Henri removed the string from the package and unfolded the wrapping. *Horse Diseases and their Treatment*. He happened on the title in a bookstore in the Passage Vivienne and thought it may be useful to him. He was familiar with every-day ailments usually dealt with by the grooms but, as he flipped the pages, he grew uneasy discovering the number of troubles a serious horse breeder had to face. Botulism, melanoma, sarcoids, spondylitis, tetanus, verminous aneurysm. Was he ready for this? Until now, he had considered horses a simple means of transport. As long as the equine was strong enough to carry him from point A to point B, and as long as they could reasonably get along with each other, he did not care what breed it was. That was his father's obsession and, on principle, not worthy of interest.

As he had recently discovered, Father's projects in breeding had not been limited to horses. After the failed attempt at designing a worthy grandson by reinforcing valuable d'Auzon characteristics, he went overboard in the opposite direction. Henri saw the woman only once, many years ago, but it was an unforgettable experience, for it resulted in yet another serious rift between father and son. He was just past twenty years old, home for Easter, the first after his mother died. After washing off the dust of the journey, he went in search of his father and was told that the general was to be found at the stables with Mrs. Davenport, the visiting horse expert.

He was there, standing erect and stretching his neck to compensate for his short stature, feet apart, fists rammed into his hips, completely absorbed by the spectacle of a woman masterfully handling a chestnut mare. The horse was his latest acquisition and had proved to be a strongly neurotic creature. Whatever her caprices used to be, she was now performing beautifully, the animal and the rider blended into one. Even though the horse was undeniably a physical masterpiece, Mrs. Davenport outshone it by her poise. Dressed in a riding habit with a split skirt, she rode astride. Holding her back straight but by no means stiff, she handled the horse with such an economy of movement that it seemed to respond to her mind rather than to a knee squeeze or a nudge of the whip. The woman radiated an aura of self-confidence with a hint of danger thrown in. She appeared smooth and intoxicating, like heavy wine.

His father must have sensed a presence behind him for he turned his head. "Ah, it's you," he said. "How was the journey?"

"Uneventful."

"Good." His attention returned to the rider and, for a while, they both watched in silence.

"A splendid creature," Father said and Henri knew that he meant the woman. "Born with a horse between her legs. A far cry from the convent-educated, poetry-reading, simpering violets one has to marry. This one, I'm sure, would not spoil a bloodline."

The insult of his mother contained all the contempt in which the general held the Villermaines, the bookworms, eccentrics, and good-for-nothings. Henri turned on his heel and headed for the house. With his luggage still unpacked, it took no more than ten minutes before he was on his way back to the railway station.

It was not until after the general's sudden death, that Henri discovered how far his father had been ready to go in order to restore the d'Auzon bloodline. He found Mrs. Davenport's letter mixed with old veterinary bills. It was dated three years later, after his disastrous marriage, which brought nothing but grief to everyone involved and sent him on a long journey away from France.

Dear Frédéric, it said, *I'm sending you post-haste a large sample of the rain scald ointment. I am proud to say that it has just recently been approved as standard equipment for the Prussian cavalry. I'm not sure whether this fact should be mentioned at the ministry, for you French dislike following foreign leads, but I cannot keep it from you. In any case, a testing of the product will soon establish its absolute superiority to any other medication. Should the ministry decide to consider the offer, I could arrange for a meeting with the manufacturer, either here in Ireland or in Paris. As usual, I'm off to spend the winter months on the Riviera but, knowing how long it takes for the army to make a decision, I do not expect to hear from you until spring when I will be back home. Should you want to contact me earlier, I will be staying at the Villa Bellamare in Nice. I expect to conclude a deal with the Russians and if Colonel Bouchard is still interested in the Orlov trotters, tell him to confirm by a telegram direct to Nice.*

As for 'hitching our horses in the same harness' subject, I have already done all the thinking that had to be done and my answer remains the same. I appreciate your willingness to allow me a good measure of independence, but I know men well enough not to believe that you would stand by your promise for any length of time. Delegating would not do either, for my children are too young and how can one delegate a business that is based solely on personal contacts? Either way, I'm settled in my widowhood and used to my way of life. I do not see how I could possibly fit childbearing into my busy schedule.

I happened to console you after the tragedy that struck your family but we cannot build marriage on such a flimsy foundation. Sooner or later, my past would begin to matter to you and that alone could turn into another disaster. As you see, dear, I'm being perfectly honest with you and am confident that in time you will agree with me. Let us not mention this again and, more importantly, let us not allow it to mar our friendship, which I value highly.

Henri could not tell how much the rebuff had hurt his father, but one thing was certain. Two weeks after the letter was sent, the general buried his hopes for a worthy heir and altered his will to benefit his sister's son. Surprisingly, Mrs. Davenport managed to remain in his good graces. In a note, found among a more recent correspondence, she thanked him for a letter of introduction and, at the same time, playfully threatened to pull his ear for an unspecified misdeed. The mental picture of the irascible general having his ear pulled was too precious for words.

Who was this crafty woman who successfully handled both horses and their owners? The question remained on the back shelf of his mind and came forth again when he inspected his Poitou estate. Located in a basin known as the Green Venice, it included hectares of lush pastures veined with waterways built under the reign of Henri the Fourth. The good king was said to be very fond of the region, which was no surprise to anyone who ventured into the green paradise.

Thanks to a capable manager, the manor and the surrounding farms had been kept in a reasonable state of repair, just on the right side of shabby. Even with the general dipping into the profits to finance his other ventures, the estate managed to remain afloat, if only barely. Now that he had become a peasant burdened with possessions and responsibility, Henri intended to make up for the stagnation of which both his uncle and himself were the chief cause. Diverting cash flow from the sugar refinery to the land, he could invest in a light industry, revitalize the estate, and provide jobs for the villagers. He had considered his options carefully. The main resources of income were wood and beans for export, wheat and dairy products. The canals yielded wild geese and a variety of fish. After considering various means of income it had come to him that the solution was obvious. Horses. The stables had stood practically empty since the war. The army had requisitioned all non-essential horses and the shortage was still felt across the country. He would have to take a crash-course in horse breeding, consult experts, and gather tips on likely sources. The Anglo-Norman Association of Horse Breeders, of which his father was a member, was the most practical starting point. Or else—and why not?—the infinitely capable Mrs. Davenport, with her international network of acquaintances, could open up other opportunities. At the same time, he would learn more about the woman and her *modus operandi*.

He wrote to her, explaining the situation and his need for advice. She responded promptly, saying how shocked and aggrieved she was by the general's untimely demise. She would, of course, consider it a privilege to be of assistance to her dear friend's son. Horse breeding could be a lucrative business if done with a clear goal in mind. Did his preferences tend to light horse breeds, warm bloods, or the heavy varieties? Did he intend to supply the army, transport, or venture into the highly profitable but risky world of racing horses? Considering his novice status, she would advise him against the latter. She was including starting budgets for several levels of operation and the average income he could expect from each. Without wanting to influence him in any way at this early stage, she recommended that he consider the French Saddle on which his father was working so hard by injecting the native Norman stock with the Norfolk Roadster and the Arabian blood. Lastly, she invited him to visit her farm in Ireland, which she and her late husband had transformed into a model breeding station and where she would be happy to introduce him to her latest exciting discovery: the American Morgans imported from Vermont.

Thus began a correspondence through which Henri was drawn into an equine world that was no less complicated than Chinese ideograms. Smoothly, and 'without wanting to influence him in any way', Mrs. Daven-

347

port had fired up his interest in biological engineering. Clearly, good horses were products of science. Seen from this perspective, Father's tinkering with expensive toys made far more sense. Still, before becoming entangled in Mrs. Davenport's yarn, he had to consider the downside of the matter. The closest veterinarian was in Niort, some ten miles away, and should an emergency occur, he would have to handle it by himself. That horses were prone to accidents, that mares often required assistance in birthing, was not news to him. However, the manual mentioned diseases he had never heard of, some of them capable of wiping out the entire stable. He had another option. The Ministry of Foreign Affairs had inquired about his availability for a diplomatic mission to China. Perhaps he should take up the offer and forget about horse breeding.

He closed the book and acknowledged his surroundings. While he had been immersed in the text, his neighbor had finished with the forms and pulled his chair to a table where a domino game was going on, and where a brunette in a magenta jacket was brushing her breasts against the back of one of the players. The two other women were still available. One of them caught his glance and rewarded him with a wink. He shook his head: No, thanks. The only time he had been with a prostitute, at the age of eighteen, he had caught a dose of clap that had greatly dampened his interest in commercial sex. He considered himself lucky to be let off with a warning. It could have been syphilis.

Why was it that each time he got himself involved with a woman something bad had to happen, ranging from merely scary to deeply tragic? Why wasn't he able to settle down and father children who would not be taken from him before he even made their acquaintance? No one knew of the twin boys and their mother who he had abandoned in China, and no one ever would. Abandoned was the right word, for how else should he qualify leaving a pregnant woman, a Christian among pagans, to fend for herself while he chose to indulge in an exciting but unnecessary expedition? His entire life would not be enough to expiate such a mistake. He should have known that the protection of the Sisters of Charity was good only when order reigned in Tientsin. He should have known that there was unrest in the region. While he traipsed inland through bandit-infested roads, helping Père David collect his precious specimens, the mission houses in Tientsin were burning down. The rebels slaughtered all priests and nuns. Very few Christians survived. Neither his sweet Chen Li nor her two babies were among the number. His sons, so he was told, were only nine days old.

If little Florence was his, would she go the way of the others? Was there a chance that the curse had run out? So far, so good. The baby had turned out to be healthy and full of life like her mother. When he held her at the christening party, the tiny fingers had curled around his index finger and held so fast that Nelly had to pry them off one by one.

"Flo is a grabber," she commented. "When she takes hold of something, she doesn't want to let go."

It was not only his finger Florence captured, it was his entire being. He felt the essence of her flow into his veins and he savored the oneness. This is what it means to be a father, he kept saying to himself, full of awe at the simple strength of it. It would be easy to love her but, with his past record, he was not sure it was wise. For her own sake, she'd better be Octave's. But he would sooner see hell freeze over than to be indebted to that blackguard.

"There is nothing further to discuss," he told him the first time they were alone. "Nelly has made her choice. You know well enough that I don't go where I'm not wanted. But if you alter the civil register before I agree, I'll choke the life out of you."

And it was doubly true now that the baby had made him experience the wonders of fatherhood.

He paid, gathered his possessions, and left the café in a combative mood. To hell with superstition! There would be no more running away, no missions to the other side of the world. He was staying. As he was passing the poster, he doffed his hat slightly. Good evening, madam. I hope you like my haircut.

Chapter 53

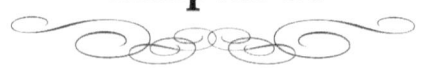

Berlin, Germany

Chancellor Bismarck opened the bottom drawer of his desk, which held an emergency supply of life-saving liquids in Bohemian crystal carafes. He poured two glasses of schnapps and pushed one of them in front of his chief spy.

"Swallow that, Stieber. You look chilled."

Wilhelm Stieber obeyed. "This helps, Your Excellency. It's a damned Siberia out there."

The chancellor's study was a cozy refuge from the January blizzard. As daylight faded behind the windows, the fire blazing in the sculptural ceramic stove began to cast playful orange reflections on the polished floor.

Otto von Bismarck settled in his carved chair, the wood creaking under his massive body. He pointed at a briefcase standing on the desk between the two men.

"What have you brought me today?" he asked.

Stieber reached for the briefcase, set it on his lap and began to work on the locks. "The French army is plotting a restoration," he said. "There's no doubt about it. There have been frequent comings and goings between Paris and London. Moreover, I have it from a reliable source in London that the emperor is having his gallstones crushed. From that, I assume that he's getting fixed for horseback riding. One cannot re-conquer a country sitting in a carriage. It wouldn't look good."

"Well, he won't have to worry about that anymore." Bismarck picked up a telegram and threw it in front of his spy. "This came when you were waiting in the antechamber. Louis Napoleon's dead."

Stieber adjusted his glasses, scanned the telegram and chuckled. "So the British doctors killed him? Tough luck for his generals. In any case, their conspiracy had all the makings of a spectacular fiasco. The man led France to a humiliating defeat and his subjects have never forgiven him for that."

"That may be so, but his death changes everything. I don't have to tell you that the situation in Germany is not all honey and roses."

Stieber nodded. Now that Prussia had dragged the Germanic tribes under one roof, the chancellor's next task was to make them like each other. And a difficult task it was. It would take at least a generation for the former kingdoms and duchies to fuse into a solid state.

"The last thing we need is the specter of Napoleon the Great raising his head in France," Bismarck said. "Now that Louis Napoleon's dead, he will become a martyr. There's nothing like a defunct Bonaparte to stir mushy patriotism in the French heart. And the young pup, how old is he? Fifteen? . . . Already sixteen? You don't say! In a couple of years, he may decide to claim the French throne and be greeted with open arms. So, what are we looking at?"

"A young vigorous Bonaparte of unspoiled reputation and with all the glory of the Great Corsican behind him."

Bismarck sighed. "Precisely! After that, it would not take long for the French to whip themselves up into a frenzy of vengeance. Germany cannot afford another war. France has learned her lesson and next time her army will be prepared. No, my friend, we must preserve the status quo."

His brows knitted in a deep frown. "That woman in Paris," he said. "The one you mentioned last time. You said that her name was Demeter?"

"Actually, it's Ceres. Your Excellency has confused Greek mythology with Roman."

"Blast it, so I have."

"An understandable error, since both are goddesses of Earth. Ceres is this American adventuress' latest incarnation. Her real name is Cornelia McKay but according to my sources she's been using three aliases."

"How old is she?"

"A little over twenty. Her resemblance to Empress Josephine is uncanny."

"I suppose you've brought a photograph."

"Several." Stieber rummaged in his briefcase. He removed a black marbled folder, untied the ribbons, and handed his boss a dozen cardboard-backed sepia pictures. "They are quite the rage in Paris."

Bismarck proceeded to study the photographs. "A pleasant package, this Ceres. What's she like?"

Stieber frowned. "Difficult to say. The reports vary. According to some, she has a temper. She's made a few powerful enemies, Victor Hugo among them. His newspaper has been maligning her repeatedly. This," he removed a newspaper clipping from the folder, "accurately sums up the situation."

Bismarck reached for the offering. The clipping was a cartoon from a French weekly entitled *A Family Visit in England*. It pictured the Goddess of Earth, clutching an armful of corn and knocking at the door of a mansion. On the other side, the exiled emperor, overcome by curiosity, stood bending at the keyhole while the empress, hands squeezing her temples, was imploring the ceiling. Their son, the young Prince Imperial, completed the scene, his features laden with gloom. Bismarck bent over with hearty laughter.

"Excellent," he said when he dried his eyes. "Excellent! A new splash of mud in the emperor's face is just what Monsieur Thiers needs to promote his Government of Moral Order."

"I smelled something of the sort when I got hold of his memo to the police prefect." Stieber was searching among the material in the black folder. "Here's a copy."

Bismarck glanced at the document. "He ordered an investigation of this Miss McKay? Interesting."

"I thought it would be worthwhile for us to look into the matter," Stieber said. "One never knows."

"Well done. I think I know what Thiers is after. He has Paris in his pocket but he needs seven million provincial votes to anchor his power. And who are they? They are the church-going petty bourgeoisie who prospered under Louis Napoleon. It doesn't matter whether this woman is his illegitimate daughter or not. What matters is that the Bonaparte closet will be open before the elections and the dirty linen aired once more. Queen Hortense's in particular."

Stieber pursed his lips and nodded. It made sense. The scandalous Hortense, Empress Josephine's daughter from her first marriage, was wed to Napoleon's brother, then King of Holland, and rumor had it that a courtier fathered Louis Napoleon. The marriage ended in shame.

Bismarck beamed. "The boy will have trouble dealing with that. His father's appearance confirmed the gossip. There was nothing in Louis Napoleon's looks that would even remotely speak of his kinship with the Bonaparte dynasty. And that's what it is all about." He slapped his thigh with glee.

He examined the photographs once more.

"What kind of hair is that?" he asked, his thick fingers designing rich waves around his balding head. "Have you ever seen anything like that?"

"You mean the coloring, Your Excellency?"

"Yes. Obviously, it grows in streaks of different hues. Some of them appear fair while there are darker shades here and there. Most unusual. Unless it's some kind of a fashionable artifice. How soon can you arrange for a wig like that?"

"Is Your Excellency planning a mischief?"

"The funeral, Stieber, the London funeral! It will be an international circus attended by reporters from the continent. We cannot miss such a golden opportunity. I intend to lend a hand to Monsieur Thiers's project."

"A diversion at the funeral?"

"Exactly. A family visit, indeed!" Bismarck chuckled. "Hire an actress of similar looks. A woman must be seen there, dressed in black, a veil obscuring her face. A brief appearance in a carriage. At an opportune moment, one of our agents will pretend to recognize her and shout her name. Knowing the curiosity of the press, the incident will snowball in no time."

Stieber nodded appreciatively. This was one of the finest from the chancellor's bag of tricks. Unexpectedly, he would strike like a viper and then watch from a distance as the poison worked its way through the victim's body.

"This McKay woman," Bismarck said, "We may need her in the near future. How do you propose to handle her?"

Stieber shrugged. "Difficult to say at this stage. I ordered only a quick probe. She must be investigated thoroughly. Luckily for us, it appears that she keeps a diary."

Bismarck's eyebrows shot up. "How do you know that, you old devil?"

"Only yesterday, I received an update from our Paris branch. Our contact at the Préfecture de Police has been copying the McKay file. What we know so far is that about two years ago, little Miss McKay was the object of a criminal investigation. The police had secretly perused her diary. It contained only cosmetic recipes and girlish blabber, which cast no new light on the case. The inspector in charge dismissed it. That was then. A lot has happened since. The diary may be a valuable asset but I wanted to make sure of Your Excellency's interest before incurring the expense of hiring a burglar."

"Get it! Besides, do we still maintain a spy in the Paris archive of the Chambre Noire?"

"We most certainly do. Misdeeds of the past can be easily used for blackmail if circumstances require such an approach."

"Very well, Stieber, have your contact rummage for anything that could lead to the McKay woman. Perhaps there's a connection of some sort."

"It shall be done, Your Excellency."

Chapter 54

Mademoiselle Pointsotte looked like one of those old maids whose opinions never mattered and who survived by picking crumbs from their relatives' table. She would have earned Nelly's sympathy had she not come armed with a letter from the now dreaded Quérat.

"I don't understand," Nelly said. "Why doesn't the agency simply pick up the mail bags and find a desk for you in the office? I don't need a secretary."

"Monsieur Quérat said that I must work with you." The woman kept her voice little above a whisper. "It's your personal correspondence and you will have to approve my answers to the letters."

Nelly winced. "As if I cared for the trash I receive! Make up a formula that fits all. Say that I appreciated their kind interest in me and enjoyed their lovely letters." What was it about whispering people that made her speak louder? Or had she simply become a shrill-voiced bitch?

"Monsieur Quérat says that personalized answers will help the sales. Also, I'm to weed out the insulting letters you complained about. You'll hardly see me, I promise."

Nelly took in the shabby dress with a starched white collar, thinned by countless washing and the bony fingers nervously threading the strings of a beaded reticule.

"You can work in the library," she said. "Thirty-six bags of mail, most of it filled with silliness, hatred, or filth. No one here has the stomach for it. Do you?"

"It's a job," said Mademoiselle Pointsotte.

* * *

Octave put the coffee cup on its saucer with a sharp clink.

"Shh . . ." Nelly hissed, cuddling Florence in her arms. "I think she is about to fall asleep."

"Did you bake those?"

She glanced at the plate of madeleine cookies and nodded. He popped one into his mouth and chewed with a frown of concentration. "Practically the same as my mother's. Your baking has improved tremendously."

"Glad to hear that. Although baking is not what you are here for, I guess."

He settled in his armchair. "In a bad mood, are we?"

"You promised to get me out of the contract. Instead, the agency plants their employees in my own home. By the looks of her, the woman is permanently short of money. She may turn into cash everything she sees and hears here. I cannot muffle Florence when she's crying."

"And I suppose it's my fault that you sign contracts without reading twice every single word. According to the lawyer, it is watertight. One wrong move and they can sue you for every centime you have. You'd better humor them in small things. You are bound to promote your image by frequent personal appearances. No one has seen you for months. Someone at the studio has talked. The rumor is out that you are pregnant. Too late, thank God. The agency wants you to make at least one public appearance looking as slim as you possibly can."

When her eyes flashed with anger, he showed his palms in a self-protective gesture. "Don't blame me! Since you don't want to deal with them face to face I agreed to act as a go-between, but I don't make the rules."

She stood up and carried the sleeping child into her crib in the bedroom. "What's that?" she asked when she returned to the salon.

"Those," Octave pointed at the table, "are tickets to *Le Roi Carotte*, a burlesque musical extravaganza with nine hundred costumes. You may as well enjoy yourself while you're on duty. It's an entire loge. Take your friends, as many as you want, so that you will not have to face the public alone. Do you want me to come as well?"

"Was this your idea?"

Octave frowned. "Why are you looking at me like that? Do you think that I'm in collusion with the agency?"

"I don't know. Are you?"

"No, I'm not!" He rose from his seat and crossed to where she stood. "Listen to me," he said earnestly, clutching her hands in his. "It's only one public appearance. There will be no more, I can promise you that. No, no, don't look away! Listen," he tugged at her hands, "just listen! They are caving in, I know that. Tassin has confided in me that he's been unhappy with the way things are turning out. They got angry letters from Bonapartist sympathizers and the government had sent an official who asked uncomfortable questions. He has to face it alone and he's thinking of resigning. Quérat's a very sick man. He's practically never there, and most of the time he sends in written orders. This cannot last. And when it's over" he squeezed her shoulders and let his hands slip along her arms, "I've a quiet place for you, a charming little house with a garden and a view of the Seine valley. Very private, and only two hours by train. I'll visit you and Florence every Sunday. You can count on me. This time you can."

She sighed and rested her forehead on his chest. "Why does it have to be like this, when the first time around it could have been so much better?"

* * *

She now had the means to have a fire lit in every room if she wished, but they still ate their meals in the kitchen. It reinforced their togetherness and Nelly could not get enough of it. Very soon, she would be alone in a remote country house with only Julie and the child for company. She cherished the morning rituals, with Claude bringing in fresh air from his early walk with Schnitzel, the lingering over coffee, and Julie coming and going as she attended to her duties.

This morning, she and Géraldine were sipping the last of their coffee, while Julie was upstairs tending to the fires. Zidore had already gone to the studio. For a change, Claude was late for his breakfast.

Géraldine swept breadcrumbs into her palm and dropped them into her empty coffee cup. "When is the performance?" she asked.

"Tuesday. And then, if everything goes as Octave says, I'll pack up and go. I'll miss you."

"You don't have to," Géraldine said sharply. "I don't see why you should exchange one prison for another. At least here you're at home."

"I feel on pins and needles in Paris."

"Once you are there, Octave will not keep his hands off you any longer. Have you thought of that?"

Nelly shrugged. "Florence needs a father. Besides, he isn't the man he used to be. He's changed."

"Has he?" Géraldine picked up a leftover piece of bread from her plate and began to pull it apart. "Listen, I should not tell you this, because Claude has forbidden me to meddle. The fact is that last week, as I was sitting in the omnibus on my way home, I saw Octave and that little milkmaid we met in Bougival coming out of a house. I got out at the next stop, went back, and bribed the concierge. He keeps the minx there in a small *garni*. A changed man? Hah!"

"So what?" Nelly said. "I'm not jealous of him. I didn't ask him to live like a monk."

356

"Dear God, what's wrong with you? Is that what you are settling for? One mistress for the weekdays, another one for Sundays, and he a married man? Has motherhood made you witless?"

"Mind your own business! You should've done as Claude said."

"No man will tell me what to do ever again. Not even Claude."

"Then why are you telling me this when he's not here?"

Géraldine smiled slyly. "There is no need for a brass band when a violin can do the job."

* * *

Nelly dropped the peeled potato into a pot filled with water, dried her hands on her apron, and inspected the cards Julie was handing her on a small tray: Rev. W. R. Bowlby, Mr. Abraham J. Lawrence, Attaché to the American Legation, and Dr. T. Evans, President of the American Association in Paris.

"I told them you were unwell and seeing no one," Julie said "But they looked so serious, that I said I'd ask."

Nelly's hand plunged into her hair. "What on earth do they want?"

When Julie stared at her blankly, she pushed a few hairpins in place and untied her apron. She glanced into a basket standing on a chair beside her. The baby was sleeping soundly.

"Finish the potatoes," she said to the maid.

None of the visitors smiled as they introduced themselves.

"What can I do for you, gentlemen?" Nelly asked when they were seated.

Reverend Bowlby cleared his throat and his gaze strayed toward Mr. Lawrence who reached into his briefcase.

"Are you a good American, madam?" Dr. Evans asked.

"Why, yes of course!" she said, watching out of the corner of her eye as the attaché removed a thick brown envelope.

"Perhaps you would care to hear in some detail what being a good American means," Reverend Bowlby said. "The duty of every American in foreign parts is to make a good impression on the local population and maintain a friendly relationship with the host country. So far, our community has done nothing but good in France. During the war, our esteemed president," he inclined his head toward Dr. Evans, "founded the American Ambulance which saved lives of countless wounded and became an example of efficiency and modern hygiene. I will not burden you with the number of charities and social events in which we participate. Suffice it to say that every member of the American Association, both men and women, has contributed his time, effort, and money to the common cause. Each of us has been a worthy ambassador of the United States of America—"

Her hands relaxed. They were raising funds for some kind of charity. She settled in her chair and politely waited for him to finish.

"—and we can no longer tolerate having the faultless reputation of our great country smeared by scandal."

"I think that you are familiar with this," said Mr. Lawrence. The brown envelope went from hand to hand, touched by reluctant fingers, until it reached her.

She stared at it with apprehension. "What is it?"

"Your contribution to the American interests in France," said Dr. Evans.

Chilled by the contempt in his voice, she lifted the paper flap. Inside the envelope she found a wad of newspaper clippings. The first one was from the *L'Intransigeant*, an Ultra-republican sheet, known to be owned by Victor Hugo. THE SCENT OF BONAPARTIST VIOLETS POISONS FRENCH HOMES, the headline said. The word Ceres repeatedly popped out of the small print.

"Go on, there is more," Dr. Evans prompted her.

She selected the next clipping. It was folded in two, and when she flattened it, she stared at a vicious caricature of herself. Dressed as Empress Josephine, she sat on a throne, her hands supporting a huge pregnant belly. The picture was headed AMERICA PAYS BACK FOR LAFAYETTE and, under the drawing, another line said, *La Ceres Founding a Franco-American Dynasty*.

Her chest contracted, seized by a painful spasm. A full minute went by, before she lifted her head and looked at the men sitting across from her, encountering the cold stare of Dr. Evans and the clear disdain of his companions.

"I was only making a living," she whispered.

Something resembling compassion warmed Reverend Bowlby's eyes. "Miss Woodridge, have you seen these articles before?"

She shut her eyelids and shook her head with effort, the muscles in her neck tight with tension.

"How is it possible?" inquired Mr. Lawrence.

"Newspapers are forbidden here. There have been articles . . . in the past . . . that upset me. I don't go out. I didn't know it had come to this."

"You must leave France immediately," said Dr. Evans.

* * *

Prostrate on top of the bed, Nelly rolled on her back when she heard knocking. Crushed by the weight of her body, the newspaper clippings rustled, reminding her of the flood of hurtful lies, mockeries, malicious gossip, and insulting speculations.

The door opened, letting in Julie. "The baby's crying, Miss. I think she's hungry."

While nursing her child by the kitchen fire, Nelly progressively calmed down. The more she thought of Ceres the more she felt detached. She had nothing in common with that person. 'La Ceres', they called her, the 'La' in front of a name signifying the highest degree of notoriety. What a vicious enemy was fame! There was a brief time when she had enjoyed the unearned attention, the admiring smiles and the autograph-signing. Ultimately, the cost was too great. What had happened to the once free Nelly McKay?

She removed Florence from her breast and reached for a towel. It was at that very moment that Mademoiselle Pointsotte chose to enter the kitchen.

"What are you doing here?" Nelly asked, her anger returning. "I told you to stay in the library at all times!"

The secretary apologized profusely and handed over four sheets of paper. "I thought that you should see this immediately, Miss Woodridge. These have come each a week apart. It could be a serious menace. A month ago, the newspapers reported a burglary at the laboratory of the Institute of Biological Studies. A case containing living vipers had disappeared."

Each sheet bore a drawing of three undulating vipers. *They are coming to bite you!* an anonymous hand wrote under the pictures.

"You were hired to destroy this type of correspondence," Nelly said, "not to show it to me. Take it away!"

"But this is different. It could be a serious threat."

Nelly shrugged it off. "Another lunatic out there, working off his frustrations on me. If I had to take them seriously, I'd become deranged myself. Here, Julie, throw these in the fire!"

When night came, the episode replayed in her mind, adding weight to the load pressing on her chest. She tossed in her bed. Public shame, poisonous correspondence, Octave's mistress. She sat up and brought her knees to her chest, hugging them, weighing her situation. Run and dodge was what she had been doing so far and it was wrong. Now she must go and face the music.

Chapter 55

The blackened ruin of the imperial palace just across the river was the reason why Mrs. Davenport always booked the same suite at the Hotel d'Orsay when she stayed in Paris. The sight of a power gone usually filled her with personal satisfaction. This time, the symbol had a crushing effect on her. This time she was frightened.

"What should I unpack?" her maid asked.

"Only overnight necessities," she answered, unbuttoning her gloves. "Have your dinner and go to bed early. We're taking the morning express to Berlin."

The maid gone, she lit a cigarette and nervously paced the room. The envelope that should have been waiting for her at the reception desk was not there. Did George Margolis get her letter at all? Did Alessandro deliver it? He was eager to be of help, but she shouldn't have had to put her trust in that enamored boy. At the time it seemed to be the best solution, as she was reluctant to drop a seventy-thousand francs deal with his father and rush to Paris at once. Yet there was so much more to lose if she failed in the present mission. Everything.

At least her seventy thousand were safely locked in a bank in Nice. As soon as this was over, she would transfer most of her liquid assets out of Britain. No one would catch her unprepared ever again.

When she heard the knock on the door, she composed herself.

"Enter!"

"Mrs. Davenport?"

"Yes."

"With Monsieur Margolis' compliments."

"Thank you."

Relieved, she seized the envelope and the man was gone, quietly, like a shadow. Seated at the table, she broke the seals and removed the contents.

Dear Amazon, she read, under the heading of Margolis Agency, International Business Investigations. *Where did you pick up the Italian puppy you sent me? I thought we had a tacit agreement not to mention — let alone display! — our side interests. Entrusting such sensitive material into the hands of a stranger is a sign of panic. Sending me your juvenile playmate is stretching the limits of good taste. You seem to be falling apart at the seams, my dear.*

As always, you demand the impossible, but this time you were lucky. The government has been investigating one Miss McKay/Woodridge/Ceres for their own purpose and since we are able to tap into their records, I had the personal report compiled in no time (see document 1).

Basically, the American community is up in arms. They want the woman gone, but the French say that she has done nothing unlawful and since she owns property in France, she cannot be officially banished. Needless to say, the Republicans in the government are enjoying the story hugely while displaying pro forma frowns. They could not ask for better timing, now that the average fickle citizen mourns the loss of Louis Napoleon and a wave of nostalgia sweeps the country.

The government investigation having been half-hearted and aimed only at satisfying the Yankees, I put two of my men on 24-hour watch and got interesting leads (see document 2).

And yes, I checked it out, and your maiden name does figure in the private accounts seized in the Tuileries after the Empire collapse. There was also a detailed report on you in the files of the Cabinet Noir. It seems that the late Duke de Morny had taken a great interest in you over the years, more than enough for Bismarck's hounds to sniff your trail and pounce on you. That de Morny had spent so much time gathering material against you can be explained only by a deep personal grudge. Lucky for you, he did not live long enough to complete his revenge. What had you done to him, you naughty girl? It will be my pleasure to find out.

For whatever it is worth at this point, I took the precaution of removing the damaging information from the archive.

I expect a proper acknowledgment of my efforts, so don't go back to the Riviera (or wherever you want to go when you are done in Berlin) without first stopping in Paris. After that unripe Italian you will need a solid dose of yours truly. Our old rendezvous near St. Cloud has been restored after the shelling damage and is very cozy at this time of the year. They have a new chef, formerly of La Forge (another regrettable war loss) and I defy you to find a better canard à l'orange. Should you feel cold, we shall warm the air by burning old documents in the fireplace.

As always,

G.

Mrs. Davenport smiled. Despite his caustic mood, George had delivered what she needed. The secret of a rewarding relationship with the opposite sex was to make oneself liked rather than loved. It was that simple.

Minutes ticked away on the mantel clock and the silence in the room continued, interrupted only by the rustle of paper as the reader turned the pages of the government report. Once finished, she returned to Document Two, the private surveillance report, and reread it.

Assignment McKay-01-73/V.& H.(report filled by Detective Vaillant,

Jan. 14th, 1873)

Locality and situation:

H. and I have investigated the property La Plaisance, situated next to the Roman Arena. The house is accessed through a passage in the rue Monge. The garden gate is kept permanently locked and is, at times, blocked by reporters and curiosity seekers, who try to catch a glimpse of the notorious Ceres. The garden is supposed to be guarded by a dog. Instead of doing its duty, it is to be noted that the animal fraternizes with anyone willing to part with food.

While the house itself cannot be seen by anyone on the street level, it can be partially observed from third-floor rooms in the neighboring rental property located in the rue Monge and from the attic above, where, with the collaboration of the concierge, we established our observation post.

Except for deliveries of bread and milk and the coming and goings of the regular inhabitants (with the exception of Miss McKay), only one outsider entered the house. My colleague H. identified her as Angélique Pointsotte, whom he had arrested three years ago for theft at the Magazins du Louvre department store. (Subsequent research in police archives revealed repeated offenses. Last released from the La Roquette female prison November 4, 1872.) Upon exiting La Plaisance, this woman secretly signaled to someone directly below our observation post.

Inquiry from the concierge revealed that the floor below our observation post was rented in February 1872 by a certain Casimir Delachaise, no known profession, and has remained unoccupied until April of the same year(*). According to the concierge, C.D. (no record in the police archives) is a model tenant and strictly solitary. She volunteered a remark that he gives her the creeps, and provided a physical description: Age 35-40, height 5'7"-5'8", slim build, black hair and beard, dark eyes, deep gash across the nose. C.D. comes and goes at irregular intervals, rarely stays overnight, and has been absent for weeks on end. However, lately he has been closeted in his rooms for long periods of time.

(*)It is to be noted, that Miss McKay moved into her property in April. The City Register revealed that, last year, the property changed hands twice. Originally owned by M. Henri d'Auzon, Count de Villermaine, it was sold to M. Octave Gaillard, photographer, and the ownership transferred to Miss McKay. As noted in the official report, both gentlemen are well known to her.

Regarding Miss McKay's rumored pregnancy, we checked the entries of the Civil Register for the past two months, both for Woodridge and McKay, and found a female child, born December 6, 1872, registered as McKay, Florence Henriette Octavie, father unknown.

Parallel developments:

At 9:50 P.M., the night of the watch, while returning from a short trip to the tobacconist's, H. noticed a man matching the description of Casimir Delachaise, carrying a cloth-wrapped object and heading for the arena. The gate being locked at the time, the man let himself in with his own key. He reappeared ten minutes later, hands empty. H. followed him at a distance to the Passage Sabotière in the neighborhood of St. Sulpice, where the man unlocked the door of a run-down curio shop. Through a crack in the shutters, H. glimpsed a moving candlelight after which the interior returned to darkness.

I visited the arena this morning at 9:00 AM, when the gate is usually being unlocked, and thoroughly searched the place. I discovered an oilcan with a long spout discarded in a bush along with a greasy rag. Oil drips in the sand led me to a small sunken gate. Upon inspection of the lock, I noticed that it had been recently oiled. I believe that the gate leads into La Plaisance grounds.

As I exited the arena, I found the entrance of the passage to La Plaisance blocked by several vehicles. One of the drivers informed me that La Ceres was giving a press conference.

I hope that the above extra effort will be favorably noted.

V.

Mrs. Davenport hunched her back, and rested her forehead on her clasped hands. Fighting conflicting thoughts, she remained in that position for several minutes. Then she glanced at the clock. The unscheduled visit would not take much of her time, provided the man was at home. She rose and went to the adjoining bedroom, where she paused in front of the mirror and studied her face. It still did not show her true age, but she could not dispel the feeling that she had aged twenty years within the last half hour.

* * *

"Stop biting your nails," Géraldine said. "You did fine. I bet you charmed them all."

Nelly obediently removed her index finger from her mouth. "I wish Claude were here already. This waiting kills me." Do we still have that sweet liquor? I need something to sustain me."

Géraldine rose from the sofa and rummaged in a cabinet. She returned with a bottle and a glass.

"Are you not having any?" Nelly asked.

"Someone has to stay cool and composed. You go ahead."

A wail pierced the air. Glad to have something to do, Nelly rushed to the bedroom and returned with Florence in her arms. The child, reassured by her mother's presence, calmed down.

"I've changed my mind. I should not drink when I'm nursing."

"As always, I've to do everything around here," Géraldine complained and downed the liquor.

Nelly was too anxious to laugh. "Tell me I've not made a mistake."

"I've already told you that."

"My stomach is in knots."

"You can face the truth. It's the lies that have been wearing you down. In fact, they've worn everybody down. I've been having indigestion from the constant worry. I don't know how many times I discussed it with Claude. Should we tell you, or should we wait until you recovered from the birth? What if the shock stopped your milk? I've heard it can happen. In the meantime, the rolling stone kept gathering moss and it became harder and harder to tell you."

They sat in silence, watching the fire in the hearth. After a little squirming, the baby dozed off.

"About the theatre tonight," Géraldine said. "Are you sure you want to do it?"

"Absolutely. I'm finished with hiding."

"Misplaced heroics, perhaps. I'd let it cool down for a week or so. Now that the journalists have seen you, you don't have to go and put yourself on display."

"This is something I have to do for myself."

"Now I can tell you how hard it's been to be cooped up at home, night after night."

"So all that talk about how good it was to spend cozy evenings at home was just hot air?"

Géraldine laughed guiltily. "Well, we've saved an awful lot of money, have we not? That fake Persian carpet in the studio is entirely the result of early nights."

They both rose when they heard the main door bang. Nelly went to the bedroom and deposited the baby in her crib. When she returned to the salon, Claude was already in, flinging his hat and coat over an armchair, while Géraldine pounced on the evening newspapers he had brought.

"Listen to this, Nelly!" she exclaimed. "Ceres Reveals Her True Identity!"

"I read it all on my way home," Claude said, taking the newspaper from her. "Let's skip the beginning and go to the essentials. Here it is . . . Questioned about Miss McKay's allegations and clearly on the defensive, Inspector Savard admitted that by her quick and decisive action, Miss McKay had curtailed the escape of a murderer. We add that she should be asked to join the police force, which has so dismally failed to close the de Chazelle case."

Nelly, who had been wringing her hands, giggled nervously. "I don't think I shall take up the offer!"

Claude turned the page, searching for the second part of the article. "Here is more good stuff . . . 'Ceres is a myth, created to excite the public and rake in money,' Miss McKay said. 'Desperate to support myself, I accepted the job. No indication was given to me that my image would serve to generate political turmoil. The only thing for which I will apologize is my failure to understand French politics. I respect this country and some of my French friends are as dear to me as my own flesh and blood. I did not stay in France to create troubles. I did it because I fell in love.'"

"Aw," Géraldine dabbed at a tear in the corner of her eye.

"In her engaging and very candid way, Miss McKay then circulated her birth certificate among the members of the press to prove that she was indeed born of legally married American parents and had no desire to pretend otherwise. It is time to put this unfortunate affair to rest. That a foreigner does not understand our politics should be of no surprise to us, who have been born in this country and often unable to understand them ourselves. But what Frenchman would not understand love?"

"What newspaper is that?" Nelly asked.

"*The Echo de Paris*."

"And the others?"

"Basically the same reaction," Claude said, grinning.

Nelly and Géraldine looked at each other, squealed with joy, and fell into his outstretched arms.

Her ribs still hurting from bear hugs, Nelly rushed to the library. "There is no need to stay late," she said to Mademoiselle Pointsotte, who was dutifully sorting letters.

"But I was about to finish everything today! Another hour—"

"Let me help you," Nelly gathered the remaining correspondence and threw it into the fire. Her elation grew to new heights as the flames engulfed the letters. "Please do tell Monsieur Quérat that I'm taking advantage of the theater tickets he so graciously bestowed on me. No one must say that I did not do my duty as stated in the contract. Goodbye, mademoiselle! I hope you'll find a better job. The gate is not locked anymore. Kindly let yourself out!"

* * *

They hastily ate a dinner of bread and cold cuts, while Julie was upstairs laying out their dresses—a cinnamon brocade for Géraldine and a slate-grey taffeta for Nelly.

Dressing up for an evening out was exciting after the long seclusion. As they stood in front of a mirror, checking out their appearance, Géraldine put her arm around Nelly's waist. "You look like you are about to cry. What's wrong?"

"It's the first time I'm leaving the baby alone. Flo is too small and helpless to be left with strangers."

"Oh, come! Julie and her aunt are not strangers. Speaking of Julie, here she is!—So, Julie, has your aunt arrived?"

"She's down in the kitchen having a cup of cocoa," Julie said. "And Monsieur Gaillard has just come in. He's waiting in the salon."

Nelly and Géraldine exchanged surprised looks. "Did you invite him?" the latter asked.

"I did not disinvite him, if there is a verb like that. I simply forgot that he had offered his escort."

"It would be a mistake to show up with a married man."

"I know. I'll deal with it."

As always, Octave looked dashing in his evening garb and Nelly told him so.

He ignored her remark. "You didn't tell me you intended to call a press conference," he said heatedly. "A grave mistake. Your criticism of Beaumont-Quérat may earn you a lawsuit."

"And I will counter sue for defamation of character. One of the gentlemen of the press gave me the advice."

Octave shook his head. "Where is your proof against the agency?" he asked. "Why don't you consult me before you make important decisions? You must take careful steps."

"All the more reason for not showing up in public escorted by you. I'm sorry that you've gone to this trouble for nothing."

Octave shrugged. "Have it your way. As for me, have no worry. I'll find other company for tonight."

"Oh, I'm sure you will have no trouble at all," she said too sweetly.

"What's that supposed to mean? I don't like you taking that tone with me."

Time was not ripe for broaching the subject of his mistress. "You're imagining things," she said and pecked his cheek. "Good night, dear."

"My gloves! Have you seen my gloves?" Géraldine asked Julie.

"Julie, promise me that Florence will not be left alone for one minute," Nelly begged. "You promise?"

Claude, his arms weighed with wraps and coats, poked his head into the bedroom. "Are you coming or not? Zidore tells me that the cab's waiting."

"Julie, get my fan!"

"Who's got the tickets?"

"The dog has vomited all over the kitchen," said Félicie, who had just come upstairs.

"What?"

"It's an awful mess down there."

"Schnitzel is sick?"

"Come, we don't have time for that," Claude urged. "God knows what he's eaten this time. He's not a dog, he's a shark."

"Please, look after him, Madame Félicie," Nelly said.

"Well now," Félicie said to her niece when the door closed behind the party. "This is going to be some evening! And to think that I was looking forward to spending it with my feet up like a duchess. Come to think of it, I don't see why I shouldn't. It's your job to scrub the kitchen floor, not mine. Besides, I never liked that dreadful dog. You go down there and I'll look after the baby. And bring me another cup of cocoa!"

Chapter 56

"The Margolis Agency is exactly what it says," Mrs. Davenport said. "Business investigations on an international scale. I make use of their services every time I consider a new prospect. You would not believe how many high-ranking people are insolvent," she added with a discreet smile. "For his established clients, Monsieur Margolis also provides services of a more personal nature. Miss Cornelia McKay is a relative of mine. My family lost contact with her many years ago and she probably doesn't realize we've been looking for her to settle a matter of inheritance. But that's not the object of my visit. It is clear from the report that a burglary is being planned, most likely for tonight. She has to be warned by someone she knows and trusts." She joined her fingertips. "You know her . . . intimately . . . I believe. Get her and the child out of there and I'll take care of the rest."

Henri d'Auzon folded the surveillance report and dropped it on the *pietra dura* table that separated their chairs. The stone inlay top depicted an antique battle scene, the only art the late general had been fond of, a fact corroborated by the paintings that hung on the walls of the main floor salon.

"What's the exact nature of your relationship to Miss McKay?" he asked.

She felt uneasy with this overgrown fellow who was probably much sharper than his father had led her to believe. The harmless bookworm reputation had left her in no doubt that he would be easy to handle but, by now, she was growing wary. There was something behind those glasses that alerted her fine-tuned intuition. She did not expect such intensity.

"Her mother Florence was a cousin of mine," she answered. "The child's name was what convinced me. I did not know Florence all that well. She was older than me and of an unusually impetuous nature. Much as I would like to meet Miss McKay, she seems to be involved in a political scandal and I cannot run the risk of encountering a journalist. The family reputation must be kept free of stains for the sake of my children. I may meet her in the near future, but this is not a convenient time." She picked up the report and stuffed it into her sable muff. "In fact, I would appreciate you not mentioning our meeting at all."

"There is little danger of running into journalists," Henri said and a flicker of amusement animated his steady gaze. "They had a large piece of your relative this morning. I assume that you did not read the evening newspapers."

"Oh, yes, the press conference. Anything important?"

"They printed largely surprising revelations. Miss McKay was very anxious to destroy her parentage myth. She went so far as to exhibit her birth certificate."

She wiped the spasm of shock from her lips. "How very unfortunate. All the more reason for me to stay away until all this fuss blows over."

"In the meantime, I shall keep your secret safe, Florence."

"I beg your pardon?"

"I don't even want to know what made you abandon your daughter. You owe the truth to Nelly exclusively. That you extended your hand when you knew her to be in danger is good enough for me."

Her heartbeat accelerated. "You are indulging in a wild guess, monsieur," she said sternly.

"A wild guess?" He shook his head. "I'd call it an accurate assessment. You see, I hold an unfair advantage over you. Even though you sign business letters as Mrs. William Davenport, I know that your name is Florence to friends. Old correspondence tends to stick around. It may be a coincidence, although I think not, that your hair is the exact same shade as that of Nelly's child. More than that, your movements, the way you carry your head when you walk, the manner in which you fold your body into a chair, and the smooth pitch of your voice are familiar to me. I even recognize the shape of your hands."

Blood rushed into her cheeks. She had never felt so effectively stripped naked and that by a fellow who sat with his arms crossed. What a stupid, stupid idea she'd had there! A written warning would have been sufficient. Was she really losing her touch? Three days ago, her life began to fall apart and the trend was accelerating. At this rate, Berlin would be the final failure.

She gave up. "Let's be brutally honest then," she said. "Is the child yours?"

"The decision is still pending."

"Who is the other man?"

"A former friend of mine." Henri rose. "Quite frankly, I'm not willing to pursue this topic of conversation. Besides, we're running out of time. I've to alert the police before going to La Plaisance."

"No," she said, getting up as well. "No official channels must be involved. Make sure they are safe tonight, and I'll get Monsieur Margolis' men to look into the matter. I've already sent him word."

"What can he possibly do that the police—"

"He owns the police. He employs the smartest of them. Problems are solved with alacrity and with no leaks to the press. Here," she removed a gold calling card case from her muff and opened it, "take this, just in case you need help in the future. If you mention my name, you'll get his full attention."

He took the card and turned it between his fingers. "You seem acquainted with the higher levels of corruption."

"Oh, please!" What her daughter saw in this irritating Goliath, she could not fathom. "I simply take advantage of what is available and I shall have no sermons from someone who does not know the value of money. A bankrupt state cannot afford loyal employees. When it comes to duty, the stomach speaks first."

He smiled and, for the first time, she glimpsed his attractive side. "You hold a very pragmatic view of life, madam. Let us make a deal then. I will not alert the police, provided you stay here and talk to Nelly. I think that she deserves to know the truth, however unsavory it may be."

She was worn-out, ill-tempered. "Don't play games with me unless you hold the right cards."

"Meaning?"

"Meaning that you'll do what I say because it's in her best interest. A man who has memorized the shape of hands is a man in love. What you really want is to bring her mother to her between your teeth like a trophy. 'See what your Henri has caught? Are you impressed, dear?' No, I'm staying of my own accord. You may ask me why."

"Why then?"

"Because if things go wrong in the next couple of days, a scandal will rock British Society and ripple across the Channel. Nelly might as well be prepared before it hits her or, better yet, get out of the way altogether. How far from civilization is your estate in the Poitou?"

"Far enough," Henri said. "Make yourself comfortable. The staff will see to your needs." He cleared his throat. "On the other hand, if you choose to leave, I'll not detain you. You are too much to swallow at one go, Mrs. Davenport."

Florence Davenport looked at him with narrowed eyes. "She'll find me here," she said.

Henri asked himself if there was such a thing as the hand of destiny. If so, Mrs. Davenport was firmly attached to it. He had been sitting at home, mulling over the newspaper articles, and gnawing at his knuckles. All these months, while he was healing his wounded pride, Nelly had had to submit to the ordeal of unwanted fame and carry a child as well. And he had thought that she was willingly participating in this tasteless business! If he was wrong in that, how much more wrong had he been in general? He was only toying with the idea, shaping it this way and that, when Florence Davenport had barged in on him and decided what to do. It was what he should have done a long time ago, had he been a real man—namely to scratch off his stiff civilized veneer, acknowledge his caveman core, break Octave's nose, and throw the woman over his shoulder. For a moment, he reveled in the primitiveness of the image before rejecting it. It had no lasting appeal. What he wanted most was warmth and complicity, the mutual surrender that fused two souls into one and made them wish they would never come apart. The trouble with that was that when not reciprocated with the same intensity, burning wishes turned into a heap of smoldering resentment. And yet was love for barter? Could feelings be weighed? One pound of my love for one pound of yours?

Although the carriage went at a brisk pace, he felt he should be up there on the driver's box to whip the horses himself. It was now about quarter past nine. Another ten minutes before he reached La Plaisance. Ten more minutes wasted on explanations. Packing baby's nappies and whatnots would take another quarter of an hour. He would not allow more. By ten o'clock, the carriage would be rolling back to his house and he would be free to organize a trap for the criminals. If there was to be a burglary, it was certainly scheduled later in the night when everybody was supposed to be asleep. He patted the revolver in his pocket. A good, simple plan.

His mind went back to Mrs. Davenport, and he winced. He doubted she had shown the general her full potential, but even at that, the man was a hero for considering her for a wife. Or a damned fool, who harbored an unconscious desire for his head to be bitten off. He doubted Nelly would be happy with the house-warming gift that awaited her. The last thing she needed was yet another scandal. But how was he to know? However, one problem at a time.

The carriage slowed down as it was laboring up the slope of the rue Monge. He reviewed the report in his mind. Unless he was mistaken, there was little of value to steal, except for a handful of jewelry. What then had justified such a long preparation? The man had rented the lodging months ago and let it sit empty until Nelly moved into her house. Why?

He looked out of the window. The street was quiet at this hour, the inhabitants staying out of the cold. Two early drunks crossed from one sidewalk to another, punching each other and laughing, to disappear into the cozy interior of a café. The sound of an accordion briefly escaped out of the door before it closed.

Then he saw him, directly under a street lamp, walking from the opposite direction. A man of average height, with a dark beard, and a deep gash across his nose. There could be no mistake whatsoever. He walked hunched over, bundled in an old-fashioned pelerine that bulged at the chest. As their paths crossed, he cast a furtive look at Henri, who lost a precious second debating whether he should have the carriage stopped. No, that would alert the man. Instead, he simply opened the door and jumped out.

As the carriage lumbered off, he catapulted himself forward. His steps resonated heavily on the pavement. The man turned his head, acknowledged the shortening distance between himself and his robust pursuer, and made a swift decision. He swiveled to face him and braced himself.

"Catch!" he shouted.

A bundle shot upwards and rotated in the air.

Later, Henri remembered the horrifying event in slow motion. He saw the object flying toward him, shedding the blanket it was wrapped in, and passing over his head. He swung around, and dived forward, stretching his arms. His fingers hooked the little body, which rolled into the crook of his elbows, and then he landed flat on his stomach, his cheekbone grazing the curb of the sidewalk.

He brought his knees under him and gathered the child to his chest. Not a sound came out of her mouth. Frantically, he checked the heaving ribcage, then ran his fingers over the plump face and encountered a cloth stuck in the tiny mouth. As soon as he pulled it out, he heard a reassuring scream of discontent. It was only then that his muscles slackened. He rose, picked up the blanket, and wrapped it around the baby.

The man was gone.

Carrying the child, Henri hastened into the passage. The lanterns at the gate were lit; he could see the light projected on the wall where the passage curved toward La Plaisance. He passed through the open gate and saw his carriage stationed in front of the house. A woman was racing toward him, followed by Mathieu, his driver.

"Murder!" she screamed. "Get the police! Get help!"

His heart missed a beat. Nelly!

Julie recognized him, tore at him, and fell on his chest. "The baby! You have the baby! Oh, thank you! Thank you!"

"Who is dead, Julie? Who is dead?"

The girl was choking with fright and he had to shake the words out of her. "My aunt! . . . The dog!"

The baby wailed ceaselessly.

"Julie, where is your mistress?" Henri shouted, and shook the maid again with his free hand. "Where . . . is . . . your . . . mistress?"

Chapter 57

Of the two other crime victims, only the dog was truly dead. The padded bonnet she wore had saved Félicie's life by a hair. When she regained consciousness, she remembered nothing of the kidnapping. The last thing she knew, she had been sitting in the bedroom armchair, baking her feet by the fire, and looking forward to a third cup of cocoa. The cup was now broken and the contents spilled on the carpet where Julie had dropped the tray in her panic. A heavy candlestick on the floor told the rest of the story.

"I swear I was not sleeping," the woman mumbled, while Julie was holding a cold compress to a swelling at the back of her head. "Nodding off, perhaps, but not sleeping, oh no! I would have heard the baby crying if need be. She was sleeping like an angel, she was, and everything so quiet . . ." She paused and her eyes rounded with sheer fright. "Holy Mother of God, I could have been murdered and met my maker without the last rites!"

As the idea took root in her mind, she began to shake uncontrollably.

"Aunt, you must go and lie down."

While Félicie embarked on a fit of hysteria, her breath coming out in rasps, the baby in Henri's arms went on crying.

"What's wrong with the child?" he asked. "What should I do?"

Julie led her aunt toward the bed and helped her to lie down. "She might be hungry," she called over her shoulder. "Put a finger into her mouth. That will quiet her."

He obeyed and the baby's lips sucked greedily at his little finger. "For God's sake, you are right!" he said angrily, too loudly in the sudden silence. "She is starving while her mother is sitting in a theater. Neglect runs in the family!"

It was too much for the harried maid. Her face contorted with anguish. "No!" she yelled, choking with tears again, "We took good care of the baby, we did! I was only gone for five minutes, I swear! I kept the cocoa warm on the stove and with the dog dead down there I didn't linger. Five minutes, that's all! Aww . . ." she squealed, "Miss is going to kill me!"

"Julie, calm down at once! You misunderstood me completely."

While Julie was mopping her wet eyes with her apron, he approached the crib and folded down the quilted coverlet. Deprived of the soothing finger, the child embarked on another fit of crying. Henri did not hear her. Transfixed, he stared at the sheet of paper inserted under the quilt. It bore a drawing of a baby tightly swaddled with snakes, their teeth sinking into the flesh.

He felt the hand of Evil rip open his ribcage, the fingers clawing his guts and twisting. Instinctively, he brought the child closer to his chest, grabbed the drawing, and stuffed it into his pocket. Nelly must not see it, ever.

As he did so, the vestibule suddenly filled with voices and the door of the adjacent salon opened. Quick steps approached the bedroom.

"Julie, where are you? Whose carriage is in front of the house?"

Nelly appeared in the door opening, her eyes taking in the sobbing maid, the shaking form on the bed, the child crying in Henri's arms, and his bruised cheek. Her eyes filled with dread.

"Pack my daughter's things," Henri said. "You are not staying here one minute longer."

* * *

It was Géraldine who took charge of gathering nappies and baby garments, while Julie tended to her aunt. Nelly nursed Florence, her free hand ceaselessly running over the baby's body, probing every inch of the tender flesh. Henri did not mention what really happened in the street. The mental picture of a baby flying through the air like a rag doll was a detail he would not offer to a distraught mother. He simply said he had cornered the criminal and took the child away from him. His grazed cheek? A slight mishap. Was he not the one who should ask questions? Did Nelly have any suspicion as to who would want to kidnap the child? Had she received any threats recently?

"The snakes!" Julie said. "Miss, do you remember the snakes?"

Henri stopped his pacing. Hands behind his back, feet apart, he faced the maid. "Snakes? Tell me about them!"

"It could be anything," Nelly said. "I've received all sorts of demented mail."

"I want to hear about the snakes."

"Mademoiselle Pointsotte brought the pictures down to the kitchen," Julie said. "Miss told me to throw them into the fire."

Claude entered the room. "I've found out how he got in," he said. "One of the windows in the library was left unlatched."

Henri acknowledged the information with a nod. "What was this Mademoiselle Pointsotte doing here?" he asked Nelly.

"She was my secretary. She was actually Quérat's employee. I merely suffered her here. Was she not the last one in the library, Julie? Could it be that—"

"The snakes," Henri reminded her. "Tell me exactly what happened."

"Drawings of snakes came in the mail. Four of them, each a week apart."

"And you did not alert the police?"

Géraldine looked up from the carpetbag she was filling. "We're used to all sorts of lunacy," she said.

"The gypsy woman!" Félicie exclaimed. "Tell him about the gypsy woman and the diary! Tell him how the cook died! Vomiting and convulsing exactly like the dog down in the kitchen. Gypsies, snakes, black magic! Blessed Virgin, Mother of God . . ." she scrambled down from the bed, ". . .this house is cursed. I must get out of here. Let me out!" She took a couple of steps and succumbed to dizziness. Claude caught her before she fell.

"Auntie, get back to bed, I beg you!" Julie said.

"I let these men in. They say they are from the police."

Heads turned toward the door, where Zidore stood with two men at his side.

"I beg your pardon," one of them said. "Detectives Vaillant and Hérisson. I'm Vaillant."

"You are late," Henri said.

"So I gather. Do you wish to make a list of the stolen objects? Lodge an official complaint?"

"Why are they here?" Nelly asked, hurriedly covering her breast. "What does it mean? Henri, you seem to know a lot more than you've told me."

"We'll discuss it when we're on our way," he said and steered the detectives into the salon.

"Are you the man who filed a report for the Margolis Agency?" he asked Vaillant.

"That's so, yes. You must be Monsieur d'Auzon."

"That's correct. I need your help. This was not a simple burglary. There's been an attempt at child kidnapping, in which both the man known as Casimir Delachaise and the woman Pointsotte were involved. He as the perpetrator, she as his accomplice." He removed the drawing from his pocket. "It was not a matter of ransom," he said. "It was an act planned by a demented brain."

376

Both men examined the drawing. "A Satanic cult?" Hérisson suggested.

Henri shrugged irritably. "Do we have time to ask questions? No, this kind of evil must be eradicated as swiftly as possible. And I want to be, must be, part of it. I understand that your services are for hire. Name your price for organizing a raid on the curio shop you mentioned in the report. It must be done tonight."

* * *

Despite the mournful mood that had seized the city after the exiled ruler's passing, the shock was wearing off and the lust for entertainment had reasserted itself. There had been enough grief during the war and Parisians were intent on enjoying this ball season before Lent.

The child sleeping in her arms, Nelly looked out of the carriage, her gaze passing over a boisterous party exiting from a restaurant. It seemed inconceivable to her that there were still carefree people in this evil world.

She turned her head to look at Henri. "This Madame Davenport, who is she? How did she know this was going to happen?"

"I'm not altogether sure," Henri answered evasively. "I prefer her to do her own explaining."

She sighed and covered her eyes. "Why? Why is all this happening to me?"

Henri shook his head. "I don't know but I'll not rest until I find the man."

"What did he look like?"

"Dark beard, dark eyes, a deep gash across his nose. I'll find him, I promise. I'll find him," he said savagely, "and when I do . . . Until then, you must not set foot out of my house and no one will be allowed in unless I give my permission."

Nelly nodded distractedly, busy with her own thoughts. *A deep gash across his nose* . . . The detail ran through her mind until it snapped into place. "Nathaira," she exclaimed. "He's Nathaira, the bearded gypsy woman! Now I know what was wrong with her face." She reached for his hand and squeezed it. "Henri, be careful! Do be careful, I beg you!"

The carriage stopped in front of a gate.

"Here is where we part," Henri said as they waited for the porter to open it.

"Are you not coming in with us?"

"The staff will take care of you. You are expected."

The carriage moved again, the sound reverberating under the vault of the *porte-cochère*, until it reached an enclosed court and stopped in front of the steps leading to the entrance. The door opened and the light streaming from it turned the servant that awaited them into a dark silhouette.

Henri got out. "You know Joseph," he said, taking Florence from Nelly's arms and helping her to step down. "And, unless she has changed her mind, Mrs. Davenport is still gracing us with her company."

"I cannot wait to meet her. I owe her everything. How good of her to come here to warn you."

"You owe her a great deal more than you think and not all of it will please you, I should imagine."

"What do you mean?"

"That is something you must sort out between the two of you. Although what she has done today has made up for the rest, as far as I'm concerned." He handed the baby over. "Take care of the child and of yourself."

"Henri," Nelly said, "for what it is worth, I want you to know that I love you."

He paused with one foot on the carriage step, his face unreadable in the shade projected by the door. A couple of seconds went by. "While I'm gone," he said at last, "think about what you just said and make sure you're not confusing love with mere gratitude. To Saint-Sulpice, Mathieu!" he called to the driver.

"I don't have to think about it!" she shouted after the carriage. "Please, be careful," she added in a whisper.

No one noticed a black form that had peeled from the carriage when it first passed through the gate and was now crouching in the darkest corner of the court.

Chapter 58

A single lantern illuminated the entrance to the Passage Sabotière. The alley way was only four yards in width and the right side was entirely taken up by the blind wall of a public laundry. On the left stood a shell-damaged building with a flaking façade and boarded windows. Halfway down the entry that foundered into darkness, the hanging sign of the curio shop creaked in the wind. The small shop was sandwiched between the condemned building and a brick wall topped with iron spikes. A man had been posted near each end of the passage, turning it into a trap. Unless there was an exit at the back, whoever was inside the shop had no chance of escape.

Henri waited as Vaillant and Hérisson forced the lock and pulled the shutters apart. Behind the shutters, a door with a glass panel opaque with accumulated dirt appeared in the light of their lantern. The lock yielded to experienced handling, and within seconds they were inside.

The lantern light traveled over an accumulation of pitiful bric-a-brac, rust, dust, and the decay of objects well past their usefulness. A cracked floor-length mirror, a cabinet with a missing door, an embroidery frame with only one support leg, moth-eaten carpets, stacks of moldy books and old newspapers. The air stank of staleness. Something moved between their feet, quickly, furtively. The lantern caught matched pairs of tiny reflections among the heaps of objects. Rats.

They found no one in the shop or in the cubicle behind. The latter contained an antiquated desk covered with an undisturbed layer of dust, the bottom of the drawers filled with mouse droppings. A steep flight of steps led to an attic under the mansard roof. They saw a rusting iron bed frame, a table, a couple of chairs, and an abundance of cobwebs.

"From the look of it, no one has been up here for ages," Henri said, choking with frustration.

Vaillant nodded gravely. "No luck so far."

"Hey, up there!"

Vaillant bent over the handrail. "What is it, Hérisson?"

"I think I've found something."

"In the dark?"

"Precisely," Hérisson said when they joined him downstairs. "As I was standing here in the dark, I noticed a draft on my face. Can you feel it as well? It comes from that direction," he pointed to a wall.

They approached the wall and Vaillant removed the candle from the lantern. Holding it in his hand, he moved along the wall and stopped in front of a plain wooden wardrobe, possibly the only piece of some worth among the junk that littered the shop. They had looked inside during their search and found it filled with more trash.

"There!" he said, when the flame flickered violently. "The draft comes from both sides. There's an opening behind."

Henri pushed him aside and seized the piece with both arms. Expecting a considerable effort, he staggered when the wardrobe gave way with ease. It was mounted on wheels. Behind it, bricks had been removed from the wall. Cold air rushed in through the opening.

The candle safely back behind the glass of the lantern, Vaillant extended his arm into the darkness. "It looks like a garden shed," he said.

One by one, they climbed through the opening into a wooden enclosure.

Henri pulled at the handle fastened to the back of the wardrobe. It moved with little effort. "This is a clever getaway. And the door over there must lead into the neighboring lot."

"Look at this," Vaillant had opened a trunk that stood in a corner and was now rummaging through the contents. He came up with something black and woolly, which proved to be a wig. The trunk contained a quantity of female clothing in gaudy colors and patterns. They were momentarily puzzled by two socks strung together and filled with a substance that felt like rice until Hérisson cleverly threw the contraption over his neck, instantly acquiring a pair of pendulous breasts.

"We've found the gypsy woman's dressing room," Henri said. The fact filled him with eager anticipation. His prey was close.

"Actually, I remember meeting the scarecrow on more than one occasion. Once seen, never forgotten," Hérisson commented. "Boldness can be an effective disguise."

Again, Vaillant's hands plunged into the trunk and this time his fingers encountered something solid hidden under the clothes. He discarded an armful of garments and lifted the lantern to cast direct light on his discovery.

"Hérisson, come and meet your old acquaintance," he said.

Both his companions bent over the trunk. Tucked in the bottom, limbs twisted to fit the confined space, was the body of a woman, clad in a thin gray dress and a stained kitchen apron.

"She must've been living close by," Vaillant said, fingering the fabric of the skirt. "No one would go out in the cold dressed like this."

"Who is she?" Henri asked.

"The Pointsotte woman, no doubt about it," Hérisson said, turning the cadaver's face toward the light. "It seems that she was no longer needed."

Henri swallowed to keep his stomach down. Close to the right temple the skull had caved in under a blow from a blunt object. The eyeball with its brown iris had popped out from the broken socket.

"Supposing he's right-handed, he whacked her from the back," Vaillant said. "I don't think he intended the corpse to rot here. He'll be back to bury it, probably in the neighboring lot. With a little patience, he'll fall straight into our—"

"I haven't the patience to wait," Henri protested. "There's a madman on the loose and I want him now, tonight. Let's see what lies behind the shed."

He seized the lantern and approached the door. It was locked but a heave of his shoulder loosened the screws of the hinges. On the second attempt, the wood around them splintered, the door falling out of the frame. This needless act of vandalism—after all, Hérisson had a professional kit of skeleton keys—temporarily soothed the rage that had consumed him since the kidnapping attempt.

They entered a narrow court enclosed by the wall of the passage and a low-squatting, windowless building with vents below the roof. A horse whinnied close by, followed by another.

"We are at the back of the Garnier public stables, I'd guess," said Hérisson. "I know the neighborhood tolerably well."

A path led them to a private house, its walls bathed in darkness, the shutters closed. Henri mounted the two steps leading to the back door and turned to his companions. After a wordless dialogue, during which Hérisson and Vaillant looked at each other and the latter nodded toward the door, Hérisson took out his passkeys. Soon after, the lock yielded to his ministrations.

They stood motionless, listening for a presence, but heard nothing but the wind rattling the shutters. There was no gas lighting but they found a couple of portable lamps nesting in the corridor niche. The house was an old middle-class residence with a kitchen and pantry just off the back entrance, a corridor leading to the two main-floor rooms fronting onto the street, and a staircase to the upper floor.

Once properly illuminated, the kitchen revealed signs of an indifferent housekeeper. A washbasin with cold greasy water contained a half-submerged iron pan with the remains of fried food still clinging to its surface. Dirty plates and cups with rings in them littered the table. A wedge of drying cheese rested on a newspaper along with a half-loaf of petrified bread. Rotting fish bones in the waste bucket poisoned the air.

Hérisson became interested in something on the floor.

"What do you see there?" Henri asked.

"A patch has been wiped clean right here. See?" he pointed at a lighter spot. "Pass me a knife!"

He squatted, ran the blade along the groove between the planks, and rubbed the gathered residue between his fingers.

"Dried blood. She was washing dishes when the blow came."

A curtain hid a cot and a rack with female garments hanging on the hooks. They found nothing else of interest on the main floor. Of the four rooms on the second floor, three were unfurnished and lack of heating had turned them into inhospitable iceboxes. The fourth one had been lived in. They found an unmade bed, a nightshirt casually thrown over an easy chair, ashes in the fireplace, a full-length mirror, and a variety of male attire in the wardrobe. A chest of drawers contained fresh linen. The deepest drawer at the bottom disclosed a grey wig on a wooden stand, a professional set of theatrical make-up and, surprisingly, four protective cotton masks to filter foul air. A small portable leather case held a collection of medicine bottles and powders.

Vaillant uncorked one of the bottles and sniffed. "Camphor," he said.

"What is it used for?" asked Hérisson, who was inspecting ashes in the fireplace, which consisted mostly of burned paper.

"It's a stimulant," Henri said distractedly, more interested in Hérisson's findings.

Vaillant shook his head with wonder. "From what I gather so far, our chap is a master of disguise. What was he up to with that wig and the cotton masks?"

"I think I can answer that." Hérisson rose from the fireplace and held out a scrap of paper. The edges had been charred by the fire but most of the writing was still legible.

after many attempts at
not answered my official resignat
address in Switzerland, your housekeeper gav

no such sanitarium existed. I keep hoping that
mistake and the remainder of my salary will b
under attack by journalists and had to close th
ployees suspended without wages until you
Regretfully, I will be forced to turn to justic
give a sign of life within the next two wee
Respectfully, Jacques Tassin

"Tassin . . . Tassin . . ." Vaillant rubbed his forehead, as if to iron out the wrinkles that gathered there. "This rings a bell. Isn't he somehow connected with the Quérat-Beaumont agency that employs Miss McKay? I worked on an assignment there roughly a year ago. This chap, Quérat, had contacted the Margolis agency with an unusual request. He wanted to invest in an existing picture-publishing house. It had to be that and nothing else. I helped to investigate several of them—bank accounts, suppliers, the usual. Beaumont's was the only one in the red and willing to accept the offer. At first, it was a silent partnership, then the original owner died suddenly—now I'm having uncomfortable thoughts about that—and, well, it looks like there's more to it here."

"Shouldn't this room be somewhat larger?" Henri asked. "Compared to others, it seems out of proportion."

Hérisson went to the corridor to check the distance outside. "You're right," he said, when he returned and counted steps between the door and the wall inside the room. "Three and a half steps short on this side."

Three pairs of eyes focused on the wardrobe. Hands clutched firearms at the ready.

"Allow me the pleasure," Henri said.

The wardrobe gave way as easily as that of the curio shop. The wall behind was a simple wooden partition covered with wallpaper, with a door cut into it.

Once the closet was lit, it was not the glass terrarium with the quivering forked tongues of live vipers that made Henri's heart faint with shock. He focused on the child-sized white coffin, padded with satin and lace, that stood on a narrow table, flanked by a pair of tall candlesticks. Behind it, hanging on the wall, Nelly's portrait by Sarah Bernhardt completed the macabre display.

Henri broke into a cold sweat. "This man . . ." he cleared his throat to smooth a way for his strangled voice, "this monster will never give up. There's no use chasing him. He'll come after her wherever she hides. And I must be there, waiting."

* * *

The man with the shattered nose crouched in the dark until the gatekeeper shuffled off into his quarters. He blew on his knuckles and inserted his hands under his armpits. For what he was to do, he needed a strong grip. Except for that, the biting cold air did not bother him. He had a store of inner heat, a feverish energy that made him feel indestructible. The incident in the rue Monge was only a glitch. Nothing could halt the grind of the machinery he had put in motion with so much care.

The main floor windows projected elongated rectangles of pale light on the iced pavement of the court and the porch lantern cast a yellow glow on the stone and brick façade of the house. When the door closed behind his prey and her child, he studied the layout. He decided to take advantage of the drainpipe in a corner, where the angle between the sculpted stones would provide him with a foothold until he reached one of the cornices of the upper floors. Once there, he would find a way in.

A handsome woman pacing in one of the main floor rooms, her arms folded across her waist, stimulated his curiosity. A hat perching on her coppery hair was an indication that she was a visitor to the house. Her manner of moving reminded him of a high-strung colt. She stopped to light a cigarette and resumed her pacing. After a couple of puffs, she threw the cigarette into the fireplace. She stood motionless for a while, as if listening to a noise outside the room, and pressed her palms against her chest, taking in a deep breath. Soon after, she smiled at someone out of his field of vision, and then he saw the McKay woman with the child in her arms. His nostrils dilated with excitement as they always did when he caught a glimpse of her.

The scene that followed puzzled him. Nelly took the proffered hand into hers but instead of shaking it, she brought it to rest on her chest and held it there tenderly. Her lips slowly formed the words 'thank you, thank you'. The other woman smiled again, but hers was an uneasy smile. She took a step back and motioned toward the baby. Nelly nodded and handed the child to her. The redhead took the bundle into her arms and inspected it with interest. Holding it, she lowered herself into an armchair and indicated that Nelly should do the same.

The conversation that followed soon took a dramatic turn. He saw Nelly's jaw drop with shock. Her features hardened. She spoke in short angry sentences, her head shaking each time the woman tried to calm her, her hand warding off whatever had been disclosed. She rose and resolutely seized the child. Turning her back to her interlocutor, she walked away. Just before she disappeared from his view, she paused, turning her head. He read her lips again and what she said was 'never'. Then she was gone.

The red-haired woman fell back in her seat and covered her face.

There was nothing else to see until the lights were lit in a second floor room. A pudgy woman at one of the two windows drew the drapes together. This was what he had been waiting for. Now he knew where to go. He approached the drainpipe.

* * *

The housekeeper finished with the second pair of drapes and turned to Nelly who stood in the middle of the room, still holding her daughter.

"This used to be Madame la Génerale's bedchamber, God rest her soul," the woman said. "That," she pointed above the fireplace, "is her portrait. She was a great lady, and I had the honor of serving her for fifteen years. Monsieur requested that the room should be used again." The tone of her voice betrayed her disapproval as if the presence of overnight guests was a desecration of this sanctuary. "The door over there leads to the boudoir. The other one communicates with a toilette cabinet. There's a brazier in there and a can of hot water. If more is needed, I'll have it brought up by the maid." She approached the bulging carpetbag standing by a chest of drawers decorated with fine marquetry. "Madam will need help with unpacking. I'll send the maid up directly."

"No, thank you," Nelly said. "I wish to be alone." She was choking with pent-up emotions, eager to give way to anger and grief.

The housekeeper shrugged. "As Madame wishes. A baby crib has been brought down from the attic. It's being cleaned up and it will be brought here before long. If there's anything else . . ." Finally picking up Nelly's mood, she let the sentence die on her lips and motioned toward the service bell.

Alone at last, Nelly laid the baby on the bed. For fear of falling to pieces when her daughter needed her the most, she had delayed her reaction to the kidnapping. Now that she could vent her feelings without witnesses, she found that they were stuck deep in her chest. She dismissed Mrs. Davenport from her mind. She simply could not deal with another shock. Sinking onto the bed, she gathered her daughter into her arms, showering tender kisses on her smooth face, her nostrils savoring the sweet smell of the satiny flesh. She loosened the ribbon and unwrapped the blanket. An odor of feces rose from the diaper but that, too, was lovable. The baby writhed and her tiny hand brushed against her face. Nelly brought the minute fingers to her lips and probed them with the tip of her tongue, keenly aware of the difference between the softness of the flesh and the slick surface of the fingernails. *Never. I could never abandon you, have no fear. I would rather sever one of my limbs than part with you. That woman downstairs is no one's mother.*

Soothed by the contact with her daughter, she slid off the bed and folded back her sleeves. The first necessity she took out of the carpetbag was Octave's revolver. It had rested in a drawer for months and she did not have time to oil the mechanism. Unlocking the cylinder, she tipped it to the side and rotated it with the flat of her palm. It turned easily around its axis with a series of slight clicks. All six chambers were loaded. She reassembled the parts, approached the bed, and slid the firearm under the pillows. Returning to the bag, she took out a pile of folded diapers and a powder shaker.

The brazier in the toilette cabinet radiated heat and a folding screen in front of the window protected the room from cold drafts. She stripped the baby, sponged her with soapy water, and rubbed her dry with a towel. She was tying on a clean diaper when she heard a soft knock at the bedroom door. It would be the crib.

"Come in," she called.

When she returned to the bedroom, she found Mrs. Davenport waiting for her. "I had to see you again," the woman said. "We should try to part on better terms."

Nelly put the baby on the bed and busied herself with folding the blanket around her. "What do you expect from me?" she asked without lifting her head. "Instant love? You have my undying gratitude for what you've done today. Apart from that, I feel nothing for you. So why don't you walk out of my life as you did twenty years ago? Since you did not care then, why do you care now?"

"Those were different circumstances. I was young then, younger than you are now."

Nelly looked at her at last. "I don't want to hear maudlin excuses. You abandoned me. Real mothers do not abandon their children, period. And to think that I've named my daughter after you!"

Florence Davenport brought her hands together and squeezed them until her knuckles cracked. "Listen to me, you spiteful prig!" she said. "It was another time and another life. Going back to it, even in memory, is like digging up a rotten corpse. Do you think I had it easy? I left my mother when I was ten and I don't think the gin-sodden hag even noticed. So, pardon me if I did not develop maternal feelings right from the beginning. I had no example to follow. By my standards then, I thought I had done quite well by you. You had a secure roof over your head and my mother-in-law doted on you. The jealous brute I married almost killed me once and I was not willing to stick around for a second try. I was only eighteen and I wanted to live. Is that a maudlin excuse?"

"You left me behind. Why?"

"Because I was leaving with nothing but the clothes on my back. I even dropped my warm shawl on the riverbank to make my death believable. Had I not staged a suicide, McKay would have gone after me and finished me for good. I'm sorry but that's the way it was. And it might have worked had you not come here to stir trouble with your looks and my maiden name. After all the effort I made to give you a respectable one!"

She sank into a chair by a console table. "I had no opportunity to divorce McKay," she said flatly, her anger spent. "After I ran away, I met another man, an Englishman. He proposed to me and I saw my chance to put an ocean between me and my first husband."

She sighed and distractedly fingered a bunch of hothouse grapes on a serving plate. "I'm not much of a believer but maybe there's something like divine vengeance. I was going to say justice, but that does not apply in this case. If anyone is going to suffer for whatever wrong I've done, it will be your siblings Philip and Sophie. You may think I'm an indifferent mother and I don't blame you, but to see my children brought down with me would be more than I could bear. I had such high expectations for them."

"I have a brother and a sister?"

Florence nodded. "Sophie is sixteen. She is in a finishing school in Switzerland. Philip is fourteen and a half and a pupil at Eton. Both have what it takes to succeed except for their shady background. I've striven to overcome it. One day, I thought, they would be so brilliant, so accomplished, that even my stuffy in-laws would have to acknowledge them." She let her index finger run along the rim of a serving tray containing biscuits and a carafe of wine. "Sophie is like you and me, she can take care of herself when need be. It's Philip that I'm most concerned about. He is at the vulnerable stage when men build up their self-esteem. You shatter that and it wrecks the rest of their life."

Like you and me. Your siblings. It dawned on Nelly that there was a continuum she could not dismiss, that no matter what, the woman sitting here was her mother.

"You are not at all as I imagined you," she said.

Florence folded her hands in her lap. "Do I disappoint you greatly?"

The answer was slow to come. Nelly examined the shining green pools of the eyes, the melting copper of the hair, and the beautifully shaped lips most men would find irresistible. "Mothers are not supposed to be dazzling."

Florence laughed. It sounded like piano keys yielding softly to a skilled hand. "I was genuinely touched when I found that you've named your daughter after me. At the same time, it burdened me with undeserved honor.

May I . . ." she extended her arms in front of her, "will you allow me to hold her again?"

Nelly nodded. They met halfway, the baby an object leading to a possible truce. Florence sat on the bed, holding the bundle in her left arm and ran the tips of her fingers over the child's face. She untied the bonnet and exposed the hair.

"She definitely takes after me," she said. "This type of auburn hair comes with a clear complexion. She'll not have to worry about freckles. Shhh . . . Don't you start to cry, my darling! Now, that's better. Look at those large eyes! Oh, what a treasure you are!"

She seemed genuinely pleased with her granddaughter and the baby responded to her touch with contented sounds. Perhaps she really had had to flee for her life. Perhaps she was a victim of tragic circumstances after all, Nelly reasoned. She joined her on the bed, sitting at arm's length. She would reserve her judgment until she knew more.

Florence's hand landed on hers softly. "I'm sorry," she said.

Nelly's hand remained limp. "Sorry for what?"

"That we should have met under such unhappy circumstances."

"Have you ever thought of me?"

"You've never completely left my mind. I know I owe you. It's too late to be a mother to you but allow me to be a grandmother to my namesake. Surely, it is not too late to be a family? Look . . ." she spread her hand over Nelly's, ". . .our hands match in size and our fingers are of the same length."

It was true. They lifted their hands and held them together, palm to palm, aligning the fingers. Everything, from the wrists to the fingertips, came from the same mold. Nelly's eyes misted over. She allowed Florence to clasp her hand in hers and draw her close.

"Oh, my darling, how good to see you!" Florence said.

They embraced in a flow of tears. Nelly could no longer fight the fact that they were flesh and blood. Florence Davenport had filled a niche.

A knock on the door interrupted the tearful reunion. This time, it was the crib.

* * *

The man landed in an unused bedroom on the third floor after a prolonged struggle with the window. He cracked open the door and, after listening for a presence in the corridor, he ventured out. The corridor led him to a servants' staircase. Too narrow and probably too busy.

He was right. Someone was coming upstairs, the bare stone echoing under the click of heels. Stealthily, he retraced his way, taking refuge in a door niche. His hand went to his pocket, the fingers grabbing a retractable knife.

Hopefully, he would not have to mess up the place too soon. His back flattened against the door, his fist clutching the knife he held pressed against his thigh. He listened as the sound of steps softened on the carpeted floor of the landing and then resumed up the next flight. A gas sconce with the flame lowered for the night lit the servant staircase, leaving the rest of the corridor in the dark. The air had the chilliness of abandon. No one lived on this floor.

Emboldened by this discovery, he walked at a leisurely pace until he reached the main staircase. The carpeted marble steps reflected dim light from the floor below. He leaned over the balustrade and observed a couple of servants: the porter and a youngish maid passing on the second floor. They advanced slowly, weighed down with an old-fashioned crib.

A crib!

He crouched on the steps, straining his ears. He heard knocking, the murmur of voices, then silence. He breathed slowly and heavily, trying to control his excitement. The crib was a new element. Made of carved wood and provided with suspended hangings, it was a patrician piece of furniture that may have harbored generations of privileged newborns. He calculated the significance of the fact and smiled. He could turn a vulgar murder into a work of art after all.

Five minutes later, the servants retraced their steps. The woman, now carrying a bucket of slops, said something unintelligible.

"Exciting," the man grumbled. "What's exciting about two women weeping?" He yawned and added, "And now the other one wants a cab. I've got to go out in this weather!"

"But the younger one was La Ceres," the woman said. "I'm sure it was her!"

"I don't give a damn. At this hour, I'd rather be in bed."

The intruder waited until they disappeared and descended to the second floor. Once there, he began to count doors. The one he was looking for should be the fourth on the right.

He approached cautiously and pressed an ear to the panel. A faint murmur of female voices. Further down the corridor, an unobtrusive door, cut in the wooden paneling that ran along the walls, would lead to some kind of convenience. A dressing room or a cabinet de toilette connected to the bedroom. Remembering the bucket in the maid's hand, he opted for the latter. Perfect, just perfect.

Chapter 59

With the flat of her hand, Nelly mercilessly pounded the embroidered quilt provided with the crib, making sure it was free of dust. "Problems? What kind of problems?" she asked as she tucked it around the baby. "What could be worse than what happened tonight? Everything else pales in comparison."

Florence dried her eyes once more and crushed the damp handkerchief with both hands. "There are people who are set on manipulating you for their own purposes and I've been chosen as their instrument."

"Why? Who are they?"

"Come and sit down," Florence patted the bed at her side and waited until Nelly joined her. "The Germans are not yet finished with the French," she said. "There has been a growing sympathy for the Bonapartes and Bismarck wants to quell it before it becomes an electoral issue. Disparaging the late Emperor may help to undermine support for his successor."

"What does it have to do with me? I've made my birth certificate public. I'm an American and I've nothing to do with their dirty games, have I? . . . Have I?"

Florence shifted uncomfortably. "After the Empire collapsed," she said, "and before the palace got burned down, documents were seized from the imperial offices. Among the files were the Emperor's private entertainment accounts. Very private entertainment." She paused allowing the information to sink in. "My name figured on the list with the sum of seven hundred francs."

Nelly sucked in her breath and clasped her hand over her mouth.

Florence averted her eyes. "Some of the filth got published then, but the public forgets fast. Now they have you, a living, breathing celebrity. They are demanding that I come forward and tell the press that you are indeed Louis

Napoleon's daughter. It's to be the starting point of a defamatory campaign before the elections. They want to remind the public of the low morality and the corruption of the imperial court."

"They? Who are they?"

"The German secret police and whoever else is behind this. They threaten that if I do not comply within a week, they will reveal the fact of my undissolved marriage to Gregory McKay. After that, if I set foot on British soil, I'll be charged with bigamy. My children by William Davenport will become illegitimate. My in-laws, who have hated me from day one, can and will claim my fortune. You, by waving around your birth certificate, have pushed me and your siblings closer to the edge of the precipice."

Nelly rose abruptly, hugged herself, paced across the room, returned, and sat on the bed again, this time away from Florence's reach. "What will happen to you after you talk?"

Florence shrugged. "They promised to keep my past under wraps. Needless to say, I'm not willing to play Bismarck's game. I've an ace hidden up my sleeve and I intend to use it. As for you," she leaned toward Nelly, reaching for her hand, "I'm sorry. When this is over, I'll make it up to you and to my granddaughter, I promise."

"Don't touch me," Nelly said.

"Dear child, you must not judge me so harshly."

"Who am I?"

Florence retrieved her unwanted hand. "Not who you think. Your father . . ." she paused and swallowed, ". . .was the duke de Morny. You may have heard of him. He may be dead but he is far from forgotten."

"The duke de Morny?"

"The man behind the Emperor. Behind, at his side, and wherever else something profitable was brewing. The crafty, conniving, ruthless son of a bitch!—I'm sorry! I should not speak like this of your father. This is the first time in twenty years that I've pronounced his name and it has poisoned my tongue." She shook her head and rose. "I'm not myself. We must meet in better circumstances and talk at leisure. I promise you that I'll keep nothing from you, and I want to hear your story as well."

"If you want to know my story, buy a newspaper," Nelly said evenly. She had reached the point of emotional saturation and felt strangely light-headed and no longer personally involved. "But I want to hear yours now. Not later. Now. You owe it to me."

Florence glanced at the mantel clock. "It's late. I've an early train to catch."

"You sent for a cab fifteen minutes ago. The man said it would take about half an hour. Now that I've been force-fed the highlights of your life, I must know the rest. Start from the beginning!"

Florence consulted the ceiling. "My life in fifteen minutes!" she addressed the plasterwork. Retracing her steps, she sat down, smoothing her skirt, her fingers combing the folds of the fabric while the clock ticked away.

"I suppose that you want to hear what I have to say about your maternal grandparents," she began. "I was born in England. My mother was a mute beast of burden when she wasn't pickled in gin, which occurred every Saturday when she pocketed her one-shilling wage. Drunk, she engaged in frightening bouts of slobbering sentimentality. Her story, as I pieced it together, was a commonplace case of the seduced maid. Dismissed when she got pregnant, she joined a gang of female farm laborers. Your grandfather, the Honorable Neville Paget, was a houseguest of her employers. He has since made his way up in the Army, collected a string of medals, and is now a gouty retired colonel. I know this because I had him investigated. Your grandmother Lizzie, on the other hand, had a drink too many, passed out in a ditch on a cold January night and is buried in a pauper's grave. That I learned when I first needed my birth certificate and had to travel in Hampshire from parish to parish to find my birthplace.

"I was born in a field where the gang happened to be slinging turnips. As soon as I could stand on my feet, I was put to work. Round and round the countryside we went, women, children, and the gang master. Farm work from April to November, stone picking in the winter months, sleeping in barns and stables. We were the lowest of the low, godless, rootless bundles of dirty rags. Accordingly, my mother shuffled from estate to estate with her head down, looking at nothing but the ground under her feet. I, on the other hand, always looked around. A curious little ferret I was then. At first, the house-dwelling people seemed to belong to another species with superior customs, and it did not occur to me that I was human as well. When I began to reason, and when I learned that my father belonged to the well-to-do tribe, I had a brainstorm. I wanted to belong as well. And I kept wanting and wanting.

"I got my first break when I was ten. One Saturday, the gang collected the wages and looked for the usual entertainment. We were near the town of Chilbolton and there happened to be a fair. And a circus parade. Looking back, it was a tired family business with patched up costumes and a couple of near-toothless lions but to me it looked like a royal procession. I forgot where I was and who I was and I followed. The director must have seen some potential in me and he struck a deal with the gang master while Mother slept off her drinking binge. Within a couple of months, I was walking the tightrope and assisting with juggling. However, it was my love of horses that shaped my career. I've an understanding with horses, always have had. At fourteen, I was Miss Butterfly, the Equestrian Wonder. By then, the sad little company merged with a larger one and I balanced on horseback in my pretty short skirt and jumped through hoops of fire in front of better audiences. And that's the end of act one.

"Act two begins in Paris and I'm the star of the Hippodrome. Only the Roman Coliseum exceeds it in size. Yes, my dear, it was a long way from the pigsties of Hampshire. I was doing exceedingly well. I led a squadron of striking Amazons and performed in the *haute école*. I lived in a cozy apartment paid for by a banker and I had a maid. By now, I was successfully aping the upper class speech and manners and liked to pretend that I was one of them. In fact, I liked to believe I was one of them. Why, when you are barely seventeen, the sky is the limit. And that was my frame of mind when I got entangled with de Morny.

"De Morny seemed the closest thing to God. Perfect manners, infinite charm, effortless wit. He was a younger, taller, and handsomer version of Louis Napoleon. Everyone knew that he was the emperor's half-brother, but no one dared to mention it in public. That was taboo. Why, you may ask, and it's a good question because our recent troubles stem from it. The reason was that their mother, Hortense, Empress Josephine's daughter through her first husband, had a record of marital infidelity. Hortense's husband, Louis Bonaparte, whom Napoleon made King of Holland, had had enough and refused to acknowledge her last son. De Morny was dumped into foster care and it was left up to him to climb the social ladder. The empire ended, the king came back from exile only to be ousted by another revolution and, finally, de Morny had his chance. The coup d'état that transformed Louis Napoleon into Napoleon III was his work. And so it happened that the bastard became a duke. There were those who spread rumors that the Emperor himself was of dubious parentage, but such people ended either in prison or in exile.

"I cared little for the rumors at the time. I fell head over heels in love. My banker lost his shine and was shown the door. Such was my love for de Morny, that I was delighted when I discovered I was pregnant with his child. A week later, a feast was given at the Court and our squadron of Amazons performed before the guests. At the end of the festivities, de Morny took me aside. 'You can help to save His Majesty from a fatal mistake,' he said. As you can imagine, he got my attention. The gist of his speech was this: The newly-minted Napoleon III was about to propose marriage to one Eugénie de

393

Montijo, who drove him insane by refusing his advances. What the Empire needed to establish itself was a virginal princess of royal blood, not a twenty-six year old Spanish adventuress of uncertain virtue. For the sake of France, His Majesty's attention must be diverted from the cunning Spaniard. I had caught the Emperor's eye during the equestrian spectacle and could be an instrument by which to relieve his stress, clear his mind, and salvage the destiny of the empire. Such a sacred mission demanded the sacrifice of individual feelings. Need I say more?"

Florence paused and combed her lips with her teeth as if getting rid of a bitter taste. "I did not change the destiny of France. My sole contribution to history amounted to a brief tumble on a sofa with an aging and less attractive version of de Morny. When it was over, an attendant slipped me a purse with money and so smooth was the transaction that I knew instantly he had long experience. Immediately, I was hustled into a carriage to be taken home. Had I had any sense, I would've left it at that. Instead, I directed the carriage to the Jockey Club, where I knew de Morny would be, forced my way in, and indulged in a screaming fit in front of his friends. How many prostitutes worked for the salvation of the Empire, I wanted to know. Was he his brother's regular supplier? Never mind his title, he was nothing but a pimp. I was not an anonymous streetwalker. I was *une grande artiste* and people paid attention to me. I could tell the whole world what kind of a family ruled France. And wasn't it true that the Emperor himself was a bastard?"

"Little did I know of the ways of the mighty. At dawn, the secret police pounded on my door. I was given time to pack a few clothes. They escorted me to Le Havre and – as my homeland was not far enough - they dumped me on the first ship leaving for New York. They told me never to come back if I valued my life."

She fell silent and appeared to be studying the carpet pattern.

"What happened next?" Nelly asked.

Florence took her time before she resumed. "America. It means freedom and opportunity if you arrive with hope in your luggage. You may suffer from the cramped conditions in the steerage, the stench, the abject food, and still step on the shore in high spirits. For an involuntary exile it's an altogether different experience. Free spirit was knocked out of me. For the first time in my life, I longed for a shield of security. I thought I had found it in the man who was to become your father. I met McKay as soon as I stepped off the ship and we married a week later. I admit that I seduced him shamelessly and fed him a diet of lies. But I was determined to be a good wife and never did I give him reason to think otherwise. McKay needed no prompting for his mad fits of jealousy. Look," she bared the top of her ear where a whitish line ran between the earlobe and the temple. "It is only thanks to my mother-in-law that I'm not disfigured. She got hold of his hand before he could do worse."

Nelly sucked in her breath.

"I escaped for the first time when I was five months pregnant with you," Florence went on. "I had barely left town before he caught up with me. Let's leave out a set of painful details. When you were born, I fell into an abyss of apathy. I lingered in bed through the winter months although there was nothing wrong with me physically. Your grandmother McKay, God bless the good woman, took care of you, while I wondered what use I was as a mother. I seriously thought of suicide but found no strength to kill myself. When the snow was gone, the will to live reasserted itself. At the same time, McKay was growing weary of my illness and I knew that my reprieve was about to end. And that's when I did what I did."

"I was told it was a boating accident."

"Yes, it's only natural that they'd have told you a charitable lie. McKay had a sort of affection for you. Was he a good father?"

Nelly shrugged. "We never had the opportunity to grow close. After you were . . . gone, he took a job as surveyor with the Central Pacific Railway. On the rare occasions he visited, I had the impression he avoided being alone with me. I was told that he drank and picked fights. He was killed in San Francisco, where a sailor hit him with an iron bar."

"Guilt," Florence said. "I believe he was racked by guilt. He was a man who could not express his feelings except when he was in a rage."

"Granny died when I was eleven."

"I know."

"You know? How is it possible?"

"I came looking for you."

"You did what?"

"I came when— Is someone knocking at the door?"

It was the manservant. The cab was waiting, he said.

Nelly caught Florence's hand in both of hers. "Is it true?" she asked eagerly. "You really came back to see me?"

"Shh . . . Keep your voice down," Florence whispered. "Yes, I went to America after my second husband died," she said. "I disguised it as a business trip. I thought I would catch a glimpse of you without anyone knowing, just to make sure you were well cared for. I hired a man to inquire. But McKay had already taken you away and nobody knew where. I assumed that you were living with him. I could do no more without exposing myself."

395

"But that changes everything! It means . . ." Nelly's lips tightened with a suppressed sob and she reached out with both arms. "Oh, Mother, you really cared for me!"

* * *

Henri climbed into his carriage. "Home," he called to the coachman. The trap was reset in the Passage Sabotière and reinforcements sent to do the same in the rue Monge and at the Beaumont-Quérat Agency. There was nothing he could do except go home and guard the fort. If only he could also fortify his mind against replaying what he had seen in the closet! The cadaver with a broken skull seemed benign in comparison. It was the compressed insanity of that shrine that froze his marrow. What sinister god was worshiped there? What rituals did he require?

Henri huddled in the corner of the carriage and crossed his arms to contain his powerless anger. Here he was, idle and seething, when he should be doing something, anything. Seething? Why was the word 'seething' suddenly important? Seething. Snakes. Seething snake. There was an old gaelic expression for it. Athair . . . No, that was not quite it. Nathair. Nathaira! A spell-casting witch. The lunatic cared for colorful details and possessed an overdeveloped taste for drama. Whatever he had in mind, it was meant to be spectacular. What frustration, what yearning led him to assert himself in such a way? More important, why had he chosen Nelly for a target?

She and the child were safe for the moment. Still, were they really? He had ordered the gate to be kept locked and no stranger to be admitted. But could he rely on that alone? He did not know the house all that well. There were parts he had never visited. The service quarters, the basement, the attic. There could be entrances that he did not know existed. There were locks to be checked and windows to be secured no later than tonight. And he thought he had nothing to do!

He leaned out of the window. "Faster, Mathieu!" he shouted. "Faster!"

* * *

The screen in the toilette cabinet was an ideal observation post. Through the split between the panels, he could see her naked, splashing water on her face. Her breasts, swollen with milk, were rather a turn-off. He did not want to be involved in base matters of the flesh. He possessed this woman more completely than any of her lovers had. She became his life. He knew her thoughts, her joys and sorrows and her lustful longings. He had stripped her to the core and had his way with her in a far more sophisticated manner than any ordinary man. He had been raping the bitch repeatedly, and taking immense pleasure in it. His only pleasure since his own life had lost meaning. When she resisted, he was pleased. It kept the play from becoming dull. Yes,

396

he had been staging an outstanding play, as witnessed by the abundant reviews in the press. Now the time was ripe to turn the farce into a full-blown tragedy.

She had donned her nightgown and was combing her hair, gazing at her reflection in the mirror, not knowing that Fate was waiting at an arm's length. Despite the obstacles thrown in his way, his progress was inexorable, the timing uninterrupted. The gift would be delivered on schedule with only one slight flaw. A well-crafted child coffin containing a body and live snakes would have made a far greater impression but, in the circumstances, the luxury crib was a good second choice. He was lucky to be given such a redeeming option.

She now stood still, the hand holding the comb poised above her head. Had she got a whiff of his excitement? Had the scent of his sweat reached her nostrils?

No, she smiled at her image and brought her hair up to try a new style. The utter insipidity of women! Their inferior minds, the primitive level of their preoccupations! The animal base of their sex!

Go now, go! Go to bed with that satisfied smile of yours. I guarantee you it will be your last genuine smile for the rest of your life. No one has the right to interfere with Honoré de Chazelle without paying the highest price.

Once more, his mind went back to the barren hills of Provence as he walked away from the railway tracks, leaving behind all hope. Again, he could feel the rough stone in his hand and the tension in his muscles as he gathered the courage to obliterate his face. He remembered the bone-shattering impact on his nose, and then nothing. How long he had been prostrated, unconscious, before the gypsies found him, he could not tell. He woke up faceless and nameless. His past was gone as was his future. The gypsies washed the blood off his face and cleaned out his pockets. It did not matter. He promised them more. The quality of his clothes convinced them that he was not lying.

In the weeks that followed, he eagerly learned the crafts of nomadic life and built a new self. So successful was he at it, that he shaped another persona in his mind. By the time he reached Paris, where he had stashed Kitty's jewelry, he had a hunger for revenge and the means to carry it out. Finding out where the woman was hiding was a matter of a few bribes. He could have killed her then, but the building of the scene, the costume changes, the planning and the carrying out the scheme were the few pleasures he had left. When the child was born, the game changed again. Why kill the women if he had the means to make her suffer for the rest of her life? The game could go on indefinitely. He was addicted to it.

She had extinguished the flame in the lamp and the cabinet was now plunged in darkness. He allowed a reasonable time to elapse before he slid from behind the screen and approached the door of the bedroom. The keyhole let in a trickle of an unsteady, dim light, a mere reflection of glowing embers in the fireplace.

Slowly, he pressed down the door handle. The door gave way with a weak complaint. He paused, his fingers grasping his knife, and listened. In the dimness of the room, he could just make out the shape of the furniture. As his eyes adjusted to the darkness, he saw her form on the bed. She was stretched on her back, a hand supporting her head, her chest heaving rhythmically. The crib stood at the foot of the bed with the curtains drawn over it. While keeping his gaze on the woman, he moved in, a step at a time, until he reached the crib. She did not move and her breathing kept its steady pace.

He peeled the curtains off. The fireplace was now directly behind him and the interior of the crib bathed in shade. Yet he saw the whitish bundle crisscrossed with a darker ribbon.

Strike! Strike now!

He lifted his arm above his head and drove the knife into the crib. It plunged in with no resistance and came out clean.

He stared at the steel of the blade as it mirrored a series of bright flashes, while his body jerked off balance. The floor was coming at him, and reached him with a brutal impact. The last thing he heard was the child, crying.

* * *

Henri was stepping out of the carriage when he heard the shots. He froze with one foot on the step and the other on the pavement, his hand clinging to the door. The whinnying horses restored him to his senses. He threw himself forward, taking the steps two at a time. The door was locked. He swore and pounded at it with his fists.

"Open up!"

He went on pounding and ringing the bell for a full twenty seconds before the door was opened by Joseph with one arm still out of his jacket. The coachman and the porter entered behind him.

Henri's hand plunged for the revolver in his pocket. "Guard the service stairs! Guard the gate!" he shouted before he leaped up the staircase and sped toward his mother's bedroom.

Clutching the revolver, he threw the bedroom door open and flattened himself against the frame. He was aiming at Nelly who stood bent over a body. The child was crying somewhere out of sight.

He dropped his arm and let Nelly come to him.

"Where is the baby?" he asked as he embraced her.

"Under the bed."

"Under the bed?"

"I knew the man was here," she said. "He was standing so close to me I could hear his breathing. I put a pillow in the crib."

"Oh, Nelly! Nelly, my love ..." Henri said and tightened his arms around her.

Chapter 60

Stieber reached the Chancellery in Wilhelmstrasse as the late afternoon shadows deepened and the gas was being lit in the offices. He left his overcoat with the clerk in the anteroom and proceeded to the Chief Secretary's office.

"What's the latest?" he asked.

The secretary discarded his pen with a frown. "Some kind of trouble," he said, "His Excellency has been summoned to Potsdam."

Stieber nodded. "I know that. I've got his telegram. It's five o'clock sharp. Still not back?"

"Not yet."

"What else do you know?"

"Only that General von Moltke is involved."

Stieber dropped the file he was carrying on the desk and sat down. "That doesn't sound good. Whenever there's a dispute between the military and the civilians, we always lose."

The secretary nodded, his long Nordic face drawn narrower by the bitter pout of his lips. "That's the unfortunate truth," he acquiesced. "The Kaiser is quite capable of standing up for his beloved army. Especially when it comes to Moltke, the Victor of Sedan. Brace yourself for thunder and brimstone."

As soon as he said it, they heard a clatter of heavy footsteps. The door opened briskly and Bismarck's round head briefly poked in from behind it.

"Stieber! My office!"

Despite years of practice, Stieber still had not conquered the involuntary collapse of his shoulders at a moment like this. He glanced at the secretary and saw something akin to pity in his eyes.

"Just as you said," he sighed.

"You blighted idiot!" Bismarck barked after he had thrown himself into the chair behind his desk.

Stieber clicked his heels, palms against the seams of his pants, the file squeezed underarm. "Your Excellency?" he croaked.

"What are you doing at the Secret Service offices? Embroidering pillows? Knitting socks? Better yet, is there an archive at all?"

"I'm not aware of any laxity, Sir."

"Then how is it you don't know the background of your agents?"

Stieber patted the folder under his arm. "Is Your Excellency referring to the Pandora file?"

"You damn well know that I am."

Stieber relaxed. "There is no background at all," he said. "The person acted anonymously."

"You mean you've been accepting intelligence reports without inquiring about their provenance?"

"Not at first. We are suspicious of anyone volunteering sensitive information. However, the reports proved exceptionally accurate and provided us with interesting insights, particularly as to the state of the French cavalry. They stopped coming after the Sedan victory."

"Give me that!"

Bismarck accepted the file and leafed through the documents. "Sit down," he mumbled without taking his eyes from the pages.

Stieber took a seat opposite him and allowed his fingers to drum a tune on his thighs.

"Hmm . . ." Bismarck closed the file and leaned back. "Who did you think this Pandora was?"

"A disgruntled French officer? Someone passed over for promotion? A royalist sympathizer bound to undermine the Empire?"

"It was a woman. An English widow. A horse breeder, horse dealer and, if I'm to believe von Moltke, a horse-whisperer extraordinaire. He holds her in high regard. Well, any idea as to who she might be?"

Stieber's face fell. *"Umgotteswillen!"* he breathed.

"Hah! Leave God out of it, he's not responsible for your mistakes," Bismarck said, his hand polishing the bald dome of his head. "I've not heard from you since before the London funeral. How was it?"

"We did not proceed. Miss McKay created such a stir in the French press the day before that any further action against her would've fallen flat."

"In that, at least, you were right."

"I'll have the McKay file classified."

"You'll have to do more than that. Von Moltke was adamant that Mrs. Davenport must be presented with a personal apology. By none other than you."

"That's . . . That is preposterous."

"His Majesty's order."

A heavy silence fell upon the room before Bismarck stirred.

"Tell me, Stieber, how did I bring Austria to her knees?"

"Well, among other things by weakening their economy with counterfeit banknotes."

"How did I annex the Kingdom of Bavaria?"

"By a forged signature of the mad Ludwig II."

"That and a hundred of similar actions built a united Germany."

Stieber sighed with nostalgia. "Those were heady times, Your Excellency."

"Honor!" the chancellor thundered suddenly. "They dare to speak of honor! They disapprove of my methods! I'm disgracing Germany with blackmail! The asinine knights with their old-fashioned morals! They'd like to believe that they've forged Germany with swords and bravery. That may well be, but who had paved their way? Who?"

"Your Excellency . . ." Stieber said softly.

Bismarck closed his eyes and silenced him by lifting his hand. "Go, my friend, go. I'm tired."

* * *

The arrival of Florence Davenport stirred attention at the otherwise sleepy railway station in Poitiers. The train contained a delivery wagon from which emerged a procession of handsome horses led by a superb Frisian stallion with silky black coat, a heavy mane and feathered feet.

"This is too much," Henri protested. "I'm not sure I can afford it."

Florence laughed. "Don't be silly!" she said. "This is Nelly's dowry."

Nelly's eyes widened. "Mother, you shouldn't have!"

Florence clicked her tongue. "What did you think? That I would allow my first-born to come to her man empty-handed? The stallion is my wedding gift for the groom," she said to Henri. "Sixteen and a half hands at the shoulder. Just the right size for you.—Over here," she called to the men that were tending the horses. "This is Patrick Donovan, and here's Joe Carpenter, two of my best men. They're thrilled to be here. So why don't you three take the matter in hand while we women catch up on the latest news?"

"And how's my precious namesake?" Florence asked as soon as she and Nelly arranged their skirts inside the waiting carriage.

"Exceptionally well considering her traumatic experience."

"Babies are hardier than is generally thought," Florence said. The carriage jolted into motion. "This is a pretty town," she remarked, glancing out of the window. "I've been admiring the landscape from the train. I've never been in this part of France. Do you like it here?"

"Very much so."

"It's quiet. Just what you need to soothe your nerves. No one will bother you again. Mr. Margolis has done a superb job, don't you agree?"

Nelly nodded. Things had been arranged to perfection. The body was discreetly carted off before dawn and dumped in the Passage Sabotière. A story of a domestic dispute with a tragic end was fed to the press. The newspapers enthusiastically heralded the police's swift action against the murderer of Mademoiselle Pointsotte and the Police Prefect gloated with satisfaction. There was no mention of Nelly or the failed attempt to kidnap the child.

"I spoke to Margolis only two weeks ago," Florence said. "They still did not know that man's real identity. Are you sure you haven't got the slightest idea?"

"Honestly, I've never seen him before except disguised as a gypsy."

"It's as if the man had no past at all. Very strange. Oh, well," Florence patted her daughter's knee, "let's talk about the wedding. A secret ceremony, no less. How romantic! The French clergy are so wonderfully accommodating."

"Henri's promised new roof tiles for the church."

"And so delightfully practical! But isn't this marriage against the church law?"

Nelly shook her head. "As far as they're concerned, Henri's marriage ceased to exist the moment he signed permission for his wife to enter the orders. It's the civil law that keeps us apart."

"The Church seems to be reasonable in comparison. And now tell me what's wrong!"

"How . . . ?"

"I knew the moment I stepped off the train and saw you two displaying false smiles. You have to do better than that to be convincing."

Nelly pursed her lips and suddenly found interest in something she saw in the window.

"Oh, come!" Florence hooked her arm under her daughter's elbow. "Is the wedding off? Is that it?" She forced Nelly to look at her. "Come on, you can tell me. If I cannot understand, who can?"

She got a moan for an answer and tears finally rolled down Nelly's cheeks. "It's Octave!" she burst with suppressed anger. "He's been poisoning us for nearly two weeks. We cannot marry as long as he stays here. It just doesn't feel right."

"Here, take my handkerchief. Octave? He's the other man, isn't that so?"

Nelly nodded. "I had no desire to talk to him after the events," she said, "although Henri said we should. I said, let's leave now and he'll get the message."

Florence waited patiently while more tears were shed.

Nelly dried her eyes, sniffing. "He's such a bad loser! As soon as he learned that we were gone, he went to the Civil Registry and acknowledged my daughter. Then he showed up here with the document in his hand and shouted at Henri that he was a kidnapper, that he had taken advantage of my weak nerves and that he had no right to travel with the child without his—her father's—permission."

Florence raised her eyebrows. "My dear, where do you find them?" she asked. "When it comes to illegitimate children, men usually run the other way."

Nelly sighed. "It's not me, it's them. It's some kind of a contest between the two ever since they were boys."

"And you say that Octave's still in the house? Why does Henri not ask him to leave? It's his property after all."

"He thinks he can't. Not after what happened."

"Which was . . . ?"

"I was unaware of Octave's sudden arrival. It was the day we hired a nurse for Florence and I was showing her the nursery. Then, as she and I were coming down the stairs, we heard a frightening commotion - furniture being overturned, china breaking. When we reached the salon, we saw Henri and Octave locked together and pounding at each other's ribs. Henri got hold of Octave and threw him and Octave landed with his groin on the fire guard."

Florence bared her teeth in a sharp intake of air. "Ouch!" she said.

"I've never heard such a bone-chilling roar of pain," Nelly said, plucking at the handkerchief. "The swelling was enormous. He spent the first week in bed and now he's been slowly waddling about. He doesn't shave and wears only Henri's old dressing gown. He's convinced he's no longer a man. Yesterday, Henri found him toying with a revolver. He could not feel guiltier had he killed him. And I'm caught in the middle of it!"

"Is he fit enough to travel?"

"Octave? He can walk and if it were up to me, he would be on the first train to Paris. But Henri says that we cannot leave a suicidal man on his own. Why do men behave irrationally when their equipment is involved?"

Florence smiled indulgently. "My dear, their equipment is their essence. But you are right. We cannot have that. Doesn't he have a wife and a child somewhere?"

"He does, but the child's not his."

"Nevertheless, it is time he went back to them," Florence said firmly.

"I'm afraid that's impossible. He hates his wife. He says she betrayed him."

"Leave it to me."

"He'll never do it. He swore he wouldn't."

Florence chuckled. "My child, you forget what I do for a living. I talk to horses and listen to men. I promise that before the week is over, he'll be eager to resume his family life."

"Do you, really?" Nelly asked hopefully.

"I've tackled worse." Florence wound her arm around her daughter's shoulders, drawing her closer. "Trust your mama, my pet! This is going to be a challenging visit but we shall have that wedding before I leave."

* * *

The night surrendered to dawn. A cat was feeding on the remains of the wedding cake abandoned on the dining room table. Voices carried through the open door of the adjacent salon where Octave was kneeling in front of an armchair occupied by Florence Davenport.

"Monsieur Gaillard," she said, "you still have five hours before your train departure. I suggest that you use them for sleep."

He squeezed her hands in his. "But don't you understand what I just told you? I love you, Florence, I love you deeply and passionately! You enslaved me the first time I saw you. I've done everything you asked me to do. I behaved in a gentlemanly manner. I renounced my paternity rights. I gave the bride away at the ceremony. What other proof of my love do you need?"

"I asked you to take these steps to heal yourself, Monsieur Gaillard. As for love, experience has taught me that passionate love is a disease. What you feel for me is the symptom of that disease. I assure you that it will not last."

Octave rejected her hands and rose. "You mock me, madame!" he exclaimed. "How can you speak so coldly of my passion for you? I ask you to respect my sentiments for you even though you don't share them."

Florence shrugged. "I don't expect you to understand the wisdom of my words right now." She rose as well. "Good night, monsieur. I intend to skip breakfast and catch up on my sleep. I'm taking this last opportunity to wish you bon voyage."

She crossed the room, before she faced him again. "I heard there was a young woman whom you used to arouse for years with kissing hands and whispering sweet nonsense until, in her fragile state, she fell victim to a

405

predator. Women have their needs too, Monsieur Gaillard. I'm leaving you with this fact to think about and act upon. In other words, go back to your family. Forgive and forget. Only then will you find peace."

* * *

The first sunrays penetrated the lace curtains of the bedroom.

"Are you asleep?" Nelly asked while attempting to free her hair from Henri's clutch.

He stirred awake. "Nelly? What's all that squirming about, my love?"

"Let go of my hair, please. You don't need to hold onto me so tight. I'm going nowhere."

"I'm very pleased to hear that."

She kissed his cheek and curled up in his arms. "I'm thinking about that boisterous Irish wedding with a banquet and music and dance, Mother offered us to make up for yesterday's secret ceremony."

"Yes?"

"It'd better happen soon. I think I'm expecting again.—Henri? Why don't you say something?"

He gave her a wide smile and kissed her brow. "For years I thought I'd never have a family. Now the blessings keep raining on me, one after another. My happiness is too big for words."

THE END

Born in Prague, and now living with her husband in Calgary at the foot of the Canadian Rockies, Iva Polansky has authored several non-fiction books in French and English. *Fame and Infamy* is her first novel. Iva is also a co-founder of Historical Fiction eBooks established in 2010. The website (hfebooks.com) offers a wide range of quality historical fiction titles.

Contact author: iva.polansky@gmail,com

Also by Iva Polansky:

Sonya's War

Biography / Screenplay

Eighty-two year old Leo Tolstoy, patriarch of Russian literature, a sage of international renown, revered by the people and feared by the government, has only one serious adversary: his loving wife Sonya.

In the fall of 1910, readers around the world, in Berlin, London, Paris, New York and Tokyo, scramble for the latest edition of the local newspapers. Tsar Nicolas II curtails his holiday in Germany and hastily returns to Russia where police and a cavalry detachment surround a remote railway station besieged by a crowd of thousands. Is this the beginning of a revolution? Well, almost. And it all started with a domestic quarrel.

Based on several biographies, personal memoirs, Tolstoy's diaries and eye-witness' accounts, Sonya's War tells the story of the crumbling marriage of two strong-willed individuals - and of family division, jealousy, madness and greed—ending in Leo's ill-fated dash for freedom.

Sonya's War is available as an e-book at www.Smashwords.com

Of Moths & Butterflies

by *V.R. Christensen*

Archer Hamilton is a collector of rare and beautiful insects. Gina Shaw is a servant in his house. Out of place in such a position, she becomes a source of fascination. A girl with a blighted past, Gina has lowered herself in order to find escape from her family and their scheming designs. All she wants is the freedom to live her life as she would wish. All her aunts want is the money she has inherited. An arranged marriage might turn out profitable for more parties than one. Mr. Hamilton is about to make the acquisition of a lifetime. But will the price be worth it?

Available online wherever books are sold.

Coming soon from the same author

Cry of the Peacock

After the death of her father, Abbie Gray finds herself the recipient of an offer to assume a place within her wealthy landlord's family. She's sceptical of the motivation behind such an extraordinary invitation, but having nowhere else to go, she accepts. While she is being groomed according to the ideals of society and of the eldest son, heir to title and fortune, the younger brothers, suspicious of her motives, attempt to expose her as a mercenary and an upstart. But when they discover that her mysterious past is disturbingly connected with their own, they are brought to reconsider. David, the elder of the two, is forced to ask himself some very hard questions about integrity, liberty and honour, and what it means to be worthy of the title "gentleman".